Paulus Cassel

An Explanatory Commentary on Esther

with four appendices consisting of the second Targum translated from the Aramaic

with notes, Mithra, the winged bulls of Persepolis and Zoroaster

Paulus Cassel

An Explanatory Commentary on Esther
with four appendices consisting of the second Targum translated from the Aramaic with notes, Mithra, the winged bulls of Persepolis and Zoroaster

ISBN/EAN: 9783337192617

Printed in Europe, USA, Canada, Australia, Japan

Cover: Foto ©Andreas Hilbeck / pixelio.de

More available books at **www.hansebooks.com**

AN

EXPLANATORY COMMENTARY

ON

ESTHER,

With Four Appendices,

CONSISTING OF

*THE SECOND TARGUM TRANSLATED FROM THE
ARAMAIC WITH NOTES, MITHRA, THE
WINGED BULLS OF PERSEPOLIS,
AND ZOROASTER.*

BY

Professor PAULUS CASSEL, D.D., Berlin,

AUTHOR OF THE COMMENTARIES ON JUDGES AND RUTH
IN LANGE'S 'BIBELWERK,' ETC.

Translated

BY

Rev. AARON BERNSTEIN, B.D.

EDINBURGH:
T. & T. CLARK, 38 GEORGE STREET.
1888.

TRANSLATOR'S PREFACE.

—o—

FEW words are required to introduce to the reader the learned author of the present work, as he is already known to English theologians by his Commentaries on Judges and Ruth in Lange's *Bibelwerk*. In Germany the author deservedly enjoys a wide reputation, for his books on religious, social, and scientific subjects are indeed legion, and his ministerial and philanthropic activity is appreciated by all classes, from the emperor to the poorest labouring man. This volume will supply a want long felt, for it elucidates the book of Esther in such a vivid and graphic manner as to make the reader realize the wonderful dealings of God with His chosen and thrice-redeemed people. Herodotus, the Talmud, the Midrashim, and other ancient books, as well as modern discoveries, reports of travellers concerning Persian customs and manners, and philological science, have been brought to bear their respective testimonies to the truth of the recorded events. To this book are applicable, to a large extent, the weighty words of the Ven. Archdeacon Farrar in the *Expositor* of January 1888, where he says, "When we study a great modern commentary we are indeed heirs of all the ages." And again : "Philology, which is a science still in its infancy, has aided and enriched our modern scholarship." The author has happily combined the topical, exegetical, critical, and the practical methods of exposition, and has offered us instruc-

tive and interesting matter on every incident touched
upon in the sacred narrative. It is a *bona fide* historical
commentary, and its parallels are striking, giving us an
insight into ancient Oriental life, and especially Persian,
as no other book of a similar kind does.

It is also valuable on account of its apologetical character.
The author holds a brief, and as a zealous advocate he pleads
Israel's cause before the nations, asks for tolerance and large-
hearted charity towards them, shows the injustice of the
repeated Haman-like attacks to which they have in the
course of their checkered history been subjected, and the
wonderful intervention of Providence in their behalf, as well
as the punishments which their covenant God meted out to
their enemies. In a word, he, like Mordecai, " speaks peace
to all his seed," and, more than Mordecai, preaches " peace on
earth and good-will towards men." The four Appendices will
be found exceedingly interesting and instructive, especially to
Biblical students. That of the First Targum will appear for
the first time in English. The author used the Amsterdam
edition, and amended the text by the light of the ספר מצח אהרן,
Fürth 1768, ספר מגלת אסתר, ed. 1698, and the Hebrew
version of Mordechai Ventura, Amsterdam 1870, and also
the translation of Fürstenthal. The Targum is divided into
eleven paragraphs as follows :—

§ 1. Introduction about Ahhashverosh.
§ 2. The acrostic concerning Solomon.
§ 3. The description of Solomon's throne.
§ 4. Solomon and the Queen of Sheba.
§ 5. The legend about Jeremiah.
§ 6. The dialogue of Vashti and her death.
§ 7. The election of Esther as queen.
§ 8. The accusation of Haman.

The author's notes, besides containing a mine of rich material, throw light on every point. By explaining the names of the ancestors of Haman, he indicates the time when the Targum was written, when the Jews were oppressed by the Romans in the time of Justinian. Such names as Pilate the governor, Felix the vicious brother of Pallas, Florus, Cuspius Fadus, Flaccus, Antipater, Herod, Vitellius, Cestius Gallus, and Rufus, might more properly be called the sons or followers of Haman. He also traces Christian ideas in this Targum as well as antichristian, e.g. in the name Bar Pandira, whereby Christ is designated. On the other hand, Mohammedanism is not in the slightest way alluded to, which proves the great antiquity of the Targum.

A word with regard to the translation of the book. I have on the whole been faithful to the author, and, as far as the English idiom allowed it, have reproduced the author's style. I am indebted to the Rev. James Neil, M.A., for his kindness in revising the translation, to the Rev. J. H. Bruhl for translating the excursus on Zoroaster, and to the publishers for their patient attention to the whole work. May it prosper on its way, and be blessed by Him who manifested Himself at all times as the Protector and Redeemer of His people.

THE TRANSLATOR.

INTRODUCTION.

———o———

1. THE book of Esther, as we have it in the Hebrew language in the canon of the Old Testament, is one of the most remarkable and instructive writings of ancient Persia. The information which it imparts surpasses in originality even that given by Herodotus; it is of the same century, but older, and is tinctured with the colour of Persian custom and life more than any other book. It was written in the capital of Persia. It brings the reader into the palace of the king;—it shows him its throne, with its magnificent surroundings. We obtain from it an insight into the inner life of the royal harem. Indeed, the little book represents a universal harem-history. It makes us better acquainted with King Xerxes, and gives us the original names of his princes and warriors. In spite of its specific Jewish-national motive, it brings us into contact with the political and religious movements that take place in the great empire. Nowhere else is the weakness of the Persian monarch so clearly exhibited as the outcome of his very possession of tremendous power, and of his considering himself as the visible Mithra. The strife which was epidemic in Oriental States, which the stories of the *Seven Wise Men* everywhere describe,[1] and which was regularly carried on between the viziers of kings and the favourite queens, is here narrated with such a vivid and historical accuracy that has no parallel. First, the queen falls on account of the intrigues of the seven ministers, then the vizier falls on

[1] I refer here to the book I lately brought out, *Sieben weisen Meister*, where the Hebrew and Greek versions in connection with Buddhistic interpretation and Oriental narrative are considered.

account of the beauty of another queen. One recognises the stamp of genuineness in every trait of the narrative; just that which appears strange at first sight proves the fidelity with which contemporary events are narrated. The doubts which modern writers have raised against this book are owing to their deficiency in the historic sense, and to their want of a thorough acquaintance with Oriental affairs. Indeed, national prejudices contributed to the undervaluing of the book. Hamanic sentiment wanted to throw a veil over the picture of the old Haman, and to declare the book a myth. Of course, the whole narrative is the expression of a national triumph over intolerance and tyranny, and betrays a national character, just as the narratives of Herodotus and of others, of the Persian wars, sufficiently manifest traits of Hellenic one-sidedness. It is a memoir written by a Jew to all his people who are scattered in the extensive countries of Persia, in which are recorded the wonderful interpositions of Providence in their deliverance from destruction, which appeared to be certain. It has no other purpose but to narrate this; it is not called upon to give information about other things; albeit it gives a picture of Persian court life the like of which is found nowhere else.

The king אֲחַשְׁוֵרוֹשׁ or אֲחַשְׁרֹשׁ is really Xerxes the First, the son of Darius Hystaspes. The name appears to be an appellative, and represents the genuine form, but which was sometimes pronounced by Greeks Kyaxares and sometimes Xerxes. It is a compound of אֲחַשׁ and רֹשׁ—as אֲחַשְׁדַּרְפַּן is a compound of דַּרְפַּן and אֲחַשׁ; דַּרְפַּן (Durban)[1] means officer, servant, and with אֲחַשׁ it means the first servant (satrap) (comp. Dan. iii. 3), so then we have to explain אֲחַשְׁוֵרוֹשׁ as meaning the chief king, or king of kings. רֹשׁ (Rakscha), the Latin *rex*, Xerxes or Xerx, is also a ξερεξ; for אֲחַשׁ corresponds to *Khsha* or *Kyax*, which certainly contains the signification

---

[1] He appears in the Manichaeic reports as Turbo, and in the narrative of Secundus as Tyrpo. Comp. my *Sieben weisen Meister*, p. 350. Comp. *Archelai et Manetis Disput.* p. 44.

of greatness or priority. אחש is also found in the name of Artaxerxes, who is named in Ezra iv. 8, 11, 23, vii. 7, ארתחששתא or ארתחססתא. This is composed of Arta and אחש, and שתא or סתא, with which the word Βίσταξ in Hesychius, meaning king, may be compared. So must the name כרש, Cyrus (the sun), be compared with κύριος, and the Persian name Darius, Dara, Darab be compared with τύραννος.

The name of the king, אחשורש, stands properly in Ezra iv. 6 between Darius and Artaxerxes. With Xerxes are mentioned in the book of Esther as his counsellors and friends, Mardonius, Barzanes, Hydarnes, Aspathines, Prexaspes, and Ahhaemenes. Proper dates are given. If nothing is said about the preparation for the war with Greece, it is because, when this was subsequently written, it was not pleasant to be reminded of the unfortunate issue of that war; yet the date of the assembly given in ver. 3, "the third year of his reign," indicates that in the year 482 preparation for the war was made. If events are narrated which have taken place in the sixth and in the seventh years of the reign of Xerxes, it is because he only returned to Shushan in the sixth year. In the twelfth year, about 474–473 B.C., occurred the catastrophe, and then follows chap. x., where we read: "And the king laid a tribute upon the land and upon the isles of the sea." This is a remarkable notice, and must be understood according to the tenor of the whole book. The narrated fact is represented as the consequence of the deliverance of Israel and of the fall of Haman. The imposition of taxes upon the land and the isles is a sign of their submission. The meaning of the passage obviously is, that since Hamanism has fallen, the power of the Persian king has risen over the land and the isles. The memoir desires to prove that the threatening against the Jews was against the interests of Persia, and that their deliverance from danger contributed to the welfare of the country. It intimates that just as Mordecai conferred a benefit upon the king by disclosing the conspiracy of his servants, so he also became the benefactor of the country in general when he was raised to the office of vizier, because he made the king's prerogatives more respected.

The appearance of Haman on the political arena was evidently the result of a religious Iranic movement. This increased the more after the return of the king from the war, where he met with disastrous reverses which naturally caused dissatisfaction. The attempt of Haman against the Jews had a deep religious-political basis; also in Palestine, as the book of Ezra narrates that the Persian statesmen wrote to the king against the Jews. These statesmen raised considerations with regard to the Jews similar to those which occupied the mind of the Pharaoh who knew not Joseph in Egypt, and to those raised by Mithridates against the Romans, and at times by Turkish sultans against the Christians. All those that did not belong to the religion of Iran were looked upon as political and ecclesiastical enemies, and therefore to be exterminated. Such ideas are not very rare even in modern States. In this sense is also the speech of Haman before the king to be understood.

A more dangerous contrivance against the Jews could not be thought of. But it was averted, and the memoir could assert that just through the deliverance of Israel the Persian power had risen and become great. In fact, the Greek chroniclers are silent concerning further Persian losses till the death of Xerxes; the battle of Eurymedon, 469, was not considered of great importance in official reports of the Persian court; besides, it took place after the memoir was written. The Persians had ceased to attack Greece, but land and isles remained under their protection.

In Persia the enemy of the king was regarded as the enemy of everything good, and even of the Deity, because he was their personified idea of God. Hence the memoir proves that the king derived only good from Mordecai and Esther. There is therefore no greater evidence of the genuineness, contemporariness, and prudence of the Megilla (scroll) Esther, than the very fact that it does not mention the name of God (יהוה). Haman accuses the Jews that they do not keep the דתי, laws, of the king. דת is the product of the mind of his royal majesty, who is the representative of the Deity. Beside him no other god must be acknowledged or tolerated. If the Jews observe the דת of their God, they do it in opposition to the king.[1] The book cannot and must not mention the name of the eternal God under the circumstances, when everything depends upon the king. The author is very careful to show that he is the friend of the king, and that his book was not written against him, but against Haman. There is not a word here against the king, although later traditions are full of mocking and hostile epithets against him. It speaks, indeed, of Haman's attempt to kill all the Jews in the name of the king, but it does not omit to mention that they were saved in his name. So, then, in the omission of the name of God, we have here a political act of prudence which it was necessary to adopt by the written contemporary, the king's contemporary. Nevertheless, the strongly-marked Jewish faith appears everywhere. The fasting which Mordecai prescribed was connected with prayer, although the form of the prayer is not given. One thought pervades the whole book, and that is, the wonderful providence by which God protects the house of Israel. It cannot be destroyed even by the malice of such an enemy as Haman. Even Zeresh his wife is represented to be of the same opinion, when she says to him : " If Mordecai be of the seed of the Jews, before whom thou hast begun to fall, thou shalt not prevail against him." With the deliverance of the Jews is connected the fall of Vashti and, to a certain extent, the Persian War, also the election of Esther as queen, the conspiracy of the eunuchs, the escape of the king, and his sleeplessness. The opposition between Haman and Mordecai is a religious and not merely a personal

---

[1] About the fanciful attempts of ancient teachers to find the name of God concealed in certain letters, and otherwise false expositions, comp. Schudt, *Jüdische Merkwürdigkeiten*, ii. pp. 311, 312.

one.   Mordecai is unwilling to bow his knee before the minister of Hom and of fire.   Through this he comes, of course, into the danger of being denounced by Haman and crucified; but in the same night the king reads of his benevolent and loyal act, and he is not killed, but is honoured publicly; yea, Haman himself must impart to him the honours which he in his vain conceit imagined were intended for himself.   The saying of Haman, that the Jews were scattered in all lands, and had their own peculiar customs, was not unfounded; but for all that, they were good citizens, and did their duty to the State in spite of their religion.   This is clearly shown in the book.   Mordecai, though in the midst of Persians, yet scrupulously observes the religious commandments; he uses the names of Jewish months and not of Persian; and it is a fable that the names of the Jewish months originated in Persia.[1]

2. The event was indeed extraordinary; never before since the time of Israel's exodus from Egypt did they pass through such great danger.   It was the first instance of the outbreak of fanaticism which in later times was often repeated.   Their whole existence throughout the wide dominions of Persia was in the balance.   The experience they received of the wonderful interposition of God in their behalf made an indelible impression upon them.   They had seen before, in their history, the appointment of fasts.   The prophet Zechariah says, " The fast of the fourth month, and the fast of the fifth, and the fast of the seventh, and the fast of the tenth, shall be to the house of Judah joy and gladness, and cheerful feasts."   But such days of redemption they had not yet experienced. Therefore Mordecai and Queen Esther resolved to commemorate the great event which they themselves had witnessed. They joined their experience of God's redeeming love with the redemption of Israel from Egypt.   As the feast of Passover was at all times celebrated with thanksgiving and praise,

---

[1] About the names of the Jewish months I refer to my book, *Literatur und Geschichte*, p. 299, etc.

so should a feast proclaim to all generations the wonderful redemption which their forefathers had experienced. In imitation of the Passover, which began with the fourteenth of Nisan, this feast was also to begin on the fourteenth of Adar. They called it Purim, to remind them of the horoscope which was placed for their destruction, but which led to their deliverance, just as the Passover reminded them by its name of the passing by of the protecting and redeeming angel. Purim also reminded them of Balaam's demoniac attempt to curse Israel, but the curse was turned into a blessing; so now Haman, in accord with Persian custom, placed the horoscope in order to find a day favourable to Israel's destruction.

The undertaking was made in the twelfth year of the reign of Xerxes, probably the twelfth month of the cycle of twelve years, of which it is said that the last was called Swine, which was considered as an unfortunate omen to the people, to whom swine were obnoxious. The thirteenth day of the month Adar was chosen, whose signification was fire, in the sense of consuming also, as March from Mars, Ares whose Greek name is from fire. The thirteenth day (*Tir*) signifies the arrow. For the king shot the arrow with the bow with which he was equipped, like the sun-god and Mithra, which we explain as meaning archer. But the arrow rebounded. Haman, his adherent, fell instead of Mordecai the Jew. The day became a day of joy instead of the horoscope of the curse. It was therefore quite natural that the day should be called Purim, lottery-day, for it was the day on which the prognostications of the horoscopian were falsified, and the threatened misfortune was turned into fortune. It was a grand thought of Esther and Mordecai, while being conscious that they were chosen by God to be the instruments in effecting a deliverance, to institute a day to commemorate that event. The people should realize a lively sense of the perpetual danger they are in on account of their faith in the midst of the heathen, so that they might the more ardently adhere to it, and never lose sight that God is their Preserver and Redeemer. Mordecai and Esther claimed to have the right which Moses possessed to prescribe a feast for the people which should not only awaken serious thoughts in their minds, but also inspire them with joy and gratitude.   When the ancient Jewish teachers ascribed to the book of Esther a certain prophetical character, it was because they foresaw the times when similar accusations to those recorded in this book would be made against the Jews, and they would often need the comfort which the feast of Purim inspires.   Indeed, the institution of this feast was the type of the Feast of Hhanukah, or of Dedication, in which Judas Maccabaeus purified the temple.   He, too, inspired by his victory over the Syrians, desired that the event should remain indelible.   Just as Esther and Mordecai made the Passover to a great extent the basis of the Feast of Purim, so the Maccabees founded the Feast of the Dedication on the prophecy of Haggai, which predicted the coming of a new time from the four and twentieth day of the ninth month (Hag. ii. 18).   We have therefore good ground for assuming the authenticity of the report that Mordecai caused the book to be written, and that he furnished the main facts.   In chap. ix. 20–23 we not only find traces of this, but also of the appointment and the observance of the feast.   (See the explanation in the Commentary.)

We observe that Esther and Mordecai must not be judged by the standard of the gospel, nor must we expect to find in them the tolerating spirit of Jesus Christ.   They retaliated and avenged themselves on their enemies in accordance with the prevalent policy and spirit of the East; but who will be so bold as to maintain that the attacks against the Jews from Byzantium to Berlin, from the time of the Crusaders to the recent anti-Semitic movement, had in the slightest possible way been influenced by the Spirit of Jesus Christ?   The Hamanism of Berlin knew no more of the Cross than Haman did, or rather they had a desire to crucify.   Mordecai had nothing of the apostle and the ascetic in him.   He retained the sole character of a praying man after his prayer had conquered; but in letting himself be invested with the office of vizier, he only wished to show in a visible manner the victory which his people had obtained through the help of God. This little book is remarkable and incomparable in the effect which it has produced upon the national and social life of Israel. Of course, the apostles rose higher to the ideal of true martyrs, because they conquered while they submitted to a violent death; but, alas! Mordecai and Esther, although they did not know the gospel, have found more imitators in the Christian Church than Stephen and Paul; and that without having to save themselves from similar dangers to those of their exemplars. The vengeance which Jews exercised was in self-defence, because their life was not safe even after the deliverance which Esther had effected, so long as the party of Haman remained alive. These would have resumed their former hostile plan as quickly as the unextinguished embers are set ablaze by the least favourable wind that blows upon them.

One must have an historic sense, and imagine himself in ancient Persia, in order to realize the true state of affairs there. Tyranny knew nothing of the right of man; and if any one obtained justice or favour, he owed it to the humour of the tyrant.

The little book considers, indeed, the whole affair of which it treats only from a religious and national point of view, and removes the history, so to speak, from the universal history of the world; but that is natural. The persecuted person thinks only of his danger and of his escape; and the believer thinks only of the wonderful interposition of God which he had experienced.

It is a beautiful thought of the Midrash when it compares Esther to the dawn of the morning. As the dawn announces the end of the night, so the book of Esther terminates in the O. T. the history of miracles.

On the other hand, the history here recorded is the first of the kind within the experience of the people. The remark of

the Midrash on chap. xi. is very significant, where, among
other enumerations of persons who were first in something,
it says, Ahhashverosh was the first buyer and Haman was the
first seller of men. For the first time was there such a
threatening in their history. Their children were once taken
away from them and killed by Pharaoh; they were also, as
a people, taken captive by Nebuchadnezzar, but their whole
existence of old and young, of man and wife, was never yet
in jeopardy. Such a dreadful danger is not to be mysticized.
We read of such in the history of ancient tyrannies and of
civil war, but from this history we get the indelible impression that we are reading of the experience of a people who
may expect renewed attacks against themselves from the
conquering nations among whom they reside. Therefore, no
book of the Old Testament has been so much commented on
and adorned as this. In its pages, not merely did a voice of
warning speak to the generations of Israel, but also a voice
of historical comfort. But it is just these many comments
and embellishments which testify to the genuineness and
authenticity of the Hebrew Persian text, because they display
quite a different spirit from that which characterizes the
original document.

3. This is already manifest in the additions which accompany
the book of Esther in the Septuagint.[1] In these the Jews have
no longer any scruple in mentioning their God; they appear
to be anxious to remove beforehand any objections which
might be raised against the narrative in Esther, and prove the
long use of the book in the congregations of the Jews.
Mordecai is represented as defending himself, by saying that it
was not pride that prevented him from rendering adoration to
Haman, but that he feared to give that homage to a man,
which God claims for Himself.

The second Epistle (*i.e.* that of the King in the LXX.

---

[1] Comp. the *Libri apocryphi veteris Testamenti graece*, ed. Otto Frid.
Fritzsche (Lipsiae 1871), with critical notes, where it is to be observed that
in the second text occurs the mistake πονίμοα instead of ταπεινοί on p. 31.

and in the Apocrypha) reveals clearly the whole tendency of these additions. It originated in Egyptian court life, and narrates of such persons who from personal motives had done harm to the princes who elevate them; it refers to examples in ancient history in which such counsellors led their kings to all sorts of evil, and also reminds of the accusations that were brought against bad viziers (as otherwise against queens) which occur in Oriental legends.

Very remarkable is it that Haman is there accused of having entertained the desire of bringing the kingdom of Persia under the rule of the Macedonians.

The author thereby intended to give the appearance of Persian originality to his letter, but he only proves the age in which he wrote, viz. at the time of the Ptolemies, who were themselves in a state of rivalry with one another in the Syrian kingdom; and there he could do it without giving offence. I have already observed in the commentary that the Syrian garrison in Jerusalem at the time of the Maccabees is designated by Josephus with the term Macedonian (Joseph. *Ant.* xii. 5. 4).[1]

We read, that in the fourth year of King Ptolemy and of Cleopatra, this letter became known in Egypt. From the fact that it speaks of Haman as a Macedonian, we may conclude that it refers to the time of war between the Egyptians and Antiochus the Great, which war terminated by the marriage of Ptolemy with Cleopatra the daughter of Antiochus (Joseph. xii. 4. 1). About the Jews the letter speaks intentionally in the name of the King of Persia, " that the Jews are far from being evil-doers, that they live under the most righteous laws, and are the children of the only and true God."

[1] Through the influence of Alexander the Macedonian, and so long as his empire lasted, Greece was confounded with Macedonia. But false readings are not rare, for, as I have shown in my comment to the Second Targum, p. 329, ought not to be read Macedonian. Dr. J. Levy in his *Lexicon* (as well as the passage in Bab. Yoma and Bereshith Rabba c. xxxvii.) is mistaken if he thinks that Macedonia stands for Media. It stands for Yawan, while מדי ought not to be translated.

The additions were evidently made as early as at the beginning of the third century of the Christian era, perchance in
order to diminish the force of the objections which were even
then raised against the book of Esther.

The most curious addition is, at all events, the so-called
dream of Mordecai. We read: "Behold a noise of a tumult,
with thunder, and earthquakes, and uproar in the land. And
behold two great dragons (δράκοντες) came forth ready to fight,
and their cry was great. And at their cry all nations were
prepared to battle, that they might fight against the righteous
people. And, lo, a day of darkness and obscurity, tribulation
and anguish, affliction and great uproar upon earth (comp.
Joel ii. 2). And the whole righteous nation was troubled,
fearing their own evils, and were ready to perish. Then they
cried unto God; and upon their cry, as it were from a little
fountain, was made a great flood, even much water. The
light and the sun rose up, and the lowly were exalted, and
devoured the glorious." The style is coloured by biblical
citations, but the story of the fight of the two dragons rests
upon an important Oriental parable. The legend is also given
by the Midrash Esther (Amst. ed. p. 94c), where the dragons
are not very correctly called חנינים, for sea-dragons are not
meant. It must appear strange, that if the dragons represent
Mordecai and Haman, then Mordecai is also called a dragon ;
but dragon here (δράκων) is nothing else than a winged daeva,
such as the Persians in particular knew. Both the good and
the evil daevas were winged. Their appearance was alike, but
they had different principles. So Astyages saw in his dream
a dragon having the wings of an eagle, and rushing towards
him. St. Jude also says that Michael the Archangel was
contending with the devil. The same meaning is to be given
to Daniel x. 13, where we read: "But the prince of the
kingdom of Persia withstood me one and twenty days; but, lo,
Michael, one of the chief princes, came to help me; and I was
left there with the kings of Persia." It is the war of the
religion of Israel against the religion of Persia. The same

is depicted in the war between the two dragons. The dream shows Mordecai as the representative of Israel, who is fought against and nearly conquered by Haman, but after Mordecai had fasted and prayed there appears suddenly a little spring from which flows abundant and refreshing streams. "The little brooks of God are full of water." "He puts down the mighty from their seat, and exalts the humble and meek." It was owing to Mordecai's personal representation of the principles of the Jews in their strife against Haman that Purim, as we see in 2 Macc. xv. 36, was called Mardocheu's day, the preceding of which, i.e. the 13th of Adar, the Maccabees celebrated with great joy their victory, and called it the day in memory of the execution of Nicanor. But the day of Nicanor is no more remembered, yet Purim remains. The same historical consideration which gave rise to the additions, namely, whether the vengeance of the Jews spoken of in Esther might not excite ill feeling among other nations against them, is also found in the Talmud (Megilla 7a): "R. Samuel bar Yehudah said: Esther sent a message to the sages saying, Appoint a feast in memory of me for the generations to come. They replied: Thou wilt thereby provoke the nations against us. She then sent them word again. The event is already recorded in the chronicles of the kings of Media and Persia." This sentence is very instructive in enabling us to get an intelligent idea of the Talmudic time. The Rabbis, in order to magnify their authority, and to preclude the supposition that a feast was instituted without their permission, and that the Sanhedrin did not even exist in Persia, have deemed it prudent to tell the story that Esther had applied to the sages to sanction the institution of the feast which bore her name.[1] Thereupon they raised the objection that the record of such an institution which commemorated their triumph over the

---

[1] [They go even so far as to ascribe to the book of Esther the authority of the divine legislator Moses. "It is written in the Law (Ex. xvii. 14), Write this for a memorial in a book." "Write this" refers to the Law; 'a memorial" refers to what is written in the prophets; "in a book" refers to the book of Esther (ibid.).—Trans.]

authorities under which they lived might be detrimental
to the Jews in exciting the hatred of the nations against them.
This fear (as we shall see) was drawn from their experience
of the time in which they lived.   She then replied, the fact is
already well known in history, there is no secret about it,
every one who reads history is cognizant of it.   This is even
given with greater clearness in the Jerusalem Talmud, according to which the Rabbis said as follows : " Have we not had
enough of impending oppressions ?   Do you want to increase
them by calling to mind the oppression of Haman ?"   R.
Shimeon ben Nahhman said in the name of R. Yonathan :
" Eighty-five elders (ומהם שלשים וכמו נביאים) have been very
sad about this affair . . . they said : Moses has told us :
No prophet should add anything from now and henceforth ; and yet Mordecai and Esther desire to appoint a
new institution !   But they did not cease to ponder over it,
until God opened their eyes and they found (a justification
for it), written in the law, and in the prophets, and in
books " (Tal. Jerus. Megilla, c. i. p. 9, W. Krotoschin).
However peculiar this Talmudic passage may appear, yet it
at the same time supplies a strong evidence of the genuineness of the book of Esther.   Who could have invented
this history, which in itself appeared venturesome to narrate,
—it contained not only elements of glory, but also elements of
danger for the people ?   It not merely strengthened the national
consciousness of Israel, but it excited also that of other nations.
The Greek and Roman Hamans were the proofs for the
Persian.   The tears of anguish which the people shed in the
Orient and in the Occident were only repetitions of their
bitter experience in Shushan.   Therefore no feast had such a
national background as the feast of Purim had.   Both the first
and the second Targums, which teem with such considerations,
were political and religious memoirs for the people.

Even the New Testament shows how great the importance
of Haman and Ahhashverosh was thought to be.   In the
Gospel of St. Mark vi. 23, Herod Antipas says to his

daughter: "Whatsoever thou shalt ask of me, I will give it thee, unto the half of my kingdom." He imitates in this that which Xerxes Ahhashverosh said to Esther (chap. v. 6): "What is thy request? even to the half of the kingdom it shall be performed." From this originated the name Ahhashverosh in the Christian legend which the so-called "Wandering Jew" bore. For Herod and Herodias are the restless ones, and therefore the name was first applied to Herod and then to Nero, who like a frog imitated the lion Ahhashverosh. Still more remarkable and recognisable is the passage in Rev. xiii. 18: "Let him that hath understanding count the number of the beast: for it is the number of a man, and his number is 666." This number is incontestably found in Hebrew letters[1] in the name המן רשעא, Haman the wicked. For it is—

$$
\begin{aligned}
5 &= \text{ה} \\
40 &= \text{מ} \\
50 &= \text{ן} \\
200 &= \text{ר} \\
300 &= \text{ש} \\
70 &= \text{ע} \\
1 &= \text{א} \\
\hline
666. &
\end{aligned}
$$

It is said of the beast that "he spake as a dragon," which reminds one of the Greek legends of the battle of the dragons in which Haman speaks. We cannot enter at large upon the question as to which of the contemporaries was regarded as Haman by St. John; but so much is certain, that even here Haman was considered as the abstract idea of the dragon and of the ferocious beast. It was therefore natural that the Jews should also in later times designate every powerful enemy who threatened to deprive them of life and property by the name צורר and Haman. Eisenmenger (i. 721) and

---

[1] We cannot enter upon an enumeration of the curious interpretations of this number which appear in every commentary, but it is to be hoped that our interpretation will finally set them at rest. Because the meaning of the apocalyptic seer—which is to be more considered elsewhere—receives the eby much light.

others had no right to reproach them with this; and what he
quotes from the book, עמק המלך, represents likewise Haman
only as the conception of the dragon, as it is done in the
Revelation. The dragon was to be assailed by the Messiah the
son of Joseph. Should they have refrained from calling Achmed
the vizier of Soliman by this name, who wanted to destroy
them all if they would not deliver to him all their gold and
silver (1523)? They had, as in the time of Haman, fasted
and cried to God; in fact, Achmed fell before he carried
out his plans, and the Jews for a long time celebrated
on the 27th of Adar an Egyptian feast of Purim (comp.
עמק הבכא, ed. Vienna, p. 76 and p. 254). Should they not
call by the same name Ibrahim Pasha, who was their most
bitter enemy (1536), and fortunately for them was thrown
over by Soliman? And if they so designated in Frankfurt
(1714) the robber and murderer Vincenz Fettmilch, was it
not because he treated them in the spirit and after the
example of Haman? Certainly no book of the Bible was so
popular among the Jews as the book of Esther. It was
inculcated that women and children should hear it read in the
synagogue on Purim; and that when all the other books of
the Bible shall lose their force in the time of the Messiah, it
and the Pentateuch will have their full efficacy. They used
to adorn and beautify the scroll, and private ones received
illustrations.[1] Schudt could not sufficiently express his
admiration for an illustrated Megilla scroll for which the
scribe asked five florins. The feast of Purim used to excite
in the breasts of the Jews triumphant as well as revengeful
feelings, for which many opportunities were given them. In
this they were not always moderate, and the reproach which
the Roman emperor brought against them, that among their
figurative representations they caricatured the cross under the
image of Haman, was not altogether unfounded; but their
persecutors were very moderate in their manifestation towards

---

[1] [There were some fine specimens of such in the Anglo-Jewish Exhibition at South Kensington, 1887.—TRANS.]

them of the spirit of the gospel.[1] The Jews used also to
show their joy on Purim by distributing gifts; every one was
in duty bound to send a מחצית השקל, a half shekel, to Jerusalem
or to the pilgrims in the Holy Land generally; and the gifts
to the poor were sent early in the morning, in order that
they might be able to prepare for the feast in the evening.[2]
And if there were no poor at the time, the money was kept
until there were some. The poor also made presents to each
other, especially of provisions. Yet a woman dared not send
a present to any other man but her husband, and so *vice versa*.
Confectionary alone was not sufficient for presents. What
Kirchner[3] reports, that the gifts sent consisted of the point of
a smoked tongue, peppered and preserved, has reference to the
passage in the Talmud Megilla 7*a*, which speaks of the gifts of
pepper and ginger. Pepper was held as symbolic of good sense,
and of more value than sweets. They feasted exceedingly well,
and practised all those customs which Christians used on Christmas. They were especially fond of the little cakes filled with
pap, which were called Kräppelchen (fritters), and which were
delightful objects, both to the young and the old.[4] Whatever
could make the poor comfortable and happy was sent to
them, because, as the author of the Mezahh Aron[5] says:
"They look, *nebich* (= poor things), the whole year for Purim."

Kirchner[6] narrates that in his time (the end of the seven-

---

[1] See my history of the Jews in Ersch und Gruber's *Encyclopädie*, ii. 27,
p. 79.

[2] About the Jewish customs, comp. notably the liturgical treatises of the
Jews, as Tania (Cremona 1565), § 39–41 ; Agur (Venice 1546), p. 80,
n. 1042, etc. ; Sefer Tashbaz (printed by Vincente Conte), p. 172, n. 14.
Comp. the compilation in Shibole Haleket and Mordecai. Also the useful
book of the Minhagim Tobim, which appeared first in Amsterdam, then
in Breslau, and re-edited by Bloch in Hanover. Likewise Simhhath
Hanefesh, Sulzbach 1797, p. 59c. Comp. also the Minhagim of Dyhren-
furt, 1692, etc.

[3] Comp. Paul Chris. Kirchner, *Jüdisches Ceremoniel*, enlarged by S. J.
Jungendres, Nürnberg 1726, p. 139.

[4] Krapf, Kräpplein ; in Silesia, Krüppel. See Frisch, *Lex.* i. p. 549.

[5] Mezahh Aron, *Jüdisch = deutscher Commentar zu Esther*, Fürst 1740, p. 51c.

[6] l. l. p. 137, note. This was in spite of the old ecclesiastical law, which

teenth century) the Jews used also to send gifts to poor
Christians on the Feast of Purim. The ancient Rabbis taught
that one could not rejoice enough on that feast, just as
Francis de Assisi said,[1] he wished it were possible that the
walls should also eat meat on Christmas; though there was
certainly a great difference in the object of joy. The Jews
then made their Purim to vie with the Christian Christmas
more than now, when many of them keep Christmas
(in Germany) as if it were their own feast. As some
Christian authors both seriously and jestingly explained
Weihnachten (Germ. for Christmas) as meaning *Wein nacht*,
" the night for wine," so were also the ancient Jewish Rabbis
of opinion that one must drink so much on Purim until he
will not be able to know the difference between ברוך מרדכי
(blessed be Mordecai) and ארור המן (cursed be Haman). It is
very curious that the two phrases are numerically the same,
viz. 502, just as the word בשר.[2] It is told in the Talmud
that R. Abaye and R. Hhananayh, having been very merry on
Purim, had by mistake exchanged their meals, but being poor,
when they came to dine together they knew not the difference.
Another Purim story which might have ended very seriously is
told of Rav. He and R. Sera dined together, and they got so
intoxicated that the former slaughtered the latter. But the next
morning God wrought a miracle, and the dead man was restored
to life. The next Purim, Rav invited his friend again to dine
with him, but he declined the invitation, saying: " I will not
risk my life this time, for not always do miracles happen."

forbade Christians accepting gifts from Jews. In the Canon Apost.
n. 70 (Patr. Apostl.), ed. Coteler (new ed. Antwerp 1698), ii. p. 446, we
read : "Si quis episcopus aut alius Clericus jejunat cum Judaeis vel cum
eis festos dies agit *vel accipit eorum festi xenia* exempli gratia, Azymi vel
quid hujusmodi deponatur," where the editors remark, that this took place
notably on Purim.
    [1] " Volo quod et parietes eo die comedant carnes si fierx potest." Comp.
my *Weihnachten*, Anm. n. 583, p. xcii.
    [2] Even in the Piut (poetical meditation) for Purim we read,—
                        כפרים עם נרדים
                    שתו ושכרו דודים, etc.

The feast was kept with great solemnity; the thirteenth day of Adar, which was formerly the anniversary of the victory over Nicanor, was afterwards observed as a fast, and called תענית אסתר, the fast of Esther; it was for the purpose of reminding them in the midst of the joys and pleasures of Purim of the great distress they had once passed through. There is no prescribed rule for it in the book of Esther, nor was it yet inserted in the index of fasts in Megillath Taanith. In the evening of the same day, the synagogue is well illuminated, and the minister unfolds the whole scroll and reads the narrative. When he comes to the passages which speak of Mordecai and of the final victory, the people repeat them after him in a loud voice and triumphant manner; but when the name of Haman is mentioned, then the young people, and especially the children, make a great noise, and knock at the benches as if they were to kill him again. The Jews were wrongly reproached for expressing their feelings of approval of Mordecai and of hatred to Haman in this dramatic spectacle. But similar scenes used to take place in the Roman Catholic Church in Passion Week, when, after the candles were extinguished, a great noise was made in imitation of the tumult which the Jews raised before Pilate. We read in an old book: "On Good Friday people rattle and make a noise in the Church."[1] And not only so, but scenes were exhibited in which Martin Luther in the effigy of an active boy received terrible blows, such as the Jews have not dealt to Haman. For the latter did only strike on wood and stone, and not men; but not so the former. Johannes Pauli tells an old story of a peasant who was frightened in the scene on Good Friday, in which, while the singing was going on, the priest put out one candle after the other, and then "every man began to beat and to strike as on such nights was the custom in the Papacy."[2] The sermons which were preached in the synagogue on Purim were pervaded by

---

[1] See my *Weihnachten*, n. 447, etc., to p. 134.
[2] Comp. *Pauli Schimpf und Ernst*, ed. Dittmar, p. 208.

an earnest tone (comp. Megilla 11*a*). R. Dimi bar Yitzhhak took for his text Ezra ix. 9 : " For we were bondmen ; yet our God hath not forsaken us in our bondage, but hath extended mercy unto us in the sight of the kings of Persia." R. Hhanina bar Papa took for his text Ps. lxvi. 12 : " Thou hast caused men to ride over our heads ; we went through fire and through water, but Thou broughtest us out into a wealthy place." R. Yohhanan took for his text Ps. xcviii. 3 : " All the ends of the earth have seen the salvation of our God." That happened in the days of Mordecai and Esther.[1] The ancient Christian Church held Esther in high esteem, as she highly deserved, for risking her life for the sake of her religion and her people. The Church knew how to appreciate the martyr's spirit, and she had a higher instinctive knowledge of the wonderful dealings of God with His ancient people than many modern theologians have. In the Epistle of Clement to the Corinthians we read : " And Esther, whose faith was perfect, exposed herself to danger when she undertook to deliver the twelve tribes of Israel from imminent destruction. With fasting and humility she prayed to the Lord, the Creator of all things, the eternal God, who, when He saw the affliction of her soul and the dangers which she encountered, delivered the people for her sake."

Clement of Alexandria[2] spoke in a similar strain : " That Esther who was perfect in faith delivered Israel from the power of the tyrant and from the cruelty of the satrap, and a single woman, bent down by fasting, resisted myriads of armed men, and by faith destroyed the tyrannical law. And she appeased the one, and the other, Aman, she removed, and by prayer preserved Israel in safety." In another place he says (*Paid.* lib. ii. p. 216) : " The one Esther we find rightly adorned. She adorned herself mystically ($\mu\nu\sigma\tau\iota\kappa\hat{\omega}\varsigma$) before

---

[1] See Tract. Bab. Megilla and Midrash Meg. and Targum I. Targum II. is in the Appendix with notes, but requires more full explanations than could be given in this Commentary.

[2] *Stromata*, lib. 4.

her king, but her beauty effected the deliverance of her people from murder." Jerome, too, writes in his letter to Paulinus: "Esther as a type of the Church delivered the people from danger, and after the death of Haman, which name signifies iniquity (*iniquitas*), she instituted a supper and a feast for posterity" (ed. Migne, i. 547). In his defence against Rufinus he says: "Let Esther be imitated, who long and silently endured the opinions of Artaxerxes, but at last corrected him by the truth" (ed. Migne, ii. 412, 413). Also in his introduction to Zephaniah (ed. Migne, vi. 1337) he speaks of Judith and Esther, who as a type of the Church had destroyed the enemies of Israel, and saved them from destruction. This honour of Esther to be a type of the Church was naturally developed from the whole Christian tradition, which regarded her as a type of the Virgin Mary. This often occurs in hymns. In a hymn, dating from the fourteenth century, we find the phrase: "Haec Esther imperatrix."[1] Another hymn from the same century is as follows:—

> "Hodie cubiculum
> Regis Hester suscipit
> Sedare periculum
> Quod *hostilis* officit
> *Aman* restans fraudibus
> Pro peccati videntibus
> Mortem mundo conficit."

Remarkable is what is contained in a Litany,—

> "O Maria, regis veri
> Virga aurea Assueri
> Iram judicis severi
> Scis lenire ut mederi
> Malit quam percutere."

Much is said of the rod, *i.e.* the sceptre of Ahhashverosh, with which he indicated his favour to Esther. Not only is Mary styled in another hymn as the rod (*virgula Assueri Aman tu mortifera sis adiutrix cleri*), but also in the famous

[1] Comp. Mone, *Lat. Hymnen des Mittelalters*, ii. 72, 157, 271, 434

poem of Gottfried of Strassburg;[1] the favour which the king
showed to Esther by the sign of the rod was the type of
the favour which God shows through the Virgin. For
Ahhashverosh was thought to represent God, Aman represents Satan, and Esther the saving Mary. Specially
strange, notably in reference to the Jews, is the moralizing
of the *Gesta Romanorum* (lat. 177), where Ahhashverosh is
compared with Christ, and Queen Vashti with the synagogue.
Vashti, who refused to come to the royal table, resembled
the Jews, who, according to the parable, refuse to come to the
Lord's Supper. Esther is the Church, which comes in her
place. Haman, the mortal enemy of the Jews, is in the person
of the Jewish people the Antichrist, who wants to hang
Mordecai, the type of the righteous.

When Queen Esther invites the king to come to her
banquet, she resembles the Church, which Christ invites to
come to partake of His body.[2]

The fast of Esther was spoken of as typical of the merit of
fasting during the Quadragesima.[3]

She was also regarded by the Church as a saint. The

[1] Comp. Genthe, *Jungfrau Maria*, p. 25, and the quotation from the
Minnesingers in Benek. *Mhd. Wörterbuch*, i. 483, *sub voce* "Gerte."

[2] *Gesta Romanorum*, n. 177, ed. Oesterley, p. 577. Owing to this honour
which Ahhashverosh received in the Church, it also came to pass that his
name was frequently given to persons even in the Protestant times.
Fritsche, a well-known theologian and liturgist, bore that name. Ahhashverosh Brandt was a famous physician who undertook a journey to
Moscow (comp. *Rhesa Litth. Dainos*, p. 351). Another by the same name
was Professor in Bremen (Hamberger, *Gelehrte Deutschlands*, i. p. 5). The
mysticism of the name of Esther found a place in Reformed circles. In
the terrible commotions which took place in Elberfeld and Ronsdorf, the
sectarian Eller left his wife Vashti, and took another whom he called
Esther (comp. Göbel, *Gesch. des christl. Lebens*, iii. 470). In England, too,
Christian women were called Esther, and shortened into Essie (comp.
Charnock, *Phenomena*, p. 41). So also the handsome wife of Casimir of
Poland was named Esther.

[3] Comp. a German sermon of the thirteenth century, ed. Grieshuber, ii. 85.
In Erfurt the 7th of September 1632 was observed as a day of commemoration of the victory near Breitenfeld, and coins were struck with the
inscription : Dies Purim Evangelicorum anno 1631, VII. Sept. Erfurt.
celebrati (comp. Falkenstein, *Erf. Chronik*, p. 709).

editor of the Bible of Royaumont calls her *une sainte femme.*
In Calmet's Bible it is said : " The Church Fathers make this
holy queen (*sainte reine*) appear as a figure of the Church of
Jesus Christ."

She is represented upon images in the attitude of kneeling before King Ahhashverosh, who reaches her the sceptre,
while this sceptre expresses tenderness.[1] Her saint's day
is differently given : May 24 or July 1. The Copts
keep it December 20. The editors of *Acta Sanctorum* decided for September 4. In old Martyrologies are found the
words : " Hester regiae " or " Hester reginae." [2] The Jesuit
Canisius remarked on this : " The beautiful and faithful, who
with the aid of Mordecai saved the whole Jewish people
from a threatening danger." A similar sentiment is found
in collections of Greek sentences—

μνήμη τῆς δικαίας Ἐσθὴρ τῆς λυτρωσαμένης
τὸν Ἰσραὴλ ἐκ θανάτου.

The poems and popular books which treat of the book of
Esther are numerous. John Chryseus wrote *Histori Hester,*
a play translated from the Latin into German, Wittenberg
1546 ; towards the end of the sixteenth century appeared
Hamanus Tragoedia, which was written first in Latin by
Thoma Naogeorgo, and then in German by Joh. M. Moeshemio
and Mag. Joh. Postio. The same has been republished in good
German by Damianus Lindner in 1607. Older than all these
is a book with the following long title : " A very beautiful,
pleasant, and comforting play from the Holy Scripture and the
book of Esther, composed in short rhyme, in which is shown
how God has at all times punished pride and self-will of the
wicked, and rewarded the piety and humility of godly men
and women." Printed at Magdeburg by Mich. Lotther,[3]

---

[1] Comp. Guenebault, *Dictionnaire Iconographique* (Paris 1850), p. 191.

[2] *Acta Sanctorum,* Bolland, Juli, tom. i. pp. 12, 13.

[3] Comp. Gödeke, *Grundriss der Geschichte d. deutschen Literatur,* i. pp. 297, 308.

1537. Hans Sachs has also elaborated the narrative. An alliterative Anglo-Saxon treatise of the book of Esther is not yet printed. It is ascribed to Aelfric who lived in the eleventh century.[1] There was also a scriptural play by Lopa de Vega, entitled *La hermosa Ester*[2] (*Comedias* appeared in Madrid in 1621, xv. p. 151). There was a Judeo-German play, entitled שפיל אחשורש, printed in 1708 and communicated by Schudt in his *Jewish Curiosities*. It is peculiar, but not without merit. This play has given occasion to Wagenseil to make the incredible assertion, and that in opposition to Cuper, that the whole dramatic art has originated among the Jews.[3] Several travellers (as, *e.g.*, Stochowe and Thévenot)[4] have reported the tradition that Safed in Galilee was the birthplace of Queen Esther. This appears to be connected with another opinion, that Safed is identical with Bethulia, where Judith lived. In the reports of Jewish travellers (as of Yihhus ha Abod)[5] it is told that the tomb of Esther is at Kefar Baram, not far from Safed. This must refer to a mural monument of Esther; as it was believed among the Jews (from Benjamin of Tudela and others) that the famous tombs of Mordecai and Esther were in Hamadan. It is told that on Purim the Jews of Safed went to the grave, and there read the Megilla, ate and drank, and made merriment. It does not appear very credible that they would do this at a grave.

The name Bethulia, which was given to Safed, in connection with the above legend, may have arisen from the fact that the Hebrew word בתולה, virgin, is found in the name (comp. Esth. ii. 19). A similar legend[6] reports that a bird flew into the room when Esther was born, as an emblem of

[1] Richard Wülker, *Grundriss der Geschichte der Angelsächsischen Literatur* (Leipzig 1885), p. 471.

[2] Comp. Ticknor, *History of Spanish Literature.*

[3] Comp. Wagenseil, *De civitate Norunbergensi*, Altdorf 1697, p. 166.

[4] Comp. Robinson, *Palestine*, ii., under "Safed."

[5] *Itineraires de la terre sainte*, ed. Carmoly, Bruxelles 1847, p. 456 (which is from the year 1537).

[6] Comp. Adami, *Deliciae*, i. 598.

liberty and intellect. What a pity that the bird did not fly into the studies of many of the commentators on the book of Esther!

4. We add a few literary notices.

With regard to the literature, see Wolf's *Bibliotheca*, tom. ii. 89. To this may be added the dissertation of B. L. Eskuche, Marburg 1734, who consulted the then known literature, and the Talmud and Midrash. The Roman Catholic commentaries are little used. That by Feuardentius was consulted by Prof. Dr. Schulze in his Commentary in Lange's *Bibelwerk* (1876). Prof. Sepp has, with respect to this book, deviated from the spirit and the piety of the Catholic expositors. Intent to bring about a church reform, he began with the revision of the canon of Scripture, which he proposed before the Vatican Council, but which rightly took no notice of it. He agitated against it with anti-Semitic hatred, but without profound learning (Munich 1870).[1] On the other hand, there are two thick volumes of commentary on Esther, which the Benedictine Monk, J. A. Nickes, published in Rome (1858), in which he manifests a spirit of piety and diligence, but he is deficient in scientific criticism and study of the book itself. Besides the books that are alluded to in Keil's *Introduction* and in Schulze's *Commentary*, I mention the following Jewish commentaries: מפתח אל מגלת אסתר, by Reggio (Vienna 1841). Abr. Aben. Ezrah, *Commentary on the Book of Esther*, edited by Joseph Zedner, London (Nutt) 1850. The Commentaries on Esther, Ruth, and Lamentation, by R. Menahhem ben Hhelbo, R. Tobia ben Eliezer, R. Joseph Kara, R. Samuel Ben Meïr, and an anonymous author, published by Adolf Jellinek (Leipzig 1855). I add to this *Liber Estherae Graece*, by O. F Fritzsche (in two parts, as contributions to the *Index Lectionum*), Zürich 1848, which he

---

[1] As regards Melito, who does not literally enumerate it in the canon, he ought to have known that already older theologians have clearly explained that Melito included the books of Nehemiah and Esther under the title of Ezra. Comp. Routh, *Reliquiae Sacrae*, i. 136.

already at this time received into the collection of apocryphal
Scriptures. With regard to poetry founded on Esther, I
refer to the notices in the *Annals of the History of the
Jews*, iii. 75, such as a drama *Usque* by Solomon, and the
epic poem *Copia Sullam* by Sarah. Of course, the most
curious of all is *Ahhashvervosh and Esther*, a drama from
the East, by Dr. J. L. Chronik (Berlin 1875).[1]

It is much to be deplored that Jews distinguished themselves prominently in introducing rationalistic and unscientific
doubts against the book of Esther, and that these were not
obscure men. It was Spinoza (see Keil, *Introd.* p. 473)
whom Gesenius, Bertheau, Ewald, Meier, etc., followed, who
placed the date of the book of Esther in the time of the
Ptolemies and Seleucian kings, for which there is no ground,
and against which everything speaks. The criticism of
Zunz was not so great as his diligent compilation of the
fragments of post-biblical literature. What Fürst observes on
the book of Esther (*Der Kanon des alten Testaments*, Leipzig
1868, p. 105) is a thoroughly unscientific conception of the
Talmudical passages about the Megilla. To the followers of
the rationalism of Spinoza and his disciples belonged also
Herzfeld in his *History of the Jews* (ii. 358). Incompre-
hensible are the insinuations of Grätz (in the *Monatschrift für
Wissenschaft des Judenthums*, 1886, p. 425). Jewish authors
particularly should take the trouble to dig deeply into the
history of ancient Israel. To catch the spirit of universal
history is a conditional qualification for true exegesis, which

---

[1] The spirit of this most curious drama is characterized on p. 89, in the
following verses :—

Ahhashverosh and Esther	They cut for the blacks
Burn the lair	The thread of the Fates.
Of the black revolution	They teach the Moors,
In pitch of infatuation.	They teach them Mores.
They wash the tresses	Born were the Moors
Of the dirty heads.	To become Kapores, etc.

Skutsche in Breslau published a humorous, satirical Purim play with
song in five acts, entitled *Haman, der grosse Judenfresser*, which I did
not see.

qualification even Spinoza and Zunz did not possess. Hasty formulas were found for hasty assertions of unauthenticity and interpolation. Anti-Semitism needed only to appropriate the exegetical arts of rationalism in order to break the stave over the people, amongst whom some so carelessly handled their own canon of the Scripture.

Paul Lagarde (Bötticher) has recently brought out about Purim a learned treatise; its conclusion is impossible to accept. I hope to be able to enter upon it at large elsewhere. With regard to the short treatise by Jules Oppert, *Commentaire historique et philologique du Livre Esther*, Paris 1864, I have referred to it in the Commentary.

CHAPTER I.

ויהי בימי—"*Now it came to pass in the days.*"

The rabbinical teachers make peculiar observations upon these words. R. Levi says (Bab. Megilla 10*b*) there is a tradition from the time of the Great Synagogue, that wherever in the Scriptures a sentence begins with "ויהי, it was," it indicates a time of sorrow and distress (צער). R. Ashe says that this is only the case when a scriptural sentence begins with ויהי בימי, "and it was in the days." In fact both views are of ancient date. In another place (Midrash Esther 85*b*) one is assigned to R. Eliezer and the other to R. Jonathan, from which we conclude that these two authorities lived in the days following the destruction of the temple, in times of great need and distress. The latter view only was the prevalent one (comp. Yalkut Esther, § 1044 [where the passage is not correctly quoted], and the first Targum). Moreover, the ancient sages found the idea of sadness intimated by the very sound of the Hebrew word ויהי, *vayĕhee*, which is similar to *woe*. The Greek οὐαί (the Latin *vae* of earlier occurrence) had the same sound and character, and was at the time used by the people (as Christ used it Matt. xi. 21, xxiv. 19 ; Mark xiii. 17). It was at that time not unusual for homiletical teachers to use, in the ecclesiastical Hebrew and in the popular Greek language, forms of expression which contained a combination of ideas in order to serve the purpose of their teaching. Even the Greek translation of Scripture offers examples: the exclamation of woe in the Old Testament הוי (especially in Isaiah) אוי is not only rendered by οὐαί, but also in Ezek. vii. 26, הֹוָה עַל הֹוָה, event upon event

A

(or R. V. "Mischief shall come upon mischief") is translated by οὐαί. This was occasioned by the sound of the word.

The five verses, concerning which the above observation is made, are as follows: (1) Gen. xiv. 1, "And it came to pass in the days of Amraphel;" (2) Ruth i. 1, "And it came to pass in the days when the judges judged;" (3) Isa. vii. 1, "And it came to pass in the days of Ahaz;" (4) Jer. i. 3, "It came also in the days of Jehoiakim;" (5) in our passage, "It was in the days of Ahhashverosh." A sixth passage was overlooked, viz. 2 Sam. xxi. 1, perhaps because it does not read ויהי בימי but ויהי רעב בימי דוד, and perhaps also from a desire not to place David in juxtaposition with Amraphel, Ahaz, Jehoiakim, and Ahhashverosh.

Now it would not be correct to assume that the observation of the Jewish teachers, of which we speak, is a complete homiletical form after their mode of thinking. It is true that all verses which begin with "it was in the days" introduce a catastrophe. They are things of impending danger which are to be narrated.

The occurrences are of a sad character. They are such disastrous events as the Greek calls συμφορά, so that this word is associated with gloom and sadness. The Hebrew word הוה is to be understood in a similar sense. Though it really means only an event, an occurrence, it has been explained as denoting mishap and mischief.

But the Jewish teachers who called attention to this, namely, that it is to a certain degree the historical style to begin a narrative of eventful catastrophes with the expression, "And it was in the days," have thereby had nothing else of more importance in view. They themselves lived in trouble and distress (צרה and צער), and only saw these, else they would have taught in a more comforting strain, that all the five catastrophes which begin with ויהי בימי, are only told for the reason that they emerge in the glorious events of the history of the kingdom of God.

Gen. xiv. 1 begins with the war of the kings of the East

against Canaan, but concludes with the victory of Abraham and with the benediction of Melchizedek, who as priest of the Most High God brings wine and bread, and says, "Blessed be Abram of God Most High, possessor of heaven and earth." The history of Ruth does indeed begin with a famine, but it ends with the joyful event of the marriage of the converted heathen woman with the Israelite in whom is no guile, with Boaz of whom sprang David and David's greater Son.

In the days of Jehoiakim (Jer. i. 3) there was indeed misery and trouble in Judea, but Jeremiah is called to see the fulfilment (i. 11). In the days of Ahaz there was fearful backsliding and idolatry (Isa. vii. 1), but the narrative only introduces the announcement of the prophet, "Behold, a virgin shall conceive, and bear a son, and shall call his name Immanuel" (ver. 14).

It is introduced with a catastrophe in order to conclude with glory. It is not told on account of the existing evil, but on account of the coming salvation. The history begins with the night, in order to conclude with the dawn of the morning. The days of Ahhashverosh serve for the purpose of revealing the redeeming grace of God. In the days of Ahaz the good tidings are declared which shall set free the whole world. The Roman historian Livy, in describing the days of ruin which came upon Rome through Brennus, says the latter exclaimed, "Vae victis," "woe to the conquered;" and he remarks, that "this is an intolerable expression to Romans" ("intoleranda Romanis vox," Liv. v. 48). But wherever the Scripture begins with its ויהי בימי, with a "vae Israelis," it reports this only in order to reveal that salvation will soon come forth, whose fulness and blessing is indispensable and unspeakable.

The Greek version of the LXX. translates the Hebrew word ויהי in all passages with "ἐγένετο," in harmony with the historical style of the Old Testament; thus in Luke ii. 1, ἐγένετο δὲ ἐν ταῖς ἡμέραις ἐκείναις, "it was in those days" (ויהי בימים ההם).

In the days when Augustus caused the Holy Land to be
taxed its bondage began; but just in consequence of this
taxing, the Messiah, who makes all who believe in Him free,
was born in Bethlehem.

אחשורוש הוא אחשורוש—"*In the days of Ahhashverosh, that
Ahhashverosh.*"

It would have been sufficient to say, in the days of Ahhashverosh, who ruled from India unto Cush; but the repetition
of the name in connection with הוא, *ille, iste qui,* is a pregnant indication of the significance of the man spoken of.

When, therefore, the Midrash Esther, p. 86a, compares
this mode of expression with similar ones, as in 1 Chron. i.
27, אברם הוא אברהם, and Gen. xxxvi. 3, הוא עשו אבי אדום, etc.,
it does so improperly. In the passages quoted, the word
הוא has simply the sense of *qui idem,* and establishes the
identity of the compared persons, as their names and epithets
do not fully sound alike (as זה, which, as a complete relative, is
like the new pers. *e'eh*). But here, where the same name is
connected by הוא, the explanation of mere identity cannot hold
good, but, through the repetition of the name, הוא receives
the meaning of the Latin *ille.*[1] And the sense is: that
famous and renowned Ahhashverosh, even more known
than Cyrus and Darius amongst European and West Asiatic
nations. The Talmud (Megilla 11a) by way of homily
remarks, that in all places where הוא occurs it expresses
the virtue or the vice of the person from beginning
to end. But the thought in connection with him, as intimated by the identifying pronoun הוא, was, that Esau was
in his character all his life long an Esau, the father of Edom,
just as Abram was by nature and grace always an Abraham
(Gen. xvii. 5). But here also the historical significance of
the expression "Ahhashverosh, that Ahhashverosh," because
it is not repeated in the Bible, was not sufficiently considered

---

[1] In *Corn. Nep.* 4 we read, "Pittacus ille, qui septem sapientum numero
est habitus."

nor emphasized. This peculiar formula does already in itself
indicate that we have to think of a famous Ahhashverosh,
and that the king of the book of Esther is none other, as
shown in the Introduction, than Xerxes of the Greek writers,
the son of Darius Hystaspes, whom the cuneiform inscriptions,
according to Lassen (*Keilinschr.* p. 165, etc.), call *K's'hars'a*,
and according to Benfey (*Keilinschr.* p. 65, etc.) *K'hshyársha.*

The twenty years of the reign of this king contain the
great decisive points which through him affected the world-
wide nations of antiquity,—the Jews and the Greeks,—and
the memorable deliverances from calamity and distress which
both experienced. The Greek histories know Xerxes mostly
only as a commander of armies, and on the battlefield. The
book of Esther reports him as he was in his court and in his
seraih. Therefore it is just these last reports, notwithstanding
that they have Israel for their central point, which show us
the external movements within the Persian empire, as the
result of former events. Bearing this in mind, it appears
clear that the opinion of R. Levi (Meg. Esther 86*b*), that
Ahhashverosh is identical with Artahhasta mentioned in the
book of Ezra, is not to be accepted, and has only arisen (as
already shown in the Introduction) from the reading of Ezra
vii. 1. He cannot be Artahhshasta (*i.e.* Artahhsharshta or
Artashsh, Artaxerxes), for the prefixes distinguish the names
of the Persian kings from each other. The termination is
mostly, as Hewdot observes (i. 139), the same letter which the
Dorians call san, and the Ionians sigma (ʂ). Comp. Khurush
(כרש), Daryawush (דריוש), Ahhashverosh, Hakhamanish, Chish-
pish (Teispes), Fravartish, Dadarshish, Serish, and many others.

המלך מהדו ועד כוש — "*Who reigned from Hodu unto
Cush.*"

This is not explanatory of the former clause, "that Ahhashverosh." It is not meant to say that it happened in the
days of the king who ruled over a wider extent of territory
than any other; for Darius had already extended the borders

of his dominion from India unto Cush; and to some extent can the same be said of Cambyses.

In the cuneiform inscriptions Darius and Xerxes have the same majestic titles. What is meant to be conveyed is, that Xerxes was not only king of Persia when this happened, but also that his dominion extended from India unto Cush, *i.e.* from east to west, from the rising of the sun unto the going down thereof.

Benfey translates a cuneiform inscription both of Darius and Xerxes as follows: "I, the mighty king, king of kings, king of populous countries, king of this great and mighty earth, far and near." Aeschines mentions in his oration against Ktesiphon, chap. xlii. (comp. Brisson, *de R. Pers.* iii. 73), a letter in which Xerxes had written that he was lord over all men, from the rising to the setting of the sun. Mardonius in his speech to Xerxes mentions the victories of the Persians over the Sakes, the Hindoos, and the Ethiopians [1] (Herod. vii. 9). Only through the repetition of the name joined by the pronoun הוא is the famous celebrity of the reigning king indicated.

That he swayed his sceptre from Hodu to Cush was merely the title of the great king. The Jewish Rabbis are therefore wrong when they interpret these words as indicating that he was a usurper, and not of royal descent (Yalkut, 1045, and therefore Rashi, *in loc.*). This cannot be maintained of Xerxes (comp. Herodotus, vii. 3), and the words of Scripture give no occasion to such an assumption. Nor could they have had Smerdis in mind; for if they had known of him, they would have also known that his reign was short. There seems rather to pervade the interpretation of the Midrash a stronger tone of antipathy and censure than we perceive in the book of Esther itself. This hostile feeling is apparently only directed against Ahhashverosh, but in reality it is meant

[1] The Sultan Soliman, when writing to Francis I. of France, called himself "emperor of emperors, prince of princes, disposer of the crowns of the world, the shadow of God over both hemispheres, ruler over the Black and White Seas, of Asia and Europe." Comp. Ranke, *Fürsten und Völker*, i. p. 5.

in spirit against the Roman emperors of the time, who certainly were often more arbitrary than the great Persian king.

Hodu (הדו), for India, is the only passage where it occurs, and shows the local origin of the book of Esther. The cuneiform inscription of Lassen and Benfey has *Hidhu*. On the other hand, Nasal, which is found in the Indian *Sindhu*, is in Zendic *Hendu*. The name denotes originally only the land of the seven streams of the Indus; it was afterwards applied to the eastern territories also (comp. Lassen, *Ind. Alterth.* i. p. 2). To derive the name Indus from the Sanscrit *ind = und*, to flow (as also Indra was explained), as the god of rain, is doubtless correct (comp. my *Engländer in Delhi*, p. 10). Darius pushed forward with his armies as far as the countries around the Indus, and subjected them (Herod. iv. 44). Their people formed the twentieth district of his dominions, and afforded a rich revenue (Herod. iii. 94).

וְעַד כּוּשׁ—*" Unto Cush."*

The usual explanation of Cush is Ethiopia, by which we are reminded of the victories of Cambyses over Upper Egypt. The LXX. has therefore left "Unto Cush" untranslated, perhaps because it was so near home. But we must call attention to something else. The name Cush is not limited by local conditions, but rather describes certain tribes of a defined mode of life; therefore Nimrod the hunter is derived from it. The Cossaei (in the present Chusistan), according to the scanty information that we have of them, are scarcely distinguished in their warlike habits from the Sakes, by which name Herodotus also designates the Persians as Scythians. That the name Cush could also be applied to these, I believe that I have shown, in that the legendary hero Rustem of the country of the Sakes (Sadjestan) appears as Cushan (see my *Commentary on Judges*, chap. iii. p. 33). They are then dark nations of Scythian (Nimrodian) mode of life, which must be understood under the term Cush. In this sense their spread becomes explicable. We can see the force of the

saying of the prophet Habakkuk, "I saw the tents of Cushan
in affliction; the curtains of the land of Midian did tremble"
(chap. iii. 7).   The name Ethiopia is to a certain degree
only a translation of Cush, for כוש or כות signifies dark.[1] Comp.
the Sanscr. *Khad*, and the Gr. σκότος.

Antiquity also clearly distinguished these formidable
Scythian nations of the steppes of Europe and Asia according
to their colours.   The extensive custom of calling the
victorious nations white and the conquered nations black
(comp. my *Magyiar Alterth.* p. 144), refers to natural marks
of distinction.   Cush, as the son of Ham, was the dark
contrast to the fair nations of Gomer, the son of Japhet,
somewhat like the dark and the dark brown nations in
contrast to the Germanic nations of light complexion.   Accordingly, it would not be impossible to think of the term
" Unto Cush" as defining the limit of the campaign of Darius
against the Scythians or Sakes; but this is out of consideration.   Cush expresses here, in general, the extreme limit.
As Homer places the Ethiopians at the setting of Helios, and
at the extreme ends of the world (*Odyss.* i. 24), so India and
Cush stand opposite to each other for the lands of sunrise and
of sunset.   It was thought that in the empire of the Persian
great kings the sun never set.   This idea the Jewish teachers
have rightly perceived, as *e.g.* Rav said, "Hodu and Cush
mark the two extreme boundaries of the world."

" *Hundred and seven and twenty provinces.*"

This enumeration also testifies to the original historical
value of our book with regard to the history of the ancient
Iran.   I should like to see an impartial acknowledgment
that this is in accord with the other credible records of the
division of the old Persian kingdom.   For the differences

[1 In the same extensive sense the Psalter of the Book of Common
Prayer renders Cush by Morians land.   Bearing this in mind, we can
easily see that the Ethiopian woman of Num. xii. 1 is Zipporah, the
daughter of Jethro the Midianite, and thus the objection of infidels, that
Moses encouraged bigamy by his example, falls to the ground.—Trans.]

which, according to Brisson (*de Regn. Pers.* lib. i. 169), were
thought to exist, are not really there. In Dan. vi. 1 we
read that Darius the Mede appointed over the kingdom 120
satraps. Whoever this Darius might have been, the report is
really not at variance with what Herodotus tells (iii. 89), that
Darius the son of Hystaspes appointed twenty governors. For
these twenty satrapies were large divisions, which included
smaller ones, like provinces and counties. The first province
consisted of Ionians, Magnetians, Aeolians, Karians, Lycians,
to which also belonged the Milyians and Pamphilians. So
also the third province consisted of Hellespontians, Phrygians,
Asiatic Thracians, Paphlagonians, Mariandians, and Syrians.
As these provinces had just six divisions, we may assume
that all the twenty satrapies had each six smaller revenue districts, called מדינה,[1] so that there were in all 120 such districts.
When Josephus (*Antiq.* x. 11. 4) speaks of 360 provinces, he
makes the mistake of assigning to each of the 120 revenue districts three governors, while he knows himself that only the 120
governors had a revision college of three superiors over them.

A closer investigation concerning the revenue provinces in
Herodotus will show that Persia is really wanting among
them.[2] The central governing country holds a special position
among the subjugated countries. Therefore there are twenty-
one countries[3] which the inscription of Bisutun[4] enumerates
(ed Benfey, p. 8), because Persia stands at the head of them.
Attention has often been called to the fact that seven tribal
chiefs have hurled the Persian Smerdis from his throne. The
passage in Plato (*De Legg.* iii. 659) which appears so obscure
nevertheless clearly shows that in his time there yet existed
to a certain degree the right and liberty which these

---

[1] Comp. מדה, מנדה, a tax, from מרד, to measure, *metior*; Sanscr. *Mâd.*
See my *Commentary on Judges*, p. 17.

[2] Herod. iii. 97, ἡ πέρσις δὲ χώρη μούνη μοι οὐκ εἴρηται δασμοφόρος.

[3] The inscription of the black Assyrian obelisk tells of twenty-seven
Persian tributary princes, according to Oppert's explanation (comp.
Spiegel, *Eranische Alterth.* ii. 261).

[4] [Bisutun means without walls.—TRANS.]

seven had established in Persia. Further on more will be told
of the seven great men (i. 14), the first in the kingdom, who
hold interview with the king, which, according to Herodotus,
was the privilege of the friends of Darius. Persia proper,
accordingly consists of seven tribes[1] or divisions, which
together with the 120 other countries make the total number
of 127 ; but it must not be overlooked that the number 127
is an indivisible one. A homily of R. Akiba declares that
Esther was elevated to reign over 127 provinces, because she
was a descendant of Sarah, who lived just 127 years (Megilla
Esther 86*d*).

Ver. 2. " *That in those days, when the king Ahhashverosh
sat on the throne of his kingdom, which was in Shushan the
capital.*"

The first verse mentions the ruler from whom the event
proceeded, to introduce the history and to throw light upon it.
The second verse exhibits the place in the kingdom where it
happened. The third verse sets forth the year of the reign,
and the occasion which produced the narrated catastrophe.
There appears, in beautiful simplicity, a fine premeditated
historical art in the composition.

In ויהי, " it was in the days of Ahhashverosh," is recorded
the whole reign of the king ; but the expression " in these
days," points out that the memorable event took place when
the great king sat on his throne in Shushan. For during the
hot season the king left the capital and took up his
residence in cooler Ecbatana in Media.[2] Some writers have
been more precise on this point, and assigned the sojourn of
the king at Shushan to the season of spring, at which time the
weather is most lovely there even now, in spite of the city
being in ruins (see Rawlinson in Ritter, ix. 302). The reason

---

[1] Comp. Ritter, *Asien*, viii. 13. Dunker, *Alterth.* 270 and 445, note.

[2] The Babylonian Jewish teachers imply a sojourn of the king in
summer and winter in different palaces in the words, היו לו שני פלטירין,
M. Esther, 87*a*.

for this may be, because the king returned to his capital to celebrate the festival of the new year in spring.

For Shushan, though very much embellished by Darius, had already been the capital since the accession of the Persian dynasty. Xenophon in the *Cyropaedia* does rightly speak of Cyrus sojourning there (lib. viii. 6). It was probably on account of its splendid situation, surrounded by mountains and streams, and abounding in fruit and flowers, especially the lily שׁוּשַׁן,[1] which gave it its name. It had already become so attractive to the older monarchs as to induce them to choose it for their residence. But this was not the only reason why the Persian monarchs made it their residence. When the Medes and the Persians became masters over the whole complex territory of the Assyro-Babylonian empire, they soon perceived that in order to become great kings they must come out of the national, local, and tribal surroundings. As the later Caliphs left Arabia and established their seat of government in Bagdad, so did the Medo-Persians leave their tribal territories in order to found the capital in the subjugated countries. Babylon could not enjoy this honour, because it would recall the hostility of the old form of government, although the assertion may be well grounded, that Cyrus resided there for some months. Shushan became, especially since the time of Darius, the official, magnificent, famous residence of the Persian kings, as it certainly had never been before. The observations which we have in the ethnographical table of Gen. x. are of inestimable value. They teach us that there was a national distinction between the nation of the Babylonian-Assyrian empire and their confederates; and not only between those who were sons of Ham, but also between Elam, Ashur, Arpachshad, Lud, and Aram, who were descended from Shem, and the nations of Madai, to which also belonged Paras.

---

[1] Spiegel in *Eranische Alterthumskunde*, ii. 623, does not give the reason why he is not convinced of this etymological derivation, but holds it as suitable. Any other explanation is not to be thought of.

When the Persians established the capital in Shushan, they found themselves in Elam, that is, outside their national country, and yet in its vicinity—in subjugated but in peaceful countries, as Strabo remarks (comp. Dunker, ii. 593).

As a centre and seat of the great kingdom the city is characterized by the appellation of הבירה,[1] habeera (meaning properly, the castle, and in an especial sense the royal castle, the residence), as Shushan is everywhere called by Nehemiah (i. 1) and Esther and Daniel, even without special personal reference to the reigning king. For in the fortified castle was the seat of the king.

In a similar manner have modern cities received a compound name, as Edinburgh, Petersburg, etc. For this reason it ought never to have been questioned that Daniel could not speak of any other capital but that of Shushan, which he calls הבירה, or that there is a difference between this and the Shushan of Esther and the Greeks (as Ritter thinks, influenced by Rawlinson). — Apart from all verbal and archaeological reasons, it must appear from the spirit of the vision of Daniel, in which he sees the decisive battles of the Medo-Persians with Alexander, that the vision took place in the centre and seat of the Iranic dynasty. It must clearly appear from the same internal evidence that the vision was seen by him near the river Ulai, because this river was connected with the great glory of the Persian kings. It flowed whither the king went—as if the glory of the royal residence went everywhere with him; for, as it is said, the great king drank no other water but from its springs.

It ought also to be observed, that though the river near Shushan is elsewhere called Choaspes (comp. the passages in Brisson, i. 1. 9, 82), Ulai and Choaspes are not on that account two rivers, as some in ancient and modern times have thought; Loftus, for instance, who deems it necessary to

---

[1] The derivation of the word is known. In Scr. *vri*, Zend. *vere*, means "to defend." Therefore Zendic *vara*, Persian *baru*. From this comes the Greek βάρις, which must again not be confounded with βάρις of Egyptian origin (comp. Sturz, *de dialecto Macedon.* p. 89).

establish new theories concerning the changes of rivers (see *Journal of the Royal Geographical Society,* vol. xxvii. p. 130, etc.; comp. Rödiger, *Zeitschr. deutsch. Morgenl. Gesellsch.* xiii. 715). But Eulaeus-Ulai is the name which Choaspes bore owing to the fact that it alone contained the pure water of which the king drank.

The Midrash has, p. 87*a*, the following homiletic legend : The angels appeared before the Lord with the complaint, " Lord, the holy temple is destroyed, and this wicked man רשע sits on the throne in joys." But their attention is called to the ways of judgment and to the changes of the times. These had come to pass in an awful manner. Shushan lies in ruins, so that one might doubt its identity. It has become a desert, an habitation for lions and hyenas. Superstitious fanatical robbers are its custodians. Benjamin of Tudela found the country deserted as early as in the twelfth century, and he describes the ruins of the palace of Ahhashverosh (ed. Asher, p. 73). He could still report of a large number of Jewish inhabitants ; but they also have gone, according to the reports of Petachia (ed. Carmoly, p. 65). Not before 1851 were extensive investigations undertaken among these ruins. But though, indeed, the proud capital of ancient Persia is destroyed, the Jews have as yet received no comforting compensation to their above complaint, for the temple in Jerusalem is also still in ruins. And certainly neither the great king of Persia nor the later Roman Cæsar must be held responsible for its destruction. The ruins of Shushan and of Babylon have not contributed to its restoration. The causes for its downfall were not political, but spiritual.

The ideas which the Rabbis in their homilies entertain concerning the throne on which the king sat, though somewhat peculiar, are yet profound. For while the words, " when the king Ahhashverosh sat on the throne of his kingdom," express only figuratively the time in which the king returned to Shushan, the Jewish interpretation takes the figurative expression in its original literal meaning. The throne was

the symbol of the royal power, and they connect their observation with its symbolic-phantastic (*symbolisch-phantastisch*)
ornamentation. They do this in accordance with the Oriental
usage and spirit.

The acquisition and the possession of a throne denotes in
itself power, as well as the besieging and the removal of a
throne denotes victory.[1] The transition of the universal
monarchies from Babylon to Media, thence to Alexander, and
thence to Rome, is represented by them as a transition of the
throne. But what sort of a throne was this ? No other but
that of Solomon, as described in 1 Kings x. 18. For the
throne of Israel which the Son of David establishes is spiritually the universal royal throne. He is represented in
prophecy as ruling over all the nations of the earth (Ps.
ii. 8, etc.).

But they embodied this truth in the type of political
dominion. They likewise made Solomon to be a real universal
king. Their historical insight appears to have been greater
than it is generally admitted, in that they also ascribe
universal dominion, *i.e.* preponderating power, to Egypt. For
they say that the throne of Solomon came after his death
into the hands of Shishak, king of Egypt, and then Asa
recovered it when he conquered Serach the Cushite. They
further assert that Nebuchadnezzar had it in his possession,
and that Cyrus sat upon it. "I have seen,[2] says Elasar bar
Yose, its fragments in Rome, but Ahhashverosh did not get
it, for only a Kosmokrator (קוזמוקרטור) had a right to sit
upon it."

The application of this word is interesting. The Midrash
applies it several times to great kings. It originated in
Jewish speculative theology, hence in the Orphic hymn it is

[1] Comp. my *Abhandlung über Kaiser und Königsthrone*, p. 23, Berlin
1874.

[2] Elasar bar Yose was, together with Simon bar Yochai, in Rome after
the war of Barcochba in the second century. When he says, ברומי ראיתי
שבריו, he may perhaps mean the booty which the Romans took from
Jerusalem, of which they put a facsimile on the triumphal arch of Titus.

applied to heaven (Hymn 4. 3), but heaven shared it and
other epithets with potentates of this world. It has been
applied by the Church Fathers, after the example of the
Apostle Paul,[1] to the tyranny of the princes of this world, to
Satan, and to demons (comp. Du Cange, *Gloss. Graec.* p. 721).

But precisely because the only potentate of the world
(קנה שמים וארץ) has alone the right to sit upon the throne,
therefore the thrones which the tyrants of the world usurp
are destroyed, and the Solomonic throne also is not restored,
so long as the son of David does not take possession of it in
spirit and in truth.

Ver. 3. "*In the third year of his reign.*"

It was in the second year after the death of Darius that
Xerxes, as Herodotus reports (vii. 7), had put down the
rebellion in Egypt, and so in the third year after his return,
he convoked a council of the princes to learn their views,
but chiefly to impart his own (Herod. vii. 8). The agreement
of this narrative of Herodotus on a secondary point with the
verse above, by itself indicates the identity of Xerxes with
Ahhashverosh, although our book does not mention the conclusion of the war against Greece. For the historical matter
of the Scripture, especially of the book of Esther, is concise
and solid, aiming to come to the point, and presupposing
the necessary limits of its report.

It does not tell of the Greek campaign,[2] because it was
known, and also because its main aim was to derive the
Israelitish history from things which were not considered of
first-rate importance. It is satisfied to narrate that it was in

---

[1] Eph. vi. 12, πρὸς τοὺς κοσμοκράτορας τοῦ σκότους τούτου. Just because the Midrash mostly uses Kosmokrator for earthly great kings is the
homily (Wayikra Rabba, § 18, p. 160a) of interest, when it says : "When I
made thee for a Kosmokrator, for a tyrant, over all men, I have nevertheless given thee no power over those who are called sons of God." The
note of Schenkel to Eph. vi. 12 is not correct.

[2] Comp. Hävernik, *Einleitung*, tom. ii. p. 340 [Eng. trans., Clark,
Edinr.].

the third year of Xerxes when the princes and the satraps
assembled in the palace, in order to intimate thereby that a
great political fact underlay the occurrence. For in order
that what is told in the book of Esther should actually
happen, there must be according to the purpose of God a
special council of the great men of the State. There must be
an important political motive, but this is of no consequence
to the narrator. It was enough for him to record the
general magnitude of the kingdom, because this only throws
light upon the coming event. An ordinary banquet could not
invest it with a psychological explanation. There was just
one campaign to which all were gathered. The Scripture
very often tells the events in Israel as apparently separate
from the events in the world, and yet they flow through
them like a river, which, in passing through a sea, does not
mingle its waters, but becomes clearer and clearer, like the
Rhine passing through the Lake of Constance. Yet the fine
threads which connect the experience of Israel with the
great powers of the world are to be found everywhere. We
seem to hear in universal history a quiet sound, an echo of
the future. Israel's history is not to be separated from the
fall of Nineveh, Babylon, and Media. Our book also, instead
of saying that there was once a great feast, when this and
that happened, quietly but instructively reminds us of the
great fact with which Xerxes was occupied at the time during
which the sudden and unexpected intrigue was brooding, a
fact which at once produced Israel's calamity and redemption. For the historian shows us both the external political
condition and the internal party intrigues of the corrupt royal
seraihs.

"*He made a feast unto all his princes and his servants.*"
Herodotus, in reporting the council of war against the
Greeks, did not need to tell what was a natural and common
occurrence, that there had been a great feast provided for all
the chiefs of the country. For his main object, according to

his manner, was to illustrate the directions of the gods, and the dream through which the great event passed. But for the book of Esther, the feast was the great fundamental ground of its historical record. From the royal table issued the narrated catastrophe. A great feast was then in itself, as in modern times, nothing extraordinary in the Persian court. The feast "unto all the princes and servants" would not have a place in universal history, in spite of its being given to the generals and potentates of the universally famous Persian expedition against the Greeks. When it is mentioned here, it is not because of the persons that are enumerated, not for the sake of the guests, but for its own sake. With the significance of the men is joined the great war, which included the germs of a new universal culture; but with the fact of the feast is connected the domestic occasion out of which proceeded the local, but for Israel the worldwide, events about Esther and Haman. These "princes and servants" of the king are more closely called *Parthemim* (פרתמים), *i.e.* the first (*fratama*, Scr. *prathama*, comp. Benfey, p. 88), and princes of the provinces (districts, מדינות). The Midrash has an interesting and instructive comment upon these princes, which certainly, on account of the corruption of the text [1] and the general neglect of scientific knowledge, has scarcely ever been considered.

The passage reads thus : " R. Eliezer says, *Parthemim*, these are two legions of the king, for no king is called Augustus until these two nominate him." And who are these ? R. Isaak said they were the דקומיוני ואנוסטיאני, when these gave

---

[1] This is seen on the same page, where there is given a homiletic definition of the word Paras, *i.e.* Persia. It is so called because it was twice severed asunder, once in the days of תרדה and once in the days of ארדיבאן. The first name should be read יתדנרדה, Jezdegerd, the last new Persian king whom the Arabs vanquished ; and the other is Artaban, the as' Parthian king whom the Sassanides dethroned. By this the age of the book is to be seen. This gloss could only have been written shortly after the fall of the kingdom of the Sassanides, about the end of the seventh century. Of course this cannot be proved to a demonstration, but it gives everywhere the impression of the Roman dominion.

counsel to Nebuchadnezzar (Titus), and he marched to Jerusalem and destroyed the temple, then God destroyed them,
and appointed others in their place; and these are, as R.
Yehudah ben Shimon in the name of Eliezer says, יבולני ובדקריאני.
The explanation of this passage, as given by Sachs (*Beiträger
zur Sprach- und Alterthumsforsch.* i. 113), is a complete misunderstanding, because it is based upon a conjectural emendation of the text instead of upon observing the general thought.
This is as follows: The Jewish commentators always proceed
from the standpoint that the various experiences of the
princes and the kingdoms of the world are to be explained
from their relation to Israel. They thus considered, not
only the history of Babylon, but also of Rome, which broke
up the last remnants of parliamentary independence, destroyed Jerusalem and Bethel, and burned the temple. The
aim of the contemporaries of the later Roman emperors was
that the Roman Senate should only be an institution in
appearance, and the real power to elect the imperators and to
keep them on the throne should be vested in the army. To
this the above comment refers. When Titus (who is to be
understood under Nebuchadnezzar) destroyed Jerusalem, he
did it—so is the tradition (which Benjamin of Tudela [1] could
still speak of in the Middle Ages)—by special order of the
Senate. For this the State was punished.

Hence comes its moral degradation. What the Parthemim
were to Ahhashverosh,[2] that exactly were the דקומיוני or rather
the דקיריוני and אנוסטיאני, viz. the Decurions and Augustani, in
Rome.[3] The Decurions were considered in the imperial
provinces what the Senators were in Rome. By the term
Augustani were understood those whom the Greek writers
call Augustalioi, βασιλικοί, officers of the highest dignity.[4]

[1] Comp. my *Historische Versuche*, p. 20.

[2] Even in later times this was the formula: "Et is esset imperator
quem Senatus elegerat." Spartian, *Didius*, 5.

[3] Comp. Salmasius, *Vopisc. Aurelianus*, cap. 33.

[4] Concerning these, comp. Du Cange, *Gloss. Gr.* p. 151. Concerning the
Augustani in similar and original meaning, Tacit. *Ann.* xiv. 15. 2: "Tunc-

They want to say that before Titus the prominent men who
appointed the emperor were the senators and consuls, but
now they are the יכולני, which stands for בלני, *i.e.* Calones,[1] and
ברקוריאני, which stands for פרטוריאני, *i.e.* Praetoriani.   The reins
of government passed from the hands of the senators into
those of the life-guards.   The cause of this is now ascribed
to the evil counsel of the patricians against Jerusalem.

But the eyes of the Jewish teachers ought not to have
been closed to the fact that the same could be said of the
Jews themselves.   They were right when they directed the
attention of their people to the history of the nations for an
explanation of the judgments of God.   The experiences which
the Roman Empire supply on this point are indeed many and
awful, only they must not conceal from themselves the cause
why they themselves lost their freedom and independence.
Formerly they were masters, but now they are servants ; once
a nation, but now dispersed.   Israel also was once a people
of Parthemim—great and free in the doctrine and love of
God—until they destroyed their "temple."

Ver. 4. " *When he showed the riches of his glorious
kingdom.*"
He proved the fulness of his royal power, in that he entertained the assembled princes for the space of a half-year,
180 days.   But this feast is distinguished from the one
mentioned in the 5th verse.   The former was the council
feast, instituted to deliberate about the great enterprise of
the king.

It is repeatedly reported by the ancient writers that it
was a custom with the Persians to hold consultations about
war and other affairs (de apparatu bellorum et seriis rebus,
Ammian. Marc.) during meals (Brisson, lib. ii. c. 131).   These
reports are to be understood to mean that their custom was

que primum conscripti sunt equites Romani cognomento Augustanorum
aetate ac robore conspicui et pari ingenio procaces, alii in spe potentiae."
[1] Tacit. *Hist.* ii. 87–iii. 33.

not like ours, to carry on important business first and then to
entertain, but they did both at the same time. The Midrash
says (876) the king manifested his greatness by displaying
before the guests the trophies of Jerusalem. So likewise
Herodotus, for the glorification of his people, represents
Mardonius and Xerxes as boasting of their hitherto achieved
victories, in order to incite to the war against the Greeks
(vii. 9). Clericus is of opinion that all the princes did not
remain together during the 180 days of the feast, but that
they took their turn, some left when new ones arrived. But
this supposition is not necessary.

Ver. 5. "*And when these days were fulfilled, the king
made a feast unto all the people that were present in
Shushan.*" [1]

It lasted seven days, and was held in the garden of the
palace. After the feastings and the consultations of the
princes, at which the king displayed his whole power which
he put in motion against the Greeks, there followed a feast
specially for the people, which lasted a week.[2] There is a

---

[1] In the *Vierzig Vezieren*, ed. Behrnauer, p. 340, we read : "The king
held a great feast, at which high and low sat at table and ate to their
satisfaction."

[2] Comp. *Epische Dichtungen* of Firdussi, translated by Schack, p. 203,—

> "Whereupon they celebrated seven days long,
> A merry feast with wine and song."

When Rustem obtained a victory there was a feast at the court of the
Shah, p. 248,—

> "After this sort, with wine and song,
> They revelled a week long."

P. 133,—　　　　"Nigh the castle in Yredsh's gardens,
> Even in the palatial chambers,
> Resounded the mirth of the festive days."

P. 47,—　　　　"The Shah, after the arrival of the expected,
> Had the royal garden decorated."

Hence the use of trees in the royal rooms (comp. my *Kaiser Königsthrone*,
p. 83, etc., and Hammer, *Gemäldsaal*, iv. 265).

passage in the *Schahnameh* of Firdussi giving also an account
of a feast lasting seven days, and according to the old Oriental
custom it is held in the delightful groves of a park. Then
follows the description, as by the epic poet, of the splendour
that was there. There were curtains of white (חור) and of
blue (תכלת) *karpas*, which originally in Sanscr. *Karpása* meant
cotton, but afterwards fine linen also.[1]

It has been observed[2] that Curtius (iii. 3. 19) describes the
cap of the Persian kings as having a white and blue stripe.
But the same author says afterwards (vi. 6. 4) that the head-
dress had white and purple stripes. Perhaps he is correct
in both passages. White and blue are the colours of the
atmosphere and of the sky (*caeruleus*).[3] These curtains
(*aulaea, vela*) were furnished with cords of בוץ (fine linen)
and purple, suspended on silver poles, and tied to marble
pillars. It is described that what was then considered as the
most costly material was used in the decoration of the garden
tents. To this class belonged byssus and purple. Many
names of the ancient materials described also their colours.
Cords of byssus are white. A Jewish teacher remarks in the
Midrash that freemen fasten their garments with cords of
byssus (c. 88).

That white was in many cases the sign of liberty is well
known. Khalid, the Arab, ordered the Taghlebites to wear
a black band as a mark of their dependence. Though colours
as marks of party distinction are no longer in vogue to the
same extent as of old, yet even to-day white is among
Mohammedans the mark of the masters of the country (comp.
my "Geschichte der Juden," in *Ersch und Gruber*, ii. 27, p. 236).
A name which should imply the use of silk is not found in

---

[1] Comp. Lassen, *Ind. Alterthumsk.* i. 250 and iii. 25. Ritter, v. 436.
The Targum, Midrash Esther 88c, has paraphrased תכלת with אייריגן, Gr.
ἀέρινός, sky-blue.

[2] Dunker, *Gesch. des Alterth.* ii. 608, note.

[3] Comp. Philostratus, *Life of Apollo*, where this tells him of the dome
of sapphires upon the royal palace of the Magi : "For this stone is dark-
blue, according to the colour of the sky."

the book of Esther. The silver poles stand opposite the
marble pillars. The former (כליו) are movable, the latter are
fixed. Both are white; for not only כסף, silver, has its name
from the colour of white, but also שֵׁשׁ is white marble, and
likewise Egyptian byssus was called so on account of its
whiteness. The great residence in which the feast took place
was named Shushan, from the white lilies which were
cultivated in the garden. The floor was a mosaic pavement
of בהט (from which came alabaster, *alabastrum*, Goth. *Alabal-
straum*, probably with the article אל, as אלבהט or אלבחט, to be
known among the Greeks and Romans), of שׁשׁ, like the pillars
of דר and סחרת.

These two words, as well as בהט, occur only once here. דר is
taken, since Bochart, to be pearl; yet the objection of Gesenius,
that the language used here can only refer to stone, has its
weight, and therefore it must mean mother-of-pearl, or pearl-
stone, as the LXX. translates. סחרת, according to Fürst,
should be read סקרת, from the Chald. סקר. If so, it must be
taken for red marble, which was very much used.[1] This
explanation is to be preferred, because thus we see the same
mingling of colour, white and red, for the floor as for the
cords of the tent. Upon this floor stood gold and silver
chairs and tables.

The description given here is so little exaggerated, that
even Mardonius had similar magnificence in his camp. The
Greeks found after their victory " tents decorated with gold
and silver, couches wrought in silver and gold, and other
precious things " (Herod. ix. 80). Xerxes had left his own
tent to Mardonius, and Pausanias was amazed at the sight of
the golden and silver beds and tables, etc. (ix. 82). It is
interesting to observe that the gloss of the Greek translation
read, instead of ודר בסחרת וסחרת, ורד,[2] and therefore translated

[1] Comp. Lamprid, *Elagabal*, 24 : "Stravit et saxis . . . porphyreticis
plateas in palatio, quas Antonisnianas vocavit, quae saxa usque ad nostram
memoriam manserunt sed nuper eruta et execta sunt."

[2] The form ורד for rose, for the first time in the Mishna (comp. my *Rose*

κύκλῳ ῥόδα πεπασμένα, roses (ῥόδα) were scattered about, for the custom of decorating with roses was then and afterwards / considered as the greatest festive ornamentation.

Firdussi describes, p. 47,—

> " There stood a golden throne 'mid beds of roses,
> Where flowers gaily shone in perfumed posies ;
> The silken carpets, precious stones of splendour,
> Gleam in the groves where lamps their glories render."

The whole description of ver. 6 begins with the word חור. In the Masoretic text the letter ה is longer than usual ; but it would be in vain to try to find a reason for the custom of Bible copyists of making some letters more prominent (see my note on *Ruth*, p. 225), and such peculiarities in the old and well-preserved manuscripts can sometimes only be explained from the casual notes of the copyists.

Ver. 7. והשקות בכלי זהב —" *And they gave them drink in vessels of gold, the vessels being diverse one from another.*"

Xenophon says of the Persians, that they were proud of possessing a large number of drinking vessels (*Cyrop.* viii. 8. 18 ; comp. Athenaeus, lib. xi. p. 465). Accordingly, there were many changes of cups at a royal entertainment in order to display the abundance of possession ; and so it is the custom even now at the festive entertainment of great people.

ויין מלכות רב —" *And the wine of the kingdom was in abun-dance, according to the bounty or hand* (כיד) *of the king, as the great king is.*"

There could be no thought of insufficiency. The expression יין מלכות, " the wine of the kingdom," is striking, for it proves also how the king entertained his guests. יין המלך would be wine of the king ; יין המלכות is royal wine, *i.e.* such

und *Nachtigal*, p. 19). The linguistic form, to which ῥόδος also belongs, appears to be found only, after my supposition in the Biblical canon, in the name Ruth (see my *Comm. on Ruth*, p. 206).

as the king himself used. It was not distinguished merely
for quantity, but for quality—the best wine, such as befits
the feasts of kings. The king himself drank only Syrian
(chalybonic) wine (comp. Brisson, i. c. 84). May we not
direct our attention to another table, at which also a king
sat? This was in Cana of Galilee. There the wine was
insufficient for all the invited guests until the mercy of their
Friend supplied them with the royal wine of the first miracle,
and turned the old drink into taste of the joy of the new
faith. What Ahhashverosh gave for the purpose of intoxication, this King gave for sober reflection upon the grace
of God.

Ver. 8. והשתיה כדת אין אונס—"*And the drinking was according to the law, none could compel.*"

The king had strictly commanded every steward to let
every man do as he liked in this matter. This order was not
for the purpose of teaching the people to be temperate in
drink, but rather to enhance their pleasure by leaving them
to please themselves without any restraint. The sense of the
passage is that it was the custom at court that, in spite of
the wine being so costly, the courtiers were to see that every
one should have as much of it as he liked to drink.[1] For
such large drinking companies all restrictions ceased. Every
one was to feel at home. The Roman custom to nominate
kings of the table and modimperatores (comp. Ursinus, *de
Tricliniis Roman.* p. 383, etc.) has no parallel here. The
Persians were great drinkers. "They drink so much," says
Xenophon, "that they cannot stand upright upon their feet,
and must be carried out." Every occasion was used by them
to get drunk. When Themistocles fled to the King of Persia,

---

[1] The Midrash explains the non-compulsion to have consisted in that
every one could drink the wine of his country. But this was a feast
especially for the people of Shushan. R. Levi says the Persians used
to have a very large cup at their feasts, which every one was obliged to
empty, no matter whether he could or not, or whether he died from the
effect. This cup the king did not have at his feast (Jalkut Esther 1048).

the latter embraced the opportunity of making a drinking feast (Plut. *Themistocl.* 28). Firdussi of the Mohammedan time faithfully represents this ancient custom. When the hero was about to march to the war, we read (p. 151), " Then music resounded, the cups were filled with wine, and the shah was merry at the feast." Rustem describes it thus (p. 481),—

> " The cups were handed round to every head,
>   And cheeks of guests have grown, like spring flowers, red."

When Kai Chosru gave a feast (p. 511),—

> " All heroes deep in lust have sunk,
>   And reel from out the palace drunk." [1]

In this revelry in the palace of the garden at Shushan every one could share; but, says the Mishna, Mordecai and his like-minded companions had no part in it. For the pious, who adore their God, and are penitent as long as they are in exile, such feasts are unsuitable.

Ver. 9. נם רשתי המלכה—" *Also Vashti the queen made a feast for the women in the royal house.*"

It was not unusual for the royal women of the East to hold feasts in their apartments for the court ladies. This we are told by Firdussi of the Princess Menishe, that she had an annual spring-feast with her ladies; and likewise Sudabe, the wife of the shah, invited her stepson Sijawush to a female feast (p. 389),—

> " The music rang, and foamed the sparkling wine,
>   The minstrels diamond decked in glittering line,
>   Loud sang."

Chardin remarks: " In Persia as well as in the whole

---

[1] Xenophon lets Cyrus accurately describe the condition of a Persian drunken company (*Cyrop.* i. 3): "You all screamed without understanding a word. You also said such funny things that caused laughter. Without hearing the singer, you swore that he sang excellently. After you rose up to dance . . . you could not stand erect upon your feet."

Orient, the women used to celebrate feasts at the same time with the men, but separate" (comp. Rosenmüller, *Morgenland*, note 705).

It might appear that the mentioning of the women's feast is unessential to the narrative, inasmuch as the catastrophe proceeded from the revelry of the men, but not of the women. But the notice introduces first the queen in the history, to make known that she was the legitimate queen, because she occupied in the royal house the same position with regard to the women as Ahhashverosh did with regard to the men. We also learn from this that Vashti was equally hilarious at her feast as her husband was at his. The Jewish teachers refer to this in their homilies, when they blame her equally with her husband as a seducer to luxury and vice, so that the women of Israel, too, caught the infection. They apply to Vashti Isa. iii. 12, "As for my people, children are their oppressors, and women rule over them." There were such four wicked women in the world, Jezebel and Athaliah in Israel, and Semiramis and Vashti among the nations (M. Esther 89*b*).

The name Vashti undoubtedly means in Old Persian, " beautiful woman," and is either an epithet, or stands for the proper name (ἡ Καλλώ). The LXX. reproduces it by Ἀστίν. In Aeschylus occurs the name Astaspes (*Pers.* 22).

Ver. 10. ביום השביעי—"*On the seventh day, when the heart of the king was merry with wine,*" etc.

Eunuchs were always in the monarchies of the Asiatic Orient the most influential courtiers. The chief officer of the army (2 Kings xxv. 19), the chief butler and chief baker (Gen. xl. 2), as well as the chief treasurers, chief guards of the harem, and chamberlains, סרסים, *i.e.* spadones, were chosen from this class. Hammer observes (*Gesch. des osman. Reichs,* v. 360) that down to modern times, with the exception of the chamberlain, the other court officers were eunuchs. Their names, he says, are usually in the East borrowed from flowers and perfumes (such as hyacinth, tulip, narcissus, musk,

amber, camphor); but as regards the names of the officers
mentioned in ver. 10, the supposition is not perhaps without
ground that they denote official designations. We are therefore in a position the more easily to explain them by introducing the Syro-Chaldaic element, because the Medo-Persian
kingdom has surely in this but entered upon the inheritance
of the great power of Babylon. Consequently we have
in מהומן the Syriac מהימן, meaning faithful, reliable,[1] a
qualification which was considered necessary, particularly to
eunuchs.

The Syriac translator therefore renders in several passages
the word סרים simply by *mehiman* (see 1 Kings xxii. 9 ;
2 Kings ix. 32). The first-mentioned in our passage was
either the chief officer of all, or a cabinet minister. The
second is בזתא, *biztha*, meaning the treasurer, from בזא or
בזה, which signifies prey, substance, riches (comp. Dan. xi. 24).
חרבונה, *hharbona*, the chief of the bodyguard, from חרב, חרבא,
"a sword." In בגתא, *abagtha*, must be understood the office
which the Turkish court designates by *kislarga*, *i.e.* the guard
of the harem, for which office eunuchs were specially suitable.
For the explanation of the word, it may be useful to draw
attention to the oft-repeated assertion of ancient writers, that
βαγῶας or βαγῶος is the Persian word for eunuch. But, on
the other hand, it is not improbable that אבגתא and זתר, *zethar*,
signify the chief baker and the chief butler. The first
comes from בג, bread, food (Sanscr. *bhag*, cf. βέκος, φάγειν),
the second from זתר = שתר, from שתה, to drink. The last
name, כרכס, is more easily explained from כרכא כרך, which
means in Syriac "a castle" or "fort," and represents the
Kapuaga or chief commander of the castle or tower.

That we have to do here with officials and not merely

---

[1] Comp. Herod. viii. 105. In Xenophon, *Cyrop.* vii. 5. 64, we read :
" That they are faithful, of this they gave the best proof at the fall of their
masters. For of no one can be shown such fidelity in the misfortunes of
their masters as of the eunuchs." Chardin, *Voy.* vi. p. 247 : " Aussi trouve-
t-on dans le pais, quils sont sans exception plus rusez, plus secrets, *plus
retensus, plus fideles* et même plus prudens que les autres hommes."

with accidentally mentioned names, appears from the added clause : "The seven *sarisim* (eunuchs) that ministered in the presence of Ahhashverosh the king." It becomes thus intelligible why these seven men received the order to fetch Vashti. Royal etiquette required that she should be accompanied by the greatest dignitaries of the State to the dining-room of the king.

The king was inebriated when he issued this order. It was not the custom among the Persians that the wives of kings should take part in such general drinking feasts. This appears from the fact that Vashti had a separate feast for the women. To this effect is what Plutarch tells us (*Sympos.* i. 1), which is repeated by others, "that the Persians never play and dance with their wives, but with their concubines." In Firdussi's poems, which are true pictures of ancient customs, it is not mentioned that the wife of the shah, but that the female singers and slaves, were present at the intoxicating festivities. True, in the well-known passage in Herod. v. 18, the Persians say to the Macedonians, "With us in Persia, it is the custom to prepare a great feast, to which also the concubines and the housewives, κουριδίας γυναῖκας, are invited;" but they appear thereby, for the sake of their pleasures, to have expressed themselves in equivocal terms. Had it been the usual custom, Vashti would have taken part in the preceding feast of 180 days, and her appearance would not have had to be postponed till the seventh day of the feast for men. The unusualness of the custom, moreover, appears from what we are told, that Ahhashverosh wanted to show the great men of the country her beauty, as they had never seen her. For Plutarch's report (*Themist.* 26) as well as Justin's (41. 3), that even the faces of the wives and concubines were not seen by strangers, is true with some exceptions. But the king being drunk, and conscious of his might, thought himself above feelings of jealousy and of the petty customs, and ordered Vashti to come.

Ver. 12. ותמאן המלכה—" *But the queen refused.*"

Plutarch says (to the ill-instructed Prince Anf.): " The Persian king held all for slaves, with the exception of his wife, over whom especially he ought to have exercised his authority." Now, just because she enjoyed extra liberty, she refused to come, for she wanted to show the other concubines the power of her charms. The Midrash (90a) explains the refusal in its own peculiar fashion. According to it, Ahhashverosh was a usurper of the throne, and Vashti was the granddaughter of Nebuchadnezzar, and therefore the legitimate heir to the throne. She sent to him this message : " When thou wast groom in my father's stable, thou wast accustomed to fetch prostitutes, and dost thou regard me as one of them ? " It is noteworthy that the word she is said to apply to him is קומיס אסטבלאטי, *Comes stabulatus, i.e.* the *Comes stabuli, Comestabilis, Conestabilis,* from which the great office of the French Connétable has its origin. (By the Byzantines Κοντοσταῦλος.) The queen refuses to come at the king's commandment by the chamberlain. If he had come himself to fetch her, she would have readily gone ; but excited as she was, like himself, through much wine, and conscious of her beauty, she asserted her self-respect. She dared to say no to the messengers, and they in their turn did not bring to the king this refusal in a mild form.

" *Therefore was the king very wroth.*"

No good ever comes from pride aroused by drunkenness. Herodotus narrates the story, according to which Kandaules, king of Lydia, had boasted of the beauty of his wife, and this was the cause of his losing his life. The Persians who came to Amyntas of Macedonia were so greedy after intoxicating drinks and things of extravagance, that the embittered inhabitants killed them. In the case above, the king considered himself greatly insulted, because his will was not obeyed in the presence of his princes and courtiers. His dreadful anger was excited, and the only person who could appease it, Vashti herself, was too proud and stubborn to come.[1]

Ver. 13. "*Then the king spake to the wise men, which knew the times.*"

The affair did not end with the king's becoming sober. The ancient writers often remark, that the transactions which used to take place during the time of inebriation were resumed after the people got sober (Brisson, ii. 131). This circumstance is instructive, as it shows the power of small things at the great royal court. The etiquette of royalty is, especially in the East, the type of authority, and the only restraining influence to which the king himself is subject. Vanity and consciousness of power have sometimes also in Christian States given rise to high political questions, because of non-observance of proper etiquette towards the sovereign. The king, indeed, should not have allowed that the queen should be fetched by main force; but whether it was possible that any one should disobey his will was a question for the highest council of the kingdom to hear and to determine. The יודעי העתים are the Magi, as they are so called, not on account of their superstition (as Clericus thinks), but because they are experienced, such as know what is proper under the circumstances; they correspond to those whom we designate as worldly wise, or savants. They are acquainted with the times and customs, are the judges concerning ceremonies and ordinances (רת ודין) in the land. It is intentionally mentioned how seriously the king took the matter in hand.

In spite of the great affairs of the kingdom which occupied

[1] In the *Vierzig Vezieren*, ed. Behrnauer, p. 107, it is told that the Caliph Harun Arrashid got into such a passionate rage, that it lasted for days, and that was because the citizens of Cairo came too late to do him homage. Just then, a female slave in placing a dish upon the table happened to spill some of its contents, so he wanted to tear her to pieces. Then she turned to him, and exclaimed : "O Caliph, God has commanded to restrain one's passion, and to forgive people their offences." This had an effect upon the caliph, his anger disappeared, and he forgave. But none had spoken in this manner to Ahhashverosh.

his mind, the apparently insignificant incident which resulted from drunkenness he could not let pass without discussing it like one of the most difficult State questions. In a kingdom such as was that of the great Persian king, nothing was insignificant. Everything that concerned his person was important. He proposed the matter before the cabinet council with all the judicial formalities, as in cases of greater concern he was accustomed to consult those who were versed in the ordinances and laws of justice (comp. Herod. iii. 31).

Ver. 14. והקרב אליו—"*The ministers before whom he proposed the matter were standing next unto him.*"

They that sat near him in the cabinet, who saw the face of the king, were the seven princes of Persia and Media. A matter which concerned the persons of the king and of the queen could only be discussed by the highest tribunal. It is known that Herodotus tells of the seven tribal chiefs of Persia, that they always enjoyed free access to the king.

Darius belonged to the order of these seven chiefs, and when he became king another succeeded to his place. For the king was the head of all, and was surrounded by seven princes, as the seven (at the time known) stars [1] surround the sun. Hence the number seven appears in all the State institutions of the Persians. To Ezra the order was issued from the king and his seven privy councillors. Aeschylus mentions seven highest officials as standing nearest to the king. Firdussi could still report of seven heroes surrounding the shah.[2] Therefore the names which are mentioned do not, as the Midrash says, signify offices, but are names of the great

---

[1] How the names of the seven stars became the names of the seven days of the week, and with regard to the astrological opinions in connection therewith, and what influence this had upon the formation of numbers, see my *Esmun*, chap. ii.

[2] *Ep. Dicht.* p. 248,—

"Kai Kawus the throne ascended,
Renewed in health, and Rustem vanquished,
Gurgin, Bahram, Ruham, Rustem,
Tus, Giw, and Guders around him."

officers who surrounded Xerxes, of the highest dignitaries,
statesmen, and generals who administered the affairs of the
State, and accompanied him in his campaigns.

It is worthy of remark that the names here mentioned
appear again in the well-known Persian histories. And it is
also of great interest and importance to the testimony of the
truth of this book, to find that Herodotus reproduces the
names in the Greek form of writing. The narrative receives
special vividness when we find at the court of justice the
same persons of whom Herodotus, on account of their
military participation in the Persian war, gives us more full
information. One caution is here necessary. The two texts
of the names must not be compared for the purpose of cor-
recting each other ; they both agree, but their variations are
due to the different pronunciation of the names by the Greeks
and by the local Jews. Moreover, great stress must not be
put on the Masoretic punctuation, which was the work of
centuries in which the Jews had forgotten the pronunciation
of these names. In order to proceed securely in this attempt
of identification, we begin with the sixth name, with מרסנא,
Marsena. One can recognise in him Mardonius the son of
Gobryas, the inciter of the war. There can be no doubt
about the person of מרס. Herodotus says (vii. 62) that all
Medes (and Persians) were called Arians. Hence the prefix
Ario, which occurs in the name Ari, is often only a family
name and not a proper one. The above מרס is the Mardos
of Herodotus, where the son of Darius and Parmys, a
prominent man, the maternal grandson of Cyrus (vii. 79), is
therefore also called by the Greeks Ariomardos. In the
same manner we learn to know כרשנא, Carshena, but which
was originally read ברשנא, as the name Barzanes (cited by
Diodorus and Arrian as of a king of Armenia, but with the
spelling of Barzaentes). Ariobarzanes is also the name of
the Persian satrap (comp. Xenophon, Cyrop. viii. 8. 4, and
the annotation of Schneider). Here is meant Artabazanes,
—for Arta (Herod. vii. 61), like Ario, is to be understood as

denoting nobility of pedigree,—who was an elder brother of Xerxes (vii. 2). Just so is שתר, *Shethar*, easily to be recognised in the strongly aspirated name of Hydarnes. One of the seven who subdued Pseudo-Smerdis bore this name (Herod. iii. 70), and his son Hydarnes was the leader of the "memorable ten thousand" in the Persian war (vii. 84). Upon the cuneiform inscriptions the interpreters read the name Vidarna as also they read Uwaihi and Kabujia for the so-called Susia and Cambyses. According to similar vocal laws, the writing of אדמתא, *Admatha*, in Esther, corresponds to *Aspathines*. The transition of the Greek *p*, *b* into the Hebrew מ is well known. *Achmetha*, אחמתא, is Ecbathana. So is Smerdis called in cuneiform inscriptions Bartya. Aspathines also was one of the seven from whom Darius rose to be king. The two names of תרשיש and ממוכן, *Tarshish* and *Memucan*, offer greater philological difficulties, but their solution can with probability be effected if the easy changes in the forms are taken into consideration.

Tarshish has indeed a resemblance in sound to the office-bearer called Tirshata, the name Theresh, and occurs in cuneiform in the name of an Armenian general of Darius, which is read Darshi (*sh*). The pointing of the Masoretes is easily explained from the fact that the name of Tarshish was too familiar to them, as standing in the Bible for a certain country and for a maritime power. But one must finally read ברשיש for תרשיש, from which the Greek name Prexaspes easily appears. This is evident from the circumstance of his position among the seven, for he stands near Admetha, whose son Asthapines was a naval captain (Herod. vii. 97). The Greek χ for the ש we have already found in the name of Xerxes. It remains yet to speak of the name ממוכן. The ו has certainly been introduced by the vocalization of the Masora. But for ממכן should be read מבכן (comp. Vidafrana and Intaphemes), or rather חבמן, so that through the interchange of במ with מב the double consonant כ was changed for a double מ. The name of Ahhaemenes in the cuneiform

Hakhamanish is to be recognised in this. This was the original ancestor of a Persian family, and of a brother and general of Xerxes. This explanation of the names receives its support from the positions in which they stand. First, the elder brother of Xerxes, then the two old and former friends of Darius (Hydarnes and Aspathines), then two younger tribal chiefs, and two younger brothers of Xerxes. The question why were just these chosen, and why are Otanes and his son Smerdomenes left out, is answered, because the cabinet consisted only of seven, and those who were entitled to cabinet rank were probably not appointed at the same time, but as a vacancy occurred ; and this was either by special choice of the king, or by other arrangements. Otanes was perhaps not chosen, for the reason that his daughter was the wife of Xerxes (Herod. vii. 61).

Ver. 15. " *What shall we do unto the queen Vashti according to law ?* "

This formal question was put to the seven princes, and it varies from the question put before the council by Xerxes, whether we should undertake the war with Greece or not, in this respect, that the latter was mainly pleaded by Mardonius and was opposed by Artaban ; but the former, although one only pronounced the decision, was in fact agreed to by all.

The description of the whole transaction is a most valuable representation of ancient court history. Not only does it teach that there were not wanting good old forms which the king was obliged to use when he desired to place 'important measures before the council of princes ; but it also shows how these forms had lost their intrinsic value when the men and the times had no longer the spirit to animate them. Of what avail are prescribed statutes when there is no heart to beat in them ? A council which is incompetent to refuse to entertain the question whether the queen was right or not in refusing to come to the revelry of her husband already manifests a dependent spirit, which disqualifies it from pro-

nouncing an impartial judgment. But they do not refer the
question back to the king, because the behaviour of the queen
gives them the opportunity of intriguing. A spirit of jealousy
has always existed in Oriental countries between persons and
corporations, who exercised an influence upon the king.
Thus far Ahhashverosh appears to have been led by his wife.
Therefore the momentary anger which she excited in him was
eagerly grasped by them as an occasion for destroying her
influence. It was so, too, according to the beautiful story
which Firdussi communicates, when Sudabe's intrigues with
the king failed, no one rose up in the council to speak for her,—

> " The princes brought their homage,
> And shouted : Death disgraceful
> Be the punishment to the shameful."

The instructive stories of the Forty Viziers, properly speaking, contain nothing else but the struggle between the queen
and the royal councillors as to predominance of their respective influences upon the decision of the king. The same
happens in all countries, but especially in the East; also in
recent times.[1] Hammer is of opinion that in the empire of
the Osmans, since the time of Soliman the Fair, the influence
of the wives was more often directed against the grand vizier.
Something of the same kind took place here; no voice was
raised either to defend or to excuse her. The king had placed
the sentence in the hands of her enemies, or, at least, of her
timid judges. If any wished to defend her, he was deterred
by the thought that he would arouse the suspicion of holding
doubtful views as to the irrevocable character of the
sovereignty of the king. Herodotus gives a fair example of
the caution practised by a timidly prudent court of justice
which Cambyses convoked, in order to decide the question
whether he might marry his sister (iii. 31). The judges found

---

[1] But it did not always result favourably to the viziers. Djemila Cau-
dahari had such great influence under Mahmud of Gasna, that Omra Altun
Tash could no longer resist it, and was obliged to resign his office. (See
Richardson, *Treatise of Eastern Nations*, German trans. p. 264.)

it difficult to say yes or no, but they perceived that he wanted
an affirmative answer, and that he would consider a negative
one as an insult upon his right to do as he liked, so they decided
that, " Whereas they did not know of any law which allowed
such a marriage, on the other hand they knew well that the
king was allowed to act as he pleases."　Here also it was not
entirely without danger to appear as a decided opponent of
the queen.　The great affection which the king had for her
might eventually cause her conduct to appear before him in a
different aspect, which would excuse her and be dangerous to
the opponent.　Memucan (Ahhaemenes) implies this in his
speech.　He lays emphasis upon the principle involved in the
act of Vashti, and makes it, to a certain degree, as a social
matter which concerns the State.　The king has in this affair
not only to consider his own interests, but also the interests
of all his subjects.　For the queen has not only sinned against
him, but by her example she has also excited the whole
country.　What Vashti had dared *to do* will be known everywhere ; and if this deed is to remain unpunished, then will
the rights of the husbands be disregarded all over the country.
The wives will refer to the example of Vashti, and repudiate
the authority of their husbands, so that בזיון, great contempt,
and קצף, anger, will enter to disturb the family peace.[1]
Memucan makes his assault upon the queen in a Machiavelian
manner.　With great subtlety he tries to conceal this under
the pretence of wishing the welfare of the people, which he
knows the king has at heart.　He gives to the accusation
such a turn of apparent impartiality, as to make it difficult
for the king, especially after the affair became known abroad,
to yield to the queen.　And there was none on the council

---

[1]According to Mohammedan custom, a woman must appear at the call of
her husband, and render obedience and subjection to him, "even should
both her hands be occupied at the time with kneading bread . . . as
the messenger of God had said (peace be upon him). 'And if it were
permitted to prostrate oneself before any one but God, I should command
the wives to prostrate themselves before their husbands'" (comp. *Vierzig
Veziere*, ed. Behrnauer, c. vii. p. 95).

board who had the courage to expose the deceitful machinations of Memucan.   For it could have been proved that the
queen by not coming to the banquet was more obedient to
her royal spouse than if she had come.

But these moral maxims had no place in the heart of any
one, perhaps not even in the heart of Vashti herself.   It
could again have been proved that the power of woman is
neither founded nor abrogated by law.   It was also certainly
known to those who sat together, that Vashti's conduct was
neither unheard of, nor that it would result in any extraordinary occurrence.   Moreover, they knew that the exemplary
punishment of Vashti would not at all alter the influence
of the beauty and amiability of women over those upon
whom they exercise the power of their attractions even in
bad things, where the will is not powerful enough to offer
resistance.   Indeed, it is in allusion to Persian manners that
the First Book of Esdras speaks of the highest and greatest
power which Zerubbabel ascribes to wives and their husbands.
He says (chap. iv. 28): " Is not the king great in his power?
do not all regions fear to touch him?   Yet did I see him and
Apame the king's concubine, the daughter of the admirable
Bartacus, sitting at the right hand of the king, and taking the
crown from the king's head, and setting it upon her own
head ; she also struck the king with her left hand . . . O ye
men, how can it be but that women should be strong, seeing
they do thus?"

Ver. 19. אשר לא־תבא ושתי—" *That Vashti come no more*,"etc.
That tyranny, which does not know even the fear of God,
is the greatest folly, our narrative teaches with unsurpassable
clearness and simplicity.   Excessive vanity demented the
king more than the wine did.   It lasted longer than his wrath.
He neither could see that the doing of Vashti was caused by
his own fault, nor the nature of the intrigues against her
whom he still loved.   In his state of excitement he had not
the sagacity either to palliate her offence or to detect the snare

which was laid against him by his sycophants. The Midrash, in reference to this, rightly calls him a שטפ—fool. Memucan's impudent accusation has for its aim to remove Vashti from the royal palace, and to give her throne to another that is better than she. From the expression לרעותה הטובה ממנה it must not be supposed that Vashti was not the queen, but one of the women of the harem, who, on account of her beauty, had raised herself to such an influential position. For although it is said that her throne should be given to her companion, another inmate of the harem, who is better, טובה, *i.e.* more tractable, obliging, and submissive, yet we must remember that this is the language of contempt, in which the vile courtier tries to wreak his private vengeance. Such examples of queens having to quit their thrones to make room for new beauties are not only found in Oriental, but also in European, particularly in modern French histories. But it must be also observed that the autocrat of the ancient great empire apparently asserted his capricious will in a legal manner, whereas the modern sultans, in their arbitrary acts, have even thrown off the external forms of legality. Chardin relates that one of the favourite wives of the shah had once besought him not to touch her on a certain day on account of her bodily condition, which made it necessary that she should have rest. The shah caused her to be examined, and when it was found that her plea had no foundation in fact, she was at once burned alive (*Voyages*, vi. 229).

Queen Vashti would not have succumbed if the royal privy councillor had not voted against her. But he used the opportunity to destroy the female influence at court. The same attempt, only in a coarser manner, was made by the viziers to avert the harem influence from the Sultan of the Osmans, Ahmed I., at the beginning of the seventeenth century. They told him that these women were witches, and had bewitched his father Soliman, so that he was entirely dependent upon them. Memucan's accusation went deeper, was more refined and flattering to the vanity of the king, inasmuch as it made the affair of Vashti's disobedience a question of principle. It was represented to him that his own position was at stake in the matter. If he yielded to her, he would be the cause of the disobedience of all the women in the country, and something dreadful might happen. But, on the other hand, it was his bounden duty, as he had the supreme power, to issue a decree that the wives must everywhere pay implicit obedience to their husbands.

Ver. 20. ונשמע פתגם המלך—"*And when the king's decree which he shall make shall be published.*"

Although Memucan's aim was to have Vashti deposed, yet he laid special stress upon this. He propounded a general principle, that disobedience of wives to their husbands was dangerous to the peace of the State. He made it appear that Vashti's deposition must be the natural outcome of this principle, rather than the aim of his advice. Should she even escape unhurt from this ordeal, such a decree, when publicly proclaimed under the sanction of royal prerogative and authority, would, at any rate, have a deterrent effect upon the women of the country. He therefore changed the dangerous and disagreeable negative verdict concerning Vashti into a positive royal decree, which should affect the women of the country generally. By this subtle device the king was entrapped into an implicit pledge of removing the queen. His own decree precluded him from saving Vashti, which would have been of direful life-long consequence to his councillors. Through the publication of a royal פתגם, official document, a reconciliation of the king with his former favourite became extremely difficult, and the intrigue which probably began already at the feast received thereby its crowning victory.

To our ideas it appears almost comical, that a king should send out a circular in which the women are commanded to render due honour to their husbands.[1] But it did not appear in this light to the ancient Persians.

[1] That this is in harmony with the Oriental mind may be seen in the story of *The Thousand and One Nights* (xxiv. 68), where it is told that a

The power of the great Persian king over his subjects was
really universal.[1]   In fact, there was not a domestic or
family right in which he could not interfere. This is evident
from the ideal glorification in which Xenophon represents the
institutions of Cyrus when developing their application. He
says that the Persian laws precluded beforehand the possibility
of the citizen thinking of evil (*Cyrop.* i. 2). Again he reports
that Cyrus had forbidden to spit or to sneeze, or even to turn
round in public places, as something to be admired (*Cyrop.*
viii. 1. 42). The companions of Cyrus cannot go hunting
if Astyages does not command their fathers (*Cyrop.* i. 4).
And, indeed, this was yet copied by the Sultan of the Osmans
in 1664, who ordered to give his kiaja 100 switches upon the
soles of his feet because he hunted of his own accord (Hammer, vi. 148). The decree which the king, on the proposal of
Memucan, issued, had not to do with the accomplishment of
an actual duty, but with the subjection of the disposition of
man to a command. Civil right was not taken from the
women, but obedience was enjoined upon them. The husbands
did not receive a substantial, but only an ideal privilege. But
just for this reason, the subtle plan pleased the adulated vanity
of the conceited king. He undertook to accomplish that
which could be done by no one. Had it been possible by the
application of external special force to restore order among the
husbands in the house, it would have been done long ago.

The Persian king must have known from his own history
and from that of his family how little the greatest force could
prevent one becoming subject to the humour of one's beloved
in the house. But being dazzled by his fancied and over-
rated omnipotence, he adopted this proposal as a means whereby

sultan ordered to proclaim everywhere : "It is not proper that any one
should follow the advice of women."

[1] The whole history about Vashti is certainly based upon a grand political thought. The Persian monarchy is founded upon the monarchy in
the family. What the husband is in the family, that he is in the State.
If his rights are disputed in the former, they are at the same time injured
in the latter.

to assert his power, and to make everybody feel the terror
of his autocratic rule. It is certainly no fable which is told
of Xerxes, viz. that when the inundation of the Hellespont
had destroyed his bridges, he gave order that it should be
bastinaded for disobedience (Herod. vii. 35). But it was
more easy for him to beat the sea than to obtain that which
his edict commanded, namely, to cause the women to renounce
their desire of governing by their own peculiar powers.
Only the truth is mightier than the women (as Zerubbabel
says); and it alone could keep their power within bounds and
hallow them. Even the command of the servant of the King
of kings, of the Apostle Paul, that women should not speak in
the churches, could not exert a compulsory force upon them.
Though it is apparently externally obeyed, yet it is only externally so.

Ver. 21. " *And the saying pleased the king.*"

The proposal of Memucan was readily sanctioned by him.[1]
No one among the ministers offered opposition. Vashti lost
her influence, probably also her life, although this is not expressly mentioned; but only that she should not come to the
king, and that her royalty (מלכות) should be given to another.
In the empire of the Osmans also, each Chasseki, *i.e.* female
favourite, had her court, her chamberlain (*kiaja*), the income
of a Sandjak, and a gilded equipage, set with precious stones
(Hammer, v. 329). But if she had been deprived of all this,
and her life had been spared, she was still to be feared by her
enemies; therefore they must have insisted that she should
be quickly executed. The enjoyment of the momentary favour
of a tyrant has often enough ended sadly. Vashti fell in a
war which is frequently carried on in Eastern courts between
the women and the eunuchs and the princes.[2] That her fall

[1] He had not the nobility of character nor the intellect of the young
Cyrus, who did not apply force to Aspasia for refusing to act as the other
wives, but treated her with gentleness. (Comp. Plutarch, *Artaxerxes*, 26.)

[2] Concerning the penalties which are meted out to the favourites when
they have displeased the sultan, Chardin writes (*Voyages*, vi. 233): "Car

did not lead to serious disasters after the king had sobered
down and calmly reflected upon it, was owing to the fact that
he undertook a great campaign, which occupied all his
attention.

Ver. 22. "*And he sent letters into all the king's provinces,
into every province according to the writing thereof, and to
every people after their language.*"

It is here emphatically declared that the decree addressed
to all the peoples was written both in the distinctive language,
לשׁון, and in the distinctive alphabet, כתב, of each nation. We
learn from this that the Persian Government did not use
a particular official language in its proceedings with the people,
but addressed them in their own dialects (comp. c. viii. 9).
The contents of this decree were, That every man should
be lord, שׂרר, in his house, and should command, ומדבר, in his
language.   Hence the decree was to be in force not only
in Persia, but everywhere, and valid not merely in Persian
language, but in every language.

The Midrash makes a peculiar remark upon this.   The
decree was written in four principal languages.   (1) לעז, Greek
(as Hellenic was considered the same as Heathenism.   The
Talmud says : "Cursed be the man who shall teach his son
the wisdom of the Greeks" (*Sotah*, p. 49*b*), comp. my *Mag.
Alterth.* pp. 196 and 338), for the purpose of singing ; (2) in
Persian, for lamentation ; (3) in Hebrew, for holding intercourse
with one another; (4) in Latin, the language which is suitable for
carrying on war.   History has taught, that in all languages,
more especially in Hebrew, the voice of lamentation resounded.
One might almost say that Hebrew literature has ceased to

le Roi . . . en dégrade les unes, changeant ces Favorites en esclaves, qu'on
en voye servir aux plus bas emplois et dans les quartiers reculez du Serail ;
il en fait châtier d'autres à coups de verge et de bâton, il en fait tuer, il en
fait même brûler les unes et enterrer les autres toutes vives."   According to
the story of *The Thousand and One Nights* (xiii. 16), Harun Arrashid
had a dark tower in which the favourites were imprisoned when they
committed an offence.

exist, since in modern times the Jews think that they need
no longer mourn.   (M. Esther, p. 91a.)

The author of the verdict under which Vashti fell was
Memucan, the last mentioned among the privy councillors.
The Midrash tries to find out the personal motives which led
him to entertain such hostile feelings against Vashti.   One
was, that on a certain occasion she had struck his face
with a slipper.   Such disgraceful treatment is certainly no
rare occurrence in the East.[1]

The second was, because his wife had not been invited by
the queen to the feast.

The third was, because he wanted to see his own daughter
promoted in the place of Vashti.   Whether the reasons given
by the Midrash were exactly the same which actuated the
hatred of Memucan or not, one thing is certain, that he could
not tolerate the petticoat government of Vashti, and that such
and similar reasons as are given by the Rabbis have often led
to such results.

That Herodotus does not mention this event is not to
be wondered at, inasmuch as it happened before the campaign.   Apart from this, it is not to be expected that he
should have known everything which took place in the inner
circle of the Persian court, and that he should have incorporated this in his brief reports of the Persian war.   There
were many writings and administrative measures issued from
Shushan, and these were of such a character as to be deposited
by all the governors among the acts of administration.[2]

---

[1] In the legend *The Thousand and One Nights*, it is told that a king
punished his son by beating him with his slipper on the face (iii. 24, ed.
König).   But the slipper is specially an instrument of punishment in the
hands of the women, as the story represents it in chap. xxiv. p. 40.   [In
Mohammedan schools in Palestine the teacher often throws a slipper upon
a delinquent boy, when he, without crying, puts it on the foot of his
master, and kisses his hands.—TRANS.]

[2] In Athenaeus, lib. xiii. p. 556, we read : "Among the Persians, the queen
must tolerate many concubines, because the king, like a master, has
the command over his wife." διὰ τὸ ὡς δεσπότην ἄρχειν τῆς γαμετῆς τὸν
βασιλία.

CHAPTER II.

Ver. 1. אחר הדברים האלה—"*After these things, when the wrath of the king Ahhashverosh was pacified, he remembered Vashti.*"[1]

This did not happen soon after the feast named in chap. i., but there was an anxious interval between. We see here how exactly even the chronology of our book shows that Xerxes and Ahhashverosh are identical. In the third year of his reign the above event took place, and in the seventh (comp. ver. 16) this which is told here. In this year Xerxes returned from his campaign (480–479), and therefore only now could the thread of the court history of Shushan be resumed (ver. 16). After the exhaustive fatigues which he went through in that war, he felt the want of the companionship of Vashti, whom he had really once affectionately loved. Formerly the ambitious desire for war and conquest had eclipsed the feelings of love to the women. Now they arose the more strongly, as in the enjoyment of a specially agreeable favourite he might forget many a care. When we read, "he remembered Vashti, and what was decreed against her," still now after three years we may suppose that he somehow connected the misfortunes of his campaign with the wrath and the severity with which he had treated her.

---

[1] Herodotus narrates (vii. 46) that Xerxes in the midst of his glory on his march to Greece had said : " In this short life there is no man either among these or others so happy, that he should not often and more than once be in such a position as to prefer death to life. For misfortunes come, and diseases rage, which make our life to appear so long, though it is so short."

When Xerxes gave expression to such thoughts, what
would not his courtiers have given if they could have brought
Vashti to life! But there was no one present to do like the
vizier of the story of the Forty Viziers (ed. Behrnauer, p. 141),
where it is told,—A king had once in his drunken hours
pronounced a sentence of death against his favourite friend, but
the vizier did not execute the order, but hid the culprit.
When the king became sober, he was in great distress of
mind, on account of the supposed death of his friend; then
the vizier rejoiced his heart by introducing the friend well
and sound. But Vashti was no longer to be got, and the perplexed courtiers did not know any other way of extricating
themselves from the dilemma but to look for another woman,
who by her especial charms would captivate the king and
would occupy his leisure, as only Vashti could, and since her
no one else. They therefore propose to the king to send out
officers [1] all over the country to bring every beautiful girl to
Shushan. They should be brought to the harem (בית הנשים),
and placed under the supervision of the הגא, viz. of the Aga
(Sanscr. *âja*), the keeper, who would introduce them to the
king after they had undergone a due course of preparation
(vers. 9, 12). Among so many, there would certainly be one
to whom the king would take a fancy, and make her what is
called in the court language of the Osmans, a Chasseki, a
favourite, in the place of Vashti. The proposal pleased the
king, and he issued an order accordingly.

One cannot but admire the simple, quiet historical style of
our narrative. Laying aside all the reports which would
only prolong our way of coming to the essential part of the
contents of the book, there is nothing omitted which would
contribute to the historical and psychological introduction and
illustration. How much was necessary to happen before
Israel could have ready help in time of need! What great
things, according to external appearance, must precede, in order

---

[1] פקידים are not common officers, but eunuchs and overseers, who bear
here this name, from the charge entrusted to them.

to make it possible that a Jewish girl by the influence of
her charms should ascend the throne of a Chasseki in the
Persian kingdom ! The great conference of all the officers of
the State, the dreadful war with Greece, and the unfortunate
issue of the same, were they not in the hands of Providence
so many stepping-stones in the path of Esther's ascendancy ?
In order to replace the loss of the special beauty of Vashti,
a woman of equal endowments must be sought for the king,
wherever and however it might be ! How many things must
subserve to the frustration of Haman's wicked plan ! The
wrath of Xerxes against Greece, and his wrath against his
wife. Court intrigues against the powerful influences of a
wife, and the vain conceit of offended sovereignty. First
drunkenness, then homicidal passion, then new excited
sensuality, were the sad instruments which preceded the
redemption of Israel. When the people were delivered, they
could well be penitent when they especially considered the
way in which Vashti—though not herself guiltless—was one
of the main causes of their deliverance. And if deep
penitence must have resulted from the reflection that a
woman like Vashti had to die a violent death in order that
the people of God should live,—what kind of penitence must
the thought call forth when we remember that Christ gave
His life in order that Israel and the Gentiles might live, and
that the apostles of the truth, walking in His footsteps, went
through fire and sword in order to save souls !

Israel passed through the conflagration of Jerusalem on
their road to conversion. In the court of Nebuchadnezzar
originated the prophecy of Daniel. Through the harem went
the wonderful intervention of Esther on behalf of her people.
The Hebrew word for harem, בית הנשים (which only occurs in
this book), does not correspond to the Arabic *haram*, meaning
sacredness, devotion, but comes rather near to the Turkish
Odalik : the Gynaeceum, the house of the women, in contra-
distinction to the house of the men. It must not be assumed
that the formation of the word implies an immoral motive,

nor that the institution of polygamy was in itself the product
of greater depravity of the human heart than the natural
man commonly possesses. The opinion of some, that the
harem was the consequence of Oriental despotism, is also
erroneous. It arose from the radical views of heathenism,
viz. that the passions of the natural man are not to be
restrained, but legalized ; and also that the natural right of a
husband over his wife is not to be controlled by moral rules,
but to be left to his arbitrary will, as an indisputable and
constitutional right. With both polygamy and despotism
social conditions of time and place were so closely connected,
that they survived in their degenerating and baneful influence
the principle of heathenism which originated them. What
we find of both, in the history of Israel of the Old Testament,
are relics of social customs, which had themselves vanished
before the thought of the living and holy God of the
Decalogue ; and even these during their continuance appeared
in their purest possible form.

The repentance of David, the deepest human self-abasement
in confession and faith, touches his pleasures in the harem
as well as the abuse of his royal power. But repentance
and faith towards the pure and holy God are wanting in
heathenism. This corrective of the deepest social wisdom
was therefore also unknown both to Oriental and occidental
heathen States. Hence the kingdom of the countries on the
Euphrates and the Tigris had become a despotic caricature ;
hence, too, the institution of the harem, and the degrading
effects, especially upon women, that were connected with it
and proceeded from it, made such progress. There is nothing
legendary in the story that is told in the commencement of
The Thousand and One Nights, that the caliph believed he had
a right to behead his wife any day.

The Persian king of antiquity, like the modern shah and
sultan, arrogated to himself this historical prerogative. In
his privilege to do everything there was a representation of
the highest power of the husband over his wife, at least so

far as external means allowed. He had the command over
the life and death of all the men, so also over the bodies and
enjoyment of all the women. Xerxes should send out a
commission all over the country in search of beautiful damsels,
in order that his longing after a favourite might be satisfied.
This was not a sudden outbreak of an unheard-of act of
violence. It was nothing else but the expression of a
universally recognised right, or rather of a heavy yoke.
When Alexander the Great did the same, and caused beautiful women from all Asia[1] to be brought to his house, he
intended also to show therewith that he completely succeeded
to the claims of the Persian great king. The harem of the
new Persian shah is supplied in the same manner. Chardin
gives an instructive representation of the process of fetching
and despatching the beauties. In some cases, in modern
times, the parents rather like the idea that a daughter of
theirs should be demanded for the harem, for they promise
themselves to obtain thereby a certain amount of influence
and interest at court. Sometimes, it is further said, the king
himself goes among the Armenians in search of beautiful
wives. It is therefore the custom among these to betroth
their daughters when still young, because such are not taken
away. But, alas! sometimes it happened that these searches
were used as a means of exercising private spite, hatred, and
revenge, and the Armenians (so-called Christians) have denounced each other when families had concealed their
daughters from the vile inquisitors of the king (*Voyage*, vi.
242). Married women were mostly spared, not because of
want of right, but because virgins were needed.[2]

Among the Mongolian shahs, it is said that the prince has
a statute right to demand the wives of his subjects. On

---

[1] Diodor. xvii. 77 : ἐξ ἀπασῶν τῶν κατὰ τὴν ᾿Ασίαν γυναικῶν ἐπιλελεγ-
μένας.

[2] In vers. 2 and 3 it is said כל נערה בתולה shall be sought. Chardin
says, vi. 226 : "Il n'y entre que des vierges. Quand on en sait quelqu'une
parfaite en beauté, en quelque endroit que ce soit, on la demande pour le
Haram et cela ne se refuse point."

account of this circumstance there was a long war in 1320, because an emir would not give up his wife, Bagdad-Khatun (Desguignes, iii. 303). In the Osman Empire also, under some sultans, such cruelty was carried on to great excess. New slaves used to be sought for Sultan Ibrahim, in order that each Friday he should have a new one brought to him as to a religious solemnity. He fancied he would like a favourite of high stature, and search was consequently made all over Constantinople for such a person ; and, after a good deal of trouble, they found at last an Armenian woman who was tall as a giant. She succeeded in ingratiating herself into his favour, so that, she became most powerful, and provoked the jealousy of the other women, until, at last, the sultana invited her to an entertainment, where she caused her to be strangled. It was then reported that she died suddenly (Hammer, v. 359).

For David also a handsome damsel was sought in all Israel; but it was in order that she might nurse the old man. After he repented he became master of himself. We read, "she cherished the king, and ministered to him; but the king knew her not " (1 Kings i. 4).

Ver. 5. " *There was a certain Jew in Shushan,*" etc.

The history passes now into that of Israel. The narrative of the selection of a virgin for the royal harem is only interrupted for the sake of introducing certain persons, in reference to whom all the reports were thus far made. These are two in number, a man and a woman, uncle and niece, guardian and minor. They form the central point of the book. They are the deliverers of Israel. "A certain Jew was in Shushan the castle." The name Yehudi (Jew) came in vogue in Southern Palestine after the separation of the ten tribes under Rehoboam. The kingdom of Judah stood in opposition to the kingdom of Israel. It still continued for a century after that of Israel had passed away, and during this time there was but one Yehudah, or Judea,

in the Holy Land. The conquest and the rule of Nebuchadnezzar obscured all preceding events. The deeds of
Shalmaneser receded to the background. By Nebuchadnezzar the holy city Jerusalem was conquered, and the
inhabitants of the kingdom, who were called Jews (2 Kings
xvi. 6, xxv. 25), were by him led into exile. These last,
through keeping closely together, in order to maintain
the national faith, have made the name Yehudi especially
distinguished. The sharp contrast between Judah and Israel
was given up in a strange land. To the ten tribes, in the
penitent sorrow of the exile, the name of Jerusalem was again
a dearly loved and cherished one. The breach caused by
the secession of Jeroboam was only repaired in the captivity.
While Israel, the ideal Biblical name, only expressed their
humiliated position before God, the name Jew became
universally known as the designation of every one who
manifested the faith of Israel. Therefore all the captives
are called Jews in the book of Esther, although it cannot be
proved that all of whom it treats belonged to the captivity of
Nebuchadnezzar, as there must have been some there who
were taken captives by his predecessor Shalmaneser.

The districts in which Nebuchadnezzar distributed the
Jews are not clearly defined. We learn only from Dan. i. 2
that they were taken to Shinar, *i.e.* to Babylon. Zerubbabel
brought back Jews who had lived in Babylon (Ezra i. 11–
ii. 1). But such also joined them who had come from Tel-
melach, Telcharsha, Cherub, and Addan, names which define
the old Elymais, *i.e.* Loristan (see my *Geschichte der Juden*,
p. 173). It is well known that not all came back under
the leadership of Zerubbabel. The permission of Cyrus for
their return home was evidently not merely an act of kindness on his part, but also an act of policy, as we shall see
farther on. It was certainly only Jewish colonies of definite
districts which emigrated. It was not of the highest importance to Cyrus to found there a new mighty State, which might
afterwards become independent, but only that these territories

should be settled by weak and thankful colonies who entertained anti - Babylonian sentiments. There yet remained behind a multitude, notably in Shushan, from which place, the residence of Daniel and Nehemiah, none seem to have been sent back (Dan. viii. 2 ; Neh. i. 1).

The man is called Mordecai. This name does not occur in Israel before the captivity. Another captive who returned with Zerubbabel is so called Ezra ii. 2 ; Neh. vii. 7. It is the name of one who was born in exile. It is according to Persian analogy.[1]

In the first syllable it corresponds to Mardonius (מרסנא), Mardontes, Mardus ; in the last it is like that of Artachaeus or Artachaes (comp. Herod. vii. 22). One is reminded of something similar in the names of Mardokempad and Mesesimordak in the Canon of Ptolemy. To say that Mordecai the Jew had his name from the idol Merodach, would not certainly be true ; but the name of the idol is itself derived from the Sanscr. *martiya*, Arm. *mart*, Pers. *merd* = man, and it does not preclude the supposition that other compounds were used with this word.[2] Moreover, when the name of Mordecai was once currently used, the Jew could bear it with as great indifference to its allusion as the Christian St. Martin could bear his name, which is derived from Mars.

At any rate, the derivation of the name — apart from Merodach—from *mart*, *merd* = man, signifying "the manly," is clearer and surer than the one proposed by Oppert, who thinks it is derived from the modern Persian *mardu*, meaning "soft." But it is remarkable that the name Mordecai is only given to a native of the captivity ; and this circumstance corroborates the otherwise evident fact, that

[1] It was not a happy conjecture of the learned Molinus of Venice (*de vita et lipsanis St. Marci Evangelistae*, Romae 1864, p. 10), that the name of Mark the evangelist was originally Mordecai, from which the Roman name Marcus was formed. It cannot be established that this was always the case with the name of Marcus, nor why it should be so (comp. *Götting. gelehr. Nachr.* 1865, p. 905).

[2] See my article "Mordecai" in Herzog's *Realencyklop.* p. 365.

Mordecai was not one of those who were exiled, as it was curiously enough concluded from ver. 6, where we read: "And his name was Mordecai, the son of Jair, the son of Shimei, the son of Kish, a Benjamite; who had been carried away from Jerusalem with the captives, which had been carried away with Jechoniah (Jehoiachin), king of Judah, whom Nebuchadnezzar the king of Babylon had carried away."

The clear and instructive intentions of the historian in the genealogical passage are evident. He points out, through the enumeration of the four generations from Kish to Mordecai, the time which elapsed since the banishment of Jechoniah, which took place before the destruction of the temple. The period of about 115–120 years which since then elapsed to the sixth year of Xerxes are exactly expressed by the four generations. We have also some intimation concerning the period of the narrative, which is assigned to the reign of Xerxes I. That Kish was a Benjamite, is only told for the purpose of distinguishing him from other men with the same name who belonged to the tribe of Levi. One might have thought it impossible that Biblical expositors should commit the mistake of making the information concerning the exile of Jechoniah refer to Mordecai himself,—an idea for which there is neither textual nor historical foundation, but rather both against it. If this had been the case, the author would have placed Ahhashverosh immediately after Nebuchadnezzar; but this could not be so, according to the narrative in Daniel and Ezra, whoever we may consider Ahhashverosh to be. The author is well acquainted with the fact that a king of Persia, of whom he reports, succeeded Cyrus; for he puts Persia before Media. If the relation אשר in ver. 6 refers to Mordecai and not to Nebuchadnezzar, there would have been no reason why the narrator should only mention the three generations Jair, Shimei, and Kish, and, indeed, why he should mention more than Mordecai's father, as he does similarly in ver. 15, where he mentions only Esther's father, Abihhail. The opinion of the Midrash, that by Kish is here to be understood the father of King Saul, is only homiletical trifling, and hardly deserves notice.

If *that* Kish had been meant, King Saul or any other member in the genealogical line as given in 1 Sam. ix. would have been mentioned; but this is not the case. Again, the opinion that this Mordecai is identical with the one of Ezra ii. 2, who returned to Jerusalem, is also groundless. First, because this one came from Babylon, and not from Shushan. Secondly, the book of Ezra itself reports that Ahhashverosh, whoever he may be, reigned after Cyrus, and therefore Mordecai would have reached an excessively great age if he had been one of those carried into exile by Nebuchadnezzar, as there were about sixty years from the banishment of Jechoniah to the return of the captives with Zerubbabel. We would reach the monstrous conclusion of the Duke of Manchester, and of the German doctors after him, which the Biblical genealogy itself destroys, if the relation אֲשֶׁר be arbitrarily connected with Mordecai, instead of, as it naturally is, with the last name. Above all things, it is necessary to be cautious of theories, for the sake of which all the hitherto received and well-established views are thrown overboard; whilst, when we follow the simple rendering of the verse as indicated, everything is beautifully harmonious.

The Midrash (Esther 92*a*) makes in its own fanciful way a peculiar and groundless assertion upon the position of the word שמו his name. It says: When the Scripture speaks of a bad man, the word שמו stands after his name, as Nabal his name; when it speaks of a good man, as here of Mordecai, it stands before. "And his name was Mordecai." But ושמו stands before Micah in Judg. xvii. 1; before Doeg, 1 Sam. xxi. 7; before Sheba, "a man of Belial," 2 Sam. xx. 1; and before others who cannot be reckoned among the good. On the other hand, the word stands after Josiah, 1 Kings xiii. 2; after Daniel, Dan. x. 1; and after the names of the best men, and, above all, after the Messiah, Zech. vi. 12, where we read, "Behold the man, Zemach (*i.e.* Branch) is his name, he shall build the temple of the Lord."

The fourth generation from the exile of Jechoniah witnessed the events of which this book treats. Mordecai must still have been in the prime of life. He had a relation Abihhail, who died and left an orphan daughter behind. This girl, Mordecai, of whose wife or children nothing is reported, took to his house, as there was no nearer relative, and he became her nursing father, אמן, from her youth. For the word אמן or אמנה implies nursing of a child from its infancy, as Naomi was the nurse of the child of Ruth from its birth (Ruth iv. 16), and as Moses said to the Lord: "Have I conceived all this people? have I brought them forth, that Thou shouldest say unto me, Carry them in thy bosom, as a nursing father carries the suckling child?" (Num. xi. 12). He cherished her as a father and mother cherish their own child; and the whole narrative shows that this was not done perfunctorily, but with his whole heart.

Ver. 7. את־הדסה היא אסתר—"*Hadassah, that is, Esther.*"

The girl was called in the house of her parents and of Mordecai, Hadassah, *i.e.* "Myrtle," Myrto, a name which in very ancient times had reference to the connection of beauty with fruitfulness; hence it was a symbol of Venus, and was therefore appropriately chosen as an epithet to the girl. Jewish women, as among other Eastern nations, have always had names borrowed from flowers. We need only refer to the names of Jewish women which have come down to us from all the Middle Ages, such as Flora, Myrrha, Blümchen, Blume, Rosa, Fiore, etc. (see Zunz, *Namen der Juden*, p. 73, etc.).

The Midrash acknowledges this in its comment on the passage. It says, Mordecai's cousin was called Myrtle, like the righteous, because she never faded, but was always blooming both in summer and in winter. They apply to her Isa. lv. 13, where we read: "Instead of the thorn shall come up the fir tree, and instead of the brier shall come up the myrtle tree," understanding, of course, by the thorn and brier Vashti, and by the myrtle Esther (Bab.

Megilla 10*b*). On the other hand, the Church Father [Jerome] refers this passage to the Apostle Paul. " At that time," says he, " when he preached the gospel in the world, and could say, ' We are a sweet savour of Christ ' (2 Cor. ii. 15), he is rightly called a cypress and myrtle tree " (*Comm. ad Jes.*, ed. Migne, iv. 538). But the prophecy goes beyond the preacher of the truth to the truth itself. The Talmudical word for myrtle is אסא, as in Syriac. Compare with it the Persian אסמוסא (see Vullers, i. 601).

היא אסתר.

Esther was the name which the girl received in the harem as a favourite of the king. R. Nehemia (in Megilla 13*b*)[1] correctly derives the name from אסתהר, or as the Targum writes it, איסתירא, after the Greek ἀστήρ, star; Syr. אסתרא ; Pers. סתארה; Zend. *stara*. And in Persian it has the special sense of the lustre of Venus, Fortuna (*sidus genethliacum*), of the morning star (see Vullers, ii. 220), as the Persians call the king, " the morning star of the throne." Such names were customary for the wives and favourites in the East. The Caliph Hisham II. of Spain gave to his beloved Radhiyet the surname of Fortunate Star (Hammer, *Namen der Araber*, p. 11).

The name of the legitimate wife of Xerxes, Amestris[2] (Herod. vii. 61–114, and ix. 169), will likewise be best explained from the compound of Amesha (אמישה) and Sitra, סתרה, meaning heavenly star. For with Amesha (heavenly, immortal) and Cpenta are also the seven genii designated, which are the gods of the seven planets. Some have thought that they could find the name of Hadassah, myrtle, reproduced in the name of Atossa, the wife of Darius. The circumstance against this is, that Hadassah is only a Hebrew word. We may rather consider that it has some relation

[1] [R. Yehudah says, that the name of Esther is derived from סתר, to hide, because she did not tell of her origin.—TRANS.]

[2] Comp. the name of the beautiful Amazon in Hyrcania, Θάλεστρις, in Diodor. xvii. 77, in respect to the latter part of the name, and of Amytis (by Ctesias), daughter of Cyaxares, in respect to the first part.

with the Persian word אתש, light, splendour, fire. With this word the Persians designated the phoenix on account of its magnificent brilliancy, and by the term אתש בהאר they called the red rose and the tulip, as the splendour of spring. Likewise the name Roxane,[1] the beautiful wife of Alexander, is explained to be derived from the Roshen Pehlvi, ראשנה, meaning "the shining one." The favourite of the Spanish Caliph Abderrahman III. was called Nureddunja, "the light of the world." A famous woman in the harem of Stamboul was called Nurbanu, "woman of light;" another in the Muhamedan India had the name of Nurmahal, "light of the harem." Famous Chassekis of the Osman sultans were called Mahpeiker, "moonlike" (this is a favourite expression of Firdussi for a girl). Mahfirus, "favourite of the crescent;" Mihrmah, "sun-moon." Other such peculiar names are as follows:—Parysatis, the mother of Artaxerxes II., in later form Perisade, "the perichild" or "angel's child;" the wife of the Caliph Mothaded was named Kothronneda, "dewdrop." An Osman Chasseki of Grecian birth was called Rebia Gulnusch, "rose-drink of spring." Favourite female slaves had such names: Dshanfeda, "offering of soul;" Sudshbagli, "the one with plaited hair" (Hammer, *Gesch.* viii. 358); Sheckerbuli, "sugar-plum;" Sheckerpara, "sweetmeat;" Sheckerchatun, "sugar-woman." This last was a princess at Delhi at the time of Firuzshah. The famous Kösem was called Ssafiye, "the pure." Jewesses also were called so (comp. Weil, *Leben Mohammeds*, p. 186), as the names of Reine, Reinchen occur among them. We conclude with the names of two wives of Darius, Phaidyme and Parmys. The former may properly be compared with Fatime of later times; but Parmys is to be taken as the reproduction of ברמאיה, the name of a cow, which according to the legend suckled King Feridon, the most renowned person

---

[1] She was the daughter of Ahmed ibn Tanlun, ruler of Egypt. Her outfit was so great, that in the kitchen there were no less than 1000 golden mortars (Hammer, *Gemäldesaal*, iv. 268).

in all Persian traditions (Vullers, i. 226). How much truth
is represented by the Oriental fable, is seen from the collection
of names of favourites which is contained in the story of
The Thousand and One Nights. We meet there with such a
name as Queen Labe (sun). The Caliph Harun had female
slaves with the names of Alabaster-throat, Coral-mouth,
Coral-branch, Moon-face, Full-moon of the full-moons, Sunshine, Pearl-necklace, Dawn of the morning, Garden-flower,
Sugarcane, and the most favourite name of all, Morning-star
(see xi. 27, xii. 102).[1]

וְהַנַּעֲרָה יְפַת־תֹּאַר וְטוֹבַת מַרְאֶה—*"And the maiden was fair
and beautiful."*

The first adjective expresses in the original, to a certain
degree, the regular beauty of her figure ; the second expresses
the gracefulness and amiability of her manners. The Midrash has a very curious homily about her age. In spite of
the text, which calls her a נַעֲרָה, *i.e.* a young girl, the Rabbis
are divided in their opinion about her age. Some maintain
that she was from forty to eighty years old. Others again
declare that she was seventy-four years old, because the letters
of Hadassah, הֲדַסָּה, are numerically equivalent to seventy-four,
and because Abraham was also seventy-five years old when
he left Haran. The sense of this homiletical peculiarity is,
that there was something very wonderful in the reception of
Esther by the king. Although she was so old, yet she so
miraculously found favour in his sight. Nevertheless the
Rabbis would not have come to this strange comment if
they had not felt the logical necessity of assigning to Esther
at this period of the story such an advanced age, in order
to make the supposition that Mordecai had already been
among the captives of Nebuchadnezzar tenable. It is their

[1] Comp. the names which, according to Oriental legend, Solomon's
wives had : Tender-violet, Shining-star, Sun-lustre, Phoenix, Paradise-
bird, etc. (Hammer, *Rosenöl.* i. 243). A heroic female slave of Alaeddin
Khiljy, to whom he entrusted the defence of a castle, had the name of
Guli Behesht, Rose of paradise (*Gemäldesaal*, iv. 218).

fashion thus to meet by way of homily historical difficulties, and solve them by combinations of letters. Now, as such homiletical solutions are contrary to reason, they just prove what they want to avoid, viz. the monstrous anachronism by which Mordecai is placed as far back as the time of Nebuchadnezzar.

Ver. 8. ויהי בהשמע—"*So it came to pass, when the king's commandment and his decree was heard.*"

The notice in this verse is not given without reason. If Esther was so beautiful, the circumstance easily explains itself why, in the midst of the great choice of beauties that were to be brought to Shushan, she was not overlooked. Jewish tradition informs us, through the Targum, that Mordecai, her guardian and second father, had kept her concealed, in order not to be obliged to deliver her to the royal agents; but people who knew her, and had not seen her for some time among the girls, drew their attention to the concealment. This they reported to the king, who immediately issued an order, to the effect that wherever it has come to the knowledge of the authorities that a man had refused to deliver his daughter, he should be hanged by the neck before his own house.

What is here told does certainly correspond to Eastern custom, but our book gives no occasion for it. The tradition originated in the East, where the search after women for the harem had become an intolerable nuisance, especially to the oppressed population. It was therefore quite natural to suppose that Mordecai did all he could, as loving parents do sometimes now-a-days, to keep Esther away from the covetous eyes of the royal eunuchs. The Midrash wanted in this manner to characterize more closely both the admirable beauty of Esther and the prudent precaution and love of her uncle. But this does not at all harmonize with the higher ideas of the narrative. Here it is precisely and instructively intimated, that no especial attention had been directed to

Esther. She was fetched in the ordinary way with crowds of
girls. As one plucks flowers in a garden to present a
bouquet to a dear friend, so they here collected a variety
of human beings from all places for sensual enjoyment,
provided they had any attractiveness and colour. The
gardener was the הגי (הגא, ver. 3), Aga, the keeper of the
women, who had the charge of the women's house. This was
the most important person in such acts as here described.
As the damsels were introduced by him to the king, his
influence and his favour was of great weight. The intention
of the narrative of our book is manifestly to show the
wonderful help which was provided for Israel for the time
of their need. This is to appear exactly from the opposite
fact, that Esther was not concealed, but at once found and
given up. The cleverness and the taste of the people who
fetched her, and of those who administered the affairs of the
harem, were also instruments of deliverance in God's hands.

Among the hundreds who were placed under the care of
the Aga, the gracefulness of Esther struck him the most.

Ver. 9. ותיטב הנערה—" *And the maiden pleased him.*"

Curtius narrates (viii. 4. 23, etc.) that it happened when
once Alexander was at a banquet, there were thirty noble
virgins presented to him; but although they were all of the
choicest beauty, yet the eyes of all were directed to Roxane,
as she surpassed them in good looks. (Quae quanquam inter
electas processerat, omnium tamen oculos convertit in se.)
The same was the case with Esther. The experienced eye of
the Aga was beyond all attracted by her, and he paid her
the best attention, and showed her favours, which were of
importance to her and her friend's future career. The
Midrash says that he foresaw that she would eventually
become queen, and therefore he was so friendly to her. But
this is false. Rather was it, that Esther's gracefulness
pleased him so much that he undertook, so far as lay in his
power, to risk everything in order to make her queen. The

pleasure which he had in her he manifested by special
exertions in her behalf, for the purpose of increasing her
natural beauty by artificial means. It is said first of him,
—ויבהל את־תמרוקיה. The original meaning of בהל, whose
organic root is הל, is represented by the German word *eilen*, to
hasten. Yes, it is clear that this German word, which does
not occur in the Gothic, and whose origin Grimm did not
discern, is connected with the Old German word *illan*, Old
S. German *ilian*. The Greek word ἁμιλλάσθαι is similarly
connected with ἅμα. The idea of hastening contains in it the
cause for doing so, an anxiety to carry out some important
duty or strenuous order; therefore also trembling, terror in
general. Here in our passage the verb בהל has the sense of
hurrying to carry out a duty and a privilege. He delivered
to Esther prior to all others, even before her turn came to
receive them, the necessary materials provided for the women's
toilet before they could be introduced to the king; and he
meant the quick despatch of this business as a favour to her;
for the longer she participated in his nursing care, the more
beautiful she would become. We read: "And he speedily
gave her things for purification, with her portions." Each
newcomer to the harem must first undergo an ablution in
order to refresh herself, etc.; and this custom is also observed
in the case of young girls, because the bath is the most
essential part, according to Oriental custom, in the process
of effecting a good bodily appearance, with which all other
adornment is connected. So then the word תמרוק has
evidently received the meaning of preparing the toilet, and
of things generally necessary for making a good *début*.

The portions (מנות) consisted of magnificent dresses and
ornaments, which were given to every woman of the harem.[1]

Not only was Esther privileged in speedily receiving everything necessary for her external appearance, but she also

---

[1] The explanation of Clericus on this passage, that by the portions is
meant food, is quite erroneous. The women naturally received food at all
times.

received seven selected slaves to wait upon her. In the
word הָרְאֻיוֹת, part. pass. pers. pl., which only occurs in this
passage, lies the significance of the selection of the servants
which were proper for her. As all who were gathered
received their share of servants, the distinction shown to her
could not have consisted in the point of time *when* she
received the servants, but in point of their *qualifications*
and appearance. They were of the very best sort. Likewise
in point of *number*, they were seven, the same number of
servants as were allotted to the great court ladies.

The Targum has a peculiar comment upon the number of
servants. In order to show how Esther could, amidst her
surroundings, remember which day was the Sabbath, it says
that she knew this from the number of her slaves; for every
day she had another to wait upon her, who was called by the
name of the day of the week, and thus when the one who
served on the Sabbath came to wait upon her, she knew that
it was the Sabbath day. It is certainly a peculiar Oriental
thought which makes a calendar of human beings. The
Targum also further gives the names of the seven slaves, and
that in a poetical and instructive manner. We have already
mentioned that the servants as well as mistresses have
poetical names, borrowed from nature. This is imitated in
the Targum; but the Jewish teachers themselves had not
noticed it before. They took these names from the history
of the creation, so that they can only be elucidated from the
things that were created in the first week. But this comment
gives undoubtedly the appearance of being tinctured with
Christian ideas. We begin with Monday, in which the
firmament or sky was created. This is in Hebrew רקיע.
The slave which waited upon Esther on this day was therefore called רוקעיתא, better רקעיתא, meaning something like
"Heaven's child." On Tuesday were created the trees, their
fruit and all vegetables, and so the name of the slave of the
day was גנוניתא, from גן, גנתא, "the garden," corresponding to
"Garden-flower."

On the fourth day, Wednesday, were created the stars of
heaven (as they are called in the Targum, Gen. i. 14, נהורין),
and therefore the name of the servant of the day was נהוריתא,
"Starlight." On Thursday were created all creeping things.
The Hebrew word שרץ is expressed in the Talmud by
רחיש, therefore the attendant of this day is named רחישׁתא,
"Butterfly." By the way, through this explanation the
reading is established, and the ג of Mezahh Ahron, etc., is
erroneous. Remarkable is the name of the slave who
attended her on the sixth day, in which the cattle and man
were created. It is חורפיתא, the diminutive form of חורפא,
meaning in Chald. and Syriac the "Lamb" (see Targ. Gen.
xxi. 29), "Little lamb." Be it remembered that *Friday* is
designated by a lamb, which certainly is in accord with the
Christian remembrance of Him who as the Lamb of God
was led to the slaughter on that day.

The seventh day is the Sabbath, the day of rest, the quiet
time. Therefore the name of the servant is רגעיתא, "Quiet."
For רגע is rendered "quiet" both by Jewish and Christian
commentators in Ps. xxxv. 20 — "the quiet in the land."
The servant "Quiet" reminded Esther that it was the
Sabbath. The day following the Sabbath, our Lord's day,
on which the light was created, Esther had an attendant
whose name was חולתא, which is best explained from חל, the
name of a rare bird, which is taken mostly, though not always
rightly, to be the phoenix (see my *Schwan*, p. L). The phoenix
is a symbol of light; and so we see here, as in connection
with Friday, traces of Christian symbolism, in which the
lamb of Friday is the risen phoenix of Sunday. But the Aga
was not satisfied with the mere giving to Esther her ornaments
sooner than to the rest, and the best of servants. He assigned
also to her and to her servants the best apartments in the
house. The phrase וישנה ואת־נערותיה לטוב בית הנשים can have
no other sense than that he changed the place where she had
dwelt into a better. But if וישנה refers to her person, then it
reads, "he wrought a change in her for the best (לטוב) in

reference to the house of the women." We may translate
the verb שָׁנָה, after the Syriac example in Acts vii. 43, by
" transtulit," " he transferred her."

Ver. 10. לֹא־הִגִּידָה אֶסְתֵּר אֶת־עַמָּהּ—*"Esther had not showed
her people nor her kindred; for Mordecai had charged her
that she should not show it."*

This prohibition testifies to his wisdom and piety. It
becomes now evident why so much stress is laid in ver. 7 on
the fact that Esther had lost her parents, and that Mordecai
had adopted her as his daughter. If her parents had been
alive, such concealment of nationality on her part would have
been next to impossible. It would have been difficult for her
to hide her origin, and the parental love and her own filial
love would have sooner or later betrayed it. But Mordecai,
who did not love her less than her own parents, had that
good sense and that judgment which are better safeguards to
love than vanity and self-pleasing, which are so often mixed
up with the better feelings in the hearts of parents. Esther
belonged to a people in the kingdom which politically and
religiously represented a marked contrast to the ruling people.
The accusation which Haman afterwards brought against
them had surely occupied the public attention of the conquerors and the priests before. At all events, it must have
been useful for Esther to conceal her descent. As she was
now exalted to such a high position, her only aim must have
been to find favour in the eyes of the king; and to this end
a knowledge of her nationality in the circle of the house of
women could in nowise be advantageous to her. Indeed it
might rather, sooner or later, imperil both the position of
Esther and that of her people. Mordecai, who was at home in
Persia, was well acquainted with the conditions of the court
and of the capital. How easily could Esther fall into disgrace,
as Vashti did, and so herself be the main cause of her
people's misfortunes (see Yalkut on the passage)! So also in
the contrary event, as the history has taught, what dangers

would ensue to Esther from her nationality being known, if
persecutions against the Jews should arise! The deliverance
which she was later called to achieve succeeded, humanly
speaking, only because no one knew that she belonged to
Israel. Had it been known, the intrigues for her destruction
would have been commenced. Add to this that the king was
perhaps favourably disposed to other Jews besides her, whose
position had to be taken into consideration; and if it had
been known that she also was a Jewess, envious tongues
would have been busy with the charge of preponderating
Jewish influence at court.

The Midrash says that Mordecai showed his modesty
by prohibiting Esther from making her pedigree known.
There is truth in this. He certainly thereby renounced
claims upon honours and presents which would have fallen
to him as her nearest kindred. Chardin says that it is still
the custom in modern Persia to give pensions to the family
of a lady of the seraglio; and the more she is esteemed by
the king, the greater are the pensions (*Voyage*, vi. 626, 627).
But Mordecai had love for his people and for his [adopted]
daughter; but he had no desire for the acquisition of money
and honours. Thus he could the more freely observe what
was going on at court. It might be asked, how was it
possible that Esther's nationality should remain a sealed
secret?[1] But the secret was in Esther's own hands, and
entirely depended upon her discretion as to the time of
revealing it. For the arbitrary and domineering spirit with
which women are sought and bought in the name of the king
is above all the petty differences of nationality, which it does
not care to inquire into. Beauty and enjoyment are sought.
The person who is admitted into the seraglio needs only to
have physical good looks. History, name, parents, and birth

---

[1] Out of this question arose the Talmudical opinion (Megilla 13*a*), that
we must not read that Mordecai took Esther לְבַת for a daughter (ver. 7),
but לְבַיִת, into the house. We are reminded of Bathsheba the wife of
Uriah, of whom Nathan said in his sermon on penitence to David, that
he had robbed her husband of the one ewe-lamb he had.

are of no account. During the time in which the Turks carried on a prolonged war with Christian nations in Europe, the sultans carried on their vicious amusements with women from Greece, Russia, Poland, Hungary, and Italy. So was the Sultana Tarshan in the seventeenth century a Pole, Baffa the powerful concubine of Murad IV. was from Venice, and Kosen the mother of Ibrahim the Vicious was a Greek. That the origin of even such distinguished persons who had left their mark upon history was unknown, is testified by the various reports concerning Churem, the favourite of Soliman I., who was an extraordinary woman. French authors say that she was a peasant woman. Other writers affirm that she was the sister of King Sigismund, so that the latter would be, of course, Soliman's brother - in - law. Others again say that she was a native of Siena in Italy, a daughter of Nani Marsigli, and had been kidnapped by robbers. If so, through her the Pope Alexander became related to the sultan. But as she is usually called a Russian, she must have come from Galicia. Count Rzewuski asserted that she was the daughter of a poor pope (priest) of Rohatyn, a small town in Galicia[1] (comp. Hammer, *Osm. Gesch.* iii. 672, 673, and 736). The Oriental legend tells that even slaves sometimes kept their origin a profound secret. A sultan said once that he did not want a favourite of unknown origin, for he feared that he would have bad children by her (*The Thousand and One Nights*, xix. p. 97). The maidens were delivered to the Aga without a name and without a history, only as so many bodies, and not even as a modern flock of camels, which possess a history, biography, and photography. The Aga had before him a multitude of beautiful faces ; and he cared nothing as to which nation they belonged. When it came to his knowledge, it was through the women themselves, who sought

---

[1] The Midrash speaks of such experience and life at court when it remarks that Ahhashverosh did not want to ascertain the origin of Esther, because various nations have severally claimed her as belonging to them.

to gain some advantage for their relations.   It therefore
sufficed that Mordecai should forbid Esther herself to tell of
her origin, as the information would not come from other
quarters.   For as soon as she was in the seraglio all access
to her ceased, and Mordecai was silent.

Ver. 11. "*And Mordecai walked every day before the
court of the women's house*," etc.

But though he asked Esther to deny any knowledge of him,
yet his anxious paternal care for her did not cease.   As an
apparent stranger, it was perhaps the more easy for him to
make inquiries about her welfare and proceedings; and so
he was daily to be seen in the neighbourhood of the court.
The Midrash thinks that he was anxious lest she should
be enchanted, a belief which to this day still exists in the
East.

Ver. 12. "*Now when the turn of every maiden was come.*"

We have here an exact description of the events that took
place in the inner circle of the house of women.   But this is
not for the purpose of telling us an anecdote from the secrets of
the harem.   It is thereby emphatically intimated how wonderful the providences were by which Esther reached her happy
goal.   We learn from Herodotus (iii. 69) that Phaedyme, in
order to investigate whether there were certain marks upon
the body of the false Smerdis, had to wait till her turn came
to be called to the king; for, he adds, "the Persians let their
wives come to them by turns" (ἐν περιτροπῇ γὰρ δὴ γυναῖκες
φοιτέουσι τοῖσι Πέρσῃσι).   This successive turn was not a
slight interval; it lasted, it is said, a twelvemonth,—a year
then, in which every newly-received woman had time to
prepare herself for the day of meeting the king.—Now such
turns were daily occurrences, consequently the number of
court women must have been about 360.   In this matter
also we see how closely our book agrees with the otherwise
known notices of classical writers, and how much light it

throws upon them. Curtius narrates (and is confirmed by Plutarch) that Darius had 360 women with him (iii. 3. 24). When Dicaearch says in Athenaeus (lib. xiii. 557) that there were only 350, the notice in our book leads us to give more credence to the report of Curtius. It is a characteristic feature of the great King of Persia that he has the liberty of having every day in the year another woman to wait upon him. This Diodorus expressly says when he narrates of Alexander the Great, that he had entirely adopted the luxurious habits of a Persian ruler. His words are: " He led with him concubines, like Darius, who were not less in number than the days of the year " [1] (" οὐκ ἐλάττους πλήθει τῶν κατὰ τὸν ἐνιαυτὸν ἡμερῶν," xvii. 77). These were to the number of 360, as Curtius expressly states (vi. 6. 8, Pellices ccc. et lx. totidem, quot Dario fuerant, regiam implebant). Yet the avarice and luxury of the princes in later times was not satisfied even with this number. The Osman sultan Murad III. had 40 favourites and 500 female slaves; but 400 appears to be the round number with the Persian shahs, as is evident from the narrative of Chardin (*Voyage*, vi. 243).

These twelve months were spent by the women in going through a course of preparation by the application of the means then usual of embellishing their bodies, and all this for one single occasion. There was never a greater caricature of monarchical and manly power, never a more legal degradation and disgrace of woman, than was manifested in the institution of the harem. Certainly it was a question of life with the selected women whether they would be raised as special favourites and queens or not. They therefore must

---

[1] For their year was 360 days (comp. Ideler, *Handb. der Chronologie*, ii. 514). Abunassr, a governor of Diarbekr, had for the number of new calendar 365 female slaves, in order to have one a day (Hammer, *Gemäldesaal*, v. p. 40). This throws light upon what is told of the Emperor Commodus (Lamprid, c. 5): "Hac igitur lege vivens ipse cum trecentis concubinis . . . trecentisque aliis puberibus exoletis quos aeque ex plebe et nobilitate collegerat."

have considered the regulation which required a whole year
of personal preparation before meeting the king as a special
act of indulgence which his refined taste dictated. It was
his pleasure to see a rivalry among the women, and therefore
full liberty was given them to this effect. Everything of
luxury and pleasure was placed at their disposal; but this was
not in consideration for themselves personally, but only in
reference to the eventual enjoyment of the king, just as a
landlord decorates a house with fine gilded paper, not for
the sake of the walls, but for his own pleasure. We have
no exact information in reference to the toilet of the women
which was given them during the year. That there was a
definite order in this respect is evident from what we read, that
six months were spent in the application of oil of myrrh, and
six months in the use of sweet odours and other purifications.

שמן המר ;מר is, as is well known, μύρρα, σμύρνα, the fragrant
resin of *balsamodendron myrrha*, which was esteemed very
precious in olden times. Famous ointments were made of
it. The Arabs, says Athenaeus (lib. xv. p. 688), generally
call ointments myrrh, because they are produced from it.
Here, without doubt, the precious ointment is meant which
in the time of Pliny (*Hist. Nat.* xiii. 3) was called "royal
ointment," because it was used by the kings of the Parthians.
It consists of a number of ingredients, among which is myrrh,
as in the anointing oil of the Scriptures (Ex. xxx. 25).
R. Hhiya-bar Abba explains it correctly by סטכת (Meg. 13a),
viz. στακτή; and in Athenaeus also we find that myrrha, called
stakte, is a kind of ointment. They understand by stakte the
drops of oil issuing from fresh myrrh. The explanation of
R. Yehudah, that it means אמפקנן, is not so correct, as ἔλαιον
ὀμφάκινον (ὀμφάκιον) is oil of unripe olives. To this very
day the Orientals like the perfume of very fragrant ointments
and pomades as well as of other odours (בשמים). "In the East
one lives and is refreshed," says Chardin (iv. 158), "by perfumes,
instead of feeling, as in our countries, overcome by them."
Eastern stories vividly describe the pleasures of the baths and

the embrocations, and of the use of rose-water and other
fragrant essences, ointments, and odorous combs, in connection
with the course that people go through for improving and
adorning their external appearance.[1]

Ver. 13. ובבׁה הנערה—" *Then in this wise came the maiden
unto the king.*"

This verse is very instructive. Every maiden that was
called to appear before the king had the liberty to use any
means which, in her estimation, might conduce to her pleasing
him. "Whatsoever she desired was given her to go with her
out of the house of the women unto the king's house." By the
term לבוא, "to go with," the Midrash finely understands that
she could choose any one to accompany her. Every one
had the right of taking servants with them, so that they
might form the background in the interview.

But it was no slight matter even for the most pronounced
belle to win the most spoiled and sensual king. And one single
meeting together was to decide her fate, either of getting a
secluded and uninfluential career, or of living all her life long a
splendid though luxurious life. For if she had failed to win the
affections of the king, she did not return the next morning to
the house of the women, which was superintended by the Aga,
but she went to the harem, the house of the concubines,
where such women were kept and maintained who belonged
to the king, and whom he disposed of according to his pleasure.

Ver. 14. The eunuch who was at the head of this second
house of women was called Shaashgaz, שעשגז, from the Persian
שאש, "beautiful," so that his name means "minister of
beauties" (as Kislar-Aga).

---

[1] We refer particularly to the narrative of Ameny (*The Thousand and
One Nights*, xx. 49). Especially instructive matter is to be found in Aelian
(*Verm. Gesch.* xii. 1), where he tells of a Greek woman that was brought
to the camp of Cyrus—women followed her whose duty was to plait her
hair and to anoint and to rouge her face. Plutarch narrates (sevenwise)
that the Sybarite women gave invitations to their friends a year before, in
order that they might have time to prepare their toilets.

Ver. 15. ובהגיע תר-אסתר —— "*Now when the turn of Esther*," etc.

All that preceded her were certainly distinguished for their good looks, but none of them had made any good impression upon the king. Finally, it was Esther's chance. In order to intimate the significance of the moment, the narrator just here adds, what he has not done in ver. 7, the name of Abihhail her father.[1] He had died early, and the education of Esther, which suited her so well in her present position, was entirely the work of Mordecai. To him, therefore, as her second father, due honour is given in ver. 7, in that she is only called "his uncle's daughter." Abihhail was the brother of Jair, the father of Mordecai. Though דוד meant originally "friend," "beloved," yet later on it came to signify "uncle," as the word uncle still retains the meaning of "a friend of the house."

So Mishael and Elizaphan are called the sons of the דוד, uncle of Aaron, for their father Uzziel was the brother of Amram (Ex. vi. 22; Lev. x. 4). So also Abner is called the son of the uncle, דוד, of Saul, for his father Ner was a brother of Kish (1 Sam. xiv. 51). The Greek name Θεῖος, Pott rightly derives from Sancr. *dhe*, to nourish (*Etym. Forsch.* xiv. 51. Comp. my *Comm. on Ruth*, p. 213); and when τήθη τηθίς is compared with it, it follows that originally it was applied to the brother of the mother, as it is mostly used so, only that it naturally was extended to the brother of the father also. The same connection of ideas must be ascribed to the Hebrew דוד. Its radical signification of "love" points to maternal tenderness in nourishing her child with her breast. דוד belongs to דד, "breast," "mamma," "nipple." Comp. שד and הד.

To the prominence which is given to the father in the Israelitish popular life is to be ascribed the fact, that דוד represents in Scripture only the patruus and not the avunculus. We may notice that it is characteristic of Roman

[1] The LXX. has Aminadab.

nations, that for the brother of both parents avunculus is usual
rather than patruus, although the former means only the
brother of the mother. (Comp. uncle, Wall. *unchin*, Albanes.
unki; cf. Diez, *Lex. der rom. Sprache*, p. 697.) In the
Targum we meet such words as אחב, viz. אחאב, father's brother.
Evidently there must have been a corresponding word, אם חם or
אחאם, for mother's brother. There can be no doubt that
from this Hebrew Ahh'em comes the hitherto unexplained
German word Oheim, and that this also meant originally the
mother's brother.

" She required nothing."

The characteristic feature which these words indicate is
very significant. The other women could not find enough
artificial means with which to make an impression upon the
king. The supplies of ornaments and other things which
they had received for this purpose from the Aga was deemed
by them as insufficient, and they demanded more in order
to satisfy their burning desire to become favourites. But
Esther cared nothing about these things. She had no such
ambitious desires. Her heart did not burn to become something which was indeed illustrious, yet not becoming to a
believing Jewess. Reluctantly she had left her home, and
reluctantly and passively she put on her ornaments, and did
not exert herself to take a single active step to reach the
pinnacle of her fellow-women's glory. She was wanted, and
ordered to appear, and therefore she obeyed the Aga in
causing herself to be dressed up for the occasion, but did
not express an urgent desire to see the pomp of the harem.
She was compelled to be there; but that was no reason for
her to profane her lips and her believing heart. This is not
to be lightly estimated. In the midst of women, who are
more jealous and ambitious than men, tempted by her own
heart to believe that she was the most beautiful of them all,
and occupying such vantage ground, to which she was to a
certain extent already committed and pledged, a desire on her

part to become the mightiest woman, or, at least, to be
crowned with the greatest honours, might have found some
extenuation. But Esther was superior to this. What she
possessed was only obedience—to her second father, and to
the necessity. But ambition, a desire to rule, lust of pleasure,
she had none. To have virtue and chastity in the heart—
when at home, under the protection of parents, is not so
difficult. But in the harem, in the midst of all the provisions
which sensuality has prepared and ordered, where everything
excites the passions, and where royal power casts its dazzling
lustre, in such a position still to remain virtuous, requires an
education in the divine law of a holy God, such as Esther
had received in the house of Mordecai.

"*And Esther found favour in the sight of all them that
looked upon her.*"

She desired nothing, and yet she received what the others
had with all their arts [vainly] endeavoured to obtain. Her
natural gracefulness of manner, heightened by a charm which
all the others did not possess, viz. the charm of an innocent
and chaste heart,—which no toilet can supply, and which
wantonness and pomp leave the more missing,—captivated
all who saw her, even before she went to the king. She
pleased all, not merely on account of her beauty, but what
is more, on account of her amiability. Her modest and
unpretentious behaviour towards everybody won for her the
respect of all. Being of a simple and contented disposition,
she excited no envy or dislike in others. In contrast with
those who preceded her, who, in spite of all the artful means
which they used for obtaining more ostentatious ornaments,
were yet dissatisfied, and therefore excited dislike against
themselves, she was satisfied with the gifts and treatment
she received. But where should the others get the charms
which only a quiet believing heart can supply in such a place?
In the house of sensuality true chastity makes an irresistible
impression upon the eyes, countenance, and demeanour. But

it was the grace of God which brought such a girl to this place; not for the sake of the king, but for the sake of the danger that was impending upon the people to whom she belonged, and to whom she was attached both in heart and belief.

Ver. 16. "*So Esther was taken unto King Ahhashverosh, into his house royal, in the tenth month, which is the month Tebeth, in the seventh year of his reign.*"

Tebeth is the tenth month in the Jewish year which begins with Nisan according to the Scriptures, and the fourth month in the Jewish year which begins with Tishri according to the traditions. The name was indigenous in Syria and Mesopotamia, where the Jews in the time of the captivity had adopted it and all the new names of the months. The statement that the introduction took place in the tenth month of the seventh year of the reign of the king, evidently refers to the Persian computation of time. Now, if their tenth month was either then called Tebeth, or corresponded to Tebeth, it would follow that, already under Xerxes, the Persian year began in the spring, as is also manifest from the spirit of the teaching of the Avesta. It would also not be erroneous to infer that the introduction of the women to the king began in the Persian spring, so that nine months had passed before Esther's turn came. The ground for the successive turns cannot be ascertained; probably it was in accordance with the priority of the selection for the harem by the Aga. The wonderful dispensation by which Esther was chosen as a favourite of the king is more prominently brought to view by the fact that her turn was not before the tenth month, after hundreds of candidates had gone before her and had been rejected. It may be asked why, if the Aga was well disposed to her, and as it appears from ver. 9 that he facilitated matters for her speedy advancement, did he not introduce her before? To this we answer, that his postponement was actuated by friendly feelings towards her, in not wishing to risk her chance, as he knew that the first were not usually successful. The LXX. and Josephus have on this a surprisingly deviating date, viz. that it took place in the twelfth month, which is Adar (δωδεκάτῳ μηνί, ὅς ἐστιν 'Aδάρ). These chronological variations did not arise from homiletical traditions, which rather adhered to the month Tebeth, but only from a gloss, which must have been made by one who was acquainted with Persian chronology. The same must have added to or explained the statement "which is Tebeth, אדר." For this is the Persian name of the ninth month, with which the tenth month of the Jewish calendar partly agrees. But the LXX. translators took this אדר for the Adar of the Jewish calendar, and consequently had added "in the twelfth month." The ancient expositors pass over any indication that the tenth of the month Tebeth recalls the sad event of Nebuchadnezzar's encompassing Jerusalem with his besieging army (Ezek. xxiv. 1, 2). In the month which had a fast day, Esther appeared before the king, that she might finally save Israel by fasting. The month of oppression and distress, caused by the anger of the king, became the month of deliverance occasioned by the love of the king.

Ver. 17. "*And he made her queen instead of Vashti.*"

The same favour which Esther experienced everywhere, she also found in the eyes of the king. "He loved her more than all the women." No other maiden found such grace before him, and she became his cherished wife, so that he set the royal crown upon her head. Jewish teachers, who did not like to entertain the notion that Esther enjoyed his love, say that it was not at all herself whom he embraced, but a spirit; while she was all the time in the house of Mordecai. But although a similar superstition was to a great extent prevalent in the Middle Ages, yet the authors of the Zohar ought to have been mindful of the fact, that in their zeal to shield Esther from contamination with the uncircumcised and vicious king, they thereby made her a deceiver.

The Midrash informs us that the king had hitherto the portrait of Vashti suspended over his bed, and now since Esther saw it, he had it removed, and placed hers in its stead (Esther Rabba 99b; Yalkut). This observation is in agreement with contemporary experience. Herodotus narrates (vii. 69) that Darius, the father of Xerxes, had a portrait of his favourite wife Artystone made out of embossed gold. The Jewish teachers quote on this occasion a remarkable saying of R. Berachia, son of Levi (Esther Rabba 92b), "When Israel was in exile, God said to them, ' You weep before me, and say that you are like orphans who have no father and mother. I will send you a redeemer, who will also be without a father.' "[1] This they apply to Esther. But she had once a father and a mother, and a second father in Mordecai. Israel, indeed, was redeemed by the Messiah, who had no human father.

Ver. 18. " *And the king made a great feast.*"

The other women were dismissed. But Esther, the king loved. The lot of these great earthly potentates was usually not an enviable one, in spite of their great pomp and magnificence. They possessed power, but no love ; they could command, but they knew little of the emotions of the heart's affection, which are extended to the person loved for his own sake. Just because they extracted sensual enjoyment by force of royal command, they were not in actual possession of love. Extravagant and luxurious persons and times, impoverish the ideal thought of true love, of husband to the wife and of wife to husband, who is also to her the image of divine creation. It is told of Khosru, the great king of Persia, that he chose the highly gifted Sherin as his favourite, but that she loved a poor artist named Ferhad. The joy also of true and inmost love grows only out of morality and out of the belief in an omniscient God. It is written : " The

---

[1] [" For it is written, Behold the man whose name is Branch, and he shall bud forth under him" (Zech. vi. 12, R. V.). Again Isa. xi. 1. Midrash of Moses Hadarshan on Gen. xxxvii. 22.—TRANS.]

king loved Esther." He found in her a different person from other women. She was modest and unassuming in her bearing. Virtue without covetousness, and obedience in spiritual nobility, not only beautified her face, but also gave her such an imposing charm that the king was moved by higher than mere common feelings when looking at her. In this for him unusual joy he instituted a feast : an Esther-feast (מִשְׁתֵּה אֶסְתֵּר) or banquet to celebrate her coronation, as this was the custom everywhere. Besides this, he gave an הֲנָחָה to the provinces, which the Chaldaic version properly paraphrases by שְׁבוּק כְּרְנָא, "remission of taxes." Just so the Latin word *remissio* means, giving rest to the soul (like הֲנָחָה, from נוּחַ), as well as release of tribute. The word ἄφεσις of the LXX., according to its ancient use, has the meaning of *dimissio* and *remissio* also in the higher senses of the word. When the pseudo-Smerdis entered upon his reign, he likewise on the ground of such a celebration remitted the taxes for three years (Herod. iii. 67), on which occasion he used the word ἀτεληίη, viz. ἀτέλεια φόρου (comp. 1 Macc. x. 34), where it is spoken of ἀτελείας καὶ αἱρέσεως, "days without taxes." Herodotus is of opinion that all Persian kings have remitted the taxes when they began to reign (vi. 59). But the Osman sultans, although they have often celebrated weddings and feasts of circumcision with great eclat, have never yet remitted the taxes on such occasions. They have rather compelled their subjects to give them presents, unlike this case, where the king gave the gifts, כְּיַד הַמֶּלֶךְ, to his subjects.

This expression, כְּיַד הַמֶּלֶךְ, is correctly rendered in the R. V. "according to the bounty of the king," *i.e.* the gifts were plentiful in quantity and worthy in quality.[1] When, in 1675, one of the most pompous feasts were held in Stamboul, every Greek family was obliged to contribute thirty aspers (a Turkish

[1] On the other hand, the ancient caliphs magnanimously imitated this royal bounty. The most magnificent wedding was that of Mamun with the daughter of his Vizier Buran. Of this Hammer, in his *Gemäldesaal*, ii. 231, reports that all the guests, including the camel-drivers and the sailors, were overloaded with presents.

coin), and every ten taxed families at Adrianople had to send six hens, two fat geese, and four ducks (Hammer, vi. 308). The delivery of other presents was also imposed upon Jews and Christians who belonged to corporations and guilds. Entirely different was the munificent action of the King of Persia ; he gave with full hands, remitted the income-tax with a joyful heart, for he loved Esther ; and he who loves gives.

Ver. 19. "*And when the virgins were gathered together the second time.*"

This verse remained obscure to former commentators, and especially in ancient times, so that the LXX. omitted it altogether. But this was very wrong. The verse occupies an important position. It closely connects the foregoing with the following, and only shows the beauty and the simplicity of the thoughts contained in the narrative. It introduces the circumstances under which a new event took place, viz. the conspiracy of the eunuchs and its collapse. This occurrence is placed close to the election of Esther as queen. In ver. 19 the contrast as well as the connection is shown : " And when the virgins were gathered together the second time . . . and when Mordecai sat in the king's gate ; " the elevation of Esther to the rank of queen had not at all interrupted the routine of the harem. Ahhashverosh indeed loved Esther, but of the tyrannical Persian lust of women he had not given up a particle. The temptation to continually acquire new wives was as strong with him as ever, and he could not subdue his sensual infirmities and love of extravagance. He did not issue a decree to recall and annul his former one for the seeking out of women, although his heart had found satisfaction in Esther. The narrator intentionally brings out the contrast. " Look," says he, "just now the king has shown that he loved Esther above all women, and yet other women are so soon sought ! " On the other hand, there is truth in that which the Jewish expositors, if they are rightly understood, seem to have surmised, namely, that the

search for new women was intentionally organized in the
court, in order that the person of Esther might possibly be
eclipsed and placed in the background.   One might easily
bring analogous cases in Oriental courts as illustrations.   The
intriguing courtiers and their retinue did not find in Esther,
whose origin was not even known to them, a person who
would patronise and support their plans and further their
influence.   This they could only secure by the elevation of
another favourite who was more intimately connected with
them.   This endeavour would not only meet with impunity,
but would also, according to Persian court fashion, be considered as an act of loyal demonstration.   The king's love
to Esther did not at all hinder him from receiving such fresh
enjoyments.   In his haughty and dark heart there was not a
shadow of the thought that such conduct was in fact directed
against his love, and against her who was momentarily
loved by him.   To this the narrator significantly alludes.
He wishes to say : " Scarcely had the feast of Esther taken
place, when they again began to collect virgins ; and so
apparently the power of the new queen had already begun
to decline."   It was then that the following event occurred,
which was of such a character that it *endangered the king's
own life, but was in the end productive of greater love and
gratitude on his part to Esther.*

" *While they were again collecting virgins, Mordecai sat
in the king's gate.*"

Not as an official, but as an independent man, Mordecai sat
in the public place before the king's palace,[1] and spent his
leisure hours, as it is the custom in the East, in hearing
news, making inquiries, and in conversations with friends
and acquaintances.   This clause is also of importance ; for not
only does it represent the external circumstance, without

---

[1] Herodotus calls the place πρόθυρα.   When Syloson came with a
petition to Darius to ask for Samos, we read : ἵζετο ἐς τὰ πρόθυρα τῶν
βασιλῆος οἰκίων (iii. 140).

which the discovery of the conspiracy could not have been made by him, but it also expresses the sharp contrast to the first clause, " While they were collecting." The seeking of new women could only have been directed against Esther, while Mordecai's sitting before the palace had no other intention [than to guard her interests], for before this he had nothing to do there except to be near the palace in order to assist his dear daughter with his paternal advice.

Before the narrator proceeds to give a detailed account of the episode, he restrains himself from what he has to say in ver. 20, and inserts parenthetically two memorable facts, viz. that Esther did not disclose her parentage and nationality, and that she now as punctually and carefully followed Mordecai's injunctions in all things as she formerly did when she was under his humble roof. The clause is remarkable from many an aspect. It reveals, first of all, a new characteristic of Esther herself. As the favoured queen she remained as modest and as obedient to her foster father as she was when she was first received into the harem. She still continued to do what he told her, as if she had still been in his house. The royal pomp which surrounded her on every side did not make her head dizzy. She had not forgotten that the whole royalty was not for her a matter of pleasure, but only a duty of obedience. Her interest was with the father out of doors, and not with the luxury inside.

Nothing else but his wisdom influenced her. Now, if the picture of Esther's character gains in our estimation through this parenthetical notice, its importance is further seen in this: Not merely because she did not disclose her parentage, and did not suffer herself to be influenced by any one but Mordecai, did she maintain her position at court (on account of which influential courtiers were searching for other and more manageable women); but also because the fact, concerning which more is to be spoken in detail, shows how wise the arrangement of Mordecai was. The knowledge that he acquired of the conspiracy he certainly owed only to the fact

that no one had paid any particular attention to him. Had
it been known that he was a countryman and relation of the
queen, he would not have been able to sit so leisurely before
the gate of the palace. The intriguers would have been
cautious with their design. Thus wisdom rewarded the one,
and obedience the other. Esther continued to be queen,
because she was no less humble now than she was when only
a poor orphan. She rose in power and influence, because, out
of gratitude to her uncle, she did not think of either. The
parenthesis is also of uncommon importance, for without it
the fact of the discovered conspiracy would have had no
significance and interest for our book.

Ver. 21. בימים ההם—" *In those days.*"

Now, after the short digression, the narrator takes up the
thread of the narrative. " In those days," says he (as they
were again collecting virgins, and) as Mordecai used to sit at
the gate, it happened that two eunuchs belonging to the
sentinels of the palace, and therefore confidential persons,
made a conspiracy against the king's life. The reason for it
is not stated, but it probably was because their ambition had
been thwarted and their influence had been damaged. Others
sought to gain promotion in a different way, by seeking to
substitute another favourite in the place of Esther; but these
thought that they could only reach their aim by murdering
the king, and substituting another in his place. Through the
wonderful guidance of Providence, the plan of the one party
must become the means of salvation from the design of the other
in reference to the king and the queen. Their names were
Teresh, תרש, and Bigthan, בגתן. The name בגתן is like בגתא
(*s. o.*), Bagoas, Bagistanes; that of תרש reminds us of תרשתא
(Ezra ii. 63); both are derived from their offices. But they
were not high officials. This is shown by the qualifying words
משמרי הסף, those who kept the door. Herodotus called them
πυλουροί, φυλακαί (iii. 140), without whom no one could enter
the castle (iii. 72). The name שומרי הסף was not unfamiliar to

the narrator, as it often occurs in the history of Israel when
they had reached the zenith of glory (2 Kings xii. 10, xxii. 4,
xxv. 18 ; 2 Chron. xxxiv. 9 ; Jer. xxxv. 4, lii. 24).

Moreover, it is said that Xerxes was at last actually killed
by conspirators. Artaban, the commander of his cavalry,
conspired with Mithridates, his confidential chamberlain, who
admitted him into the bedroom of the king during the night,
and so he stabbed the king with his dagger while he was
asleep (Diodor. xi. 69. 1). But this time he escaped assassi-
nation. It is emphatically told that the conspirators were
watchers of the threshold, the guard at the entrance of the
gate. From this it appears probable that Mordecai, who was
loitering about the gate, and unnoticed by them, overheard
their treacherous conversation. Josephus thinks that a Jewish
slave was one of them, by the name of Barnabazus, who
betrayed them to Mordecai. The Jewish commentators are
of opinion that Mordecai understood their language, inasmuch as he spoke seventy languages; and the proof they
give of this is, that another man in Ezra ii. 2 is called
Mordecai, whose name stands near the name Bilshan, which
they take as an adjective meaning linguist. The language
they spoke was the language of Tarshish, טרסאי. How they
come to this strange idea can easily be guessed. The name
of one of the conspirators was תרש, which reminded of תרשיש,
which is sometimes explained as standing for Tarsus in Cilicia.
But it is curious to note that with this Mordecai the Benjamite, according to the Rabbis, a Barnabas stands in confidential and fraternal relationship, and he is conversant with
the language of Tarsus, like the Apostle Paul, who also had
a Barnabas for an intimate friend and companion ! The
LXX. does not even mention the traitors by name, but simply
speaks of them as commanders of the body-guard ($\dot{a}\rho\chi\iota\sigma\omega\mu\alpha\tau o$-
$\phi\acute{u}\lambda\alpha\kappa\epsilon\varsigma$). Josephus used a manuscript which read הרש
instead of תרש, for he calls him Theodestes. Mordecai dis-
covered the plot by his wisdom and by his observation, which
his love to Esther inspired. Was he not sitting day by day

F

in the square before the palatial gate for the very purpose of being vigilant, and yet to be unobserved? And when he was quite certain (וידע) that the king's life was in danger, so that he could substantiate his accusation, and that this would not fall upon the head of Esther, he at once acquainted her with the fact. Evidently he must have kept up a continual correspondence with her, as appears from v. 20, and so the queen revealed it to Ahhashverosh. A searching investigation was immediately made, the accusation was proved, and both eunuchs were hanged on the gallows. Upon this mode of execution we shall speak farther on. The incident was a wonderful interposition of the great Redeemer of Israel, who thus already made known His name. Without this, Esther might perhaps have fallen a victim through the instrumentality of a new rival. But now she had saved the king's life. She had told him that it was Mordecai from whom she had learned the secret of the conspiracy, and he had his name duly registered in the archives; but to reward him, he had momentarily forgotten,[1] and Esther, acting on the advice of her friend, was silent on the point. He would have been exalted to high rank, had she said that he was her uncle and foster-father. But she obeyed, and said nothing. The instruments have been prepared for the hour of danger and of deliverance. The Midrash adorns the above fact with many quaint sayings; but there are some valuable thoughts among them.

According to it, the conspirators wanted to poison the king by putting a snake into his cup of wine or coffee. When they saw that this plan was discovered, they indeed hastily removed the snake; but when the investigation of the affair was made, lo, in order to save Mordecai's head, there the snake was again in the cup. The story of the

[1] Even in the history of Germany it occurred, as Archenholz narrates (*History of the Seven Years' War*, 7th ed. p. 462), that the court preacher Gerlach had warned Frederick II. against the treachery of Warkotsch, and saved his life; but his fidelity was not acknowledged nor rewarded.

snake in the cup[1] is borrowed by the Midrash from the experience and notions of the time. King Xerxes was not exactly a John, who, according to the Lord's promise to all His disciples, might drink from a cup in which a snake had full play, without being hurt. The Midrash further says of the wonderful providence of God, that the king's anger against his servants was like that of Pharaoh against his in order that Joseph might be set free from prison; and that the anger of the servants against the king happened in order that Mordecai might become instrumental in the deliverance of Israel. In answer to the question whether Mordecai was right in his intervention to save the life of such a king, the Midrash says: Jacob blessed Pharaoh, Joseph interpreted the king's dream, and Daniel prophesied to Nebuchadnezzar. The pious of Israel have always been obedient to the existing authorities, and have always done what they could for their welfare. This exhibition of loyalty, as in the case of Joseph and Daniel, so also here, became the means of the salvation of those who showed it. The king had certainly not appreciated the spirit and the sentiments of Esther. He was accustomed to his wives esteeming his life of the highest consequence. When Darius recovered from sickness, through the instrumentality of the clever Greek physician Demokedes, he sent him to the house of the women, in order that they might see him who saved his life; and they gave him rich presents (Herod. iii. 130). For the life of these women was, after the death of their king, very sad and miserable. The report of Athenaeus, that the Persian king was guarded by 300 women, has no other sense except that to none was his life so precious as to them. Ahhashverosh, indeed, rejoiced that Esther saved his life, and she gained in his estimation, and

---

[1] The narrative of the noble Omar Ben-Abdul-Aziz has taken hold of the Oriental legends, which tell that he was poisoned by a treacherous servant, and from the poison he became green like as grass (comp. Tutinameh, *übers. v. Rosen*, ii. 139).

secured her position against possible rivals. But the tyrannical selfishness of an Oriental mighty king is neither diminished nor refined by such catastrophes. They are to him usual acts and occurrences that are bound up with government. Holding unlimited power over the lives of thousands, his heart is not softened nor his wisdom increased by an exhibition of dutiful love. He had not, indeed, forgotten to condemn the conspirators, but the reward due to the deliverer, and the warning lesson which the hostile assault was intended to teach him, these he had forgotten. This is evident from the narrative farther on, when it reaches its tragic height. Through extraordinary interventions, that which was prevented from happening helped to prevent other things from happening. The failure of the attempt to murder the king, and his omission to reward Mordecai, were factors in the frustration of the plan which hatred and caprice had formed. But it also proves that the preparatory steps taken by the king, as recorded in chap. iii., although they were intended to prevent similar catastrophes, yet they did not proceed from a sense of dereliction of duty and love on his part, but were entirely based upon his right of exercising his arbitrary will.

CHAPTER III.

Ver. 1. "*After these things.*"

The narrator in our book has not undertaken the task of giving a complete history of Ahhashverosh. His chief object is to report the circumstances which were connected with the drama of the danger and of the deliverance of Israel. True, he gives the exact dates in which the recorded events happened, but at the same time we must remember that he does not write annals of the Persian court. He rather very ably places those events in succession after each other which have any ethical tendency or bearing upon the history, in spite of the intervals of time which lie between them. The disaster which Haman seeks to bring upon Israel is to him the hinge upon which his history turns. All these things, he implies, must necessarily have happened, in order that the plan of an angry man should be frustrated. Instead of giving us diffusive reflections, he lets the facts speak for themselves. He does not speak of the miracles which these successive occurrences reveal, but he makes it clear that Haman only becomes powerful just at that moment when the exaltation of Esther to the position of queen, and when the saving of the king's life through Mordecai had taken place, and not before.

"*Haman the son of Hammedatha the Agagite.*"

The narrator reports his elevation by the king after the preceding events had taken place, but omits to indicate the ground for this elevation. Regarded superficially, there seems to be no connection between these events and his promotion, nevertheless they form the historical basis or the ladder upon which he climbed up to his high position. There is a well-known Persian tradition, that in the reign of King Vistaçpa, later Gustasp, the religion of the Avesta was introduced into Persia (Spiegel, *Avesta*, i. 42, 43). Although it has been questioned whether this Vistaçpa is the same as Hystaspes, the father of Darius, yet the identity of the names may be established from the fact that the house of Darius was particularly zealous for the doctrine of the Zarathustra. It is remarkable enough that we do not meet with the name Hystaspes, except in the case of the father and the son of Darius. This king says of himself, in the inscription of Bisutun, according to Benfey, p. 12, as follows: "I have again restored the temple, and the worship of the protector of the kingdom and of the gods." Xerxes also, if the few notices we have are an indication, was closely connected with, and influenced by, this religious cultus. A magus by the name of Osthanes (see Pliny, 30. 1) accompanied him on his war expedition, and was commissioned to propagate Persian doctrines, and an Iranian priest had even ordered the destruction of the temples and the images in the hostile countries. In the elevation of Haman we must therefore see an approval of, and participation in, his religious zeal. The whole activity of Haman betrays religious sentiments, and his name has a religious sound.

Haman (הָמָן) is to be derived from the wonderfully holy Haoma, or Hom, who was thought to be a spirit as well as a sacrificial potion, possessing life-giving power (Spiegel, *Avesta*, ii. 75). The significance of Hom in the Persian sacrificial service was at all times known (Omomi in Plutarch); and as it was connected especially with priestly functions, we may infer from this that one who bore a name which was derived from Hom, was endowed with priestly qualities. In fact the name הָמָן, Gr. *Omanes* (like Otanes, Azanes, Hystanes), does not occur in the classics as a name of any Persian, and only the inscription of Bisutun (Benfey, p. 14) contains the following passage: "A man named

Martiya, son of Chichikrish, who lived in Khuganaka, a
Persian city, rose in the Susian kingdom, and said: 'I am
Umanish, king of Susiana.'" Though it is doubtful whether
the letter "u" is in the name of Umanish, but the context
shows that the name is similar to Haman. It says that a
man in Shushan (where Haman lived) arrogated to himself
the royal title of Umanish. And it is precisely of such a
person, that we may presume he was actuated by religious
motives. What enhances the probability of the identity of
Haman with this person is the name of his father, המדתא,
Homdata [as in Pherendates], "the gift of Hom." The
appellation of Hom was then, like the functions of the priests,
hereditary in the family. We may also assume that the third
epithet of Haman which sounds as a family name, Agagite
(אגגי), is closely connected with it. The Jewish commentators
have, forsooth, woven a good deal of fantastical interpretation around this name, but which in no other point comes
near to the historical truth save in this, that they give to the
hatred of Haman against the Jews a religious colour. But
their saying that Haman was a descendant of Agag, the
king of Amalek (1 Sam. xv. 8), who descended from Esau,
Jacob's brother and enemy,—and hence his hatred of the
Jews was hereditary,— cannot be proved from history, although
their pointing out an historical contrast in Haman, as we
have already shown, is certainly correct. The Midrash goes
even so far as to give a whole list of names which form the
genealogy of Haman up to Esau, but in spite of the corruption of the text, it can be seen that the names mostly arose
from the Rabbinical views of the morality of this generation.
First, names are given which denote "bad qualities;" then
figure as the ancestors of Haman those persecutors of the Jews
in the Herodian-Roman era, who are of Idumean and heathen
origin.[1] The genealogy of the Targum is for this reason

---

[1] The passage in the corrupt text, Amst. ed., compared with another, is
as follows (a similar genealogy in Herod. vii. 204, viii. 131):—

בר (al. אליפלוטס) אפלוטס בר בוזה בר סרח בר אגניא המדתא בר המן ית

remarkable, because we get thereby a clue to the time when
it was written; but it does not contribute anything to elucidate the epithet Agagite in connection with Haman. In
our opinion, it is quite improbable that Haman should be a
descendant of Amalek.[1]

For the son of a certain Hamedatha, a man whose name
was derived from Haoma, must be of pure Medo-Persian
descent. If the narrator had wanted to say that Haman was
really an Amalekite, he would have at once written Amalek
instead of Agagi. Agag was indeed a king of Amalek, but
what is told of him in the Book of Samuel cannot stamp
him as a type of Haman, as he rather suffered than executed
judgment. One cannot also assert that the narrator, in calling
him Agagite, wanted to represent him as the ethnical as well
as the political persecutor of his people, as Amalek was, for

---

[2] דיוסיס בר פרום בר מעדי (מאה .al) בר בלעקן (פלקן .al) בר אנתימרוס בר
הרידום בר שנר בר נגר בר פרמשתא בר ויותא בר אנג בר סומקי בר עמלק
בר לחינתא דאליפז בוכריה דעשו.

[1] To read בנר אנטיפטר, אנטיפדום פלקום פעדי פלרוס ליוסיס פלטום.
The translation according to the corrected text is: Haman the son of Hamdatha of Agagi, son of Stench, son of Robbery, son of Pilath, son of Lysias,
son of Florus, son of Fadus, son of Flaccus, son of Antipater, son of Herod,
son of Refuse, son of Decay, son of Parmashta, son of Waizata, son of
Agag, son of the Red One (Rufus), son of Amalek, of the whore of Eliphaz,
son of Esau. These are, with the exception of Lysias, a Syrian general,
entirely names of Roman persecutors of the Jews; and Antipater and
Herod, who were Idumeans, and therefore sons of Esau, have a place in
the ignoble roll because of their similarity of character with the rest
(comp. Targum, ed. Amsterdam, 58d).

[1] The Midrash, as is usual with hostile parties, tries its best to stain
Haman's pedigree. It declares him to be a descendant of a prostitute, as
the nickname bastard is common in the East. However, Hammer tells us
(Namen der Araber, p. 50) that the expression is not a nickname among the
Turks, but rather a term in praise of natural gifts [so also among the
Jews.—Tr.]. Yet it is not always so, for when used by Ibrahim, the Osman
sultan, it was certainly not an expression of praise (Hammer, 58d). That
Agagi represents the ethical hostility of Haman may be seen from the
analogy of the LXX. on ix. 21, when it calls him Μακεδών, inasmuch as
the hostility of the Syrians, in the time of the Maccabean persecution,
was designated by Macedonian names. The garrison of the castle, whose
expulsion was for a long time commemorated by a feast, was also called
Macedonian (Joseph. Ant. xii. 5. 4).

this would have been unique in Scripture. In that case, he would have explicitly named Amalek. Apart from this, it did not even occur to the interpreters to ask whether, according to 1 Sam. xv. and 1 Chron. iv. 43, which record the destruction of the whole race of Amalek, there could still be any one descended from him. But Haman does not even feel and act like an Amalekite, for he does not begin to persecute the Jews before the independent bearing of Mordecai excites his indignation. If the narrator had wanted to designate by the appellative Agagite an enemy of the Jews, he need not have added in ver. 10 the words צֹרֵר הַיְּהוּדִים, "the Jews' enemy." There can therefore be no doubt that the word Agagite has received the prevalent notion from the punctuation of the Masoretes.

The similarity of the letters of אֲגָגִי with the name of the Amalekite king led them to this punctuation, so that by way of jest they might transfer the character of the ancient enemy of the Jews to Haman. But this change in the punctuation is the more interesting, as in all probability an honourable title was changed by it into a polemical one. For Haman bears this appellation in the first mention of him. If it is not a nickname given to him by the Jews and reproduced by the narrator, then it must be a Persian name, which is somewhat connected with the purport of the father's and the son's names. It is very probable that in אֲגָגִי is to be found the New Persian גֻּאַאגֶה, Guageh, which means a man of authority and dignity, and therefore is also used as a title of honour (Vullers, Lex. i. 735). But it has also the sense of a comrade or companion, one who belongs to the same corporation, which is perhaps more characteristic, as we shall afterwards show. The LXX. reads Βουγαῖος instead of אֲגָגִי, and thereby prove that they, at any rate, had not thought that he was a descendant of Agag. They seem thus to have thought of Bagoas, which was also the name of a number of royal confidants of Alexander the Great.[1]

[1] Comp. Curtius, vi. 5. 23: "Inter quem Bagoas erat specie singulari spado . . . cui is Darius fuit adsuetus et mox Alexander adsuevit."

But the Bagoas were eunuchs, and Haman was not. Perhaps we may recognise this Guageh (Gogeh) in the name Gyges, who was a favourite among the retinue of Candaules of Lydia, and who afterwards became king (Herod. i. 8).

"*And advanced him, and set his seat above all the princes.*"

The elevation of a man at court was figuratively represented by the elevation of his seat in the presence of the king. The highest seat was occupied by the king, and the one who sat the nearest to him was the most honoured and distinguished.

When the hero Rustem was to be rewarded by the shah, we read (Firdussi, ed. Schack, p. 266),—

> "And Rustem, with the adorning crown,
> Sat nearest to the lofty throne."

When he quarrelled with Kai Kawus, and his friends persuaded him to remain, they promised him—

> "Thy seat a throne as for a king."

Therefore at great conferences of princes, the various dignities were displayed by the various elevations of the thrones they occupied. When the German kings came during the Crusade to Constantinople, the emperor occupied a higher throne than they.

Geiseddin Balbun, the ninth prince of the Ghurid dynasty in Delhi, permitted only those of the fifteen expelled kings who formed his court to sit on lower seats near him, who were descended from the caliphs (comp. my *Kaiser und Königs-thron*, p. 49). When Apollonius of Tyana came on his fabulous journey to the Indian sages (Phil. iii. 16), Jarchas sat upon a high seat, the other sages upon lower ones, and to Apollonius was offered, as a mark of special honour, the throne of Phraortes the king (17).[1] Such elevations through personal

---

[1] The famous Vizier Melekshahs, Nisamolmülk, narrates in his auto-biography, of the great honour which was shown him. He alone rode on horseback, the others were on foot. "From this moment I sat upon

favour of the rulers were not unusual in Oriental courts, especially in times of peace, and under weak princes. It is told by Ktesias of a eunuch under Darius Nothos, that, through the favour of the king, he succeeded in getting all the power at court into his hands. So also it is told of Bagoas, under Artaxerxes II., that he and the Greek Mentor had so much ingratiated themselves into the favour of the king that they had more influence than the king's own friends and relations, πλεῖστον ἰσχῦσαι τῶν φίλων καὶ συγγενῶν τῶν παρ' Ἀρταξέρξῃ " (Diodor. xvi. 50). The elevation of Haman must surely have a special significance, for all the courtiers and guards were compelled to fall down before him and to render him homage as to a king.

Ver. 2. *" All the king's servants bowed down and did reverence."*

Servants of the king included all the courtiers and guards. The expression corresponds to the New Persian Gholam, of which Malcolm says (*Gesch. Pers.* i. 185) Gholam, or slave, was the title of the body-guard of Eastern princes. When the son of a great Persian nobleman is admitted into the guard, he claims the title of Gholam-e-shah, or " slave of the king." " Slave " was the usual title by which the rulers when angry addressed the highest officials, as pashas and grand viziers. To the demented Ibrahim, sultan of the Osmans, his grand vizier said : " You are the caliph, the shadow of God upon earth, and what enters your mind is divine revelation ; however absurd it may appear, it has a hidden meaning, which your slave[1] respects, although he does not understand it " (Hammer, v. 399). The religious power which the adulating minister

---

the wished-for horse, and all the great and eminent men walked by my stirrups " (Hammer, *Gemäldesaal,* v. 71). So the Barmekide Giafar at the court of Harun was allowed to sit alongside the caliph.

[1] Aloisius Gritti was the plenipotentiary ambassador of Soliman I. in his treaties with Charles V. In the official communication of the sultan, as given in a Latin report, are the words, "Aloisius Gritti sclavus meus eo proficiscitur " (Hammer, *Gesch. des osman. Reichs,* iii. 137, note).

ascribes in these words to the sultan is an exact copy of the
flattering words which were used in very ancient times to
Eastern rulers. "The important thing with us," says Artaban to
Themistocles (Plutarch, *Th.* c. 27), "is that a king is worshipped,
and is looked upon as the very image of God." The Babylonian and Assyrian princes had names which in themselves
indicated the people's high reverence for them. The saying of
Solomon, according to the Muhamedan legend, that a great king
always includes the prophet, but the prophet does not always
include the king (*Rosenöl*, i. 234), does not reach to the height
of that which Cleo dared to say to Alexander the Macedonian
(Curtius, viii. 5. 11): "The Persians did not simply out of
piety worship their kings as gods, but also out of wisdom, for
the majesty of the kingdom is a refuge of salvation." For
this reason he also advised him to accept prostration and
adoration like a Persian king. For this custom had not,
properly speaking, among the Persians, and generally in the
East, a slavish, but a religious sense. They did not bow down
before a worldly, but rather before a spiritual power. Hence
the same homage was also due to the images of the king.
Philostratus narrates in the *Life of Apollonius* (i. 27) that all
barbarians who came to Babylon were first obliged to adore
the image of the king.[1] When, therefore, the king ordered
that the same honour should be shown to Haman as to himself, it was a recognition that he was his *alter ego*. Hitherto,
so long as Mordecai sat at the gate, *i.e.* since Esther became
queen, no courtier had received such honours, though, as
Plutarch reports, Xerxes had chosen his brother Ari(a)menes
next to himself. Perhaps it is necessary to explain this as
connected with the inherent dignity of the office of Haman,
which corresponds to his name. There may be some connection between the New Persian Gogeh and the idea of

---

[1] In order to show distinction to his general Dshewher, the Caliph
Moiseddin of Egypt commanded his governors to dismount from their
horses before him and to kiss his hand, a distinction which is generally
only due to princes (Hammer, *Gemäldesaal*, iii. 214).

spirituality in more ancient times, as Benfey (*Gr. Gr.* i. 134) joins the Sanscr. *akkha*, "pure," with the Greek ἄγιος, which in Persian life was applied as an epithet to distinguished pious and great men, and which Burnouf (*Yaçna*, i. 16) finds again in the name Achaemenes.   The surname Sofi, which the Persian shah, who had established his new seat of government at Ispahan, bore with his family, likewise meant "pure," and referred to the ascetic habits of the otherwise political and warlike house, even before Ismael's accession to the throne.

"*But Mordecai bowed not down*," etc.

This refusal of Mordecai to render adoration to Haman arose perhaps from an opposite cause from the refusal of the Greeks.   They considered such an act as mean and degrading, because, as the Spartans said afterwards, it is not their custom to fall down before a man (Herod. vii. 136). The Athenians punished Timagoras for performing adoration (Valer. Max. vi. 3, Ext. 2).   Pelopidas nobly declined it— because he looked upon the Persian king as only a man, to whom he would in nowise render divine honour.   When Themistocles was a captain in Persia, he thought it his duty to perform such homage, on the ground that it would please God who had so exalted Persia (Plutarch, *Th.* 27).   But Mordecai had just the opposite motive for his refusal.   He saw in the adoration which the king demanded for Haman, not merely an act of etiquette to a man, but an act which involved the recognition of false gods.   Daniel and his three young friends submitted rather to every hazard of their lives, than to recognise the existence of any other deity but Jehovah. The word כרע, here used, expresses the sense of falling down, as in the adoration of idols, and it is therefore not used in the history of Israel to denote polite homage paid to kings and those who are high in authority, or strangers, but the word שׁחה instead.   It is analogous to כנה, Gr. κυνέω, and προσκυνέω, expressing the same act of worship.   But before Elijah as a man of God the captain falls down (2 Kings i. 13).

In the time of the same prophet there were only 7000 who did not bow the knee, כרע, to Baal (1 Kings xix. 18). In the time of Hezekiah, he and all that were with him bowed themselves, כרע, and worshipped the living God (2 Chron. xxix. 29). Mordecai could not fall down before Haman as the reflex of a false lustre of a false god. For the prophetic words ring through all Israel: "To me every knee shall bow, every tongue shall swear."

The Persian history, Dshami, which Hammer in *Rosenöl*, ii. 3, quotes, narrates of a governor of Caliph Omar, when he came for the first time to Persia after its conquest, that the inhabitants according to the Old Persian manner fell down before him, as the servants of Ahhashverosh fell down before Haman. When the governor saw it, he also fell down. And as they all rose from their knees, he asked before whom they fell down. They replied, "Before thee; but thou, O prince, before whom didst thou kneel?" "Before God," said he, "to whom alone worship belongs." Thereupon Omar sent ambassadors, who forbade the people to fall down except before God; and consequently the Persian custom did not become one of the Muhamedan ceremonies. But instead of this, the Muhamedan and Osman sultans made the kissing of the hand, and especially of the garments, obligatory, as the humiliated Tatarchan when he lost his power was no longer received with pomp by the sultan, but was satisfied to kiss the coat of the grand vizier (*Gesch. des osman. Reichs*, iv. 644).

The Midrash has its explanations of the subject in question, which were employed in the homiletical discourses in the synagogue. According to one, Haman had actually worn an image of an idol upon his coat, for the purpose of compelling the people to worship him, and thus Mordecai the more resisted. In fact, this remark only shows that in the view of the authors of the Midrash, Mordecai's refusal to fall down arose from religious scruples. Stranger still is another glorification which they bestow upon Mordecai. Haman had really been Mordecai's servant. They were once both sent out on a military expedition. Both had a separate division to command, but Haman carelessly spent all the provision and ammunition before he could take the enemy's fort; for he relied too much on himself, and he would have been dismissed with disgrace had not Mordecai saved him. But this he did on condition of Haman becoming his slave. And therefore Mordecai refused to make obeisance to his own slave. The national vanity, as represented in this fiction of Haman being a slave of Mordecai, has overlooked the fact, that it gave to the former the character of humility and submissiveness in certain circumstances, and to the latter a want of refinement and duty towards a comrade in arms.

Ver. 3. *"Then the king's servants, that were in the king's gate, said unto Mordecai, Why transgresseth thou the king's commandment?"*

It is a sign that they had greater concern for Mordecai than for Haman, that they gave him timely warning, instead of at once accusing him. They called his attention to the danger before him. Not for the sake of Haman, but because it was a law of the king, which could not be transgressed without peril. Mordecai knew this, and yet remained. He could, indeed, withdraw from the conflict, by not appearing at the gate, but his love to Esther forbade it. He would not leave this post of loving duty at all hazards. But should he be killed, his loss to Esther would be irreparable. Yet his courageous faith in God triumphs over these difficulties, and he is sure that no ill will happen to him, as no ill happened to Daniel in his stedfast opposition to idolatry. He could not reckon upon escaping harm on the ground that he as a Jew refused to fall down before strange gods, nor could he depend upon the assistance which Esther might render him at a critical moment, for his whole plan, according to which he strictly bound her to be silent upon her origin, would have been frustrated; but he trusted in God, who would surely protect him, whether he fled or whether he remained at

the gate. Nevertheless, the **servants of** the king contributed
to the acceleration of the danger; and this unseemly trait is
perfectly characteristic of the friendships and companionships
of such worldly people. They had encouraged him every day
to render homage, till at last he had told them that he was a
Jew, and could not do it. When he gave them this reason for
his refusal, it was because he considered it as amounting to
idolatry. Naturally, the courtiers, being themselves heathen,
could not comprehend his reason. It did not appear to them
clear why he, because he was a Jew, should be exempted from
a duty which they were obliged to perform. Certainly, they
might have calmed themselves and let the matter go until
Haman himself had noticed it, or until it had altogether passed
into oblivion. But their exaggerated zeal for upholding the law
was incited by their vexation at the stubbornness of Mordecai,
and so they denounced him. What Haman had not yet noticed,
they now told him in order to learn, whether a Jew had
the privilege of not bowing before him. They also wanted to
see whether Mordecai would remain stedfast after Haman's
attention had been drawn to his conduct. They are just
עבדים, servants, slaves, excited by curiosity, their pride offended,
displaying slavish zeal, without any regard as to the danger
to another man's life whose conscience they ought to reverence,
and whose character they ought to admire. But at all events,
they represent to Haman that Mordecai refused to pay him
homage, only for the reason that he is a Jew. Haman learns
that it is not a personal matter, but one of principle with him.
Not wilful disobedience, but religious legal ground underlies
his refusal. Haman had not noticed anything in particular
in Mordecai hitherto, but now he pays close attention. He
gives Mordecai to understand that he has his eye upon him.
The emphasis in vers. 4, 5, is upon the words (אשר הוא יהודי):
"*that he was a Jew.*" "*And Haman saw that Mordecai
bowed not down.*"[1] This shows that he did not notice it

[1] The anger of Haman is explained by the following remark of
Herodotus, i. 134: "When Persians of equal standing meet, they kiss

before. "And he was full of wrath." A man of refinement would have overlooked and excused it, as no personal slight was intended. But the vain parvenu was vexed that anybody should have the courage to refuse homage to him, even him (as vain men think), and to expose him to the ridicule of the courtiers (as little souls think) if he did not break down the stubbornness of Mordecai. A noble-minded man would have respected his conscientious religious scruples; but a puffed-up man, as Haman was, did not consider the person, but the principle involved in his refusal, and the ground upon which it was made.[1]

Ver. 6. "*But he thought scorn to lay hands on Mordecai alone.*"

The haughtiness of the man was too great to be satisfied with taking vengeance on Mordecai alone. The offender appeared to him too small a person to hurl all his thunderbolts against, and yet too important a person to be left alone. He must avenge the disgrace which was so publicly cast upon him by Mordecai in the presence of the courtiers, and obtain such satisfaction for himself as may have a deterrent effect upon others. But if he called Mordecai alone to judgment, it might be understood as an act of private and personal spite, which would not redound to his honour, but would rather bring hatred and intrigue upon himself. So he lays stress on the fact that Mordecai, as a Jew, incurred the guilt of transgressing the royal decree. Looking from this standpoint, he found it easier to wreak his vengeance upon him. In this way he could conceal his personal malice under the

---

each other upon the lips instead of saluting. But if one of them is inferior to the other, they kiss the cheeks; and if one of them is quite an inferior, he falls down and worships the other."

[1] The comparison of the French Minister Villéle with Haman was not quite a happy one; he is reported to have said, when he reached the pinnacle of glory, "Only two persons, Labourdonnaye and Delalot, did not, like Mordecai, bow the knee before me" (comp. Münch, *Gesch. der neuesten Zeit*, v. 195).

cloak of zeal for resisting the rising influence of Judaism.
He thought he could earn merit for himself by vindicating
the interests of the State, while at the same time avenging
his offended pride.   Should Mordecai fall in the midst of
a general massacre, there would, of course, be no suspicion
that he met with his death for the trifling offence of refusing
homage to him.   For it would be said that the king simply
put down the rebellion in general.   There would also then be
wanting an avenger and an accuser.   This psychology of the
hatred which brooded in Haman has undergone a manifold
development in Oriental courts, where the powerful have
often to be cautious in exercising vengeance, because the way
to it lies always between the mood and the caprice of the
autocrat.   Great and small citizens have at all times sought
to give vent to private hatred and personal passions under
the pretext of patriotism, and of seeking to promote the
welfare of the State.   Many an ambitious office - seeker,
who either possessed no qualifications or was unfortunate
in his demands, became by this process converted from a
royalist to a rebel.   The offended pride of Hassan Ibn
Sabbah, which was provoked by Melekshah and his Vizier
Nisamolmülk, contributed to the establishment of the
ancient sect of murderers, the Assassins (Hammer, *Gemäldesaal*, v. p. 19 ; comp. Weil, *Kalifen*, iii. 205).   The Jews
experienced this plentifully.   The hatred which they were
made to feel during 1500 years not always arose from
religious zeal, but very often was occasioned by personal
discord on account of some slight offence to somebody.
In a speech of defence before the King of Spain, a Jew
said strikingly enough : " We Jews are like mice, upon
whom all throw the guilt when some one has nibbled a
little cheese " (Shebet Jehudah, chap. viii. and chap. lxii.).

It was remarked before that the names of Haman might
be indicative of his priestly origin.   If this be so, and if we
may take Haman as in some degree connected with the
family of those religious persons whom the Greeks and

Romans specially call Magi, then the way in which Haman
observes that Mordecai is a Jew, and at once decides to
strike the whole of Judaism root and branch, would be
more explicable from a psychological point of view. It
was consistent with the character of a Magus to direct his
attention to the Jews, and their opposition to the customs of
the country, in order to constitute the supposed misdemeanour
of Mordecai into a principle of rebellion. Just such a person
would be inclined to stir up the religious animosities of the
people against the whole Jewish nation [as, alas! we have
witnessed in more recent times, and that in the midst
of the boasted civilisation and culture of the nineteenth
century!].

If Haman had been merely a secular vizier, one would
have thought that he would pour out his wrath only
upon Mordecai and his family. If his refusal of homage
only concerned the transgression of a royal decree, then
surely he alone was the guilty party. But Haman regarded
Mordecai as a representative of a religious persuasion, and
therefore he wanted to destroy the whole of Judaism. He
did not consider it merely as an offence against the majesty
of the king, but also against the established religion of the
country, and hence his great wrath. The whole perception
of the dramatic conflict between the Jewish-believing
Mordecai and the Persian Magus gains in clearness if we
place them in sharp contrast to one another. We have
shown that the name of Haman, Agagite, is a Masoretic
change of the New Persian נואנה. The word has the meaning
of "fellow-comrade," and therefore appears to be in connection with תאש, socius, consors (see Vullers, i. 414). But
now the Jews, at least those of Talmudical times, call a Magus
and priest of fire by the Hebrew name חבר, which, in every
sense of the word, means "a companion," "fellow-disciple,"
"comrade." In consequence of this, its signification is
the same as נואני, and tash, "wise man," "learned master,"
"house-father." Thus it appears that in the surname

אגני,[1] which Haman bore, is expressed his titular name as a member of the order of fire-worshippers and Magi, with which also his other names perfectly agree. The fire-ministers and Magi were, at any rate, hostile to the Jews down to the times of the Sassanides. With the appearance of the Sassanides began also in Persia restrictions upon the Jewish cult, because with them was completed the restoration of the Persian fire-worship (see my " Gesch. der Juden " in *Ersch und Gruber*, ii. 27, p. 184 ; and Spiegel, *Avesta*, i. p. 18).

The Talmud frequently mentions the hostility of the חברים, *i.e.* the Magi, who, in contrast to the Parthians, have oppressed the Jews (comp. the passages in the *Aruch, sub voce*, whence Buxtorf and Hyde, *relig. vet. Persar*, p. 360). Therefore the Jews remember them with scorn and aversion. They explain Ps. xiv. 1 : " The fool, נבל, says in his heart, as referring to the חברים," the " companions." So also the Muhamedans usually call them by the nickname of Philiva, *i.e.* fools, instead of Kalivan, " fire-worshippers."

But when the Jews gave to the Magi the name of חברים, it must have corresponded to a similar name which was peculiar to the whole order, and which was perhaps handed down in the New Persian נואנה. It is interesting to notice, that as this at the same time was the designation for " house-father," so also does Spiegel trace back the name Mobed, μανίπτας, *mopet*, to Sanscr. *umâna-paiti*, " house-father " (*Avesta*, ii. p. 15).

The name חבר for Magus is manifestly older than the time of the Sassanides. This is especially seen in Isa. xlvii. 9–13, where the prophet addresses Babylon in these words : " The loss of children and widowhood in their full measure shall come upon thee, despite of the multitude of thy sorceries, and the great abundance of thine enchantments " (חבריך).

---

[1] Oppert quotes from the Sargonidic Inscriptions, " Countries like Agag and Arubanda in Media " (Spiegel, *Eranische Alterthumskunde*, ii. 247). Even if Agag should mean a country in Media, it would not militate against our view, as the Magi were considered Medians.

And further, in ver. 12: "Stand now with thine enchant-ments," חֲבָרַיִךְ; and ver. 13: "Let now the astrologers, the star-gazers, the monthly prognosticators, stand up and save thee from the things that shall come upon thee." So, then, there is a close relation between the name חֲבָרִים with חָבַר, which the prophet in olden times[1] used to designate magic, and which was also included in the word *societas*. Indeed, this idea receives support from the fact that the Jews, acquainted with such passages as Deut. xviii. 11, where חֶבֶר is used for "enchantment," have transferred its meaning also to the verb חבר.

The prognosticators, astrologers, and Chaldeans formed a separate caste, society, and fraternity in Babylon. Diodorus says of them: "They form a society in the State similar to the priests in Egypt . . . they are famous in astrology, and very diligent in augury. Amongst them science is trans-mitted through the family."[2] The same is said of the Persian Magi. "The religious service of the Persians is like a priestly order, transmitted from father to son."[3] It is therefore to be understood that חברים, companions, was their titular name, as covenanted members, just as *sodalis* was the appellation of the Roman priestly associations [Titii Augustales], or as the name fratres Arvales, from *frater*, was applied in Rome to Christian orders in the Middle Ages, and to societies in modern times. Even among the Jews חבר was a titular name, which implied that he who bore it participated in the spiritual communion of a certain society. The name חברים received then the same general sense as Chaldeans and Magi.[4] According to its etymology, it expressed as little what the associates did as the other names; but as all magic

---

[1] Comp. *Bibliotheca-Antiquar.* i. 635, 860, etc.

[2] The beautiful passage is fully given in *History*, ii. 30.

[3] Sozomen, *Hist. Eccl.* ii. 8, *of Brisson*, p. 383. [Rashi on *Tal-Shabbath*, p. 11, distinctly affirms that the Persian priests were called חברים; but from Kiddushin, p. 72, it appears that some Persians were called so who were natives of Atabur, 2 Kings xv. 12.– Tr.]

[4] See Chaldeans and names of priests in Herod. i. 151.

proceeded from the Magi, so from the knowledge possessed by the חבר proceeded the formation of the word חָבַר, which expresses this knowledge, to divine and to pronounce enchanting formulas. Thus, therefore, חָבַר has received the meaning of magic, and חבר (also in Arabic and Persian) came to signify "to know," "to investigate;" as Knobel[1] rightly maintains we should read, in Isa. xlvii. 13, חוברי שמים, "astrologers," instead of הוברי. It is not necessary to assume, with Schelling,[2] a mixture of these names with the deities of the Kabires.

When Origen says (*contra Cels.* vi. 23) that neither Jesus nor His apostles have borrowed from "the Persians or Kabires" (Περσῶν ἢ Καβείρων), he indeed alludes to the famous classical name Kabires, but he means the name of the Chaberim, the Persian savants, as he can only speak of these. But when the Arabs have applied to the Parsees the name of Gheber, or Caphir, it is probable that this was because they wanted to express by this name their scorn for them, and to show that they did not consider them wise men, but infidels.[3]

To the special arts of the חברים, the wise men of Mesopotamia and Iran, as well as to the ancient wisdom in general, belonged horoscopy, *i.e.* the observation of the relations that subsist between the movements and the position of the stars, and their reciprocal influences upon the life of man.

The prophet speaks in the passage quoted above "of the monthly prognosticators of the things that shall come upon thee." As they pretended to be able to foretell fortune or misfortune, success or failure, good or evil days, by means of horoscopy, so their science for kings and statesmen was not of slight importance. It was evidently in vogue at the Persian court. The Magi must have latterly been called Chaberim,

---

[1] See his *Commentary on Isaiah*, p. 353.

[2] *Die Gottheiten von Samothrake*, pp. 111, 112.

[3] Just as *pagani* is from *pagus*, so somewhat similar is the Arabic כפר, from which, as applied perhaps to heathen, was derived the meaning, "to deny," "to doubt." The Hebrew כפר, *texit*, is quite remote from this meaning.

not without reference to this science. Pliny narrates (*Hist. Nat.* xxx. 2), in the name of Osthanes, the royal Magus of Xerxes, that there existed a magic from the stars. The astrologers who accompanied Darius, Curtius calls by the common name of Chaldeans; but the astrological idea pervades the name and the legend of Zoroaster (Zarathustra). The star which the wise men of the East saw appear at the birth of Christ, receives its significance only when such divination is connected with the truth announced by the Magi. An instance of this is given us in ver. 7, where we read :—

> "*They cast the Pur, that is, the lot, before Haman, from day to day, and from month to month, to the twelfth month, which is the month Adar.*"

The narrator translates the word פוּר by גּוֹרל, which means "share," *pars, sors*,—just as we use the word "lot" in a religious sense. The New Persian has also an analogous word for pur.[1] It is not necessary to bring the New Persian בּארה, *pars, segmentum* (comp. Vullers, i. 317 ; Rosen. *Narrat.* p. 110), to elucidate the meaning of פֻּר, פוּר. For inasmuch as the "lot" here spoken of was cast from day to day, and from month to month, and finally fell on the twelfth month Adar, it must evidently refer to the horoscope which was set up, and whose apparent indication of fortune the Greeks, as well as the Romans, called the result of horoscoping, κλῆρος, or *sors*. Indeed, the prophet may allude to this when he says מוֹדִיעִים לחֳדשׁים, "the monthly prognosticators" (Isa. xlvii. 13).[2]

It fell before Haman, *i.e.* "he caused it to fall," he made observations and obtained the result. If the meaning of אנני is really found in נואנה (with which the Sanscr. *sakhja* is to be compared) as a Persian expression for חבר, then the know-

---

[1] Hyde, *de rel. vet. Pers.* p. 195, says : "Notandum est quod Persae vulgo sunt proni ad pronuntiandum, p pro b, unde scribunt Panaem pro Banâm et Deypâdur pro Deybâdur," etc.

[2] The lot was, according to Herod. (iii. 128), customary among the Persians. For when thirty men volunteered to follow the expedition against Oroetes, the lot was cast who the chosen ones should be.

ledge of Haman in the use of the horoscope gains through this
a clearer explanation. The narrator has already indicated this by
the mentioning of "Haman, son of Hamadatha the Agagite," as
hachaber, or אגג, is equivalent to חמר, fire-worshipper magician.

Sors, *pur*, the result of setting up the horoscope, was so
termed, as according to ancient ideas every day and every
hour had its allotted fortune, which was suitable to the various
undertakings and exercises of the will of man. How these
observations were made, the ancients have left us an abundance of information. It did not merely depend upon the
position of the planets, but more particularly upon their relation to the zodiacal signs, every one of which controlled a
month. In reference to this, the Chaldeans, as Censorin
expressly narrates, had a special era, *dodecaeteris*, consisting
of twelve years, " which the horoscopians made applicable, not
to observations of sun and moon, but to other purposes,
because they say that in it revolve weather, fertility of
crops, drought, as well as diseases and conditions of healing"
(*De die Natali*, cap. xviii.). Scaliger is of opinion that this era
was still in use by the astronomers of the East in the Middle
Ages.[1] The years of the era had different names of animals.
The first year was called Mouse, and the last had the name of
Pig. What form of horoscopy it was that gave to Haman
the twelfth month (the Jewish Adar) as favourable for his
enterprise against the Jews, is difficult to establish. The
Jewish exposition (Megilla 13*b*) tries to show that he found
out that he could not harm Israel in any other of their
months but Adar, because he knew that Moses died on the
7th of that month; but he deceived himself, as Moses was
also born on the 7th of Adar.[2] [So it was not an unfortunate

[1] Isagog. *Chronolog. Canon*, lib. iii. p. 181 : "Ea signant sua tempora
Persae, Chatai, Tartari, Turcae, sed Indi praecipue." Likewise in his notes
to Manilius, comp. Eschenbach, *Epigenes de Poesi Orphic* (Norib. 1702),
p. 165*a*.

[2] [The reason for assigning the same day of the month to the birth and
death of Moses is given by Rashi, *in loc.* Because he said : "I am an
hundred and twenty years old this day" (Deut. xxxi. 4).—TRANS.]

day for them after all, as the end proved.] The Midrash
(93b, followed by the second Targum) is more explicit as to
the reason why the other months were less favourable for his
purpose. " When he came to make observations in the month
of Adar, which stands under the zodiacal sign of the fish, he
exclaimed : ' Now they are caught by me like the fish of the
sea.' But he noticed that the children of Joseph are compared in the Scripture to the fish of the sea, as it is written :
' And let them multiply as the fish in the midst of the earth '
(Gen. xlviii. 16)."

This thought did not, of course, enter Haman's mind,
but perhaps he made use of the Persian customary idea,
that the twelfth month is propitious for taking action
against the hostile principle under the figure of serpents, by
the writing of amulets which would kill them (Hyde, *de rel.
vet. Pers.* p. 258). But surely more suitable is what Manilius,
among many other things, says of the zodiacal sign of the
fish : " The star does not come out at the beginning of this
sign. Hateful gossip and poisonous tongues are bestowed
upon men, who bring bad words to ears unaccustomed to hear
them. Thus the faults of the people are blazed abroad by
these ambiguous tongues " (lib. iv. 5. 574, etc.).

The narrator mentions the time when Haman made investigations concerning the lot. He says, בחרש הראישן הוא־חרש נסן,
" In the first month, which is the month Nisan." It must be
taken for granted that he understands by the expression, "the
first month," the first Persian month, as he paraphrases the
word *pur* by the Hebrew הוא הגורל, *i.e.* the lot. Otherwise it
would have been sufficient to say, in the month Nisan, for he
wrote for Jews. But he wanted to specify which month it
was in which the lot, according to Haman's scientific observations, was cast. Just because it was a horoscopy, it depended
upon the month. The Jewish month Nisan had no particular
advantage to offer for Haman's purpose, but the first Persian
month had certainly its significance. The Persian new year
undoubtedly tallied in ancient times with Nisan, for as an

astronomer of the Middle Ages says, " Their first month always
began when the sun entered the zodiacal sign of the Ram." [1]
This ram is the symbol of Nisan. The specification in the
book of Esther, therefore, confirms the oldest authentic notice
of this description. New year was from time immemorial,
in the opinion of the nations, exactly the proper time for
attempting to ascertain the future. We still find in the book
Sadder, a Persian compendium of doctrines (in Porta 66), that
it is necessary to offer sacrifices and to feast on the first day
of the new year, for the welfare of the coming year depends
upon it. [2] The superstition which has fastened itself upon our
new year, and also upon Whitsuntide, by the practice of
lotteries and the seeking to ascertain the future by means of
oracles, is to be traced back to the highest antiquity. It is at
all events very remarkable, that on the feast of Epiphany, *i.e.*
January 6, there was a custom to play a game with beans,
by which lots were cast to elect the king of the feast.
On the same day was commemorated the arrival of the Magi
of the East to seek the new-born King. Again, the same
day is also the chief festive day of the first week of the new
year among the Persians, properly the great Neurûz. [3] It is
not previously mentioned that the king did not enter upon
an enterprise without first casting the pur. The omission
would not have appeared strange, if we had not the notice in
ver. 7. And this is the more important, as with it is connected the memorable day when the whole disaster was to
take place. It brings out the fact prominently, that Haman
put the arts of astrology into motion, in order to secure the
destruction of Israel. He had likewise set in array the
wisdom of heathenism against the people and the will of
God. The diabolic character of his hatred is shown in that
he called the lottery of divination to his assistance. It is
not so much the personal antipathy of one man towards

---

[1] Ideler, *Handbuch der Chronologie*, ii. 547.

[2] See Hyde, *de rel. vet. Pers.* p. 465 ; comp. Spiegel, *Avesta*, p. 100.

[3] We shall enter upon this more particularly in another place.

another man, but the hostile sentiments, which make use of
the hidden arts of magical calculations, in order to make sure
of the enterprises that are here characterized; the casting of
the lot is here considered as an unusual mode of procedure.
For it expressed the fanatical zeal of Haman, who not only
applied his official power against Mordecai, but also his
magical arts against the people of Israel. Therefore the
report in ver. 7 is properly the central point of the whole
narrative, though the author only mentions it, as it were, in a
whisper. The contrivance of Haman against Israel is thereby
represented, not merely as an act of tyranny against the
people, but also as a rebellion against their God. Through
the casting of the lot, Haman, as shall be more fully shown
farther on, is placed in the rank of the magicians of Pharaoh,
and near Balak, who sought by the curses of Balaam to hurt
Israel. He casts the lot in the new year as though he wants
to have the fortune of the star for himself against a people
which, as he well knows, has a peculiar religion and an
especial reverence for God, as appears from ver. 8. The
drawing of a lottery at the court of the king was in itself no
extraordinary thing. The wisdom of the Magi was consulted
in all important affairs. This is what Pliny means when he
says : "This wisdom has assumed in the Orient the command
of the kings" (xxx. 1). Later times give an illustration of
this. That the descriptions of Chardin [1] of the Persian court
of his time are perfectly suitable to antiquity, we do not
assert. But among the Oriental princes of the Middle Ages
there were no politics without astrologers. Through these
they made their own wishes and intentions legitimate. The
Mongolian Khan Hulaku destroyed the Caliphat, because the
astrologer said that the house of Abbas must fall before him.[2]
Even the Osman sultan requested Frederick (1769) to send

[1] Comp. particularly, *Voyages*, tom. v. ; *Descript. des sciences*, xi. p. 76,
etc. : "On consulte les Astrologues sur toutes les choses importantes et
quelquefois le Roi les consulte sur les moindres choses par exemple s'il
doit aller à la promenade, s'il doit entrer dans le Serail," etc.

[2] Malcolm, *Gesch. v. Pers.* ii. p. 73.

him three expert astrologers. But his answer, "That his astrology was an efficient army and a full treasury," it appears, did not quite please the sultan, for he then turned to the Emperor of Morocco, with the request to send him an astrologer, saying, "That although the knowledge of all secrets is only with the most high God, yet it is legitimately allowed to cultivate the knowledge of the true moments of the day and of the night." [1]   But though similar astrological polities existed in the court of Xexes, yet the casting of the pur for Israel had just as distinct a significance as the arts of the Egyptian magicians and the curses of Balaam. For, not what these generally were in the habit of doing, but what they *did* against Israel, could be taken into consideration. The narrator does not forget to note that this happened on the first month of the twelfth year in the reign of the king. It appears that in the view of Haman this twelfth month was particularly favourable for his design.

The second Targum calls the man who assisted him in the casting of the die, Shamshai the scribe. This is one of the interpretations of which the Midrash is fond. Among the enemies who sought to hinder the rebuilding of the temple in Jerusalem by writing a denunciatory letter to King Artahshasta against the Jews, was one Shamshai, the scribe (Ezra iv. 9). It is to be noticed that his name is apparently derived from the adoration of the heavenly lights, and signifies "sun-servant," as Epiphanius also knew a sect by the name " Sampsaei," translated by Ἡλιακοί.

On the other hand, the Midrash has another beautiful explanation : At the moment when Haman challenged the diabolical chance of the lot of the stars against Israel, a divine voice was heard exclaiming, "Fear not, congregation of Israel ! If thou wilt repent towards God, then the lot will befall him instead of thee." Instructive is also the parable by which the Midrash scoffs at the vain haughtiness of Haman, who wanted to soothe his offended vanity by the adoption of

[1] Hammer, *Gesch. des osman. Reiches*, viii. pp. 328 and 428.

destructive measures against the people of God. "He is like,"
it says, "to a bird which built its nest on the seashore.
One day the waves swept the nest away. Then the bird got
angry, and wanted to empty the sea and fill it with sand,
which naturally enough caused great amusement and laughter
among its companions."[1] So foolish was also Haman, who
thought to annihilate the people for which God had appointed
such a past and such a future. Like the little bird was also
a smaller Haman, or rather no Haman, but only his scribe
Shamshai, who, it says, had such a thirst for wisdom that
even the Sea of Tiberias could not quench it. He drank it
all out, and yet was thirsty as before.[2]

Ver. 8. "*And Haman said unto King Ahhashverosh.*"

The horoscope was set up by Haman's instruction and in
his presence, therefore it is expressly said, לפני המן, before
Haman. The king knew nothing about it. Haman only
now communicated to the king what had been in his mind
for a long time (ver. 8). For he wanted not only, as he
thought, to be himself secure, but also to have the result of the
horoscope investigation, and to be able to say in the language
of Schiller, "Die rechte Sternen-Stunde ausgelesen sei, des
Himmels Häuser forschend zu durchspüren" (Wallenstein,
ii., vi.): "I have deciphered the right hour in the stars, by
searching its traces in the celestial mansions," before coming
to the king. And when he did so, his opening statement was
more devilish than his former action. "The stars do not lie,"
but he did lie, and with fine diplomatic words entrapped the
unsuspicious king. One could not better represent the art
with which Haman sought to win the king, both by what he
said and by what he did not say, than it is done in ver. 8.

---

[1] The parable of the strand-snipe (Sanscr. *tittibha*) is found in India, of
which the people say, "It considered itself one so important that it slept
on its back, and stretched forth its legs in order that the sky should not
fall down." The Indian fable has only changed the end (see Max
Müller on *Hitopadesa*, p. 97).

[2] Michelet, *Gesch. der Bibel*, Prague 1865, p. 11.

ישְׁנוֹ עַם־אֶחָד—"*There is a certain people.*"

He does not call it by name. The name would bring their
glorious history to remembrance. The name would in itself
have contradicted many a subject which he was desirous to
mention.   It was, moreover, properly speaking, an act of
treachery against the king himself which Haman had in
hand ; inasmuch as the protection of the Jews had been the
policy of the Iranic dynasty ever since Cyrus.   For it was
just in opposition to Babylon, against which Cyrus revolted,
that the Jews were favoured by him and restored to their
land to form a faithful advanced guard.   Darius adopted the
same policy when the Magus Gumata (Pseudo-Smerdis) fell.
It may be supposed that Xerxes would not have consented to
Haman's request even on that account.   For Haman speaks
as the Magi had spoken.   Because he knew this, he entirely
suppressed the name of the people whom he was arraigning
before the highest tribunal in the land.   Besides, the name
Jews was extensively known.   The king must have known
how many of them were living in Shushan.   Had he not in
the name of the Jew Mordecai been saved from the treachery
of his servants ?   Therefore Haman says ישְׁנוֹ עַם, " There is
somewhere a people."   In the other three passages where the
word ישְׁנוֹ occurs, it has the sense of " some one, somewhat,"
connected with it (Deut. xxix. 14 ; 1 Sam. xiv. 39, xxiii. 23).
Here it expresses, besides, the scornful tone with which
Haman speaks of the people which he disdains to name.
He depreciates the importance of the nation, in order the
more easily to attain his end.   It is כָּפוֹר וּמְפֹרָד, "scattered
and separated among the nations."   The people of whom
he speaks has no national consolidation.   It is without a
national bond of union, and therefore also destitute of the
means of offering a possible resistance.   Repressive measures
against it would require no sacrifice and might easily be taken,
for as scattered and separated fragments, it has neither power
nor importance worth thinking of.   He speaks of the Jews as
if they were gipsies, and the question had concerned a tribe,

without a history, vocation, commonwealth, and connection. So, also, we find in elementary books of later times Jews and gipsies placed in juxtaposition, though it may not have been done with Hamanic intentions. But the despicable way in which Haman speaks of Israel to the king, was not disadvantageous to his design of representing them as very dangerous subjects to the State. He therefore adds, True, this people is scattered among the nations, but they are found in all the territories belonging to the king. He notices a fact whose historical truth is, indeed, of importance, and could not be gainsaid in any age. The fault he has to find with them, is a matter that concerns the whole country. And now come the principal objections to them : שׁונות מכל העם דתיהם, their laws are diverse from those of every people. By these laws are to be understood the religious precepts which divided Israel from the inhabitants of the Persian kingdom. The word דת is only used for the decrees of the king and of God. Of the king, because he was considered as the embodiment of divine power, and therefore his orders were looked upon in the same light as if they had been issued by God. They were irrevocable. The word occurs in the book of Esther in this and other passages only in reference to the king. Now, when such statutes of a people are spoken of, no others are meant than their religious customs, for they cannot have another king, and other precepts, דת, cannot be used. This is evident from its etymology. But so great was the importance of such decrees as were issued by the king, that owing to their religious character they inseparably combined justice and equity. Hence in Pehlvi דאת, New Persian דת, meant "justice," "righteousness," as well as "chance," "destiny," and "fortuitous event." The surname which the ancient Persian kings are said to have had, from Kajomors to Gustasp, was that of דאראן, *dadan;* compounds of this word are applied as appellatives to the king and to God (Vullers, i. 779–81). To it corresponds the Greek θέμις in Homer, which is only applied to a holy statute. The oracles in Dodona were called θέμιστες Διός, "decisions given by Zeus." Θέμις ἐστί corresponds to the Latin *fas est*. It is interesting to compare the various ideas formed among different nations with the statutes and customs given to men for their observance. Among the Iranians, statutes are considered as gifts (Sanscr. *da*, δίδωμι, dare); among the Greeks, as ordinances (τίθημι ; cf. Sanscr. *dha*); among the Romans, as proclamations (*fas* is derived from *fari*, and *lex* from *legere*). But the Roman view comes nearer to the Hebrew idea of revealing which the word דבר, אמר (δεκάλογος), contains. However, what is here said applies only to radical words which disclose ancient divine commands in human rites.

The דת, says Haman, which *this* people considers obligatory, differs from those of the whole nation. When this difference was emphasized, it amounted to a passive disloyalty to the king. For it did not fully recognise the claims of the דתי המלך, the statutes of the king. It indeed regarded them as the laws of the potentate, but it denied their religious basis. Haman must have desired that the king should draw such a conclusion. For the nations of the Persian kingdom greatly differed in language, costumes, and manners. This was even a matter of pride to the ruler, that his powerful sceptre extended over such a heterogeneous conglomeration of peoples.

Herodotus, in his description of the Persian kingdom, portrays its manifold character in a very drastic manner. Haman therefore must have intimated that the difference between the Jews and the other nations is not so much in their external dress and language, as in their sharp religious contrast, in their acknowledgment of a God who is different from the gods of the other nations, who, although they vary among themselves, yet are at one in describing to the great king of Persia divine honours. But this people would not do that, because they would thereby acknowledge a principle which is against their religious convictions. This was, of course, derogatory to the dignity of the king. The king provided himself with all sorts of symbols and ordinances, in order that he (to use the words in the treatise of Mundo, which is ascribed to Aristotle and edited by Apuleius) " should be venerated as a god." But Haman is not yet satisfied. He wants to show the actual consequences which follow, when other laws are carried out than those which emanate solely from the king's will. It is not to be assumed that their different religious opinions are merely matters of sentiment, and it is sufficient that they by their actions show themselves to be obedient Persians (as, *e.g.*, Mordecai who had saved the king's life). The consequence of such diversity of principles is that " they do not practise the king's laws " (דתי המלך אינם עשים). Is not Mordecai's refusal to kneel before *him* a proof of this statement ? But Haman, with the subtlety of the serpent, avoids mentioning individual cases of disobedience. He generalizes his accusation that the whole Jewish people, on account of their religious laws, do not respect the commands of the king.

By this he did not mean to convey that they refused to pay taxes, but he referred to their denial of divine honours to the king, which denial as a people they dared to make throughout all the territories of the kingdom. This they everywhere do with their self-willed stubbornness, and show publicly, that they prefer their own laws to those of the king. In the book of Daniel, we see that his rivals went similarly to work, and when they could not point to any omissions in his duties as a citizen, they said : " We shall not find any occasion against this Daniel, except we find it against him concerning the law of his God " (בדת אלהה, Dan. vi. 6). But his resistance to the king's law, because it was against the law of God, must cost him his life. The three pious men, Hananiah, Mishael, and Azariah, were likewise placed by their enemies in a strait between the obedience they owed to the king's command and the worship which was due to God alone ; and they were ready to die in defence of the latter. But Haman made the charge general against the whole nation, that they rejected the authority of the king altogether. Had it been

a question concerning a single person, Haman would not probably have wasted one word more. " But they are many
(said the king), a whole nation. Would not the State suffer by
your proposal ? Shall they not be tolerated because they are
useful citizens ?" This objection of the king, Haman at once
removes. He tells him that they are a profitless people, and
do not deserve any such regard. The damage which might
possibly ensue by leaving them to enjoy rest (להניחם) is not
equal (אין שוה) to the profit which their removal would
bring. And he hastens to add,—noticing that the king had
thus far approved of his speech, and wishing to remove any
financial consideration which might have seriously occupied
the king's mind,—" If it please the king, let it be written
that they be destroyed (לאברם),—not merely be banished or
their goods spoiled,—and I will pay 10,000 talents of silver
into the treasury [1] to compensate for the possible damage."

The subtlety with which Haman tickles the conceited king,
could not be more accurately presented, than it is in the
specification of the sum of money which he was ready to pay
for the slaughter of the Jews. It is self-evident that the
king was to understand that this sum was to compensate
him for the loss the royal treasury might sustain, as soon
as he issued the order for their destruction. As he
formerly spoke so slightingly of the significance of this
people, that it mattered very little to the king whether
they existed or not, one should have expected that he, in
order to confirm his low estimation of them, would have
offered a very small price for their heads. But the cunning
Haman had the avarice as well as the vanity of the king
in view. The sum was, in fact, not a small bribe which
the king might be induced to take, notably when Haman
himself guaranteed it. Had he offered a small sum, it

---

[1] גנו, גנזך, is the treasury, Zend. *ganza* (Sanscr. *gandscha*), *gaza*. The
amassing of solid gold and riches in the treasuries is only peculiar to the
East in respect of show. In itself it is the case everywhere. Meissner,
in his *Humiliated and Exalted Esther*, p. 62, etc., has collected the descriptions of Oriental treasuries from travellers of the seventeenth century.

might have offended the king, and aroused his suspicion
that Haman's only intention was to make profit by the
bargain. Exactly because he so depreciated the people, and
made out it was of no consequence to the king whether
they lived or not, he for that very reason named a high
sum. Thus he entrapped the king from two sides, from one
by tempting his avarice with the large sum, and from the
other by tempting his pride in implying that it must be a
trifle to him to lose a multitude who were only worth the
price of 10,000 talents. It must be a large sum if the offer
should not offend the pride of the king, and must so excite
his vanity that he should, as is shown in ver. 11, turn it into
a generous gift to himself. Ten thousand talents of silver
were a considerable sum for the Persian king. כִּכָּר (of
round form, cake, as the Greek φθοῖδες χρυσίου, gold cake; cf.
Böckh, *Metrolog. Unters.* p. 51) was a Babylonian talent which
was stamped in silver in Persia; therefore Haman says he
wants to let the silver be weighed or stamped. As such
it was 3000 shekels and 1000 Attic drachmas in value. In a
round sum, 10,000 Babylonian talents were about £4,000,000.[1]
With regard to the higher or smaller value of the sum, we may
obtain more decisive knowledge by comparing the contemporary
value of the currency generally. The parallel notices in the
books of Ezra and Nehemiah with those in Herodotus make it
appear that it was a very important sum. In Neh. vii. 70,
72, we are told of the offerings which the returned captives
brought for their sanctuary. They were 41,000 darics of
gold and 4200 minas of silver. How exact these statements
are, and how they agree with the money value given by the
Greek writers, appears from the fact that the 21,000 darics
which the fathers apart from the people gave, are of the same
value as the 4200 minas; for five darics are equal to one mina.
Now, as one talent has 500 darics, therefore the value of the

---

[1] [According to Mr. Berewood, a Babylonian talent of silver was £218,
15s., so that ten thousand talents would be £4,680,000; but it is uncertain
whether they were Hebrew, or Babylonian, or Grecian talents.—TRANS.]

whole contribution was over 80 talents, which indeed was a large
sum for the poor captives of those days to raise. But it appears
insignificant by the side of the 10,000 talents which Haman
offered as a price for the whole people. Very important also
were the valuable things which Ezra received from the king as
the property of the temple. We read (Ezra viii. 26): " I even
weighed into their hands (that is, to the priests) 650 talents
of silver, and silver vessels 100 talents, of gold 100 talents; "
total, 850 talents. To this were added 20 bowls of gold =
1000 darics, or 2 talents. So then the whole temple treasure
did not even amount to 1000 talents.

Herodotus has given us particulars about the revenue which
the several provinces of the Persian monarchy contributed.
The provinces which paid in silver had to calculate in
Babylonian talents (iii. 89). The whole sum which was
collected from Babylon and the rest of Assyria (where the
Jews were in great numbers), amounted annually only to
1000 talents. From Egypt came 700 talents. The sum
raised in Shushan and the whole adjacent territories was
not more than 300 talents. The whole income from the
Persian Empire, apart from the gold dust of India, was no
larger a sum than 7600 Babylonian talents in silver. To
this certainly must be added the revenue of 210 talents
from the Lake of Moeris, and 140 which remained in Cilicia
for the payment of wages.[1] So, then, the sum which Haman
offered was about equal to the whole annual income in silver
from the whole empire. For, according to the standard of the
Euboeic talent, which was also valid in Persia (for all, *e.g.*, who
delivered gold were obliged, according to Herodotus, to pay in
the Euboeic talent), the income of the Persian king amounted,
with the exception of the gold dust of India, to 9540 talents.
This agreement of the offer of Haman with the silver revenue

---

[1] On this occasion, while mentioning the particulars given by Herodotus,
we cannot do otherwise than call attention to the difficulties which
they occasion to historical expositors. As they are so very important
we shall endeavour to solve them in the supplement.

of the king has also an exegetical value.[1] Considerable numbers of Jews were only to be found in the chief States of the Persian kingdom, and for these alone Haman offered the king as much as he derived from all,—a very great sum apparently for the people which was represented to the king as worthless. But the speculation of Haman was, as already remarked, strictly correct. The greater the sum was, the more flattering it appeared to the fancy of the great tyrant to waive it. It must have been thought enormous, if Ahhashverosh should boastfully reject it. Haman knew his master well enough to guess that when he once enjoyed his confidence and smiles, matters of finance would not be so exactly weighed in the balances. The Oriental sultans were liberal in taking as well as in giving. Haman could comfortably offer such a sum to the king, for if he at all entered into the bargain of selling the Jews, he need not trouble his head any further about the money. He who, like Ahhashverosh, delivers up a people, without question, investigation, or consultation why and wherefore he should do so, does not want to make a business of them, but only to show that he is the grand lord, who treads nations under his feet; and yet the more boastful he is,—as it here appears,—the more he is in reality only the slave of his ungoverned passions. What Haman has here done, in offering the king money for the lives of others, is by no means a thing unheard of. At the court of the Seldshukian princes, Mohamed was offered a great sum of money by his grand vizier for the life of an eminent man whom he hated — viz. Alaeddaulet Abul Hashim in Hamadan. Mohamed, who was not so generous as Ahhashverosh in giving, but extraordinarily greedy of receiving, entered upon the bargain. But when Alaeddaulet heard of it, he offered

[1] The Oriental legend, which better portrays the life and the spirit of the East than its authentic history, teaches also analogies on this point. In the legend of King Heykar, one king demands as tribute from the other "the triennal income" of his country, and about this there arises the prize fight of the spirit (*The Thousand and One Nights*, ed. Habicht, xiii. p. 86).

the king a greater sum for the life of the vizier, and the bigger bid obtained the victory. Of course Haman concealed his plan and hatred under the flimsy pretext of political prudence and necessity. It is a matter about a disobedient and hostile people. He reckoned upon the distrust of the king after the experience which he had gained in his dealings with the Greeks in his unfortunate expedition. Similar devices for killing all the Christians of the Turkish Empire were made several times at the court of Stamboul under Selim I. and Murad IV.; and even so late as 1770 the fanatical Mufti Perisade Osman Efendi declared his opinion, that such a massacre was a necessity. But when the Sultan Ibrahim, 1646, meditated a similar plan of killing the Christians, it was his Mufti who dissuaded him, by telling him that the stars were not favourable to his intended enterprise (Hammer, *Gesch. des osmanischen Reiches*, v. 390). By this opinion the right to kill all Christians was not contested. As also the right to kill all the Jews was claimed by the Roman emperors as successors to Titus, and this supposed right was commuted into the imposition of a head-tax.

Ver. 10. "*And the king took his ring from his hand and gave it to Haman.*"

The name טבעת which the ring bears comes from its use in the act of sealing. The seal was dipped (טבע) in a coloured liquid, and then pressed upon a document. Thus the seal-ring received its name from the action, because a seal without a ring was not customary in the East. For the ring which was worn on the finger was the symbol of the person having control and power over his will. The seal of the king included all his power. A document which bore the impression of the royal seal (*sigillum*) demanded unhesitating obedience. It was considered as a divine law, and irrevocable (see chap. viii. 8). Therefore with the king's great seal was transferred royal power. Not before his dying hour did Alexander the Great deliver his ring to Perdikkas. History

very characteristically narrates of the Emperor Tiberius, that
with his last breath he convulsively held his ring in his
clutches (Suet. *Tib.* 73). The Oriental legends about the
peculiar virtues of the seal of Solomon, by which he had
power over demons and spirits, are only figurative representations of his royal power. Only to an *alter ego*, or uncon-
ditional representative of the will of the king, could the royal
seal-ring be delivered. This, in a modified form, became for
the purpose of State administration the custom in the court
of the Turkish sultans, where, for a long time, it was customary
at every accession to the throne to order four imperial seals
to be made, three of which, in circular form, were given to
the highest officers; while the fourth, in quadrangular form,
the sultan reserved for himself (Hammer, *Osman. Reich.* viii.
199). No one could execute the work which Haman
undertook without obtaining from the king extraordinary
power. By putting on the ring which the king wore on his
own finger, he was thereby invested with royal authority.
The narrator, in recording this act, repeats the designation:
"Haman, the son of Hamedatha the Agagite, the Jews'
enemy," in order to call attention to the impending calamity.
The ring stamped him as the Jews' enemy, and his receiving
it—remarks the Midrash, strikingly—produced a greater
impression upon the Jews than the prophecies of all the
prophets did, for they were led to repent of their sins.
Haman is now distinguished with the name צֹרֵר הַיְּהוּדִים,
"persecutor of the Jews," "hater of the Jews,"—a name
which is applied to no one else in the O. T., but which the
Jews have ever since applied to all those whose blind prejudice caused them to be Jew-baiters, and who were influenced
more by feelings of fanaticism, envy, and avarice than by a
desire to ameliorate Israel's condition, and to lead them to
repentance and to salvation. The expression is chosen with
particular reference to more ancient usage. The enemies of
Israel and of their God are often so styled. The word צֹרֵר in
the sense of enemy (in the singular and plural) occurs, besides,

in some passages in Ex. and Deut., in Amos v. 12; Isa. xi.
13; especially in the Psalms, where שׁרר stands often for צרר
(comp. Ps. xxvii. 11, liv. 7, lvi. 3, lix. 11). But more probably
the narrator had Isa. xi. 13 in his mind, where it is said of
the enemies of Judah (צררי יהודה יכרתו), "They that vex Judah
shall be cut off."

Ver. 11. "*And the king said unto Haman, The silver is
given to thee, the people also, to do with them as it seemeth
good to thee.*"

The haughtiness of the king is extreme. He gives to
Haman the ring, without receiving first the price of the
bargain. Therefore he adds, that he makes him a present
of the money. Haman should give nothing, but he can take
what he likes. As Haman said, "if it please the king" to
destroy the Jews, he would give him money; so now the
king says he need not give anything, and may do "as it
pleases him." We must observe that the king does not say
that he makes him a present of the people in order to
destroy them (לאבדם), but only that he may do with them
as he likes. Has he not noticed the brief hint of Haman,
or does he think that this is merely his avaricious speculation?
The narrator gives us an insight into the tyrannical carelessness and indifference with which Ahhashverosh listens to
Haman. How readily he gives him the seal of authority to
deal with a whole nation as he likes, without a single
question or investigation! For he merely says, "The people
(העם) also is given to thee," without mentioning them by
name. He looks upon the order simply in the light of
granting a favour to Haman. What can scarcely excuse
him is his confidence in Haman, in that he believes that
Haman is patriotic in his declaration that the people (העם)
are really dangerous to the State. It is the peculiar character of Oriental tyrants to have too much confidence in
their ministers. The more a ruler is careless and capricious
and absolute in power, the more boundless is his confidence

in persons whom his autocratic will has raised to high offices of State. Of the noble Giafar the Barmekide, it is told that he possessed such power, that he first spontaneously adopted and executed the most important affairs, and then reported about them to the caliph, who merely used to say, "All right, Giafar." This gave rise to the mocking verse which Abu Pharaon made upon Harun, and which, according to Hammer, is as follows :—

> "Thou thinkest that thy hand rules the empire ;
> Thou art mistaken indeed ;
> Thou art nothing but the puppet, whose wire
> The hand of the great man does lead."

But Ahhashverosh is not in the hands of a Barmekide, but in those of a revengeful man.——At the conferences which the ambassador of the Hungarian pretender to the throne, Zapolya, had with Ibrahim Pasha in 1533, the latter boasted of his power, and said, " My master has also two seals; one he wears himself, and the other I wear; for he does not want to see any difference between himself and me " (Hammer, *Osman. Reich.* iii. 129). Against this Ibrahim the Jews complained, as against a second Haman ; and they rejoiced in like manner when he fell (Joseph ha Cohen, *Dibre khayim*, p. 103, ed. Amsterdam).

Ver. 12. " *Then were the king's scribes called in the first month, on the thirteenth day.*"

This date must have been perfectly known to the narrator, for the letters of the king must have been prepared from the day of the first month to the corresponding day in the twelfth month in which the execution was to take place. But this was the thirteenth of Adar, as is expressly stated in chap. ix. 1. And as the edicts were issued to the Persian authorities, it must have been in accordance with the Persian calendar, with which the Jewish must have been brought into harmony. It must therefore also be assumed that the thirteenth of the first month agreed with the Jewish. But was it without any significance that Haman should choose the thirteenth day of the

month for the starting-point of his diabolical hatred ? He had
cast the lot from day to day in order to find out the month in
which he might strike the Jews. The thirteenth day of
every month was called by the Persians Tir, and this has still in
the modern Persian the meaning of " lot," " share," and " part "
(Vullers, *Lex. Pers.* i. 486). We cannot refrain from other
considerations which throw light upon the choice of the
thirteenth day. It is necessary to remember that beside
other four months of the Numa which have thirty-one days,
the ides of the Roman calendar falls upon the thirteenth, and,
with regard to the full moon, the time of the month was
reckoned as so many days before or after the Ides (cf.
Ideler, *Handb. der Chronol.* 239). So also it is known that
Macrobius (lib. i. cap. 15) adheres to the explanation that
" Idus signifies the day which divides the month, for *iduare*
means in Etruscan the same as *dividere*." The full moon
divided also the old Indian months into two parts—the
bright part was called *cuklapaxa*, and the dark part *krish-
napaxa* (see Lassen, *Ind. Alterthumskunde*, i. 824, etc.). Likewise, we find in Persian dictionaries that the planet Mercurius
was called by them Tir. But concerning Mercurius-Hermes
the ancients had, to a certain extent, the notion that he was
the god of light of the lunar year. It was thought that Isis,
the Egyptian moon, was descended from Hermes, and that
Hermes has his seat in the moon, and goes about with it in
its rotation. He has also added the five leap-days to the
lunar year, and he, as is elsewhere more fully told, liberated
Mars, *i.e.* Ares, who was chained in the thirteenth month,
whereby the arrangement of the leap month (among the Jews,
the second Adar) is indicated (see my *Drackenkämpfe*, p. 65).

The connection of the thirteenth day with the planet Tir
may yet be instructive from another aspect. It is thought
that Tir is nothing else but a part of the compound *tistrya*, the
star Tistar, which the Parsees have ever invoked as the most
illustrious and mighty (comp. Spiegel, *Avesta*, i. 273), which
notably gives rain. But it appears to me that the very name

Zarathustra, in a reversed form, means " the son of the star." It is undoubtedly this star which the gospel tradition knew as the star of the Magi, the Persian wise men. Then the tradition would also be remarkable, because the arrival of the Magi at Bethlehem is assigned to January 6, and this was reckoned as the thirteenth day from the 25th of December, the assumed birthday of Christ, as it still goes in modern times by the same name of the thirteenth, in reference to the three kings (Melchior, Caspar, and Balthazar), among the people of North Germany and of the Netherlands.

However, there is something more certain and sure. If we may believe that the designation of the thirteenth day by the name of Tir had reference to the full moon, we should rather decide for the connection of its significance with Tir, " an arrow," which was contracted from *tigr* (comp. Tigris, *tigra*, τόξον, τίξευμα). Pliny says the Medes call Tigris an arrow (see Bötticher, *Arica*, p. 28). The arrow is an ancient emblem of the moon as well as of the sun (hence of the moon and sun-gods). Even the name itself of the fourth month, which is the same as of the thirteenth day, viz. Tir, receives an explanation from this, not so much, of course, according to the later Persian calendar, where the year began with spring, but after a computation of time, of which the year began in September, which was so much in use in the first Christian centuries in the East, that it became the official era in Constantinople (Ideler, ii. 359). In this era the fourth month corresponds to the zodiacal sign Sagittarius, whose symbol is the arrow, or, as the Jews call it, " the bow." The constellation of Sagittarius appears in December, hence the arrow-throwing god of the Lycians, when winter came, hid himself in Patara.

All this undoubtedly throws much light upon the intention of Haman to destroy the Jews on the thirteenth of the month. The arrow is the symbol of death, of sickness, of disgrace, and of blasphemy. Poisonous words are compared to arrows (Ps. lxiv. 4). False tongues are called deadly arrows (Jer. ix. 8).

The apostle speaks of the fiery darts of the evil one (Eph. vi. 16). In a similar figurative sense the Greeks used the word ἰός; and in Persian " to shoot one with an arrow" means, to wish evil to any one, or to slander him (see Vullers, i. 483).

The importance of the arrow and the bow in the Persian kingdom is well known. A coin bore the image of a bow, and an archer hits better than an edict. The bow was manifestly the symbol of the king himself, and represented his victorious and ruling power like the sun, hence the Persians were depicted upon the coins as standing with the extended bow, ready to shoot (Vullers, *Arsac. Imperium*, i. p. 50, Paris 1728, etc.).

On the day of the arrow, Haman sealed a death warrant against unprepared Israel.

"*And there was written according to all that Haman commanded unto the king's satraps, and to the governors that were over every province.*"

Haman had received the authorization from the king, and " it was written," not, " they wrote," for the writers were only instrumental in the act, and wrote, so to speak, what the grand vizier dictated. He caused these letters to be addressed to the אחשדרפנים. That we are to recognise in this word, both according to the sound and sense, what is known from classical authors as satraps, or satrapa, satrapes, there can be no doubt. The Σ, comp. σύν and ξύν, is reproduced here by חש, as in אחשורש, for the Ξ in Xerxes. The א is, besides, only a Semitic prefix; therefore the form of Ἐξατράπης for satrap, by Theopomp, can be recognised as Semitic pronunciation (comp. Pott, *Etymol. Forsch.* i. lxvi.). In a similar manner the Jews have reproduced later Greek words which begin ξ by appending an א, and by כם, to which corresponds חש here; or ξενός by אבסן, and ξύλινον by אבסלן. — Likewise, it is certain that אחשדרפנים perfectly corresponds to the Old Persian *Khshatrapawan*, as it was read upon the inscription of Bisutun by Benfey (comp. *Die Pers. Keilinschrift*, p. 18), and, in fact, we may read

אחשדרפונים. It means the administrator of a government
(*khshatra*, domain, and *pawan*, according to Benfey, from
the Sanscr. *pâ*, to govern), as Herodotus calls satrapies ἀρχαί.
The second part of the word פונים (sing. פן or פ) is doubtless
found in the modern Persian *Ban* (באן), possessor, commander.
The Greek form teaches that *Khshatrapawa* was also pronounced *Ksshatrapa*. After the fall of the Old Persian
monarchy there were, properly speaking, no more satraps.
The different Oriental kingdoms have given different names
to their governors. When we find the old word שתרפ,
sitrap, in Persian dictionaries, it looks as a reintroduction
of the Greek name into the Persian. Under the caliphs
the governors of provinces were called Wali, or sometimes
Amil, as Hammer remarks (*Länderverwaltung unter dem
Chalifat*, p. 11), and Emire or Nabbe (pl. *newab*, whence in
a maimed form, Nabob) were the names of representatives.

But Haman did not only write to the satraps, but also to
the פחות, governors of single districts. There were twenty
satraps of the king (see ver. 1); but in the several satrapies
were *medinoth*, *i.e.* revenue districts, to the number of 127,
including Persia proper. At the head of these stood the
פחות, and therefore the first were entitled "the satraps of
the king," *i.e.* governor-generals; while of the second it said,
"who were over every *medina* or district." Now we must
remark something about the meaning of the name פחה, pl.
פחות or פחוות. It was not only a name of a provincial
administrator in the Persian, but also in the Assyrian and
Babylonian Empires. The most ancient notice of this name
we find in the kingdom of Solomon. Nehemiah held the
office of a פחה in the Persian kingdom. That this office consisted in collecting the taxes may be seen from Neh. v. and
1 Kings xx. 24. To explain this very extensively used word,
it is necessary to compare it with ancient Greek notices, for
it must seem strange that satrap had become Grecised and
פחה not. Now we must remember that Hesychius uses
πάχητες, "rich," "eminent," in the same sense as Herodotus

speaks of the πάχεες as the aristocrats of Naxos (v. 30), the eminent men of Aegina (vi. 91), and of the rich Sicilian Megareans (vii. 156) as πάχες. To the same effect we read in 1 Kings x. 15, that Solomon received gold from the kings of the mingled people (or of the West), and from the פחות הארץ ; which cannot in the strictest sense mean governors of the country, as they were not called so in Judea (see 1 Kings iv.), but must likewise be understood as a general name for the rich and the eminent of the country. Why Thenius (*Bücher der Könige*, p. 169) should conclude, from the mentioning of this name, that this chapter is of later date, is difficult to see. The connection of פחה in a figurative sense with παχύς, which has also the natural meaning of fat, has nothing astonishing in it. It is exactly in the nature of the Oriental dialect to associate riches and eminence of a person, in a figurative way, with the size and appearance of his body, and to express the two ideas by one word. The Psalmist calls the mighty of the land דשני ארץ, *i.e.* "the fat ones of the land" (comp. Isa. v. 17). In like manner is this the case with שמן (comp. Judg. iii. 29 ; Isa. xxx. 23). It has its analogy in the Greek παχύς, at least according to Pott (*Etymol. Forsch.* ii. 221), Sanscr. *bahu*, large. Hesychius has the gloss βαγαῖος μέγας, πολὺς ταχύς. It is evidently to be read παχύς, and refers to similar forms. פחה is still to be recognised in the modern Turkish pasha, formerly written basha, bassa, and was also a general title of honour which was bestowed upon learned men (Hammer, *Osman. Reich.* i. 56). And what is here remarkable is, that in the placing together of satraps and pashas in the book of Esther, we have the ancient Oriental designation of governors side by side with that given by the modern Moslem State (probably the last of that description).

The State secretaryship of the great king of Persia was evidently a very extensive institution, for the many nations were not managed and governed with uniformity after one single scheme; they were allowed to have their own particular language and customs; the orders which were addressed to

them from the throne were sent to them in their own language
and writing, It is emphatically stated that **every province
and people** received the letters in its own peculiar writing
(כבתבה) and language (כלשונו). This is explained by the fact
that they were not merely directed to the satraps who were
Persians, and to the inferior governors (פחות), but also to the
princes (שרים), who belonged to the people themselves. For
as the officers of the first rank were called governors of the
king, and of the second rank pashas of the provinces, so these
were called princes of the people (עם). Indeed, the contents
of the letters concerned them the most; for, to a certain
extent, it was a call for a united national war against one
people that was scattered among them all. Haman in his
diabolical subtlety did not merely write to the satraps, lest he
should provoke disapproval, as it would have appeared to
them as an arbitrary act. Nor did he write merely to the
administrators of finance, lest these should demur on the
ground that the exchequer would suffer by it; but he specially
wrote to the chiefs of the nations, to inflame their local
popular antipathies against the Jews. The bureaucratic board,
which was instituted for the better management of local
affairs, and for the instruction of the people, when measures
were transmitted to them in their own language, should
become the instrument in his hand of exciting hatred and
passion. Thus does the abuse of power change the best
organizations into instruments of death. It is not the
institutions and constitutions of a country which secure
prosperity to the people, so much as the spirit which pervades
the hearts of the rulers who put them in motion.

Ver. 13. " *And letters should be sent by posts into all the
king's provinces.*"

The actual despatch of the letters is not yet told in vers.
12 and 13. The former speaks of their style, and the latter
of their contents. The sending out of the letters is recorded
in ver. 15. The words, the letters to be sent (נישלוח, Niphal

Inf. absol., which occurs only in this place), are connected
with ver. 14 and explanatory of it. The runners (הרצים)
were the royal post. "Nothing in nature," says Herodotus
(viii. 98), "surpasses those messengers in swiftness. For as
many days as the journey would occupy, so many men and
horses are provided, one man and a horse for each day's
journey, and neither snow nor rain, nor heat nor night, can
hinder any of the runners from finishing his course with the
greatest speed. The rider transmits his message to a second,
and the second to a third, and so on, until it reaches its
destination. This running course of the riding messengers
the Persians call Angareion." The messengers themselves
were called Angaroi. The word אגרת, letter, which occurs in
chap. ix. 29, is therefore hardly to be explained from a
Hebrew root, but must be taken as a contraction of אננרת.
The modern Persian clearly shows this in the words *engare*,
engariden, a "writing," "document," "codex" (though in
Vullers it is used only in the abstract sense of thinking).
The Talmud Erubin 62*a*, gives the Persian names of letter-
carriers מוהרקי and אברנני, and so the first is clearly explained
from מוהרק, Arab. paper (see Freytag, iv. 216), by the modern
Persian מהר, a seal.

The second name, Rapaport (in *Erech Millin*, p. 6) explains
from *angari* ; but this is a mistake, for it is to be read אברדני,
from the Persian *berden*, to carry. In Arabic we have still
the name of a letter-carrier, ברידה, *tabellarius* (Freytag, i. 106).

    *" To destroy, to slay, and to cause to perish, all Jews, both
young and old, little children and women."*

The contents of the writing were to the effect that all Jews
should be totally exterminated ; and the expressions used were
evidently chosen to convey the climax of cruelty. First the
command is להשמיד, to destroy, *i.e.* their communal institutions, their domestic peace, their welfare, and their property.
But this is not yet enough, so it is followed by the more
cruel word להרג, to put them all to death at the edge of the

sword. But lest any official might out of pity let some of
them escape, another more revolting expression is added,
וּלְאַבֵּד, "and to cause to perish," all without distinction of sex
or of age. When Haman first made his proposal to the king,
in ver. 9, he used the word לְאַבְּדָם, to lose them; but he did
not explicitly say that he meant to kill them, for he would
have attained the object of his request if they had only been
banished from the country. But lest the provincial authorities should interpret this ambiguous expression in a mild way,
he specified the manner in which he wanted them to be
destroyed, namely, by slaughter. Some commentators have
thought it so improbable that such an edict should be issued,
that they have thrown doubt upon the genuineness of the
whole book. Such critics only displayed their complete
ignorance of history and of the spirit of Oriental rule.
Attention had rightly been called to the misdeed of
Mithridates king of Pontus (Grot. *in loc.*). The manner
in which he ordered the Romans to be slain is literally the
same as the one narrated in our book. Appian (xii. cap. 22)
reports : " He sent secret orders to all the satraps and the
mayors of cities, that they should within the space of thirty
days fall upon the resident Romans and Italians, upon their
wives and children, and upon all freemen of Italian origin,
and kill them, and throw them away unburied, and take their
goods and possessions, partly for themselves and partly for the
King Mithridates." . . . " These secret orders Mithridates
sent to all at the same time. When the appointed day
came, there was wailing and lamentation in the whole of
Asia." Mithridates was also an Oriental tyrant, and acted in
a measure according to old tradition. It was to him an act
of vengeance as well as national policy, which Haman likewise in his plan presented before the king. But the Romans
were a mighty people who had penetrated Asia victoriously,
whilst the Jews formed, throughout the whole country, subjugated peaceable communities. Mithridates therefore was
the executioner of national vengeance, but Haman sought to

I

avenge his own personal spite.   For the latter fearful motive
has also many analogous examples in the Orient.   Specially
cruel appears the deed of Alaeddin Khiljy Sultan (in the
beginning of the fourteenth century).   Some Mongols whom
he had dismissed from his service were accused of treachery,
and in consequence of this he caused all Mongols, it is said
15,000, to be slain in one day.   Mohammed, the victorious
Shah of Chowaresmier (in the beginning of the thirteenth
century), had conquered Turkestan, and had given to the
conquered Osman Khan, who was uncommonly handsome, his
daughter in marriage.   But this man, being inwardly as
coarse as he was outwardly fair, had no sooner settled in
Samarkand, than one fine morning he undertook a massacre
of all the people of Chowaresmier, so that his own wife, the
daughter of Mohammed, scarcely escaped.   Of course he
himself did not escape vengeance afterwards (comp. Hammer,
Gemäldesaal, vi. 172 and iv. 197).   Shah Abbas of Persia,
when he no longer needed to tolerate the disobedience of the
inhabitants of Ghilan, issued an order in 1634 that all the
people should be killed (Malcolm, ii. 30).   European history
also is not without such examples of tyrannical cruelty.
Prominently among all is the fearful sanguinary St. Bartho-
lomew night.   For those who were then killed were not
strangers, but Frenchmen, friends and guests.   Yea, even
those who had been invited to weddings were cut off without
pity.   Here the king himself and the princes imbrued their
hands in blood.   They were more bloodthirsty and guilty
than Ahhashverosh, who was deceived by another, and mis-
led by his own arrogance.

Ranke, in his *French History* (i. 332), says that about 3 o'clock
the alarm-bell began to ring ; then the people rushed everywhere into the houses of the Huguenots, in order to kill them
and to rob them of their property, crying, " It is the king's will,
and he has commanded so."   Orders were given by word of
mouth, and these were carried with the speed of lightning
from city to city to excite fanaticism.   According to moderate

statistics, in Paris alone 5000, and in the country 20,000, people were massacred.

The Jews were scattered in all the provinces of the empire (Joseph. *Jewish Wars*, vii. 333), but they lived everywhere together in separate communities, as was the peculiar custom in ancient times. The various nationalities of a city did not reside promiscuously, as in a modern city, but in separate quarters. For this reason jealousies were more frequent, and hatred and passion were more easily excited against each other. In the cities where Greeks and Syrians dwelt together strife never ceased. It could not therefore be difficult for Haman to excite fanaticism and avarice, either of which is always, even without external impulse, the source of the other. Joseph. *Antiq.* xviii. 9. 9, gives a remarkable example of this from Seleucia. The Greeks and the Syrians were always quarrelling. But the former were generally defeated, because the Jews took part with the latter. "Now when the Greeks had the worst in this sedition, and saw that they had but one way of recovering their former authority, namely by preventing union between the Jews and the Syrians, they every one discoursed with such of the Syrians as were formerly their acquaintance, and promised they would be at peace and friendship with them. Accordingly they gladly agreed so to do; and when this was done by the principal men of both nations, . . . they fell upon the Jews, and slew about 50,000 of them; indeed, the Jews were all destroyed, excepting a few who escaped," etc. A similar quarrel arose at Caesarea between the Jews, the Greeks, and the Syrians as to the ownership of the city, in which the Syrians played a double game; and though overcome by the Jews, the latter were at last severely punished by the Romans (Joseph. *Jewish Wars*, ii. 13. 7). There is a history of the entire extermination of the Jews in Persia under Abbas II. in the year 1666. It is not authenticated, but it may possibly be an imitation of the narrative in our book (see Schudt, *Jüd. Merkwürdigk.* i. 1. 26-32).

" In one day, even upon the thirteenth day of the twelfth month, which is the month Adar."

It may seem strange that Haman should have left the governors such a wide space of time for the execution of the order, but it was because the horoscope had cast the die for the month Adar ; and this turned out to the salvation of Israel. On the other hand, a long interval was desirable for himself, as it would leave the various executioners time to prepare for decisive action on the appointed day. The objection to this, that the Jews might in the meantime have fled or provided themselves with places of refuge, does not hold good, for whither could they have fled ?　In such a case the whole extensive empire would have been their universal prison. And if the communities had desired to emigrate, would they have been suffered to do so ?　And even if they had been willing to forsake their faith and nation, would they not have been hindered from doing so ?　For when one wants to destroy a person, he strengthens him in tenacious adherence to his religious system out of hatred. The command of Haman was violent and cruel enough before the actual deed. He played with them, as the cat with the mouse which she has already caught. He let them have breathing time, during which they should prepare to die, to lament their fate, and to fall into despair. The horoscope had decided for Adar. In the 13th of the first month, the day of the arrow, the decree was issued, and till the 13th of Adar, *i.e.* a whole year, the angel of death was hovering over Israel, and pierced their souls before he touched their bodies.

" And to take the spoil of them for a prey."

That שלל represents war booty is well known (comp. my *Comm. on Judg.* p. 60).　It is therefore usually connected with בזז, to plunder.　Pott (ii. 153), who compares it with ἁρπάζειν, is surely right, rather than Benfey.　The writing of Haman regards the Jews as enemies of the country, whose subjugation is determined upon, and whose hostility is of so enormous a nature, that slavery would be too mild a punishment for them. The Persian monarch had power enough to deal as he pleased with those who were under his dominion, and of whose power of resistance he had nothing to fear.

The Jews have experienced a similar fate in their subsequent history, if not in being threatened with death, at least in having their property confiscated. The German-Roman emperor used to claim the right, during the Middle Ages, of levying a head-tax from them, on the ground that he was the heir of the conqueror of Jerusalem, and could do with them as he liked. The Emperor Charles IV. said expressly, in a rescript: "All the Jews belong, themselves personally and their possessions, to our exchequer, and are in our hands and power, so that we are authorized to deal with them according to our pleasure." It was again a relic of the old Oriental law of conquest, which was upheld against the Jews in Christian States, and aggravated by religious sentiment, such as we find in Haman's order, when Albert Achill, the Margrave of Brandenburg, published the following political law: "When a Roman king or emperor is crowned, he has everywhere the right to take the goods of the Jews that are living under his dominion, and also to take *their life, and to kill a certain number of them*" (see my "Geschichte der Juden" in *Encyclop. Ersch und Gruber*, ii. 27, p. 86).

Ver. 14. "*A copy of the writing to be given out for a decree.*"

The explanation of פתשגן is not without certain great difficulties. It does not appear that the compound פתבג, " royal bread" (Dan. i. 5), Zend. *paiti*, Sanscr. *pati*, Pers. *pád =* "king," "lord," and בג, "bread," comp. Greek βέκος, bread, throws any light upon it. Nor can it be compared with פתגם, " word," "edict," which is in Persian פינם, פיהם, for the two words have no relation to each other. It is certainly like פרשגן in Ezra. With regard to its meaning, we find a difference of opinion already among the oldest commentators.

Some of them thought that the two words in Esther and in
Ezra are of different meanings, which is surely not the case.
The LXX. has rendered the word *pathshegen* in Esther by
antigraphon; hence came into Lexicons and into most modern
versions the word "copy" for it. But this is clearly an
hypothesis of the LXX., for it renders *parshegen* by *diasaphesis*
and *diatage*, which corresponds to the paraphrase of the Targum, *diatagma*. But it is also evident that *pathshegen* and
parshegen are inseparable, because the second half of the
compound never occurs for "writing" or "copying." In the
passages in Ezra there is no mention of a copy, as they only
speak of one letter. The satraps could not have sent a copy,
but the original, to the king. So also in our passage, the
word cannot be understood in the sense of a copy. We must
therefore take antigraphon in the sense of "contents," "purport," "tenor," as Jerome rightly renders it by "summa." To
obtain this meaning, it is not necessary to adduce the modern
Persian בהרשת, Arab. פהרש (Castelli, *Lex. Syr.* p. 738; Vullers,
ii. 698).[1] Other Orientalists, as Oppert and Gildemeister,
have thought that the word is composed of the Old Pers. *fra*
(Sanscr. *pru*, Lat. *pro*) and *ahanhana* (= *çanghana*), which
means order (see Fürst, *Lex.* ii. 244). At all events the
syllable שֶׁגֶּ demands consideration. It may dialectically be
compared with *signum*, whose original idea was likewise
"mark," "character," and "contents." Pott hit upon a good
idea when he reminds us of a Sanscr. form, *sangna* (*cognitio*)
(*Etym. Forsch.* i. 183). *Signum* is, in fact, nearly related
to γιγνώσκειν, with which the Zend. *znâ*, Sanscr. *yna*,
cognoscere, are connected. *Parshegen* and *pathshegen* cannot
be better rendered than by "intelligence," "observation,"
"contents of a letter." Only in the sense of *argumentum*,
cognitio, could the Targum translate מכתם, Ps. lx. 1, and
משנה, Deut. xvii. 18, by *parshegen*; but for the latter, other
editions have merely *parsha*.—The contents of the writing to

---

[1] The attempt of the Targum to derive the word from פרש, "to explain,"
may be correct for this, but untenable for *parshegen*.

the authorities was published (נגלוי) to the populations, in order
that they might be ready for the day of the execution. These
were no private instructions to the authorities, but rather open
orders to the people. The intention of the publicity was in
order that the Jews might be prevented from a possible flight.
Thus the prospect of the coming event increased the hatred
and mistrust of the heathen against them, severed all the ties
which had hitherto held them together, and extinguished every
humane feeling of pity in the breasts of the people, by harden-
ing their hearts during this long interval of respite. The
tyrannical command caused the Persian people to prepare
themselves as for a feast. They were to provide themselves with
weapons, and to be ready and eager for the prey.[1] Fanaticism
and avarice do not need much time to be inflamed. But
Haman thought that the more the idea was held out to the
people that on a certain day they would have a chance of
robbing the Jews, the more they would calculate upon it as
sure. Men must be prepared for joys and for sorrows, for
benevolence and for hatred, in order to drink of their cup to
the brim.

In ver. 15 may be seen how vividly graphic, and yet
how plain, is the description of the narrative. While the
messengers run—for they transmit a royal order (therefore
hamelech)—the command is published in Shushan. What a
dreadful command! Life and property should be taken from
hundreds of thousands, parents should see their children
killed before their eyes, and children should stand as silent
and helpless witnesses of the slaughter of their parents;
and while this is being proclaimed, Ahhashverosh and Haman
sit down at the table and drink. Just now an arrow is
shot, giving the signal for the butchery of thousands, and
Haman sits silent at the table of the deluded and fickle king.

---

[1] The Midrash Esther 94a, describes this beautifully in its own homiletical way. When a Jew went to market to buy meat or anything else,
there the Persian met him, and said scornfully, "To-day you still buy and
pay your money; to-morrow I shall kill you, and plunder all that you
possess."

Wine flows abundantly into the cups, but the numberless
tears which flow from many dim eyes are forgotten. It is
not more tragical in Shakespeare's *Richard III.*, act iii. scene 1,
where Glo'ster is represented as inciting to acts of new
atrocity, and saying to Buckingham, " Come, let us sup
betimes, that afterwards we may digest our complots in some
form." For the banquet of Ahhashverosh gives less the
appearance of a complot than of the malicious triumph of a
treacherous enemy.

" *But the city of Shushan was perplexed.*"

The accustomed explanation of the word נבוכה cannot
easily be adopted. Commentators have generally followed
the LXX., which renders it by " *ἐταράσσετυ*," " the city of
Shushan was horrified," deriving the word from the root בוך,
which means " rolling," " turning," and is cognate with אבך
and הפך. Jewish grammarians have given occasion to this
interpretation (see Kimchi's אוצר השרשים, p. 72). On the
other hand, the predominating ancient Jewish opinion on the
word was, that it is derived from בכה, " to weep ; " so the
second Targum, etc. Of course it was thought that the weeping
refers to the resident Jews alone,—an opinion which Jerome
followed, for he says, " Cunctis qui in urbe erant flantibus ; "
and another scholium has the word " Judaeis" instead of
cunctis. And the LXX. also renders in other passages forms
of words which are likewise derived from בוך by κλαυθμός,
" weeping," as, *e.g.*, Joel i. 18 ; Micah vii. 4. But it is
necessary to limit both significations, as they are due to the
homiletical expositions of later Jews, and both are untenable
objectively. The word *nevucha* (" perplexed ") cannot apply
to the Jews, for we read only in chap. iv. 1, " Now when
Mordecai knew all that was done." Only now commences
the description of the effect which the publication of the
decree had produced upon the Jews. Apart from this, it
would be extraordinary to intimate that the Jews are meant
by the word " city," when iv. 3 expressly relates that wher-

ever the report of the decree came, " there was great mourning
among the Jews, and fasting and weeping." But if, as is
undoubtedly the case, this is predicted of the whole city of
Shushan, the question arises, why should *nevucha* be taken
in a sense which implies that they were horrified, amazed,
and confounded at the event which had actually been
ushered in ? Did it come all of a sudden upon them, that it
took them by surprise ? When the king *had long before* placed
the prospect of plunder before them, it can scarcely be
supposed that when the longed-for day had actually arrived,
the people were smitten by feelings of compassion for the
poor innocent Jews. The first Targum foresaw the objection,
and tried to meet it by the remark, that the city got confused
by the discordant, tumultuous voices that were heard, of joy
on the part of the heathen, and of lamentation on the part of
the Jews. But in ver. 15 there is only expressed the deeds
and the behaviour of the heathen against the Jews. Then in
chap. iv. comes the contrast afforded by the description of the
misery it had produced among the Jews. In נבוכה, therefore,
there can only be intimated a parallel to the drinking of the
king with Haman. When Naomi returned with Ruth to
Bethlehem, we are told " that all the city was moved about
them " (תהם), *i.e.* her return in such a poor condition, accompanied by her young daughter-in-law, excited wonder and
gossip, but does not necessarily imply that feelings of
sympathy were aroused. In the same sense we must take
the word *nevucha*. The edict of Haman did not arouse
compassion towards those against whom it was directed, but
formed only a subject of gossip and conversation. While the
decree was issued to kill thousands of Israel, " the king and
Haman were merrily drinking wine, and the city of Shushan
was full of gossip." I think that נבוכה may be derived from
a form of נבך cognate with נבח (in the onomapoetic meaning
of *latrare*), " to bark." From the Gk. βάβω, βαβάζω, " to
prattle," usually in a secondary bad sense (fut. βάξω),
comp. *Odyss.* viii. 408, ἔπος βέβακται, from which βάβαξ,

βαβάκτης, " gossiper," " crier," are derived (Suidas, etc.).   It
is certainly the onomapoetic form, and it has doubtless an
affinity with the French *babil*, *babiller*, and the English
babble.   Again, נבך may be compared with it, because the
נ is only a prefix peculiar to Hebraisms (see my *Comm.
on Judges*, p. 120).

The condition of Israel was sad in the extreme.   Their
annihilation was impending,—their enemies were drinking,—
and their neighbours were gossiping.   Where else were they
to seek help, but in repentance towards the living God !

CHAPTER IV

Ver. 1. "*Now when Mordecai knew all that was done.*"

He got to know, not only that which was evident from the published edict, but also the whole transaction of Haman with the king (see ver. 7). The order to the city of Shushan declared perhaps only what should take place there on the 13th of Adar, but he knew that Haman's plan made provision for the destruction of the Jews in general. The resentful vizier had not told the king what was the design of his hatred, but the courtiers suspected it (iii. 3); and it *must have reminded* Mordecai, and touched him to the core. The more he got to know the whole condition of things, the greater was his terror. It was not a mere caprice of the king, but a systematic, premeditated plan. If at any time he had cause to weep and repent, much more now. There was only one friend left who could help in this extremity, God alone; and before Him confession of sin, and heartfelt supplications must be made.

The Midrash has for the explanation of the words, "and Mordecai knew all," invented a heavenly scene, which as a homily may not have been without effect upon the synagogue. The things which had come to his knowledge were not human, but divine. The prophet Elijah had informed him of the accusation of Satan against Israel, that they had transgressed the law and worshipped idols. In consequence of which, judgment was decreed. But the prophet Elijah called upon the patriarchs to come to the rescue, and Moses had advised, that inasmuch as judgment had not yet actually gone forth, it was yet time for Israel to repent of their sins;

and if they did so, the sentence of condemnation would be
revoked. Elijah came to make this known to Mordecai. It
is clear that exegesis does not gain anything by the contribution of this legend. Mordecai did not need that Elijah
should come and instruct him in the duty of repentance and
supplication, when the whole existence of Israel was called
in question.

"*Mordecai rent his clothes, and put on sackcloth with
ashes.*"

What Mordecai did was a sign of personal as well as of
public mourning. When Jacob heard of the supposed death
of Joseph, we read that "he rent his garments and put on
sackcloth" (Gen. xxxvii. 34). David did the same when
mourning for his sons. But the symbolism out of which
these signs were formed contains thoughts which go beyond
the mere idea of mourning. Achilles mourned in like manner
as the pious of Israel, and there is nothing to prevent us
from assuming that in his display of these external signs of
anguish he recognised the idea of repentance (*Iliad*, xviii. 23).[1]

They only show that the whole ancient Western Asiatic
world anticipated the word of the apostle, "The wages of sin
is death." These external signs of mourning are also therefore
public, and so to speak, political and patriotic, because
mourning and repentance flow from the same source. The
custom of throwing earth and ashes upon the head of a corpse
at burial by the bereaved arose also from the idea, that the
mourners had brought vividly to their remembrance their
state of mortality. For dust has the similarity to decomposed
matter. Dust and ashes represent the disfigurement of the
face and of the form of the one buried. Homer says:
"Achilles deformed the lovely countenance (ᾔσχυνε)," and
that in contrast to the washings and the anointings which

[1] With regard to the literature on this subject, see generally the article
of Leyrer in Herzog's *Realencyclop.*, and in respect to the Greek, Pauly's
article in the *Realencyclop. of Antiquities*.

were used for the beautifying of the body. But ointment
upon the head, with its fragrance, was the symbol of life, an
emblem of the fragrant flower; just as the flowing hair upon
the head of a Nazarite was the type of *a portable altar which
the holy man should be*,—and dust or ashes upon the head
was the symbol of the person disfigured by death, and of man
who is destined to die, reminding the mourner that he is
but dust. The rending of the garments and the putting on
of sackcloth were inseparably connected. Together they
expressed the opposite of life and enjoyment. It was considered as a renouncement of the world when the comely
garments were torn asunder, and when the coarse sackcloth
was put on. It was a giving up of the joys of life on
account of death. When one mourned with these external
signs upon him, he indicated thereby that he was mindful of
the transitoriness of all earthly things, and of the insipid
vanities of the world. Plutarch narrates of one whom he calls
superstitious as follows: " He sits outside wrapped up in a sack
or shabby garments, he rolls himself naked in the dust, and
enumerates his sins and delinquencies one by one, that he
has eaten or drunk this or that, that he has gone in a way
which his tutelary spirit forbade him " (Plutarch *On Superstition*). The same did pious Job, who rent his garments, sat
in ashes, his head covered with dust, while his friends sat
in like manner near him. The only difference was, that the
pious and patient sufferer knew what he wanted when
displaying these symptoms of his sorrow. But to Plutarch
and to heathenism these things became unintelligible. However, although gloomy customs like these, as well as those which
were most beautiful, became in time instruments of ungodli-
ness and superstition, yet we cannot fail to recognise that
they originally possessed the inherent thought of repentance,
and for this reason became the pictures of mourning and
death. Albeit among the Syrians and Orientals in general,
they did not call forth true repentance and confession of sin
before God. Ahab did the same as Mordecai, when the

ascetic prophet Elijah declared to him the judgment of God.
"He rent his clothes, and put sackcloth upon his flesh, and
fasted, and lay in sackcloth, and went softly" (1 Kings xxi.
27).   The King of Israel did so in consequence of the
preaching of Elisha (2 Kings vi. 30).   When the pious
King Hezekiah heard the blasphemy of Rabshakeh, "he rent
his clothes, and covered himself with sackcloth, and went into
the house of the Lord" (2 Kings xix. 1).   But the prophet
Joel exclaimed: "Rend your heart and not your garments"
(ii. 13).   For hypocrites and worldly people used to put on
sackcloth in order to appear as prophets.

Mordecai's mourning was not merely a conformity to a
custom, but it was sincere, heartfelt, and true.   And this
mourning was repentance.   The Midrash shows deep insight
into his state of mind when it represents him as a penitent,
first of all for his own personal sins, not casting the guilt
upon others, and then repenting for the sins of his people.

"*And went out into the midst of the city, and cried with
a loud and a bitter cry.*"

These words of the narrator are not without significance
and difficulty.   The whole manner of mourning at that time
could in itself be only intelligible by publicity.   It was to a
certain extent an ecclesiastical custom, bearing the external
and visible signs of instruction and exhortation to the
spectators.   At public calamities mourning was necessarily
a public affair.   "In the streets," exclaims Isaiah, "they gird
themselves with sackcloth ; on their house-tops, in their broad
places, every one howleth, weeping abundantly" (xv. 3).
But Mordecai does not sit down in ashes and sorrow, but
"he goes into the midst of the city."   Yet surely this is not
a Jewish city, it is Shushan, the residence of the Persian
king.   Its inhabitants are the very persons who have the
task entrusted to them of murdering him and all his kindred
on the 13th of Adar.   Why does Mordecai go to them
with the cry of penitence and mourning ?   The LXX. has

sought to explain this by adding a clause, "A people is about to be destroyed which has done no evil." But the added clause is an explanation of the Midrash of that time, and has no exegetical force. In the first place, the penitent garment is unsuitable for making remonstrating reproaches. He was penitent, as the Midrash elsewhere says, because he recognised that his nation had sinned before God, and therefore he could not have said that they had done no evil. In the second place, the lamentable cry to excite the sympathy of the people would have been in vain, for they could not grant it. The king's order precludes all private sympathy, and also self-defence, according to Persian usage. Plutarch narrates, that Teribaz the Persian once successfully defended himself against people who wanted to seize him and carry him off as a prisoner; but when they told him that they came by the command of the king, he at once threw down his sword, and extended his hands to be bound.

The Jewish commentators say that he went into the city in order to make known to the Jews what had happened with regard to them. But they must have known this, as it was everywhere proclaimed. Perhaps he knew it before they did, and indeed he knew more than the proclamation contained. If this be the case, we might expect that the same would be said as occurs in ver. 16, that he gathered together all the Jews that were present in Shushan.

When "he went into the city," it must have been in reference to his mourning and penitent cry. Therefore the opinion of Clericus is very singular, that "Mordecai cried so loud and so bitterly, because he was convinced of the wrong that he had done to Haman in refusing to adore him." In that case Daniel must also have done wrong in resisting the impious commands of the tyrant. It is not the lamentation itself which is striking, but the lamentation, on the way to the city of Shushan, before all the Persians, and as far as the court of the king.

It is interesting to notice the contrast between Mordecai

and the prophet Jonah, of whom it is written, that he went into the city, viz. Nineveh. At that time Jonah was not penitent, but he preached repentance; he did not preach to Jews, but to the heathen of the whole city; and the lowest citizen as well as the king listened to him. Mordecai, on the other hand, was himself a penitent; his appearance was a forcible wail; his voice sounded of judgment to come: but only upon the Jews. The king and the people were struck dumb in perceiving that they were to be the executioners of this judgment. But Mordecai was as good a witness as Jonah. The latter was the witness of God before the heathen; the former, his own witness, in that he declared himself to belong to the people of God in the presence of the heathen. Mordecai belonged to the most prominent men of Israel, for he was descended from the captives who were carried away with King Jechoniah (ii. 6). To these belonged the best class of Israel, as the poor were left behind at home (2 Kings xxiv. 14, 15). Mordecai " sat before the gate of the king." This certainly implied a degree of respectability. Herodotus (iii. 120) informs us that those who sat before the gate of the king were eminent Persians. This is confirmed by what we read in chaps. ii. and iii. He had facilities of detecting the conspiracy, and could maintain himself against the demands of Haman; for it was not entirely unknown that he had saved the king's life (see chap. vi. 2, 3). But among the Jews especially, it was no secret that the foster-child of Mordecai was the queen. How else could she have issued such an order to them as in chap. iv. 15 ? They must have known her when yet in the house of her uncle. How easily, at least in the opinion of the Jews, Mordecai could now save himself! The people are generally inclined to overrate influence at high quarters. If he placed himself under the protection of the queen, who would dare to touch him ? Haman himself would not enforce the law against him, if he knew, what he does not know, that this Mordecai possessed such personal protection. With these thoughts in the minds of the Jews, Haman, as the author of their national misery, would have appeared before them as the only one who could save the life of Mordecai. But Mordecai removed their fears or comforts in this respect by appearing publicly in his mourning dress. He did not remain sitting at the gate of the king but was not ashamed to go forward with ragged garments before all the Persians, and to acknowledge himself as one of that people who were under sentence of death. He went into the city with the cry of repentance and of sorrow, in order to show himself before all others as a fellow-sufferer with his people. In taking part in their national sorrow, he does not want to assume any other position, but he wishes to show that he is ready, if needs be, to share with them the common fate that Providence may have in store for them. This he makes known by his wailing all over the city, that Jews and Persians may be convinced of his earnestness. All heard it; he did not desire to escape the notice of the Persians, and the Jews he wanted to arouse by his example to similar acts of repentance, and to strengthen them in their faith. No other Jew needed to go in this manner into the midst of the city, for no other knew so much of the depth of the misery they were in as he did. He desired that the report should go forth that it is Mordecai himself who goes about in sackcloth and ashes. Not ashamed to be known as belonging to the persecuted people, he went back to the king's gate, but not, of course, to his old place, to which he could not come.

Ver. 2. " *For none might enter within the king's gate clothed with sackcloth.*"

The historical originality of our book could with certainty be established by this casual remark, for it proceeds from the radical idea underlying the Persian religious system. The doctrine of the Old Persians was perfectly dualistic. To the principles of good and evil—the powers of Ahuramazda and Ahriman—corresponded the categories of clean and unclean in the affairs of daily life. That which had any reference to life was considered clean, and that which had reference to suffering and death was considered unclean. Therefore a corpse, with all that appertained to its burial, mourning, and the mourning garments, was unclean. The sacks, or, as we should say, the gloves, which the bearers wore on their hands, were to be buried (see Spiegel, *Avesta*, ii. Introd. xviii.). In the third Fargard of the Vendidad, vers. 36, 37, we read: " What is the most unpleasant thing on earth ? " Ahuramazda answered: " When, O holy Zarathustra, the wife or the son of a holy man goes on the perverted way, covered with dust and dirt, and makes a mourning speech " (Spiegel, *Avesta*, i. p. 80). According to Anquetil, ed. Kleucker, ii. 311, the passage reads : " When a righteous man, a woman, or young person covers the head with dust and goes and comes with weeping and mourning." Now this was naturally only the case among the Parsees, whilst Mordecai conformed to the custom of mourning as practised among his people. But the King of Persia was the visible representative of Ahuramazda ; and therefore what was unclean could not approach his person, his room, or his palace. His house was as the temple of God. No one who, whether in thought or in deed, had participated in the arrangements of a funeral, or was otherwise connected with dead creatures, could enter his apartments. His palace was to a certain degree the seat of the holy fire. Of this it is written in the book Sadder (ed. Hyde, p. 476, n. 80), that " whosoever brings a corpse or anything in connection with it, is said to produce misfortune for himself and others." The castle of the Persian king had an outer and inner court. At the gates of the latter the courtiers, as well as Mordecai, were in the habit of sitting. But when he was clad in sackcloth and ashes, he could only approach the outer court and wail.

Ver. 3. " *Whithersoever the king's commandment . . . came, there was great mourning among the Jews, and fasting, and weeping, and wailing.*"

We read in Deut. iv. 30 : " If thou shalt return to the Lord thy God, for He is a merciful God, He will not fail thee, neither destroy thee, nor forget the covenant of thy fathers, which He sware unto them." Of this promise Israel always thought in distress, and also now. Wherever the deadly edict came, there they remembered that God alone was their last resort for help and deliverance. In times of terror and persecution, Israel, when repenting and turning to God, experienced the preciousness of His word. Where else was there at that time a people upon earth who possessed a similar source of comfort in such an hour of distress ? What would the descendants of the Milesian Branchides have done if they had received a similar communication that they were to be totally destroyed ? (Curt. vii. 5. 51). They would have appealed trembling for pity, with ropes upon their necks and naked ; for so used the inhabitants of besieged cities in the Middle Ages to supplicate the besiegers. But the Jews have no thought of this, they do not put their trust in human artifices, they turn to the Lord their God, who commanded them to apply to Him, but with a penitent heart, in the time of their need ; their whole history is but a chain of mercy from their Lord in heaven. They do not appeal to the king at Shushan, but to the Judge of all flesh. They come with penitence, prayer, and lamentation. They appoint days of humiliation for all the congregations. The manner of their mourning is the old-fashioned one. The traditional customs were observed, which only require a new heart and a lively faith to become new also. They consist of fasting, weeping, and wailing (*zom, bechi, misped*). The prophet Joel when preaching to Israel on repentance and conversion said in the name of God : " Turn ye unto me with all your heart, and with fasting, and with weeping, and with mourning" (*zom, bechi, misped*), ii. 12. In the war in which all the tribes were engaged against the tribe of Benjamin, they could not obtain the victory until they repented with fasting and weeping (see Judg. xx. 26, and my Comm.) At the commencement of the time of the Judges,

when Israel received a message from an angel or messenger of
God who reminded them of their history, they wept, and the
place was called Bochim—" weepers " (Judg. ii. 5).   To
mourning belonged—apart from fasting and weeping, when
it was especially on account of the dead, and on account of
national sin—the dirge or lamentation, the מספד, from ספד,
" to lament."   Most of the expressions for the signs of mourning are borrowed from observations of the conditions of
nature.   Thus אבל, " to mourn," is borrowed from the fading
and drooping condition of a plant, and generally expresses the
mourning condition of man.   One can notice it in his bearing ;
if he is humbled and crushed down, then he is an אבל, " a
mourner."   Therefore Isaiah speaks of " those that mourn
in Zion " (lxi. 3).   They are such as deplore the lamentable
condition of the kingdom of God, not merely by putting on
black garments, but by being contrite in heart (comp. my *Irene*,
p. 17).   As בכה, *bacha*, " to weep," surely arises from the
observation of the drops of tears flowing from the eyes, so that
it was taken as akin to the Greek πηγή, " spring," and the
German *Bach*, " brook," so also ought the grammarians to
have long ago accentuated the kinship between the Hebrew
ספד and the Greek σφαδάζω.   For among Oriental and other
nations, excited movements of the body, and striking upon the
breast, are generally tokens of mourning.   As an animal kicks
about when it is pricked and wounded, so does the uncultured
man when he feels inward pain.[1]   So is the Greek πένθος,
" wailing," to be explained by πάθος, passion ; and so also
κόπτεσθαι has the double signification of " striking " and
"mourning;" so is *plangere* originally synonymous with *tundere*.

But the Scripture uses the word ספד only in its secondary
meaning.   It is the solemn mourning for the dead which used
to accompany weeping.   Of Abraham we read that " he
came to *mourn* for Sarah and to weep for her " (Gen. xxiii. 2).
The prophet Ezekiel announces to Israel that they will be in

[1] Of the horse, which on account of its pain threw down Cyrus,
Xenophon says : "σφαδάζων ἀποσείεται τὸν Κῦρον" (*Cyrop.* viii. 1. 37).

such an extreme state of terror and of stupefaction that they will neither be able to mourn nor to weep (xxiv. 16). In the word ספד was not expressed the unarticulated sobbing and sighing, but the spoken lamentation. In Jer. iv. 8 we read: "For this gird you with sackcloth, lament and howl" (הילילו). The substance of such lamentation we hear in 1 Kings xiii. 30, where it resounds at the grave of the old prophets: "Alas, my brother!" or as we read in Jer. xxii. 18: "They shall not lament for him, Ah my brother! or, Ah sister! they shall not lament for him, Ah Lord! or, Ah His glory!"

In later times the Jews called those who held such funeral orations or sermons by the name of *Saphdanim* (ספדנים), who it has been thought are the persons to whom Job alludes in chap. iii. 8, when he says: "Let them curse it that curse the day." Excessive lamentation for the dead was inseparably connected with excessive praise of them. Therefore in Berechoth 62a, it is strictly inculcated that the funeral orators will have to give an account for making a great ostentation. Among the public rites in connection with mourning, the *misped*, or "dirge," or "oration," was after all the most insignificant part. Hence the index of the fast days which we have under the name of Megillath Taanith, from the time of the destruction of the temple, constantly reminds us that lamentations must not be made. That is, that the fast days should be observed with sackcloth, ashes, and weeping, but without that additional and non-essential *misped*.[1]

"*In sackcloth and ashes also the most prominent wrapped themselves up.*"

The Hebrew שק ואפר יצע לרבים cannot otherwise be understood. It is not merely *multi*, "many," by which לרבים has been translated since the time of Jerome, as in the second Targum.

---

[1] [This only refers to certain weeks in which a feast occurred. The prescribed ceremony for fasting is: the ark is to be carried into the street, ashes to be placed upon the heads of every one, and the eldest is to deliver an exhortation (Taanith, i. 15a).—TRANS.]

Only the first Targumist perceived that in this supplementary word there is something more expressed. When, namely, it is said before, that wherever the sad news came, there was great mourning among the Jews, it would have been superfluous to add that many sat in sackcloth and ashes. No, the word " *rabim* " must have the same sense as in Job xxxv. 9, " prominent," " rich," " mighty." As in Isa. liii. 12 it is predicted of the Messiah, that He will have the *rabim*, the " great people," for His portion or booty, and not merely the poor and the needy, so the same word marks the contrast here. The great and rich men of Israel also did not disdain to put on sackcloth and ashes, which with them was really a sign of sincere repentance. A similar contrast is found in Isa. xv. 4, where judgment against Moab is announced. The armed men of Moab (who are not usually tender-hearted) cry aloud : " His soul trembleth within him " (see Delitzsch, *Comm.* p. 205). This explanation agrees with what was said before of Mordecai. No one shirked the duty and the need of repentance.

There were many in Israel who in spite of their exile had amassed riches and lived in pleasure, and were eminent, like Mordecai ; but none of them despised the external signs of repentance and conversion towards God. The " *rabim* " forsook their luxurious ottomans and couches, and laid themselves down (יצע) upon beds of sackcloth and ashes, as Job did. This expression, as well as the custom itself, passed into the asceticism of the Church. So we read, *e.g.*, of the clergy in the *Consuetudines* of the monks of Clugny : "Cineres, qui in capite jejunii fratrum, olim pœnitentium hodie fidelium omnium capitibus imponuntur . . . benedicti conservantur ab Infirmario, ut Morientibus fratribus cum cilicio substernantur " (comp. Du Cange).

It is just the complete penitence to which the Jews gave themselves up, just their reliance upon the mercy of God, and the committing of themselves into the hands of their heavenly Judge, which explains the insertion of ver. 3 to connect the preceding and the following verse. Ver. 4 begins the history of the deliverance from the distress. Their first human support was, that Esther had received the news of what had been decided by Haman with regard to the nation. This was occasioned by Mordecai's appearing before the court of the king in sackcloth and ashes, so that he attracted the notice of the people of the palace. One would have expected the narrator to report without interruption : " And Mordecai came before the king's gate in sackcloth and ashes ; and then the maidens came and told it to Esther." But as this is not done, it shows the profound thought which pervades the report, in spite of its brevity. For if the insertion had not been made, it would have appeared as if the deliverance of the Jews was entirely ascribed to the fact that Esther was the queen, and to nothing else. But in Israel is manifested that when a people is to be saved, it can only be through repentance before God. When this has taken place, then natural and human assistance comes as a matter of course. For this reason Israel's universal humiliation and repentance is first narrated, and then the history begins with the human deliverance, in which Esther was the chief instrumentality.

Ver. 4. " *And Esther's maidens and her chamberlains came and told it her.*"

They have not told her of the edict against the Jews ; of this she only heard afterwards, vers. 5 and 6. In the house of the women, which was secluded and perfectly inaccessible, nothing was as yet known of the State edict. As the queen had no share in the affairs of government, nor could even have an interview with the king without an especial summons (ver. 11), what did the activity of the grand vizier concern the harem ? Perhaps the report of his doings would have penetrated the secluded house ere this, if the origin of Esther had been known at court. But why is it said " her maidens and her chamberlains told her " ?

The context leads us to guess the reason for the twofold notice. Esther had constant intercourse with Mordecai, otherwise the discovery of the conspiracy (chap. ii. 22) would not have been possible. Besides, Mordecai used to sit before the gate of the king, that he might learn how Esther fared. This intercourse made him an object of notice to the servants of the queen, and it is natural when they missed him in his usual seat at the gate of the court, that they should come and tell it to their mistress as something very strange. But when the maidens said that they did not see Mordecai within the court, because it was unusual for them to leave the house, then the *Sarisim, i.e.* the eunuch chamberlains, most likely added that he was seen sitting in the open space before the gate in a most lamentable condition, clothed in sackcloth and ashes. The more such a mourning dress was against the spirit of the Persian law, the more astonishment would he occasion in the eyes of the courtiers. Indeed, it was owing to this circumstance that the sentinel did not let him pass within the court.

But when the maidens and the chamberlains brought this report to Esther,—

> "*Then the queen was exceedingly grieved; and she sent raiment to Mordecai.*"

The formation of the word לחלחתתל, from חול, portrays by its reduplicate sound the terror which this news caused to Esther. But what was it that made her so afraid? As she was unaware of the political ground of her uncle's sorrow, she must have thought of some other, *e.g.* that a dear relation of his had died, for whom he was in mourning. But this also could not have been the only ground of her dismay; for it would not explain why she sent him raiment. If that were the case, why should she interfere with his conforming to a Jewish custom of long standing? However, her sending him raiment was not a compliance with a Jewish, but with a Persian custom; and this notice also is a remarkable testimony to the original source of our book in Persian life. The modern Persian liturgy has still the following rubric: "When a person dies, the relations, especially the nearest, have to care for his soul. Among the rites that are to be performed belongs an outfit of garments. For new garments must be given which, at least in modern times, become the property of the ministering priest, who puts on the first in the third night after the death of the person, the second on the third day, the third six months afterwards, and finally the fourth on the anniversary of the death" (Spiegel, *Avesta*, ii. p. xli.). In the Persian Canon Sadder (chap. lxiv., ed. Hyde (ed. 1700), p. 467) we read: "The more magnificent the garments shall be, the more honour thou shalt have. Without garments there will be shame before the heavenly assembly." There is no doubt that we find traces of this custom in the Judaism of a later age. A legend which the book מעשה contains, reports of a certain Rabbi Ponim to whom the spirit of one departed appeared, saying, that it came from Paradise, and requested him to mend the torn sleeves. For it was ashamed to walk in Paradise in a ragged garment, chap. 213 (comp. Eisenmenger, ii. 212).

Now the above throws light upon the act of Esther. The Jews in Persia, especially those who like herself moved in Persian society, had to a great extent embraced the notions and customs of the Persians. So thinking him to be a mourner for a relative, she sent him the new raiment as a filial duty, and that he might be able to resume his intercourse with her. And this also explains why she was so horrified when she heard of his appearance as a mourner, because she knew that as such he was considered by the Persian law unclean, and therefore must not come near the palace. But in her great love to Mordecai, and sympathy with his sorrow, she involuntarily removes the veil of mystery that was hitherto hanging over her origin before the eyes of her household. She sends him garments, which is just what only relations do to mourners. "How is it," must the messengers or those who saw it have asked, "that the queen sends garments to the mourning Jew?" Nevertheless the mystery was not yet disclosed, for the hour of redemption had not yet come. Her origin still remained an obscure puzzle to her

companions, and a holy secret between her and her uncle.
But we see in this again a clear proof of the truth, that it is
love which becomes the instrument and occasion of succour
in every distress. Mordecai refused to accept the garments.
He did not wear them for a dead person, but in penitent sorrow
for a people who were doomed to die. He did not put them
on, but he said nothing. He did not wish to betray the
secret to the messengers. If he had desired to say something
to her, he could not have refrained from making allusion to
her nation. But this he could not do without being sure whether
he might trust the messengers. With her, love had broken
through the bounds of caution ; while he, in wisely sending
back the garments, gave her an intimation that the ground of
his being in deep mourning was another and more appalling
one than the loss of a friend. He led her, in fact, to conclude that some great danger had befallen, or was threatening,
all her kindred, otherwise he would not so promptly send back
the sympathetic gift of his beloved niece, which was the only
possible means of continuing his intercourse with her.

Ver. 5. " *Then called Esther for Hathach, one of the king's
chamberlains, whom he had appointed to attend upon her.*"

Esther, ever since she became queen, had not diminished
her love and respect for her uncle. Her heart had not
become proud, and she did not look down haughtily from
her high position upon her relations. How much her heart
beat for Mordecai may be seen from the terror which seized
her when she heard that he was in mourning ; still more so
from the decision she came to when he had returned the new
garments. The sending of these was indeed already fraught
with danger with regard to the secret of her pedigree, but it
was done on the spur of the moment ; and now she increasingly
hazards her secret, deliberately and consciously, out of the anxiety
that she has for her friend. The word וַתְּצַוֵּהוּ, " she charged him,"
is emphatic; the chamberlain is strictly charged to obtain information from Mordecai of what has occurred, and to bring it

straight to the queen, no matter what it might be. Her anxiety was too great to allow her to dread lest the chamberlain might possibly through this obtain the clue to her greatest secret.

Ancient Jewish interpreters have understood Hathach to have been Daniel. But the sense they meant to convey by this explanation was, that they thought Hathach was a Jew, and therefore Esther sent him on such a confidential errand. But this conjecture is not only unnecessary, but also contradicts the context of the narrative. True, one might think that she would have preferred to choose a Jew, if he were at hand, for the discharge of this important and delicate business; but this man was the chamberlain whom the king had appointed to attend upon her. Had she had a Jew near her who knew what was going on, she would have been informed of it long ago. He would have been known to Mordecai, who would have transmitted the sad news to her at the very first opportunity. Under the supposition of the messenger being a Jew, the psychological fact of her anxiety to learn the grounds of Mordecai's sorrow, joined with her fear lest her secret should leak out, would remain in inexplicable obscurity. Hathach was a eunuch; as such he was appointed chamberlain of the queen, and therefore a proper person for her to send on a confidential errand. The termination of the name Hathach reminds us of the same termination in Mordecai's name (Mordach) as Artachaeus, Artachaies (see above), it may be supposed that it is in Greek Otaches, like Otanes and Otaspes. The etymological explanation may perhaps illustrate it from the Zend. *pazend, jatan,* Huzvaresh, יאת,[1] as *nomen dei* (comp. Ized). The eunuchs were generally more faithful to their mistresses than other servants.

Phaedyme also, the wife of Cambyses, and then of pseudo-Smerdes, must have had a reliable servant in order to transmit the dangerous message to her father (Herod. iii. 68). It is touching to read of the fidelity of the eunuch Tyriotes which he displayed towards his mistress, the wife of Darius Codo-

[1] See Vullers, *Lex. Pers.* ii. 1542. [Buhlen compares ﺱﺝ merely.—Tr.]

mannus, even after her death, and this at the hazard of his
life (Curtius, iv. 28).

Ver. 6. "*So Hathach went forth.*"

He went, that is to say, from the palace and its enclosed
walls into the open space where Mordecai now sat, and
told him of the order of Esther. Consequently, Mordecai
understood that Esther had full confidence in her messenger,
and so he communicated to him everything. Mordecai's
message in return was surely not without danger, for it contained an accusation against the powerful Haman. It revealed Esther's Jewish origin, and it demanded from the queen
something which might seriously affect her. He let her know
through the messenger all that "had happened" (קרהו); he
did not conceal from her the fact of his refusal to bow before
Haman (for this can only be meant by the word "happened,"
because it is connected with the sum of money which Haman
offered to the king), and that his conduct had provoked the
wrath of the vizier. It was necessary that Esther should be
informed of everything, in order that in case of need she
should be able to expose the trifling and mean motives
which induced Haman to persecute the Jews. What Mordecai did at the time was surely with a good conscience.
It at all events served to bring the issue clearly before
Esther, for the sake of whom he was sitting at the gate, and
brought upon himself great danger. The queen must have
been touched by observing that Mordecai had remained
stedfast in his fidelity to God and in his love to her, and
that he did not swerve either from the one or from the other.
He did not bow before the idols, but he also did not desert
the gate of the king. How mean must Haman appear in
the eyes of the king, when Esther would be in a position to
tell him that he rewards the piety and faithfulness of such
a man by alluring the king to issue such a terrible edict
of persecution against a whole innocent nation, and that,
forsooth, because his vanity had been offended! Mordecai

was well informed; the transaction of Haman with the king
was not unknown; yes, even the exact sum which the subtle
and clever vizier offered was known. We read that Mordecai
stated to Esther "the exact sum of the money (פרשת הכסף)[1]
that Haman had said (אמר) he would pay to the king's
treasuries;" in reality he did not pay it, as the king made him
a present of it. But he is not satisfied with a mere verbal
communication; he sends her the document of the royal
proclamation, in order that she should see that the information is not founded upon mere hearsay reports, but upon
written evidence, and be convinced of the fearful condition of
the Jews in the country. But he does not stop with his
simple narrative. He joins to it a request. When Esther
through her chamberlain astonished him with the present of the
garments, and had made anxious inquiries as to the causes of
his mourning, he at once saw that she was inclined gradually
to make known her origin. At any rate, he believed that he
had the right to set her free from the pledge of secrecy which
he himself had imposed upon her (ii. 20). Her inquiry had
not arisen from mere curiosity, and he gives his report also
not for its own sake. He tells Hathach "to disclose it"
unto her, and "to charge her" (להגיד ולצוות) he should tell her
that it is her uncle's and her benefactor's request, and command,
that she should make use of her royal prerogative, and seek an
interview with the king to obtain help from him. She had
"charged him" to let her know what had happened, and so
he now "charges" her to obtain succour. She did so as his
queen, and he does so as her uncle. "She should go in unto
the king and make supplication unto him, and make request

[1] The word occurs again in chap. x. 2. It must not be compared with
parshegan, as in this evidently Persian word *par* is only the preposition.
But it clearly belongs to the Heb. *parash*, to be distinct, which meaning
may suffice both passages. For both contain the idea of greatness, height,
and expansion. In the above, Mordecai communicates the highest sum, as
we would say. Chap. x. 10 speaks of the expansion of the greatness which
Mordecai had obtained. *Parash* means originally "to spread," "to unfold,"
and so it came to be used in the sense of "explaining" and "illustrating."

before him for her people." Such weeping and supplication
for grace before the king was not an unusual thing; the wife
of Intaphernes, Herodotus narrates (iii. 119), went with weeping and wailing before the gate of the king (like Mordecai),
until Darius was moved with compassion and granted her at
least some favour. From the beloved queen Mordecai could
especially demand that she should do this for the sake of her
people. It would not have been extraordinary that a queen
should intercede in behalf of the sad lot which had befallen
a strange people; how much more reason was there that she
should do this for her own, especially as Ahhashverosh did
not even know that she belonged to the condemned nation,
and perhaps did not even remember the name of the people
whom he had so rashly appointed to die.

Ver. 11. "*All the king's servants and the people of the
king's provinces do know.*"

Esther is frightened at the request of Mordecai, but she
does not decline to comply with it. It corresponds with her
feeling in the matter, though her feminine weakness makes
her hesitate and shudder at taking the step, that she declares
that she would gladly do it if she could. She would obey
his order to go to the king, but he ought to know that
this is no easy thing to do. It does not depend upon her
to speak to the king when she wants. His own wives
can see him only when they are specially called, and her
influence over him is not yet paramount, as thirty days had
elapsed during which he did not even think of her. And
should she even dare to go to him uncalled, and should he
be so benign as to receive her when he is sitting upon the
throne, she could yet not address him unless he held out
the golden sceptre to her, and beckoned her to approach
nearer. She does not actually decline her uncle's request;
she does not say that when the king summons her she would
not petition him for mercy to the Jews; but she evades and
postpones it, and makes it dependent upon the whim of the

king. In fact, the court regulations were so as Esther said. It is well known, as Herodotus narrates, that at the fall of the false Smerdis the only persons who could obtain admission to Darius without being called were his six companions. But this oft-quoted passage is not enough to explain fully the words of Esther. The majesty of the great Persian king was not only inaccessible without his permission, but also no one dared to speak to him without his beckoning on them to approach. For he was the human representative of Ahuramazda. That Alexander the Great imitated the manners of the Persian king we have proofs in many descriptions. Phylarchus in Athenaeus (p. 539, comp. *Fragm.* ed. Lucht, p. 100, ed. Brückner, p. 36) says, that while Alexander sat on the throne, "no one of his great friends and servants dared to approach him." Ephippus in his description says: "As he sat with majestic look, there was a solemn silence before him." This was the Oriental idea of solemnity and awe with which the august majesty of a king is surrounded.

When an English Embassy was received by Shah Abbas of Persia, we read: "They entered into the audience chamber, where the first officials sat round the walls like statues, not moving a muscle, and dead silence prevailed." No one, even at the present time, approaches the King of Persia without the repeated order from the king to do so. Fraser reports that a courtier, who had made his fortune, when he was asked to come near, answered, "I do not pray to be commanded to approach (*mí souzum*), I burn to do so."[1] Herodotus tells of a similar sending of messengers to and from the harem. The daughter of Otanes became first the wife of Cambyses and then of pseudo-Smerdis. Her father sent a messenger to ask her whether her husband was the real Smerdis; she replied through a confidant, that she would make the investigation at the risk of her life, but she must wait until her turn came when she would be called by the king (iii. 60).

Here also there was an understanding between Esther and

[1] Comp. my *Kaiser und Königskronen*, p. 172.

Mordecai with regard to the king, but a friendly one. She was requested by her foster-father to dare to approach the king without his special permission, but it was in order that she should ask for mercy in behalf of an innocent people.

" That whosoever, whether man or woman . . . who is not called, there is one law for him, that he be put to death."

The sense of the peculiar form אחת דתו להמית is that the law makes no exception. אחת (דת, fem.) expresses that the law is absolute and of universal application. Esther wishes to say, that she is subject to the same law, and if she transgresses it, no exception or excuse will be made, although she is queen. For in "the coming to him" (אשר־יבוא) is included the address to him, because she would not come without having to ask him for something. We can see from Dan. ii. 9 that this indicates a standing rule. The King Nebuchadnezzar demands from his courtiers, to give him without fail the interpretation of his dream. "If you are not able," says he, "then there is but one law for you," חדה היא דתכן, *i.e.* "there is but one sentence for you in all circumstances, whatever excuse you may make."

" Except such to whom the king shall hold out the golden sceptre."

The expression שרביט occurs only in the book of Esther; it is the form of the Masora for שרבט, and its relation to שבט is as the Gr. σκῆπτρον to σκήπτω (σκηπτοῦχος). The linguistic comparison teaches thereby that the Hebrew letter ש has indeed the sound of *sh* (as in שלי, σκυλάω, etc.); and the various pronunciations of *shebet* and σκήπτω rests upon similar dialectical differences, as *sch* does in German dialects, which in Low German has completely the sound of *sk*.

The sceptre is said to be golden, just as Homer calls it (ii. 1. 15 ; *Odyss.* xi. 91), where the priests and seers carry it in the name of their gods. The sceptre of Achilles was embossed with gold (ii. 1. 246), as Voss translates, or had

golden nails. Gold was generally the appendage of royal
dignity. Everything belonging to Oriental kings and to
antiquity was ornamented with gold, and was called golden,
as a crown, a throne, a chair, and pillars. In the Middle Ages
they used to speak of "golden Rome" (*aurea Roma*).[1] Wallace
tells of the Burmese, that when they spoke of anything belonging to the king, they qualified it by the word gold, and therefore they spoke of his golden ears and golden feet (*Denkwürd.
Indien*, p. 33 ; comp. my *Kaiser und Königskronen*, p. 127).

The sceptre is the royal staff of authority. Odysseus takes
the royal staff of Agamemnon in order to command silence
and order (*Il.* ii. 185). To whom permission was given
to speak in the assembly, to him the herald handed the
sceptre (*Il.* xxiii. 568 ; *Odyss.* ii. 37). The inclining of the
sceptre forward towards the visitor was the sign of permission
given him to come near. Kings and gods (priests, and in
caricature wizards) work and beckon with the staff. The
form שׁיט for "stretching out," "extending the arm" with the
staff, only occurs in Esther. It may be dialectically compared
with the Lat. *tendo* and the Greek τείνω.

Ver. 12. "*And they told to Mordecai Esther's words.*"
This additional clause is surprising, for it is already said in
ver. 10, "Then Esther spake unto Hathach, and gave him a
message unto Mordecai." But it must be so understood that
Mordecai made inquiries from others with regard to the custom
at the Persian court, and they confirmed Esther's words, that
it was really only at the risk of life that one could appear
before the king unsummoned.

Ver. 13. "*Then Mordecai bade them return answer unto
Esther.*"
Ancient commentators felt it strange that from ver. 13 the

---

[1] [R. Akiba promised his bride ornaments under the term golden Jerusalem, *Nedarim*, p. 50*a*. Perhaps the Hymnologist borrowed from the
Talmud.—TRANS.]

name of the messenger Hathach does no more occur, while it is repeatedly mentioned in vers. 5, 6, 9, and 10. The Midrash has from this circumstance developed a legend, viz. that Haman had killed Hathach because he acted as a messenger of Mordecai. It need hardly be remarked that such violent procedure is in perfect harmony with the spirit that prevailed in Oriental courts; yet we cannot accept the legend, as it is at variance with the true exposition of the passage. We may rather explain that the further omission of the name of the messenger by the narrator, was owing to the fact that he had more important subjects to relate, compared with which what became of Hathach was of no consequence.

" Think not with thyself that thou shalt escape (as) the king's house more than all the Jews."

The answer of Mordecai will appear the grander the more earnestly we consider it. He does not say to her, first of all, " If thou canst not save the people, at least save me, and the house of thy father, for thou belongest to the unassailable house of the king." This would have been natural enough under the circumstances. But we see that with him there is not a moment's consideration of personal interest and safety. He thinks of nothing else but of the salvation of the whole of Israel, and of its providential calling. There can be no question with him about the individual, when the existence of the whole nation is at stake. He does not want to be saved alone, nor to be an exception in the hour of danger. He demands from all his people the duty of holding together, and first of all from Esther herself. For she alone is in a position not only to be saved herself, but also to save others. Therefore it is her bounden duty to be anxious for the salvation of her people, even if she should thereby lose her own life, and become the first victim. Mordecai's words are closely joined with the report of Esther, that it is impossible to come to the king spontaneously without risking one's life. But when going to the king in such a manner includes the possibility of obtaining deliverance, why not run all hazards! What worse thing can be expected? If she is killed in her attempt to save others, then she will die the death of the martyr, as her people *should* die! Of course, Esther is in the house of the king: Haman does not even know that she is a Jewess; and should he know it, he would not dare to enforce the law against her. But this exceptional position is only so far valuable, if she herself will not make an exception. She can make use of it in order to save her people, but it offers no security to her own safety when all Israel are cut down. It is a thing of daily occurrence that a favourite wife should lose her life—as was the case with Vashti. But that a people like Israel, having such promises and hopes in store for them, should be totally destroyed, would indeed be an unheard-of occurrence. If, therefore, Esther should think of using her advantageous position to save herself and her family by separating herself from Israel, the probability is that she herself will be lost, and that they will be saved. Israel's whole history is composed of wonders of salvation. When they were persecuted by Pharaoh, when they were in the wilderness, when they were surrounded by enemies on every side, they were always delivered in an unexpected manner. It is more sure, Mordecai firmly believes, that Israel will in some way or other be delivered out of this trouble, improbable as it may appear, than that Esther should receive security for her own life if she declines to do her duty. We can clearly see that he wants to impress her with two thoughts: first, that Israel was always delivered in an extraordinary manner; secondly, that it was an extraordinary providence which exalted her to the royal throne. "Who knoweth," says he, "whether thou art not come to the kingdom for such a time as this?" *i.e.* whether the one did not happen to secure the other. The answer of Mordecai is a masterpiece of eloquence. He who had loved and cherished Esther as a daughter, seeks now that she should risk her life for the deliverance of Israel. He wills it, because he believes

in the deliverance, because he draws from the history of Israel
the hope that they cannot become extinct, and because he
sees in the wonderful exaltation of Esther the way to the
deliverance. This he puts before her consideration with
all the paternal urgency and authority which he has still
reserved for himself with regard to her. He begins with
destroying every illusion of Esther, that she is in danger
by speaking to the king, and would therefore prefer not to
risk her life ; and he concludes with comforting her that
she shall save her life, just because she will not flee from
the danger. It is not the danger which is of decisive
moment, but the moral aim for which it is sought. He con-
vinces her that escape and silence would be of no avail to
her, but that courage and acknowledgment have hope,—not
for her own sake alone, but for the sake of Israel which has
such a history ; and yet for her own sake, who was formerly a
captive orphan, but is now become queen. His chief design
was to plant in her heart faith in an overruling Providence,
and then she would have nothing to fear.—He was the right
man to do this, because she knew how very much he loved
her. He would not advise her to sacrifice her life needlessly.
Such confidence is necessary in order to have such a faith,
which is superior to human anxieties and precautions. That
Esther was capable of having such faith, is evident from her
former and later conduct.

Of verbal peculiarities in the passage may be mentioned תדמי,
from the Piel דמה, which has completely the sense of imagin-
ing, as from it is derived the word דמות, image (imagio,
imaginari).

Remarkable is the position of להמלט בית־המלך; Mordecai
says: Do not imagine to escape "as[1] house of the king."
Esther might think that even when all the houses of Israel
would be sacked, her royal house would naturally be spared.

---

[1] [So the Rabbis understand the word בית in 1 Sam. vii. 17 as meaning
wife, from which they infer that wherever Samuel was there was also his
wife.—Trans.]

We must not take the words to mean "in the house of the king," the household which she had formed for herself. They stand in contrast to the expression in ver. 14, "Thy father's house." Mordecai thinks that Esther perhaps imagines that as a royal house it would escape, so he says, "But when Israel shall be delivered, then wilt thou and *thy father's* house perish." In seeking to save thyself, those who are with thee in the royal house may perhaps be preserved; but if thou shouldest nevertheless perish, then the house of thy father will be totally destroyed. The fall of male and female favourites in Oriental courts, as we shall see in the case of Haman, brought with it the fall of the head and members of their families. Mordecai wants in this manner to raise her moral courage, by showing her the disgrace which she would bring upon herself when, although Israel would be delivered, she would fall together with her family, himself of course included, although she had not attempted anything for their deliverance. It would be a disgraceful death.

Ver. 14. "*For if thou altogether holdest thy peace.*"
החרש תחרישי. The infinitive represents the continuance of silence, "If thou shouldest altogether be silent, and suppress thy concern in the matter." Esther should speak for her people, whether she is called or not called; she should attempt to fascinate the king by her manner and speech, as she can at other times, and more especially now, when it is a question of life or death to her people. The derivation of the verb " to be silent," from the noun חרש, "dumb," "deaf," has been contested ; yet the idea of Gesenius, who adduces the analogy of dumb, obtuse, of κωφός from κόπτειν, is before all others to be preferred. The verb חרש, to cut, to work in art, is doubtless from the Greek χαράττω. As from this is χάραξ, "stake," "pile," so has הרש come to mean a "blockhead" or "stupid fellow," who cannot open his mouth, as *stipes* and *truncus* in Latin. The biblical colloquial describes by the word חרש, a dumb man, under the notion that he is like a

piece of wood, without life, dull and awkward. That חרש was actually used in the sense of " stake," " pile," is seen from the meaning of חֹרֶשׁ, a " wood," " bush ; " Chald. חורשא ; Samarit. ארשא. The word has the signification of silence also in the Arabic. When חרש has the meaning in Persian of " rough " (*homo impolitus, rudis*), it is only a confirmation of the above given derivation. But Vullers is mistaken when (*Lex. Pers.* i. 675) he wants to join it with חרש, *ursus*, which is from quite a different etymology.

> " *Then shall respite and deliverance arise to the Jews from another place.*"

Mordecai is in full assurance of faith that Israel cannot be so shamefully annihilated. He is quite certain that ways and means will be found for their deliverance. He sees an earnest of this in the wonderful exaltation of Esther. But should she refuse to act, deliverance will come in spite of her. The words רוח והצלה occur only in Esther, and have arisen from the influences of the captivity, *i.e.* they manifest Aramaic forms. רוח is ἀναπνοή, as the Chaldaic Targum uses. The time will come when Israel, as one that has escaped breathless from persecution, will be able to breathe again freely. הצלה is an infinitive substantive of נצל, " the deliverance ; " comp. the Chaldaic להצלה in Dan. iii. 29.

> " *And who knoweth whether thou art not come to the kingdom for such a time as this ?* "

The expression "who knoweth" occurs particularly in Ecclesiastes as an exclamation of despair in not knowing what is to come. But it is quite differently used in this place, where it is an exclamation of certainty in the ways of providence, which man does not know as to detail. Mordecai is not a prophet who can say with certainty that Esther's errand will be successful, but he has faith enough to see in her going to the king—difficult and dangerous as it is—a way of deliverance. He cannot describe the result in detail, but he is sure that it will be an important turning-point in the history of Israel, and that Esther was not raised in vain to occupy such a high position. The exclamation מי יודע, "who knoweth," is here also an exclamation of faith, as in Joel ii. 14 ; Jonah iii. 9 ; Ps. xc. 11. For when the Psalmist says, "Who knoweth the power of Thine anger, and Thy wrath as he should fear it ?" he believes in the anger of God, the mystery of which had only overwhelmed himself. But the words of Mordecai to Esther were not intended to implant despair, but faith, in her heart. For it is faith which ascribes Esther's exaltation solely to a special guidance of providence ; and however adventurous and sublime the demand of her uncle may appear to her, the extraordinary circumstance of her becoming queen should only act as an incitement to duty, and she should be ready to give her life for the salvation of Israel.

Ver. 16. "*Go and gather together all the Jews that are present in Shushan.*"

Esther is ready to act in accordance with Mordecai's request. She certainly had not said too much of the danger which she would have to encounter, but in spite of it she does not resist his demand any longer. She is ready to do everything for her people. It is no common hazard which the woman and the queen undertakes. Clericus was of opinion that Esther only displayed timidity when she thought of the possibility that the king might kill her for venturing to transgress the rules of etiquette. But he overlooked both the awful importance that was connected with etiquette and the feelings of a woman's heart. The coming and going of the women to the Persian king depended entirely on his caprice. This caprice was inexorable law. Vashti had lost her life because she did not come, although she was commanded ; might not the same happen to Esther, who came although she was not commanded ? Be it remembered also what the coming of Esther to the king must imply. It must appear in his eyes as a self-willed request for that for which at other times his lust summoned her. This was then debasing to her feeling. She thought the king would misinterpret her motives and regard her profession of fidelity to her people as the flimsiest pretext.

The wives had to wait till it pleased the king to call them. Therefore she thought that if she came and found him in ill-humour, not only might she lose her life, but also her honour, which is worse. She would be dishonoured among her fellow-women of the harem, who considered it honourable patiently to wait until their turn came.

And did Esther know whether she would, even under the most favourable circumstances, succeed with her petition? What if she did not overcome the influence of Haman, and if the order of massacre were not withdrawn? And if she failed, what then! She would in vain have exposed herself to be misunderstood. She would have lowered her royal dignity. Henceforth, even if her life should be spared, she would be an object of hatred and intrigue. If her desire should not be fulfilled now, she must sooner or later succumb.

It is necessary to judge the deeds of men by the circumstances in which they are placed. Torn asunder from the conditions of life of which they are the outcome, they lose for the most part all significance. In itself the seeking of an interview with the Persian king, who is the husband, is certainly no wonderful thing. But when we review the circumstances under which this was done, then Esther appears to have displayed greater heroic courage than the famous Roman women, who out of patriotism were ready to die ; or of the Pythagorean women, who would rather have their tongues bitten off than be silent. Just because Esther put her throne and life at hazard, without having any prospect of a certain result—therefore she sent Mordecai word : " Gather together all the Jews that are in Shushan." To what place ? Into the synagogue. She says בנוס, gather them into the בית הכנסת, " house of assembly," the Hebrew form for synagogue. What shall they do there ? They should fast for her three days

(צוֹם).[1] Fasting was in the O. T. the symbolic form of prayer, as well as the garment in which the suppliant appeared. It represented the attitude and the disposition under which alone true prayer could take place. The man who is not hungry does not ask for food. Out of a luxurious life does not flow the longing after spiritual things and after God. The body must first be mortified before the soul is full of faith. Fasting has no selfish aim. If it does not by fervent and spontaneous prayer spiritualize the body, it loses its value. The sanctification which it offers to the body must be the vessel of the God-loving soul. If this is not the case, then fasting is absurd. Therefore the prophet blames the fasting of Israel when it is severed from true repentance and love (Isa. lviii.). Jeremiah shows that fasting and prayer are inseparable. "And the Lord said unto me, Pray not for this people for their good (for grace, לְטוֹבָה); when they fast, I will not hear their cry" (xiv. 11, 12).[2] The character of the fasting required by Esther from Mordecai is also given in Neh. i. 4, etc.: "I sat down and wept, and mourned certain days, and I fasted, and prayed before the God of heaven." In the same way is fasting understood in the New Testament. When Jesus tells the disciples the reason why they could not drive out an evil spirit (Matt. xvii. 21), He does so by saying, "This kind goeth not out but by prayer and fasting." Thus He describes the devoted, penitent, and holy disposition by which alone the suppliant may accomplish such a thing. So also does the apostle join together fasting and prayer (νηστείᾳ καὶ προσευχῇ) (1 Cor. vii. 5). The ancient Church laid great stress upon fasting, inasmuch as she found herself surrounded by a society that lived in luxury and extravagance. It was considered as a disciplinary measure, and as a means by which an individual might overcome self. There were not

[1] The word occurs for the first time in the O. T. in Judg. xx. 26. Concerning its etymological connections, see my *Comm. on Judg.* p. 176.

[2] Jerome says on this passage (ed. Migne, iv. 771, 941): "Jejunia et preces et victimae et holocausta tunc proficiunt cum recedimus a vitiis flemus antiqua peccata."

wanting in those days men who in the spirit of the prophets spoke against the abuses of fasting. Augustine comments upon the above passage of the apostle thus : " Christians may say, ' Let us fast and pray and give, for to-morrow we die.' But of the two sentences, I prefer that they should say, ' Let us give and pray,' instead of the other, ' Let us fast and not give.'" Far be it from the thought that the apostle considered the highest good, *i.e.* salvation, to consist in the exercise of the bodily powers of man.[1] Similar words Augustine uses in another place, quoted by Suicer from Severian : " Fasting has two wings, prayer and almsgiving, without which it cannot move." Again in his commentary : " Wilt thou that thy prayer should fly to God, give it two wings—prayer and almsgiving."[2] In his letter to Casulanus, Augustine writes, " I, at all events, find in the writings of the apostles and evangelists, and in the whole document which is called the N. T., that fasting is prescribed ; but on which days to fast and on which not, I do not find. Therefore it is the business of the ministers of the Church to arrange these according to necessity and usefulness."[3] What is said with certainty is, that to prayer belongs a spirit of fasting. By the appointing of certain fast-days, the dignity both of fasting and of prayer is lowered. Discipline of the body, moderation in eating and drinking, the crucifying of one's lusts and propensities, is the daily fasting which is necessary, and without which the Lord's Prayer cannot be repeated. It does not matter whether one eats meat or fish on this or on that day, or begins to satisfy his old appetite for eating in this or in that hour. This is [only] work and external appearance, and does not increase the strength of life in and prayer to God. Esther wants three days to be devoted to true repentance, earnest

---

[1] Oratio 151, cap. 6 (*Opp.* ed. Migne, v. 1. 812).

[2] On Ps. xlii. cap. 8 (*Opp.* ed. Migne, iv. 1. 82).

[3] Ep. 36, cap. 11 ; but the last sentence : " Itaque ad Ecclesiae pastores id spectat pro necessitate vel utilitate ecclesiae decernere," I find in the quotations of older editions (cf. Beyerlinck, *theatr. vitae humanae,* iv. 300), but not in the ed. Migne, *Opp.* ii. p. 147.

prayer, and intercession on her behalf before God, and says that she will do the same in her palace with her servants. One might have thought it would have been enough if she had done so herself, but in her humility she has no confidence that her prayer alone will bring the desired answer. Besides, it is not her own, but the people's affair; the people fast and pray for themselves when they do so for her. She appoints the duration of the fast to be three days, night[1] and day, in which nothing should be eaten or drunk. Of such long fasts, the life of the synagogue affords no other examples; but it is correct to begin to reckon the commencement of the fast with the evening of the first day, as is the case with the Day of Atonement. It did not, however, conclude, like the Day of Atonement, after twenty-four hours had elapsed, but continued till the end of the third day. It lasted then about forty hours, and ended when Esther went to the king, as it is believed, on the third day. The space of time would then be like that in which "the bridegroom is removed from the disciples" (Matt. ix. 15), viz. from the crucifixion to the resurrection, therefore the ancient Church had a fast of forty hours, strictly speaking, and afterwards forty days. This is undoubtedly the passage of Irenaeus, as Bingham proves (*Opp.* ix. p. 180), for the remark about counting together hours of the day and hours of the night will only then have a meaning if we place a comma after ὥρας. It appears that recent Roman Catholic writers have also maintained that there was no distinction between the forty hours' and the forty days' fast.[2] When we remember that the number forty

---

[1] We read, "Three days, night and day." The word night standing before day, shows that the fast commenced with the night. [It was an established custom among the Jews, both in biblical and post-biblical times, to regard a part of a day as a day.—TRANS.]

[2] Prayers of forty hours' duration have been appointed in the Roman Catholic Church since the sixteenth century. There was a fraternity who devoted forty hours to prayer in memory of the death of Christ. The Pope ratified this rule in 1560. On account of ecclesiastical abuses, especially in France, Clement VIII. appointed such a period of prayer for all churches in 1592.

was already in the Old Covenant a number used in reference
to repentance, judgment, and expectation, as in the flood, in
the sojourn of Israel in the wilderness, and in connection with
Elijah, etc., we can see the reason why Esther's fast should
last exactly forty hours. Curiously enough, the Midrash
places the command of Esther to fast in the time of the
Passover (p. 94, etc.).

Esther has by this long fast imposed no slight task upon
herself and upon the people; but she sees in this the only
hope. She knows the danger of her action. "I will go unto
the king," she says, "which is not according to the law"
(אשר לא־כדת). This דת, "law," is like the law of God. It is
inviolable; death is the wages of its transgression. If men
in general, if Israel in particular, had in like manner feared
to transgress the laws of God, their peace would have been
more lasting. But, at all events, the punishment of the
transgressor by the Persian king was sure and unmerciful;
but our God is full of mercy and love in all His judgments.

"So let it be!" she exclaims, "I will do what lies in me.
Do you your part, fast and pray. And if I perish, I perish
as the victim of obedience and love (כאשר אבדתי אבדתי)." The
whole force of these thoughts lies in the repetition of the
verb. She gives by this expression free vent to her pent-up
feelings of misery and woe, and to her determination, whatever may come, to submit to the will of God. We have a
similar passage in Gen. xliii. 14, where Jacob, after having
refused for a long time to let Benjamin accompany his
brethren to Egypt, at last, being pressed by a higher law of
love and duty, quietly consents to his going, and exclaims,
כאשר שכלתי שכלתי, "And if I be bereaved of my children,
I am bereaved." Neither exclamation contains an expression of indifference or of despair, as Ewald maintains
(*Hebr. Gram.* 8th ed. p. 865). Therefore the translation of
Arnheim in Zunz's Bible, "I am anyhow lost," is entirely
false.

Ver. 17. "*So Mordecai went his way.*" ויעבור.

The translations hitherto given have not hit upon the sense. If the word meant merely "*abiit*," "he went away," or as Arnheim translates, "he went about," it, having a definite and well-known meaning, would not have been chosen to express this idea. We must not depart from its sense of passing over. We have in it, when *locally* spoken of, a local portraiture. Therefore those Jewish interpreters who understood by it, transgression of a law, still retain its proper meaning. It is maintained in the Talmud that Esther's three days' fast began two days before the Passover, and included the first day; and this is incorrectly thought to be proved by chap. iii. 12. Consequently, it is asserted that Mordecai transgressed the law of the Passover (Rab. in Bab. Megilla 15*a*; Midrash Esther 94, etc.). No other view is found in the first Targum. For the words ונכסם ובנם, "sad and excited," are not the translation of ויעבור, as Levy (*Chald. Lex.* ii. 116) supposes, inasmuch as they are immediately followed by ויעבר; but they merely mean to say that Mordecai was very sad to be obliged to transgress the joy of the feast (חדות חנא). How can Levy ascribe to the Targumist the derivation of the word "anger" from עבר? Another explanation of the Midrash likewise testifies that the word is to be understood in the sense of passing over or transgressing. According to which, Mordecai was displeased with Esther for profaning the feast; but after being better instructed by her on the subject, ויעבר, "he transgressed" his words,[1] *i.e.* in the dialect of the Talmud, he withdrew his words. It is impossible that this word should have been chosen without a purpose, and R. Samuel (Megilla 15*a*) felt this, and explained that Mordecai passed over the other side of a lake or river. Samuel, who himself lived on the other side of the Euphrates, is for this a good authority. The castle of Shushan was situated near the river Ulai, as we know from

---

[1] Sefer Meg. Esther, "Er überfürct seine Red." [This verb is used in the sense of transgressing in Hos. vi. 7. In Micah vii. 18 it means "passing by transgressions."—TRANS.]

Dan. viii. 2.   The royal castle was the real Shushan, and it is of this that the ancient writers speak when they describe the city as situated near the Eulaeus or Choaspes (Herod. vii. 7 ; Curtius v. 1 and 2, etc.).   Mordecai was in the royal fortified town, and transacted his business with Esther before the chief gate.   The Jews resided in another part of the city. When he wanted to go to them to gather them together, he had to cross the water to come to the Jewish quarter. Benjamin of Tudela in the Middle Ages still described Susa as lying on both sides of the river, and connected by a bridge across it.   So then we see that the word ויעבור has a local and graphic meaning, and we cannot have a better testimony for the topographical knowledge of the narrator than we have in this word.   In עבר is contained the idea of passing by or passing over.   But Mordecai did not pass by, but he passed over the river, like Abraham and Nehemiah,—certainly not the Euphrates, but the Ulai, into the capital of the captivity, —not to rejoice before God with thanksgiving, but to pray to Him in deep sorrow and in earnest repentance.

CHAPTER V

Ver. 1. "*Now it came to pass on the third day.*"

The emphasis which the narrator puts on this date seems to indicate that he had the thought in his mind, that the third day in Holy Scripture marks important facts in connection with the kingdom of God. A pious Jewish narrator chose on this occasion this formula in remembrance of the third day on which God gave the law to Moses in the midst of thunder and lightning (Ex. xix. 16). This third day was the beginning of a new life for exiled Israel. Out of the darkness of death the sun arose in his brilliancy. What God, through the prophet, said to Hezekiah (2 Kings xx. 5): "I have heard thy prayer, I have seen thy tears; behold, I will heal thee: on the *third day* thou shalt go up unto the house of the Lord," had also happened here. After two days of weeping came deliverance. The prophet Hosea says: "After two days will He revive us; on the third day He will raise us up, and we shall live before Him" (vi. 2). It was on the third day after the day of suffering that Christ rose from the dead, to raise others too. It appears as if the Midrash was thinking of these parallels, when it ascribes to Esther as having cried out in the moment of her great anxiety and anguish of soul, when she had to appear before the king, "My God, my God, why hast Thou forsaken me?" (Ps. xxii. 1). She repeated the very words which were understood by the Jews as referring to the Messiah, and according to Christian interpretation, which had their complete Messianic realization when they fell from the lips of Jesus on the cross.

"*That Esther put on her royal apparel.*"

וַתִּלְבַּשׁ מַלְכוּת, "she put on royalty," is a form of expression

chosen with great precision, and means more than "she put
on royal apparel." She appeared before the king in the full
array and attitude of the queen. She wore the crown which
he himself had placed on her head (ii. 17). The whole κόσμος
βασιλικός is meant, of which Diodorus relates, that Alexander had placed it again on the head of the Persian queen
(*Bibl.* xvii. 38). The additions in Josephus and in the Greek
Apocrypha bear already the Midrash character. The queen
came to the king.

"*And stood in the inner court.*" הפנימית.

Fürst is of opinion that if פנים should be connected with
פָּנִים, the sense would be opposite, viz. "face to face" with
Ahhashverosh. But this is not even the case with ἐνώπια,
"the face," expressing the inner walls of the chamber, and
means just the opposite of προνώπια, which signifies the
external side. The use of the word face in Hebrew, as well
as in Greek, comes from the covering of the face; the veil
being considered as the door to the face. When the veil is
opened, the inner part of the face becomes visible.

Ver. 2. "*So Esther drew near and touched the top of the
sceptre.*"

When the king saw her standing, she gained favour in his
sight; he was not angry with her because she came without
being called, as she feared would be the case. She found him
in good humour. When Bathsheba came to King Solomon,
her son, he rose up to meet her, bowed himself unto her, then
sat down on his throne, and seated her on his right hand
(1 Kings ii. 19). Of course, Ahhashverosh did not receive Esther
with the same politeness. Yet the report of Plutarch (in his
treatise about the badly instructed prince) is correct, that the
Persian kings did not treat their wives like slaves. And
Esther wore the crown upon her head; and she did not
prostrate herself at his feet, as others were obliged to do, but
he saw her standing (עומדת), and he beckoned to her with the

sceptre, as one beckons with the hand, as a sign of salutation and of invitation to come near.[1] The poet Zachariä uses the imagery of night as a queen, "Lo, the solitary night beckons with the leaden sceptre " (*Adelung Lex.* iv. 1563).

It is worthy of remark, that by touching the sceptre she intimated that she had a petition to the king. The sceptre represented royal power; this she touched, because she needed it very much. Nothing more was certainly expressed by the touch; for with the King of Persia, everything that was to be obtained by petition, be it the smallest trifle or the life of a whole nation, was considered as a grant of grace. Amongst the Jews of old the custom was, that a petitioner who desired the grant of a great favour from any one, fell down before him and took hold of his feet, as the woman did to whom Elijah restored the child alive. This was a sign of humility, in the same manner as touching the knees. Pliny says, " The knees of man contain a certain amount of sacredness in them, according to usage of nations. The petitioners touch them; they stretch out their hands to them; they pray to them, as to altars, perhaps because there is vital power in them " (" fortassis, quia inest in iis vitalitas," *Hist. Nat.* xi. 45). But this is not correct. The feet or the knees of man were touched out of humility, because the petitioner did not arrogate to himself worthiness to such a degree as to enable him to touch the higher parts of the benefactor's body. He therefore prostrates himself upon the earth, and can only touch the foot or the knee.

The custom among the Greeks, for a petitioner to touch the chin, had a different significance. Thetis did so when she laid her petition before Zeus (*Ilias,* i. 501; comp. viii. 371, ὑπ' ἀνθερεῶνος). This also Dolon would like to do, to obtain mercy from Diomedes, but he does not succeed (x. 454), where Crusius in his Commentary on Homer explains,

---

[1] What the Midrash reports, as well as Josephus and the Apocrypha, that the king was so angry that Esther fainted, and that angels accompanied her, etc., are entirely legendary homilies of the Jews of a later age

that it was the knee, and not the chin, which was touched. It is not this passage only to which Pliny refers when he speaks of it as a general custom among the Greeks. There was even a particular word, ὑπογενειάζειν, for it. The underlying thought of the custom was, that by caressing and flattering the chin the petition would be granted. It had nothing to do, as Rosenmüller will have it, with the Oriental notion of the sacredness of the beard, for it was peculiar to many nations. Grimm quotes from Gudrun 386 similar customs. It is remarkable, at any rate, that *genu*, Sanscr. *ganu*, knee, is evidently cognate with *gena*, γένειον, Sanscr. *hanu*, chin, and yet the two customs had different fundamental thoughts. Touching the knee was an appeal for mercy, but touching the chin was an act of flattering the supposed tender part of man.

To be sure, the humiliation of Esther in presenting her petition in the palace of Shushan was not like that of the Venetian Ambassador, Francis Dandolo, before the Pope in 1312. He appeared before the Pope in the presence of many guests upon all fours, and carried an iron chain upon his neck, and thus lay under the table like a dog until his petition was granted. When he bore after this the name of *Cane* (dog), he deserved it less than Diogenes, who did not know how to flatter (comp. Leo, *Gesch. v. Italien*, iii. p. 70); and still less than the pupil of Diogenes, who, when asking a favour of a superior for some one else, touched him on his thigh. That person became enraged, for he expected that the supplicant would touch his knee. " What," exclaimed Crates, " are the thighs not also thine ? " (Diog. Laertius, vi. cap. v. n. 7.)

Plutarch (on Cold) mentions that a petition was not refused in Persia when the petitioner carried fire, or went into the water. The same custom is still observed among the Turks, and Hammer adduces many examples from the years 1638 and 1655 (*Gesch. des osman. Reiches*, v. pp. 239, 630).

Esther does not touch the knee as a dependant, nor the chin as a woman ; she touches the sceptre of royal authority, because from this she seeks deliverance. In fact, the Persian tyrant arrogated to himself divine power. With his sceptre he dispensed life or death. When the ancient Christians established petitionary courses (*supplicationes*), and often called them stations, they based them on the idea that they caused the cross to be carried before them. This is spiritually, but not in the sense of material superstition. The cross is the true sceptre of the great King of Grace. He who touches it in his heart will live.

Ver. 3. "*What wilt thou, Queen Esther?*" (אסתר המלכה.) Esther came at the time when the king held a reception. This appears from the circumstance that "the king sat on the throne." At such a time those who had any business to transact with him presented it. This throws light upon the question of Ahhashverosh, "What wilt thou? What canst thou, O queen, want? What has brought thee into the reception room?" It is the language of gracious favour, in which he expresses his astonishment that the queen should also have something to ask.

"What is thy request? It shall be given thee even to the half of the kingdom." Nowhere does the sublime munificence of the Persian shahs appear to greater advantage than in their readiness to bestow great favours. The more powerful they considered themselves, the more they fancied they could give everything. "Ask what thou wilt, express thy wishes," were the haughty phrases with which they as divine beings thought of bestowing a favour. The more so here, where Esther, wearing a crown upon her head, asks a favour. As queen she is, as we say, half or part of him; she is his companion in the government (in name and by favour), therefore he says to her, "Ask what thou wilt, thou shalt have to the half of the kingdom." This was naturally only a benignant phrase, to show Esther his love for her, and the claim she has upon him.—Yet it happened that on similar occasions whole provinces and cities, *i.e.* the revenues from them, were really given away.

Ver. 4. " *Let the king and Haman come this day* [1] *unto the banquet.*"

The caution which Esther uses in her invitation is for us the finest characteristic of Oriental conditions.

She has two things in view, in order to succeed in her attempt to get the edict revoked. It must first become clear to her that Ahhashverosh is indeed so favourably disposed to her that he will also fulfil his promise according to her mind. For that he will keep his promise was sure, but the realization of it was often worse than the refusal. When Darius, son of Artaxerxes, realized the promise that was given him to have the beautiful Aspasia for his wife, he indeed received her, but she was very soon snatched from him ; and this also led to his lasting disgrace and to his final ruin (Plutarch, *Artaxerxes,* 26). When Pythius the Lydian was encouraged by former favours from Xerxes to beseech the king to leave behind one of his five sons who accompanied the expedition, his wish was fulfilled,—he was left behind, but cut into two parts, which were placed on each side of the road, and then the army passed through them (Herodotus, vii. 39). Secondly, she wanted Haman to be present when she made her petition. She thought she must not give to Ahhashverosh the opportunity of talking the matter over early with Haman, and that the latter must not have time to accomplish his design, or at least to arrange for his escape. In inviting Haman, too, she avoided giving the appearance of her petition being detrimental to his interests. Haman himself must consider the invitation as a special sign of her regard for him. We see that Esther manifested in her undertaking a bold as well as a prudent spirit. But the life

---

[1] [This is in Hebrew, יבא, הַמֶּלֶךְ, וְהָמָן, הַיּוֹם, Yabo, Hamelech, Vehaman, Hayom. From this the Rabbis prove that the name of God is mentioned in this book, for the initial letters of these four words compose the name Jehovah. The same form so many words in chap. i. ver. 20, only in a reversed manner from the final letters. But they do not account for the omission of the name of God in the Song of Solomon, as it is uncertain whether the word יה in viii. 6 is the name Jah or a suffix.—TRANS.]

of a whole nation was at stake, and it was her love to them which nerved and inspired her resolutions. It was a great distinction to Haman that the queen invited him together with the king to her banquet; but she learned already from the favourable reception she met from the king how much she might depend upon his attachment to her, and also what weight she might place upon his regard for Haman. She experimented to a certain degree as to the relations in which Haman really stood to Ahhashverosh.

Ver. 5. "*Cause Haman to make haste, that it may be done as Esther hath said.*"

This shows that the king at once appreciated Esther's zeal. Without a moment's hesitation he granted her very first desire. He had not the slightest suspicion that his minister harboured any ill-feeling against his consort, and he might even have joyfully congratulated himself that the relations between the government and the harem were those of peace and harmony and mutual respect for each other. There is nothing more instructive for powerful autocrats than to observe the great weakness with which they rule. The haughty potentate who believes that he is able to do everything, gropes as a blind man in the dark about the designs which others out of passion and despair are laying for him. While he fancies that he, like a human god, can dispose of life and death, and of happiness and misery, others play with his humour as with a ball. The haste with which he makes Haman come is but the dawn of a gracious morning. Haman hurries unconsciously to judgment, of which he himself was to be the instrument as he was its guilty cause.

Ver. 6. "*And the king said unto Esther at the banquet of wine, What is thy petition?*"

From the repetition of this question Esther gathered hope. For when the king gave audience to her, he must have seen that the invitation to the banquet was not her only object in

coming to him. He must have understood that she had a
petition which she wanted only to present at the banquet,
where according to Persian custom it could more easily be
granted (Hammer, *Gemäldesaal*, ii. 162).   During the drinking of wine, the king used to consult with his family about
the affairs which were brought before him.   The Persian
kings were often tried and harassed on such occasions by
petitioners who took advantage of their benevolent disposition.
When Xerxes had promised Artaynte to grant whatever she
wished (Herod. ix. 109), she asked a present which his
wife Amestris gave him, and whose jealousy must thereby have
been provoked.   When he again promised to grant a similar
petition to Amestris, she demanded that Artaynte should be
delivered up to her, that she might avenge herself upon her
(Herod. ix. 110, 111).   Such things were of daily occurrence, and they took place in every department of Oriental
life.   Procopius relates (*Pers. Gesch.* i. 5) that the Persian
shah under the Sassanides had once told a man to ask any
petition he liked, and so he asked something which was
against the law : to visit the prisoners " in the house of
oblivion."   Almamun the caliph said once to a girl, " Ask
what thou wishest;" and she asked the liberation of his enemy
(*The Thousand and One Nights*, ed. Habicht, xiii. 14).

When, therefore, the king remembered at the banquet that
Esther had touched the sceptre, and that apparently he had
not satisfied her desire by his coming, he then really showed
devotion to her, and a readiness to do her a favour, and that
in the presence of Haman.

" *What is thy petition* (שְׁאֵלָתֵךְ) ? *and it shall be granted
thee : and what is thy request* (וּבַקָּשָׁתֵךְ) ? *it shall be performed.*"

The ideas of שְׁאֵלָה and בַּקָּשָׁה are not the same. שָׁאַל signifies
to ask, to demand an objective thing, as *rogare*.   What is
asked is granted (נתן) by the gift of an object.   When
Ahhashverosh first spoke kindly to Esther, he did not imply

that she might have a שְׁאֵלָה, a tangible thing to ask. It
looks as if the first term was concealed in it. But now he
adds to what he said the first time: מַה בַּקָּשָׁתֵךְ, "What is thy
wish?" The substantive form בַּקָּשָׁה occurs only in Esther
and in Ezra, while the verb בקש is found in the whole of the
O. T. It has been overlooked that its meaning "to wish" is
lexicographically established. The German word *wünschen*,
Eng. "wish," is derived from it. Thus the Hebrew בקש
(*vaksh*) corresponds closely to the Sanscr. *vaksh*, *vanksh*, Norse
óska, Anglo-Sax. *vyscan*, Eng. "wish" (comp. my *Eddischen
Studien*, p. 99). Wishing has more of a subjective character.
The king therefore says to his wife, as to a wife, "What is it
that thou wishest, what is thy heart's desire? Whatever it
be, petition or wish, of a general or of a personal nature,
speak out, it shall be granted."

The king considers himself as possessing the power which
the legends and fables ascribe to those who, as spirits and
wizards, allow their beloved to have wishes. When God
appears to Solomon, He says, "Ask (שְׁאַל) what I shall give
thee" (1 Kings iii. 5). When Elijah takes leave of Elisha,
he says to him, "Ask what I shall do for thee" (2 Kings
ii. 9). Ahhashverosh fancies himself like the God of truth
and like the powers of fiction, to be able to grant petitions
and desires of the heart.

"Even to the half of my kingdom it shall be performed."
He repeats at the banqueting table what he said in the
inner chamber. From this and other examples it appears
that Herodotus (ix. 110) could not have meant that the king
only grants petitions once a year at his dining table. This
happened especially when he gave a public dinner on his
coronation day. This mistake of Herodotus has conduced
to the false explanation which he has when he says: οὔνομα
δὲ τῷ δείπνῳ τούτῳ, περσιστὶ μὲν τυκτὰ, δὲ τὴν Ἑλλήνων
γλῶσσαν τέλειον. The last word τέλειον, a complete feast,
is surely not a translation of τυκτά, a connection which

could scarcely be if τυκτά be Greek joined with τεύχομαι, τυγχάνειν. Therefore the attempts hitherto made to explain the word have been in vain. It appears to me that τυκτά has the analogous sense of γενέσια, "annual feast," "throne feast," "coronation feast," and it is therefore to be derived from the Persian *techt*, meaning a throne. This throws light upon the narrative in the Gospel of Mark (vi. 21). Herod in his vain conceit entirely imitates the court fashions of the great Persian kings (as the German princes in the seventeenth century aped the fashions and extravagances of the court of Louis XIV.). He also had a feast to commemorate his accession to the throne (τοῖς γενεσίοις αὐτοῦ). The names of his courtiers (though of Macedonian origin) are in accordance with those of the Persians, μεγιστᾶνες. When his daughter dances, he says to her, "Ask of me whatsoever thou wilt, and I will give it thee." And again, "Whatsoever thou shalt ask of me, I will give it thee, unto the half of my kingdom." Thus he imitated the language of Ahhashverosh, which was familiar to him.

Ver. 7. "*Then answered Esther: My petition and my request.*"

She still keeps back her petition. She sees indeed that she has found favour in the eyes of the king, and has good reason to believe that he wants to do what she will ask him; and yet she hesitates. "Ah, indeed," she says, "I have a petition and a wish; but if thou wilt show me a favour, then come once more with Haman to my entertainment, and I will tell it thee then." What she does now is entirely calculated with respect to the nature of the king. She makes him curious and expectant; she excites in him a still greater desire to be kind and gracious by timidly telling him to observe somewhat of her difficulty and embarrassment which necessitates a postponement of telling her desire right out; she assures herself of his love, when he, the tyrant, who is not in the habit of exercising patience, agrees to come once

more to the banquet. She increases by this the proofs of
her feigned respect for Haman, so that he dreams of being
quite secure. She psychologically prepares everything as
best she can, before she ventures upon the great stroke, which
in spite of the favour of the king may become dangerous.
The two intervening days have a wonderfully tragical character. While Esther trembles all over with excitement and
uncertainty, while she stands between life and death, with
full consciousness that the fate of a whole nation depends
upon the success of her enterprise, she must at the same time
appear in the character of a cheerful wife, of an interesting
hostess, and of an illustrious queen. Nothing about her must
betray that she sees in the cup of wine a reflection of the
blood of her people; nothing must indicate that Haman the
dreaded favourite was invited not to meet with honour, but
with judgment. The simple narrative conceals a conflict of
thoughts of a highly dramatical character. The sorrowful,
prudent woman must overcome two men who hold the destiny
of thousands in their hands; she has no weapons for the
warfare except her charms and her insight into human nature.
But her trembling heart soon found help. Through the
guidance of God, who is not named, things take place which
pave the way for such a success far beyond her knowledge
and calculation. Just then, when she could not withdraw,
when delay was no longer possible,—for " to-morrow I shall
make known my request,"—events happen which powerfully
influence the mind and disposition of the king. There was
only one night [1] between one banquet and the other; but it
was long enough to announce to Haman and Mordecai an
unexpected catastrophe. Esther is to experience, that when
one pursues a great plan, it is not necessary for him to fret,
nor to think that the result is entirely dependent upon his
own power and wisdom.

---

[1] An Arabic proverb says, " The nights are pregnant with many things,
and give birth to them before the dawn of the morning" (Hammer, *Gesch.
der Ilchane*, ii. 291).

Ver. 9. "*Then went Haman forth on that day joyful and glad of heart.*"

" On that day," for on the next day there was an end to his joy. To-day his heart was still elated, that he was the first man in the country, and was in great favour with the king and queen, and in fact he had reached the goal of his ambition. It is true that generally an invited guest received special distinctions, as Themistocles received (Plutarch, *Th.* 29), and as the Cretan Timagoras (according to Athenaeus, quoted by ancient commentators) ; but they do not form a strict parallel to the case before us. Here Haman laid stress upon the fact that the queen invited him, that she invited no one else to give the king the pleasure of his company, that therefore she must esteem him beyond measure; and the pleasure was enhanced when he reflected that the attendance at such banquets generally turned out very dangerous to the viziers, but in this only honours awaited him. At any rate, it appears clearly from Haman's glee that he was quite unaware that Esther belonged to the people against whom he had issued such cruel orders ; otherwise his merriment would have been moderate. He was the more pleased when he thought that he had not noticed any jealousy on the part of the queen concerning his predominating influence over the king. All obstacles appeared to have been overcome by him. He had no longer any rival. Henceforth all must bow before him.

" *Mordecai sat in the king's gate ; he stood not up, nor trembled before him.*"

Now also he did not take any notice of Haman ; he did not bow before him, nor did he stand up to compliment him, nor was he convulsed either by fear of or respect for him. And Haman was full of wrath that the Jew, the commoner, should not bow before the *Magus* and favourite of the king. In his vanity he was ashamed that the other courtiers had seen Mordecai's boldness. He was afraid that they would think that after all Haman cannot be so all-powerful, if a man like

Mordecai dares to ignore him. Still excited with his self-glorification, the conduct of the Jew appeared to him intolerable. Certainly he knew that this could not last long, for his destructive decree had already been published everywhere; but the time for its taking effect had not yet come, and should he till then tolerate the contempt of Mordecai? The thought occurs to him to wait no longer, and to order at once that he should be killed; but ‎‏ויתאפק‏‎,[1] he restrained himself. Ancient commentators[2] have not understood why Haman did not at once make short work with Mordecai; but they were deficient in insight into the customs and spirit of the East. The arbitrariness of the absolute shah is on the one hand a burden to the great, and on the other it secures freedom to the humble people. The unlimited control of the king over life and death, to decide according to the whim and mood he was in, prevented his subordinates doing the same. For the nearer they were to him, the more they were exposed to the same treatment.

The position which a grand vizier like Haman occupied was an exalted one, but not the less dangerous. He had to take good care not in any way to give the appearance of arrogating to himself the prerogatives and functions that belonged to the shah. He was surrounded by enemies who were jealous of him. There were many others who wanted to supplant him, and the intrigues of the seraglio might become at any moment dangerous. To do away with Mordecai in a quiet manner was in itself an easy thing for him, but he feared the consequences. When we read above (iii. 6), "But he thought scorn to lay hands on Mordecai alone," it means that he did not think it worth his while to risk his position for such a man. It was permitted to everybody to sit at the gate

---

[1] ‎‏אפק‏‎ is rightly compared with ‎‏אבק‏‎, to wrestle; its meaning is certainly the German *fassen*, "to take hold." And ‎‏התאפק‏‎ is to be taken, like the Greek ἀναλαμβάνειν ἑαυτόν, in the sense of taking hold of oneself (*se colligere*). In sound it is like the German *packen*, Sanscr. *paç pax*, *capere* (see *Dieffenb. goth. Gloss.* i. 343).

[2] This applies even to Clericus; but these misconceptions always arise from an inclination to follow a complete unhistorical criticism.

of the king.   This law was recognised even under the Turkish
sultans.   Jews and Gentiles could appear before the gate
either to present a petition or to pay homage, just in the same
way as all could place themselves before the sun to be warmed.

The idea was that all had the liberty of receiving the beams
that shone from royal majesty.   Now, this being the case, if
Haman had privately killed Mordecai, the intriguers of the
palace would have eagerly reported to the king that Haman
had murdered one that had placed himself under the protecting
wings of the king, and who appealed for protection ; that he
encroached upon the rights of the king to pardon a criminal,
and that he had done this from personal spite and vanity,
without asking for authority, and before the very holy gates of
the king.   The mistrust of the king would thus have been
aroused, the enemies would have gained time to complicate
matters further, and the consequences would have been incal-
culable for him.   Haman thought of all this, therefore he
restrained himself from adopting harsh measures at present,
until he had first consulted with his party.

Ver. 10. "*And he sent and fetched his friends, and Zeresh
his wife.*"

Every one of the great men who had obtained power had
his party.   In this the absolute government did not differ
from the modern constitutional forms of government.   It is
therefore such a party meeting which Haman at this moment
calls together.   The occasion for it is not his encounter with
Mordecai, but the new good fortune which he believes has
befallen him.   The narrative has for this reason an extraordinary dramatical character, since it presents Haman as
seeing in the invitation of Esther the crowning of his ambition,
while she was actually preparing measures for his fall.   Having
become the attached friend of the king and queen, how
powerful is his position !   So he gives a kind of account of
this to his friends and to his wife, for they share in his honours
and power.   It is wonderful enough that to-day he describes

to them all his glory, while, unknown to him, the to-morrow will strip it from him entirely. He shows them how rich he is—how numerous are his sons—also the number of his faithful adherents upon whom he can rely. He further communicates to them that he enjoys the highest confidence of the king, who has bountifully lavished his honours upon him ; and that of which he is still more proud is, that the queen was quite partial to him, and had so distinguished him as to invite him only, together with the king, to her banquet. In fact he pours out his whole joyful heart before them,—for really more pleasures he cannot expect.[1]

Ver. 13. " *Yet all this availeth me nothing, so long as I see Mordecai the Jew sitting at the king's gate.*"

He tells of this vexation also. He is, forsooth, ashamed to tell of the real ground of his vexation. He simply but emphatically gives them to understand that his joys are embittered by being obliged to see Mordecai at the royal gate. The more we consider Haman as the representative of a religious party, the more force we see in this complaint brought before them, as it is intended to awaken their general interest in the matter of the Jew being still tolerated at the gate of the king. But what is to be done ? Let them give advice, for his honours and his attempts are as much theirs as his. But their interests will certainly not be furthered if the Jew should still be suffered to sit at the gates of the king.

Ver. 14. " *Then said Zeresh, his wife, and all his friends unto him.*"

It is evidently correct to take this name as related to Zairi, gold. Other Persian names seem to have the same compounds (Zariadris, Zariaspa); it is the same name which Jewesses of a later age frequently have, like Zahab (gold) Chryse, and in Germany, etc., Golde (see Zunz, *Namen der Juden*, p. 71).

[1] Comp. " Die Gesch. eines Veziers," in Mirchond's *Histor. Samanid.* ed. Wilken, p. 85.

Naturally they are not merely Jewish names, as the name Chryse is mentioned by Homer. The German name Goltrat (in ninth century) has some connection with this (in opposition to Förstemann, *Namenbuch*, i. 543).

Thus also in the house of Haman Zeresh represents the decisive and regardless person. She speaks first, and proposes the worst means. Her fanaticism excites the whole party. Her diabolical subtlety soon finds its condemnation through the fidelity of a noble and obedient wife. What she advises Haman to do is to use the moment, and to act decisively while he has the opportunity. Now he stands on the pinnacle of favour with the king. A day must not be lost; *to-day* he must proceed to act, and is sure of success. He must by no means delay, for who knows what changes may come in the interval? "Let a gallows be made" — then go to-morrow to the king. Has not the king presented thee with the whole of this people, because they are contrary to the law of the empire? Why then dost thou not quickly execute this obnoxious man? Go and do away with him, and then when thou goest again to the banquet of the queen, nothing will vex thy soul! This advice was certainly clever and bad enough, and would have been carried out, if a mightier arm from heaven had not frustrated it. A gallows fifty cubits high should be erected. With regard to the mode of execution we shall speak later on. She wants to intimate that this individual is guilty of high treason. So high should the gallows be, that it may be seen far and wide what happened to the man who offended Haman. The height of the gallows for the enemy should proportionally contrast with the high position of the person against whom he had sinned. A Persian cubit was three digits longer than the common Greek (Olympic) cubit, as Herodotus says (i. 178), where, without doubt, he means Persian or Greek δάκτυλοι. Böckh decides for Persian. Accordingly, the Persian cubit had 24 digits, and was in proportion to the Greek as 8 : 7, and contained 234,274,286 Persian lines (*Metrol. Untersuch.* p. 219).

But this prudence came to nought. However short the time was in which her plan was to be carried out, it was yet too long; judgment came sooner. The apparent exaltation of Haman was really his fall. It is dreadful to think that he intended going to Esther's banquet with a complacent countenance after he had murdered her dear friend. But what is even more striking, that the cruel deed fell upon himself. What he has so long postponed, viz. the punishing of Mordecai, in order not to give a handle to his enemies, becomes now, when he thinks he may safely execute it, the stepping-stone to his fall. The height of fifty cubits becomes at last the picture of the depth of his fall. His adherents and Zeresh have rejoiced with him in his triumphs; and so they fall with him in the abyss of destruction.

CHAPTER VI.

Ver. 1. "*On that night the king's sleep fled from him.*"

No one has command over sleep. When, therefore, in ancient times sleep was represented by the figure of a lion, it was because the lion subdues all, and does not suffer himself to be subdued. The great king wanted sleep, but sleep would not be caught; like a flying butterfly, it continued coming and going. Why could he not sleep? It need not have been on account of fear or sordid cupidity (*sordidus cupido*, Horatius, *Od.* lib. II. *ad Grosphum*). Was it because he had taken too much wine—of which it is said that it drives away sleep? This also need not necessarily have been the case. It often happens to kings, and especially to Oriental despots, that the care and responsibility of government, their remorseful consciences and gloomy forebodings, deprive them of sleep. Suetonius (cap. 50) tells of Caligula, that he so suffered from sleeplessness, that, tired of lying in bed awake, he used to get up and stand or roam about the rooms of the palace. Procopius reproaches the Emperor Justinian with being cursed with sleeplessness, so that he is obliged to roam about the whole night (*Hist. Arcana*, ed. Bonn, pp. 81, 82). Similar restlessness of conscience and sleeplessness is reported of the energetic but cruel Caliph Al-Mansur (comp. Hammer, *Gemäldesaal*, ii. pp. 70, 89).

Of the Turkish sultan, Selim I., it is told that he was in the habit of passing most nights in reading books, without sleeping at all; sometimes he would have others read to him, or talk to him about the affairs of the State (Diez, *Denkwürdigkeiten von Asien*, i. 266). In the history of Ahhash-

verosh, that sleepless night was illumined by the torch of a
people's emancipation from worse than slavery. It caused his
mind to meditate upon the past. The night often becomes
a means of awakening serious reflections. Quietness and
leisure cause the mind to collect its powers, they rouse the
conscience, they bring to remembrance what is lost, they set
free from the excitement of the daily routine; and happy
is he to whom they are as a ladder to God, to whom belongeth
the mysteries of salvation and redemption.

"*And he commanded to bring him the book of records.*"

It is also known from other sources that the Persian kings
had every service that was rendered to them entered in
historical books.[1] Of Phylakus we read in Herod. viii. 85,
that he was recorded as a benefactor of the king, and such
were called "ὀροσάγγαι." This word has surely not been
correctly explained by Rosen and Bötticher (*Arica*, p. 20);
it has rather a connection with the Persian *Ersans, Orosans*,
אראנוש, *dignus*, "worthy," and means even now in modern
Persian *beneficium*, "benefit" (Vullers, *Pers. Lex.* i. 79). Likewise Herodotus reports (viii. 90): "As often as Xerxes saw
that one of his men distinguished himself by some act in the
naval battle, he made inquiries about him, and the secretaries
registered his name, and his captain's, and his family name,
together with the name of the town from which he came."
To the same effect Xerxes wrote to Pausanias (Thucydides, i.
129): "The service will remain in my house for a continual
remembrance" (which examples were already noticed by
Grotius, though not correctly explained). It is not to be
assumed that the books in which the names of benefactors
were inscribed are different from the general chronicle of the
kingdom, for the events of the court were also the events of
the kingdom. There was a royal and grand reason for so

---

[1] A similar book was kept by the Byzantian court. See Codin in *Lib.
de Offic.* τοῦ ἐπὶ τῶν ἀναμνήσεων. Even Scriver mentions it in *Zufällige
Andachten*, iv. n. 30, p. 25.

greatly valuing every service rendered to the king as to put it
on record, so that it might be brought from time to time before
his remembrance. On the one hand, what concerned the king
was considered worth remembering; and, on the other, such a
record was an incitement to his subjects to attachment and
submission. What is gained now by receiving decorations
and titles was gained at that time by having one's name
inscribed in the chronicle, and by the title Orosang. But in
every case the preservation of historical facts, however little
in themselves, proved their beneficial power. Recalling to
mind past events is always instructive and useful. The
cherishing of remembrance may become the means of leading
the individual to a higher life. In our narrative the finding
of the forgotten fact in the book of records, becomes an
important factor in the deliverance of Israel. Ahhashverosh
is warned against bad deeds, and inclined towards good ones;
Haman already finds the commencement of his condemnation.
How much, indeed, the occurrences of this night humble all
human foresight! In that night all those machinations of
revenge, spun in the dark, are scattered; and while Esther still
trembles, because she thinks that she alone must be the instrument in Israel's deliverance and Haman's fall, the foundation
thereof is already laid by a higher hand. The greatest achieve-
ments of men are only portions of coinciding interpositions,
which the spirit of truth orders and directs in history.

Ver. 3. *"And the king said, What honour and dignity
hath been done to Mordecai for this?"*

The thing was indeed of the utmost importance. The life
of the king had been at stake. What greater thing can be
for the king than the remembrance of this event! Should
not he who had saved his life be royally rewarded! It was
against the dignity and the pride of the great tyrant not to
acknowledge this on a grand and magnificent scale.

But though the rewards were generally entered in the
book of records of the court, it was omitted in Mordecai's

case. This circumstance surprised the king the more. It was not only that he felt grateful to his benefactor, but also that it was an offence to his majesty that the record of the empire should have nothing to show of a reward to the man who had saved his life from the conspiracy. " What honour and dignity " (יקר וגדולה), he asks, has been done to Mordecai for this, for such he deserves who has rendered so great service to the king ? The courtiers reply, Nothing has been done to him ; and they lay the blame upon others. This reply of " Nothing " excites in the king mistrust and ill-humour. A man who detected and denounced the conspiracy of his eunuchs has received nothing ! May it have been that those whose business it was to propose such a reward were dissatisfied with the king's escape ?

Did his courtiers manifest no zeal and joy in the good deed, even so much as to mention the benefactor's name with approval and praise ? Mordecai did not ask anything—and who, with all these meritorious services which he had rendered to the royal house, would have remained content without receiving a reward either openly or clandestinely ? He had no friends whom he could expect to recommend his case and to promote his interests. Courtiers protect others only when it is to their own advantage. Mordecai was a free and independent man. He did not send in any petitions, and did not court any one's favour. How should *he* receive anything ! Merits alone are not enough for obtaining a reward. These examples reveal to us the hollow condition of the whole royal power. The king does not even know whether deserving servants receive any recognition, where those who surround him keep them in the dark. He cannot even show gratitude, which is his chief duty. What a caricature is such a shah who demeans himself like a god ! Have no confidence in great men, nor in princes, says the Psalmist. But this is our comfort, that the heavenly King knows all things and knows our heart,—that there is no nepotism in His kingdom, —and that His willingness to give to and atone, does not depend upon a priest. The table of the Lord's Supper, where He thinks of those for whom He died, belongs to Him and to no one else.

Ver. 4. " *Who is in the court ?* "

The indignant king wants to carry out at once what he has omitted before. It is not so much out of regard to the person of Mordecai that he is so urgent, but rather on account of his own pride. He is vexed to think that there should be a man in existence who had saved his life, and who could say that he had done it gratis. Officers were at all times waiting in the court to receive orders. The king does not want to lose time in causing any particular person to come, in order to bestow the delayed reward. The first man who is in the outer hall court should do it. The king does not even think of Haman. Now, although it was something unusual for a man in the high position of Haman to make his court visits at the dawn of the morning, yet this time he was there at that very moment. Never was there exhibited a more frivolous and thoughtless judgment than that shown by many critics in their light estimation of the value of the Book of Esther For surely there can be no more beautiful description of the impending dramatic catastrophe than that with which the whole of this book is full. At the moment when the mind of the king has but one thought, to compensate Mordecai with the long-merited honour and dignity, and so much the more because it ought to have been done long ago,—at the very moment when he looks for a person to carry it out properly, just then, Haman makes his appearance on the scene. What does he want? To ask for an authorization from the king to hang this same Mordecai on the gallows which he has already erected. Haman was in a hurry. Early in the morning the execution should take place; on that day he should see Mordecai no more in his accustomed seat; for he could no longer bear to behold the obstinate Jew. Before he goes to the banquet of Esther with a triumphant heart (to

the banquet of Esther, the adopted daughter of Mordecai,
though he knows it not), Mordecai shall be no more.
The removal of this faithful man would, in his opinion,
enhance the honour of enjoying the good things at Esther's
table.

But time is not given him to make his proposal. Before he
had yet left his house his doom was already fully developed.
Scarcely has he arrived when he is summoned to appear before
the indignant king. Mordecai, who knows nothing of what is
going on, is the object of a wonderful conflict of ideas and
intentions in the royal sleeping apartment. One wants to
honour him, and another wants not only to degrade him, but
also to hang him on the gallows. Spectators, too, are there
who observe these strange coincidences. They are the servants
of the king (נערי המלך), who know of the gallows which Haman
had erected for Mordecai, and now hear of the purpose of
the king to reward him. They act like genuine courtiers,
and do not reveal to the king the intention of Haman out of
fear of this man ; nor, from jealousy, do they communicate to
Haman, even if they have time to do so, the thoughts of the
king. Haman in his vanity, and still dizzy with excitement on
account of the special favours which he experienced yesterday,
sees in the circumstance that he is called in so quickly, a
happy omen for himself. Never has any one fallen so blindly
and so self-deceived into the snare of destruction as he did.
What is written in Ps. xciv. 21, "They gather themselves
together against the soul of the righteous, and condemn innocent blood. But the Lord hath been my tower," was now
fulfilled. Of course it afterwards received a greater fulfilment.
"When they shall go to and fro" (German trans.), says Hos.
vii. 12, "I will spread my net upon them." This was so in the
case of Haman.

Ver. 6. "*And the king said, Let him come in.*"

Even the highest minister is not so eminent as not to accept
the orders of the king; for in point of fact all his officers are

his slaves. Certainly, the king cannot make Haman responsible for Mordecai not being long ago rewarded for his deed, since at that time (iii. 1) Haman had not yet been exalted to power. But the suspicion and the ill-will of the king towards him are seen in the fact that he does not tell him what had passed during the night, that he does not ask him anything about Mordecai, that he does not even mention his name, or give any reason why he wants to reward him. The general abstract question : " What shall be done unto the man whom the king delighteth to honour ?" shows that he has no confidence in Haman. He cannot trust him to say the right word, if the person upon whom the honour was to be conferred does not please him. And the king had a right to suppose that that person could not be beloved by Haman, or else he would have long ago asked for some acknowledgment of his services. A man with such merits, who had received nothing, is surely not a friend of the momentary favourite. There was a tone of ill-humour towards Haman in the general question which he put to him, inasmuch as he was of the highest rank among the court officials ; but Haman does not see it. In his infatuation even the vagueness of the question appeared to him to have but one definite meaning, namely, that it contained a very flattering recognition of himself. He was so sure that he saw everywhere success to his efforts. When the king called out, " Let him come in," it was no honour to Haman that he, the first and best man, should act merely as an instrument of conferring high honours upon a man who was his subordinate. But he believed that he had found in the early audience to which he was ordered a new sun of royal favours which was to shine down upon him. When he was so early in the day and so specifically asked as to the manner in which a favourite should be honoured, he thought it could not possibly refer to any other person than himself. This, he explained to himself, must be the reason why he, and no other, was called in, and why the king did not mention any name, lest he should perchance in his modesty fail to do justice to his merits. How vain, indeed, is the wisdom of these children of the world! They fall into their own traps. In his self-love he ascribes to the king such a tender conscience as purposely to make the question a general one in order not to hurt his delicate feelings, and so he thinks of using his opportunity of asking a good deal. He thinks, too, that he would at the same time flatter the king by placing the honours to be conferred in the highest possible scale; and with all this he hypocritically pretends to be impartial, as he does not yet know whom Ahhashverosh means.

Ver. 7. "*And Haman said unto the king.*"

The foolishness of haughty and yet servile men repeats itself. When Xerxes allowed Demaratus, the Spartan, frankly to ask what he wanted, he asked to have the crown of the king placed on his head, and to be led through the city in the same manner as the king was. According to Plutarch (*Themist.* xxix.), Mithropaustes, the king's uncle, said to the vain Greek: "The king's crown could not cover a brainless head; and should he even hold the thunder in his hands, he would still not be Zeus." Seneca, who tells the same story (*De beneficiis*, vi. 31), properly says, that he was deserving of a reward so long as he did not ask for it. The parallels which Clericus adduces are not properly to the point. Haman proposes, for the person to be honoured, the same distinction as Demaratus asked, only in a higher degree. The individual concerned should be arrayed entirely as the *alter ego* of the king; he should put on the royal apparel, he should ride upon the king's own riding horse, and he should wear the king's crown. Haman, who thinks that all this will fall to his lot, wants thereby to appear throughout the whole of Shushan as the "other I" of the king, in order to subdue all his opponents. As if he were the king himself, one of the foremost princes should lead the horse by the bridle during the procession through the city, and should proclaim before him: "Thus shall it be done to the man whom the king delighteth to honour." All this has its deep foundation in Oriental life.

The Hebrew word כתר, "crown," is none other than the traditional Greek κίταρις or κίδαρις, the tall Persian imperial hat which we sufficiently know from coins (see Spanheim, *De praest. et usu numism.* i. p. 470). Such town-criers as Haman here asks, we often meet in Oriental histories (Gen. xli. 43), —also when one was led to be disgraced. Just as here the crier is to proclaim the reason for the honour, so also he was called to proclaim the reason for dishonour. In a story of *The Thousand and One Nights* (ed. König, xi. 19), the Imam of the place is led through the city, seated upon a camel backwards, and a crier goes before him and proclaims: "Thus are those punished who mix themselves up in affairs without being called to do so." Also the leading by the bridle on such occasions is a well-known custom (see Hammer, *Rosenöl,* ii. 33).

It is a shrewd remark of the old Jewish commentators, that although Haman had also asked for the person to be distinguished, the ornament of the royal Kidaris (Keter), yet afterwards we read only of the apparel and the horse. They concluded from this, that Ahhashverosh did not permit the crown to be given. It is true that ver. 10 does not mention the crown, yet this does not conclusively prove that it was not used. On the other hand, the words "apparel and horse" imply that the officer to be appointed as attendant had special functions to discharge besides robing, putting on his spurs, and holding the bridle.

How exquisite was Haman in the wishes of his vanity! How smart he thought he would look when he would plume himself in royal magnificence before all his friends! How he would tower in grandeur even over all the highest of the kingdom, the Parthemim! (comp. chap. i. 3). But pride comes before a fall, and the higher he thinks himself to be, the deeper he falls into disgrace. The prophets could not teach a more striking lesson than is taught in the history here.

Ver. 10. "*Then the king said to Haman, Make haste.*"
These are friendly words, but they fall like thunderbolts

upon his ears. Apparently they are unimportant orders, but
they shatter his pride as a stormy wind breaks a reed.
The king had evidently anticipated that Haman would think
that he was to be so highly distinguished. Therefore he
thought if he made him the groom to Mordecai, it would
be in itself a lesson to him. Then he noticed that his
servant wanted to play the king, and this stirred up jealousy
in his breast, as is the case with all. tyrants. And yet
with all this he thought : Haman considers such a con-
descension upon my part a mere act of grace. He wants
to be reckoned among the great Parthemim of the kingdom ;
his wishes shall be granted. To them would fall the honour
of holding the horse's bridle of the person to be distinguished,
and he shall have that honour. But Haman hears of the
new dignity with a shudder. For this honour is his shame.
When he thought that these great dignities concerned himself, it pleased his pride to be attended by a compeer ; but
now he is singled out to attend upon the man whom he
abhorred from the bottom of his heart, words cannot
describe the galling annoyance which this command caused
him. What, he ? Impossible ! But who else ? That
Mordecai, whom he just now was about to hang on the
gallows ! That decided enemy of his ; that Jew of whom he
was going to make an example, and let him feel his power
before he breathed his last breath, upon him he should
attend all over the city ! How could he look after that in
Mordecai's face, if he should happen to meet him ; and what
will the people of the city say when they see Haman
invested with the office of stable - boy to such a man as
that ! It is necessary to realize the vanity, intoxication, and
false security which possessed Haman's soul in order to
see how low he sunk when he heard these words of the
king. While he dreams of the glory of becoming an "*alter
ego*" of the king, he all of a sudden is made to feel the
entire pressure of his humiliation. If the whole psychological
process which was going on in the vain man's mind is

considered, one would find that the judgment of Haman has no parallel in the whole history of the world, nor has there been a humiliation of a statesman or any other great man like his.   Many conceited Ministers of State have been sternly rebuked and dismissed.   The Persian history offers an example in the case of a vassal of Mahmud of Gaznas, who made another run like a slave by his horse, and soon afterwards had himself to run in like manner by the horse of him whom he had humiliated, and to live in the prison which he had built for him (Malcolm, *Gesch. v. Pers.* i. 204).   But the ground of his fall was an external one.   Haman fell from the enormous height of his vanity.   He fell at the feet of him whose deadly enemy he was,—and before a man who was innocent,—whom, in spite of his piety and fidelity, he so cruelly persecuted. He was at the same time wounded in his pride and in his conscience.   One must indeed be like Haman, a willing Persian courtier, now as abjectly slavish as before he was wicked, in order to endure the humiliation that he had to undergo.

Whilst he apparently showed unconcern in the matter, and acted as if he felt nothing amiss, and left the king as an obedient and zealous servant to discharge his duty with regard to Mordecai, his cowardice was greater than his vexation.   One can sufficiently realize the scene which took place when he met Mordecai at the gate of the king.   Mordecai must have for a moment imagined himself to be like that Hassan in the fable whom Harun Ar-rashid in his sleep arrayed in the gaudy dress of a caliph, and brought into the magnificent apartments of the palace. "His mouth must have been filled with laughter, as one that dreameth" (Ps. cxxvi. 1).   But the uppermost feeling of his heart must have been that of praise rather than of victory.   He then learned a fresh meaning in the words of the Psalmist, "The Lord alone doeth great wonders;" "The Lord releaseth the prisoners."   For in what other mood could a believer in the living God of love and truth express his astonishment at seeing the author of all enmity against his people coming in the name of the king to be his servant, whilst he and his people are still mourning and fasting? His heart must, of course, have palpitated when he heard that Haman, his implacable enemy, is to lead him riding through the royal town. The proud vizier is to be his herald and slave; but he realized at the same time the full assurance of hope, that if this can happen, God will surely not forsake His people, but will redeem them in a marvellous way.

When Haman afterwards lost his life on the gallows, his death-agonies were nothing in comparison to the humiliation he had undergone when he humbly begged Mordecai to permit him to wait upon him. The agony was great enough when he was obliged to decorate another, and in this case a Jew. But it was quite unendurable when he remembered that everybody knew how he hated Mordecai; that the latter had not paid the slightest respect to him; and, above all, that Mordecai was aware of his wicked plan, and would rejoice at its overthrow. Haman judged every man by his own standard. He could not appreciate a servant of God, as Shimei could not appreciate David in humiliation. He therefore suffered, not only in reflecting upon his own miserable condition, but also in pondering upon the achieved triumph of Mordecai. It would be worthy of the pencil of the greatest artist to picture the two faces as they stand opposite each other. That of Haman, who, in spite of the enormous internal vexation which breaks his heart, looks externally courtly, complacent, and careless, — and that of Mordecai, solemn, emaciated by much fasting, prayers, and tears; and yet with a halo about it, arising not from joy over another man's misfortune, but from a heart attuned to gratitude to God. His eyes are not directed towards Haman, but towards heaven. " I will lift up mine eyes unto the mountains, from whence cometh my help."

Now the king looks intently upon Haman to see what effect his words would make upon him; he therefore repeats the order twice, " As thou hast said," and, " Let nothing fail of all that thou hast spoken." Horace, while in his first satire narrating the parable of Tantalus, uses the well-known sentence : " Mutato nomine, de te fabula narratur." A tone of irony pervades the words of the king : Do not err, " de te *non* narratur." There is no thought of thee, but carry everything out as thou hast said.

We find a grand antithesis in the parable of Nathan before David. As if Nathan had asked : What shall be done to the man who has done this ? David's anger is kindled against the man, and he says, " The man that has done this shall surely die ! " And Nathan says : " Thou art the man." Thou hast pronounced thine own sentence. But here is David, a penitent sinner, seeing in the parable of Nathan a picture of himself, and soon applying it to himself; and the judge is not Ahhashverosh, but the living God.

The explanations given to this passage by the Rabbis are more of a triumphant than of an exegetical character, as might be expected from them, when later similar experiences brought it vividly to their remembrance. The reader in the synagogue, when he comes to this passage, raises his voice as if momentarily triumphant; but these are notions suitable to them, and not in accord with the spirit of the ancient witnesses in the Old Testament. It is certainly an idea borrowed from Oriental life when they represent Mordecai as putting his foot upon the neck of Haman when he mounted the horse. Such things occur (see Hammer, *Gemäldesaal*, v. 45), but the humiliation of Haman's soul was much greater.

Ver. 11. " *And caused him to ride through the street of the city.*"

Rehhob (רחוב), street, is an open space. The Oriental towns had a free space for riding and racing, something like a

hippodrome, which is called Atmeidan in Constantinople.
Upon the open space where equestrians and equipages appeared,
Haman was to lead Mordecai in procession. It may also
mean the principal street, the broad way leading through the
city. He was to display him before the greatest number and
the most prominent of the people.[1]

Ver. 12. " *And Mordecai came again to the king's gate.*"

The pious man was not changed by the honour shown to
him; he did not esteem himself the better for it. In his
view things were as before. The people were still in danger.
Whether his life is now secure, this did not enter his mind
to inquire. He was sufficiently conversant with Persian
customs to know that this incident had in no way changed
the situation of his people, and that what had been conferred upon him was only a self-glorification of the king
himself. So long as the decree which threatened destruction to
his people was not revoked, there could be no progress. Yet
he was sure that God would wonderfully send help. So he
resumed his place in sackcloth and ashes. He, who had just
now attracted the envy of all the spectators who saw him
wearing the king's crown upon his head, is now seen sitting
at the royal gate, and covered with the mourner's garment.

But how much happier was he in his mourning than the
one who hurried home with bated breath! Haman looks now
as an אבל, "a mourner," who had just returned from the
burial of his beloved, for he comes back from the grave of
his insolent pride.

How provoking to him was the ride of Mordecai through
the city; while the people hailed him who had saved the
king's life, he is laughed at and mocked by everybody, and
Mordecai in envied array looks down upon him. He must

[1] The story of the Princess Hind, who avenged herself on the cruel
Hedshadsh by causing him to hold the bridle of her camel in her procession, is a romantic contrast to the above, and taken from later Arabian
life (See *Rosenöl*, ii. 33).

hold his tongue, and hold the horse by the bridle, and perhaps
be kicked by it.   At length the ride is over ; he went home
hurriedly (נדחף, " impelled "), crushed (which is properly the
sense of אבל, mourning), and having his head covered, as one
that is ashamed to be seen and recognised, and he related to
his family what had happened.

How different was the scene in that house from that
described in chap. v. 11 !   At that time he was inflated with
recounting his successes, his influence, his favours,—and only
one anxious thought troubled him, how to get rid of the
obnoxious Mordecai who sat at the gate,—but now he fully
realized shame, vexation, and disappointment, which far over-
balanced his former enjoyments.   Then it appeared so easy
to put Mordecai out of the way ; but now he is not only
still alive, but is recognised and registered as a benefactor
of the king, and who had triumphed over him in the presence of all the inhabitants of the city.   All the members
of his family hung down their heads.   It was an unheard-of
disaster.

> Ver. 13. " *Then said his wise men and Zeresh his wife
> unto him, If Mordecai, before whom thou hast begun to fall,
> be of the Jews,*" etc.

How much worldly wisdom and admonition does this verse
contain, especially when we compare it with chap. v. 14 !
On the former occasion of the party gathering, Zeresh was
the first boldly to advise the immediate execution of Mordecai, and the " adherents " only chimed in, while nothing
was said of the wise men.   But now the adherents are silent,
Zeresh is in the background, and the wise men are the
speakers.   Among a class of men such as are gathered here,
it is not principle or conscience which decides a point, but
the measure of its success.   When Haman was successful, everything that he did was considered wise by them, but now they
have not even a word of comfort for him.   At that time they
instigated him, now they blame him.   Did they not then

know that Mordecai was a Jew? Had not Haman expressly told them so? Now they act as if they hear it for the first time! What else was the cause of Haman's disgrace but their advice! Why did not they then moderate his temper by saying, "Never mind Mordecai, let him sit,"—but they urged him on to hang him at once. Had this not been done, the present occurrence would not have turned out so badly for Haman. He would not have been present on that morning at the palace. Another person would have had to discharge the irksome business. But of this neither his wife nor his friends take any notice, they again pretend to be wise as before. We could have told thee at once, they say, what the result would be, "Why hast thou begun with that fellow?" And Haman is in that evil state of falling out of the frying-pan into the fire of his false and self-righteous friends. Remarkable is the expression חכמיו, "his wise men." It seems in itself to indicate the irony of the narrator. Fine wise men were these! They ought to have given him better advice before! Of what avail is the announcement to him now? But the mentioning of the "Hhahhamim," who were with Haman, contains also an instructive significance. That Haman's whole position was a quasi-spiritual one, belonging to Parseeism, we have already attempted to show above. This accounts for his being surrounded in his high office by other such Magi, who are sometimes called הברים and sometimes "wise men," like the priests of Egypt, to whose office belonged divination and astrology, as we have seen above. But their wisdom consisted in their superstition in results. Only just now they find a reason for their ominous prophecy.

But what causes them to declare that because Haman has fallen before Mordecai, he will always continue to fall? The misfortune which has befallen him appears to them as a bad omen. The Jews, thought they, are his enemies; he has undertaken a dreadful work against them; whether it will succeed or not, no one can tell. But now this misfortune

has happened to Haman. If it begins so, prophesies superstition, it must go on in the same way to the end. Mordecai
is a Jew; and if he is unfortunate with him as an individual,
it is a sure prognostication that he will be equally and more.
so in his attempt against all the Jews. The conclusion they
come to is not with regard to the Jews *per se*, but only in so
far as the experience in the case of the individual Jew Mordecai leads them to infer what will be Haman's fate with
regard to the whole nation. This is pure belief in fetishism.
When Indians have to remove a heap of stones, if before
they proceed to the task they are hurt by one stone, they
will leave the stone and abstain from the work altogether.
Of the high morality, according to which Haman as an
intriguing traitor and murderer must fall, they were not in
the least conscious. Superstition, of course, has not seldom
carnal forebodings that are fulfilled in the spirit. In fact,
the God of Israel is a living God, who, because righteousness
and truth are His attributes, reveals them unto men, especially unto those who trust in Him that He will not give
them over to destruction. Not because Haman fell the first
time he will continue to fall, but he began to fall because
the time of judgment had come. Universal history bears
testimony that persecutions of believers never brought a
blessing to the persecutors. The saying of the wise men of
Haman has an important comforting truth far above their
knowledge and understanding; only not in the national and
carnal sense in which the Jews understood it, but in the
extensive sense that "Blessed are they that have been persecuted for righteousness' sake: for theirs is the kingdom of
heaven" (Matt. v. 10). No one will prosper who wantonly
persecutes innocent witnesses of the truth. Hamans have
never been wanting, but they have all fallen.

Ver. 14. "*While they were yet talking with him, came
the king's chamberlains.*"
Behold, their gloomy conversation is yet dispelled for a

while by a ray from the sun. Royal messengers yet come to
the house, and bring a new invitation to Haman to come in
haste to the queen's banquet. He is still accompanied by a
royal retinue through the city to the palace. Mordecai may
see that there is not yet an end of Haman.—But he saw him
for the last time. It was but a deceiving lustre. Destruction
lay beneath it. He was fetched in order to be held more
securely. Probably Esther had heard what had happened to
him, and feared he might not come. What took place in the
morning encourages her for the act at noon. They were still
(עודם) speaking of the misfortune when the message arrived, in
consequence of which he so shamefully fell, to rise no more.

CHAPTER VII.

Ver. 1. "*So the king and Haman came to banquet,*" etc.

We have here a repetition of what was told in chap. v. 5, but this repetition is for a very significant reason. Esther wants to make an experiment at the table with the king and Haman, which will be decisive of life or death.[1] If she succeeds, then her people are saved; if she fails, then she is lost too. The invitation to the second banquet is not in vain. Observing the changeable mood of the tyrant, she tries first to ascertain whether the kindly disposition which he has shown towards her on the former occasion still continues. And she was not disappointed. He asked her, as at the first time, to express her wish, whatever it might be. He treated her now with the same tenderness as he did then. But she had also during the interval received some tokens of encouragement. Haman's humiliation had in the meantime taken place. It was now known that his position with the king was not so unassailable after all. Esther had seen that Ahhashverosh himself had really no antipathy against the Jews, otherwise how could he have conferred such high honour upon Mordecai, and that through the medium of Haman? It was now clear to her that every persecution that was started against the Jews was only an intrigue of Haman, of which the king, properly speaking, knew nothing. All this was revealed by the wonderful night in which the king could not

---

[1] Amestris, the wife of Xerxes, asked for similar permission to avenge herself against the wife of Masistes at a banquet; but that banquet was of another kind, and that petition was influenced by different motives. Herod. ix. 110.

sleep.—Esther saw in this the hand of her God, stretched out to render assistance in the time of need, and she was inspired by new courage.

Ver. 3. "*Then Esther the queen answered.*"

Her reply shows a decided and determined tone,—"Now, if thou art fully in earnest with thy kindness, and thou really wishest to show me a favour, know that my heart has no desire for playthings, my petition does not crave for female pleasures, I do not ask for money or for dress,—I have no court intrigues and eunuch stories to speak of with thee, but of a matter upon whose issue depends life or death, shame and destruction. Thou expectest, O king, a petition which shall supply thee with pleasure and amusement; I must speak of such things as will excite thee to the uttermost. Thou sittest at table and art desirous to be merry, but I bring a petition before thee which will cause thee pain. But thou hast promised me to grant my petition; then spare my life, which I fear is at stake. Thou hast expressed a willingness to fulfil my wishes; then give me the life of my people." The royal feast becomes all at once a tragical scene. The king listens, is astounded, and becomes excited; Esther begs for her life. Who besides himself can threaten it? Who *dares* to threaten her whom he cherishes and loves? All in the dining-hall are dumb-struck and trembling. The king's brow is clouded; while Esther with her calm and plaintive eloquence, which the occasion and the subject have inspired, looks handsomer and more dignified than before. The force of her tremulous voice the author portrays in reproducing her speech in an abrupt form. It should have been, "If I have found favour in thy sight, O king, and if it please the king to grant my request (לתת את שאלתי), let my life," etc.; but she in her excitement puts life before petition, and people before request.

Ver. 4. "*For we are sold.*"

"There was a bargain made about us, and that for the

purpose of our being destroyed, slain, and annihilated." The
words להשמיד להרג לאבד do not exactly represent a climax,
but show that Esther chose the strongest words she could
find with which to express the fate of her people. שמד, to
destroy, by removing a thing out of sight; אבד, to let a thing
perish by plucking it out by the root, and that, too, by
slaughter, therefore the word להרג is added. But notwithstanding Esther's excited feelings, which were natural to her
under the circumstances, we must not overlook the fact that
she made a masterly calculation of the nature of her husband,
and ordered her language accordingly. She does not say to
whom she and her people were sold, nor does she name the
people that were sold. She places herself in the front, and
says: " I and my people." For she has to do with a fickle
man, whose will is governed and determined by his momentary
passion and humour. There is nothing to be gained by a
mere plea on the point of justice involved in the question.
Here the heart, the vain heart, is required to be inflamed by
representations which might flatter his fancy of possessing
unlimited power. She must not say that he has sold her, for
what *he* has done must be well! and she must take care not to
assail *him*. Therefore she does not even name the sold people,
—perhaps he is reminded of his own deed; and the Jews are
too despicable to him. So she mentions herself first,—for at this
moment she was more valuable to him than a whole people; that
she was sold, whom the *king loves* so much that he generously
offers her half of his empire; that *she* was sold, whose beauty just
now at the table fascinates more than ever. This is what she
emphasizes, and whereby she seeks to win the tyrant. " I and
my people," she says. The impression of the speech gains all
its force from the insertion of the personal pronoun. The
people do not suffer for her sake, nor she for the people's
sake. She who belongs to the king, and whom he loves, is
sold. Who can dare to sell his wife? Yea, even so much
as to estimate the value of the person he loves! He wants
to give her half of his kingdom, if she desires it; and she

begs him with bitter tears to save her from the death to which she is sold. "To be sold" was, besides, an expression applicable only to slaves. Quintilian says (viii. 1): "As under the term city (*urbs*) is understood Rome, so by the term *venales* are understood slaves." When Roxolana got to be the favourite of the Turkish Sultan Suleiman, she was reproached by her envious rival with being *carne venduta*, "sold flesh." Roxolana then called herself so before the sultan, as an excuse for no longer approaching him, for as "sold flesh" she considered herself unworthy to do so; and this contributed to her complete victory over her rival (Hammer, *Gesch. des osman. Reiches*, iii. 728).

"But if we had been sold for bondmen and bondwomen."

This turn in Esther's plea is still more beautiful and impressive. One cannot represent in a few words the whole of the rare position of a Persian shah. "If it were nothing further," she says, "but that we had been sold as slaves, our lives would then be spared, and we could entertain the hope of eventually regaining our liberty,—in that case I should not trouble thee so much. It would not have been worth while to disturb thee just now and spoil thy appetite." For these pregnant words, although the adversary could not have compensated the king's damage, כי אין הצר שוה בנזק המלך (or R. V. "for our affliction is not to be compared with the king's damage"), are calculated to flatter the Persian tyrant. True, צר means "enemy," but in the abstract also "distress," "tribulation," "misfortune;" and even if it is insisted that the article points to the enemy, still it must be conceded that the emphasis cannot be on the person, but, as it is a participial form, rather upon the act of the enemy. For "the adversary" is no other in the second than in the first,—it is always the same Haman,—but the mischief would be of another character if it were only to end in slavery. The word הצר, therefore, means the evil which the evil one has done to Israel. Esther's meaning is as follows: "The enemy,

or the enmity, if it threatens such things to us, would not
have been considered of sufficient value (אין שׁוה) to disturb
the king (בנזק המלך)." True, indeed, that נזק has the meaning
of damage, and may radically be compared with *nocere* ; and,
in fact, is used in Ezra (iv. 13) to denote the damage done to
the revenue, and other acts of enmity to the king. And yet
it cannot be here, as some have supposed, that Esther meant
to convey to the king that she and her people would rather
suffer slavery than cause him any pecuniary damage ; for in
both cases, whether they were sold to be killed or into slavery,
pecuniary damage must ensue. But in the flattering language
of the etiquette of the Persian court, to disturb the king
was tantamount to damage or injure the king. When the
king was disturbed in the enjoyment of his dinner by being
called to pass judgment upon sad cases, it was considered as
an injury done to him. Esther nevertheless does it—only
because her life and the existence of her people are at stake.
She would have rather gone into slavery than cast a gloom
upon the joyous hours of the king. But she cannot act
otherwise. She is compelled to speak out. With this explanation agrees that of an African Rabbi, quoted by Ibn
Ezra in his commentary on this book (ed. Zedner, London
1850, p. 29). One reading of this passage in the LXX. is
indeed remarkable : οὐ γὰρ ἄξιος ὁ διάβολος τῆς αὐλῆς τοῦ
βασιλέως, for αὐλή certainly does not mean here the court of
the king, but is a Greek form of the Hebrew עַוְלָה, viz. "the
injustice," "the evil deed," against the king.

Ver. 5. "*Then spake the king.*"

The words of Esther could not fail to produce the desired
impression. They were so forcible and so full of good sense.
She spoke from the depth of her heart, and yet with full discretion. Her high position as the beloved wife of the king,
her beautiful appearance, her graceful manners, her heart-
rending plea, her bitter tears, and above all the justice of her
cause, called forth sympathy mingled with indignation from

every impartial heart; and the king's wrath was specially
kindled, seeing she had touched the delicate spring of his
immeasurable vanity. For he knew of nothing. He had
long ago forgotten the thoughtless grant that he had made to
Haman in one of his capricious moods, and if memory still
served him, he was quite certain that the sale of the queen
formed no item in the contract, and that her name was not
even mentioned on that occasion. And now he sees that the
whole scheme was after all designed to deprive him of her.
Undoubtedly it was an intrigue which caused Vashti's fall,
but she had to some extent brought it upon herself by
her disobedience, and he was not present when she was
sentenced; and yet how sorry he afterwards was for his rash
deed. But now somebody, without his knowledge, sells
his wife to death,— his wife who is so obedient and so
loving. One sees in these words that the narrator describes
the king's anger, in that he repeats the word ויאמר, "And
the king Ahhashverosh spake and said to Queen Esther."

"*Who is he, and where is he?*" (הוא.)

This question expresses his burning indignation. There is
some one who dares that—who is he? Where in my kingdom does the man live who has the audacity to act thus
towards me, whose heart is full, *i.e.* whose heart is filled with
such impudence as to do so?[1] The LXX. pretty nearly reproduces the sense by ἐτόλμησε, "that durst presume" to do so.
Arnheim renders it freely, "who had the haughtiness," etc.
The first Targum exaggerates his excitement still more, by
representing him as saying, "Who is the audacious, the
criminal, the rebel, who ventures to do this?" Esther,
impelled by the trouble of her heart, and noticing that the
king was inclined to do her justice, gains confidence, and
without regarding the presence of him whom it concerns,
freely speaks her mind.

---

[1] [A speech like that in the N. T. Acts v. 3, "Why hath Satan filled
thine heart?"—TRANS.]

Ver. 6. "*An adversary and an enemy,*[1] *even this wicked Haman.*"

"That one after whom thou inquirest, the oppressor and enemy, the one who wants to murder me and my people, who has sold me—now, with flashing eye and angry mien she lifts her finger and points to her guest, ' that Haman !'—he is not far from here ; we need not seek him ; he sits at our side, that man there—Haman is this wicked one !" It is a dramatic scene beyond comparison. Haman's blood runs cold. Such a storm he had never anticipated. How should he know that Esther was a Jewess ? Had he known it, he would have adopted quite different measures. To defend himself now he knew was impossible. The faces of both, of the king and of the queen, deterred him. He knew well how the king looked when he was angry.

The Oriental legends frequently describe the dreadful look which Harun-Arrashid assumed when he detected a piece of roguery. Abdolmelik, king of Damascus, says one of these legends, did not make the slightest movement. He was quite like one petrified. Harun assumed all at once such a dreadful tone, that the unfortunate prince gave up his throne not so much on account of obedience, but on account of the terror which overwhelmed him. The surprise made him stiff and benumbed.[2] נבעת, from בעת, to become " alarmed," " terrified," figuratively and really φοβεῖν.

Ver. 7. "*And the king arose in his wrath.*"

The king was so angry that he did not speak a word, still less did he give Haman the opportunity to speak. Excessive blind wrath generally follows tyrannical conceit. In the same proportion in which Oriental tyranny permits itself to make superabundant grants, is its blind wrath when its

---

[1] The observation of Ibn Ezra, that צר means an open enemy and אויב a hidden enemy, is at any rate not confirmed here, where Esther uses both expressions to heighten her hatred.

[2] See *The Thousand and One Nights,* ed. Leipzig 1790, i. 124 and 407.

infatuated vanity is offended. The Oriental legendary world
is full of representations of pure downright passion, which,
against whomsoever it may be directed, whether he deserves
it or not, is thought to be so natural, that it is to the
Oriental mind an adornment of the most ideal king. Upon
the quality of relentless passion are founded the Eastern
novels and stories about various catastrophes, and sons and
wives and viziers are its habitual victims. That which befell
Haman here was experienced by Hikar, the most virtuous of
all viziers, as is told in a very instructive Arabic narrative.
Intrigue knows usually how to excite jealousy and anger, and
an investigation concerning the right or wrong of the accused
is considered unnecessary.

חמה, "heated fury." The king became hot on account
of glowing excitement. Rosenmüller has collected some
examples to show that when an Oriental king rises angry
from the table, then there is no mercy for him who was
the cause of it (*Morgenland zu Buch Esther*, No. 718).
The sense is that the king withdraws his favour from him,
as the sun departs. His going away means the same as
the vanishing of the sun, the cessation of the light of mercy
and of life. The royal dining-hall was close to the garden
of the palace, whither the king went as a sign of his being
angry, and to cool himself.[1]

"*And Haman stood up to make request for his life.*"
Haman read his fall in the face and in the movements of
the king. But as he was haughty when prosperous, so now
he is without manliness in ruin. He falls upon his knees
before his accuser to beg for life. He is not ashamed to
ask mercy of her whose people he wanted to kill without
mercy. He lies at her feet, to whom he owes his sudden

[1] Not like Sulpicius Severus, of whom we read (*Hist. Sacra*, ii. 111):
"Remembering the enemy, he delayed a little. And in order somewhat
to deliberate (*deliberandique gratia modicum secessit*), he turned aside."
This is not the manner of an Oriental prince. The going away was a
sign of anger.

crushing defeat, crying and sobbing for help. He beseeches
her to save him, who had just now called him a traitor and
an enemy. Of course he could have said that he did not
then know that she was a Jewess, and that his proposal had
no reference to her. But how could this plea move Esther's
compassion, when all the efforts she had thus far made were
in behalf of her people? But seeing that she alone has
influence with the king, he cringes before her after the
manner of knavish cowards, who do not mind begging from
any and everybody if they think they will get what they
want. They do not blush, for they are destitute of self-
respect. And so Haman lies prostrate before Esther's feet
crying for mercy, and not minding the contemptuous and
wrathful glance which she deigns to cast upon him. Esther
would not and could not forgive him.—To speak a good word
for him now, if she were disposed to do so, would be to
undo the whole work that she has done. The angry king
feels himself deeply offended. Who should now save Haman?
While he is still kneeling near the divan upon which Esther
sits, the king returns from his walk in the garden and
finds him in this posture. It is quite true what Plutarch
(*Themist.* 26) tells of the jealousy of the Persian kings with
regard to their wives, but the words which the king addresses
to Haman, "Will he even force[1] the queen before me in the
house?" do not contain jealousy, which would be absurd, but
biting irony. It cannot be mercy, thinks the king, that thou
seekest from her whom thou hast so atrociously offended;
thou canst have no hope that she would forgive thee; so it
may be that thou art so audacious as to lay hold of my wife

---

[1] כבשׁ. LXX. βιάζειν, in the well-known sense. Clericus has translated
this classical word by "*subagitare*," for this word is still more used by the
Latins in this sense than "*subigere*," especially in the popular language of
the comedians (comp. Terent. *Heaut.* iii. 3, 6, etc.). Old Meissner (p. 112)
has not understood the irony, for only in ironical bitterness has the
exclamation any sense. The same was the case with Vorstius, who, for
this reason, rendered the expression of Sulpicius Severus by "*appetitam*,"
which is a weak emendation (p. 203).

in an unwarrantable manner! He that could be so bold as
to devise a plan for killing my own wife, who could abuse
my confidence in order to betray the love of the king, such a
man is quite capable of making an indecent assault upon the
queen in my presence! In these awful ironical words lay
the sentence of death for Haman. They manifest the fury of
the king, who does not stop to consider that Haman was
unaware of the origin of Esther, nor does he think of the
people whose lives were at stake, but only of the audacity
which could make his wife an object of hatred. And this
irony contained an accusation against Haman, which was in
itself enough to procure the forfeiture of his life. Therefore
scarcely had the words escaped the king's lips when Haman's
face was covered. The covering of the face of a criminal
arose from the idea that he is henceforth no more worthy to
behold the light of which the king was an emblem. That
with which he was previously only threatened when the king
went out to the garden,—when the sun departed,—he is now
made to realize after the king's return,—he must see the sun
no more. He is a guilty criminal, and has no more right to
see the sun. Guilt is in itself defilement like death.[1] The
voluntary covering of one's own face is different from its
being covered by another. Mourners do it spontaneously,
because they feel as if under judgment; but when the faces
of others are compulsorily covered, it is a sign to them of
judgment, to intimate to them that they are condemned.
The first do not want to see the light, the second no longer
need it. The explanation of Ibn Ezra, that it was customary
to cover a man's face who had provoked the king, is correct.
To this effect the reference of Curtius is also a happy one,
who reports that when Philotas was seized by order of

---

[1] The faces of the dead are covered. This brings painful recollections
to me of the time when I had to cover the face of my dear departed
wife. In a story of Lübeck, the dying monks are said to have been seen
in the monastery in a time of cholera with covered faces, as if they were
already prepared for burial (see Deecke, *Lübische Geschichten und Sagen*,
p. 120).

Alexander, he was brought with covered face to the place of the king (*velato capite ad regiam*) (vi. 22. 8). We are even informed further that this was done with an old rag (*obsoleto amiculo*), while his hands were tied to his back. Therefore Cicero rightly ascribes the origin of the formula, "Lictor, tie his hands, cover his face, hang him on the accursed tree," to the time of the Roman kings, as he thinks to Tarquinius (*superbissimi et crudelissimi regis*) (*Pro Cajo Rabirio*, p. 3, etc.).

In fact, as Livius (i. 26) informs us, this punishment was already applied under Tullus Hostilius to Horatius, on account of the patriotic murder of his sister. His father pleaded for him, saying, "Should the hands which have shortly before carried arms and obtained dominion for the Roman people be tied? Should the face of the liberator of this city be covered?" So Horatius is sentenced to pass with covered face under a beam as under a yoke. The covering of the face signified his guilt.[1]

This evidently was also the theological ground in the practice among the Romans to pray, and to offer sacrifices with covered heads.[2] By this, a sense of guilt was acknowledged and confessed; and Plutarch's explanation, that the Romans did this to humble themselves, is the right one, while other explanations are flat and constrained, and only rarely applicable. Tertullian (*Apolog.* cap. 30) rightly says: "We pray with uncovered head, because we are not ashamed," —*i.e.* Christians pray without fear, not as condemned, but as reconciled,—"for love casteth out fear." Naturally this is also the meaning of the words of the apostle when he says

---

[1] At all events, I believe that I have given to this remarkable passage its proper meaning. For it has been often quoted and misinterpreted even by Göttling in *Römische Staatsverfassung*, p. 159.

[2] Comp. Brisson, *de formulis*, i. 32, but the custom is not there explained. When Suetonius (*Vitellius*, cap. 2) reports that Vitellius, after his return from Syria, adored the king "Velato capite," it was not necessarily an Oriental practice, but rather the flatterer rendered homage to the emperor in the same way as was done to the gods.

that a man should not have his head covered, whatever the
covering may be, when he is praying or prophesying (προσευ-
χόμενος ἡ προφητεύων), for Christ is his head. The doctrine
was not, as Oosterzee thinks, against the custom of the Romans,
but more particularly against that of the Jews. Not only
the later Jews, as he says (on 1 Cor. xi. 4, p. 107), had this
practice, but it existed from time immemorial (as in the case
of Moses at the bush), and especially at the time of Christ
and the apostles. The theological idea contained at that
time in the covering of the head during prayer is proved from
the use of the word עטף in connection with prayer, which
the Psalmist employs to express " covering the face in sorrow,
or being overwhelmed with affliction " (Ps. lxxvii. 4, cvii. 5).
The act of covering of the face in the case of a mourner was
in itself not different from that of a suppliant. In both the
feeling of repentance is presupposed to exist. The mourners
in this way bemoan only one object of temporal loss, while
the suppliants have in view the whole relation of man
towards God. When we read in Moed Katan 24a, " Every
covering which is not as the covering of Ishmaelites (pre-
Mohamedan) is not a covering," it refers not only to
mourners, as Levy thinks (*Chald. Wörterbuch*, ii. p. 210),
but to prayer in general (comp. *Sefer Agur*, ed. Venez.
1516, p. 4a). And this covering consisted in putting on the
Talith (praying garment), and did not exclude the proper
covering of the head. Hence we read in Tract Shabbath
10a: " He put it on, covered himself, wrapped himself up
(מתעטף), and prayed." This practice went so far that it
became indispensable to every religious and spiritual act,
so much so, that even God in heaven was pictured as a
Rabbi covered (רעטיף) with a garment as white as snow
(Targum on Song of Solomon, v. 10), and as it is added,
" He studied during the day the law and the prophets,
and during the night the Mishna " (Eisenmenger, i.
p. 6).[1]

---

[1] [Comp. *The Old Paths*, by Dr. M'Caul, p. 439.—TRANS.]

222BOOK OF ESTHER.

In the dreadful words which the king uttered to Haman, the courtiers perceived the sentence of his condemnation. He was covered.

Ver. 9. *"Then said Harbonah,"* etc.

When courtiers are unsuccessful, then all their glory is at an end.[1] Former jealousy breaks now out in open hostility. Former cowardice gives place to bold accusation. Haman's manner and conduct was of such a haughty character as to preclude his making loyal friends who would stick to him in misfortune. Besides, Harbonah may not have been one of his friends at all. The scene took place in the apartments of the queen. Harbonah was one of her eunuchs, who belonged to her party, and now supports her victory by his remark. The word גם also is explained by modern commentators (Bertheau and Keil) in such a way as to imply that Harbonah added to what other eunuchs had said. But this is erroneous. It is most characteristic. The accusation of Esther against Haman was that he had sold her with her people. This embittered the king the more, that he had presumed to sell his wife. He considered it as the highest act of treason. And so Harbonah adds: "It is not this offence alone that he has committed, but he has also conspired against the life of Mordecai, who has saved his majesty's life, and who has just now been honoured by the king.[2] Haman was quite ready to execute him on the gallows fifty cubits high." The word "also" (גם) refers then not to Harbonah's speech, but to Haman's treachery against the king and his friends. It is very curious that, as in chap. iv. so here, the name of Jews is passed over in silence. It is not said that the people who have been sold are Jews, nor does Harbonah say, as it stands elsewhere, "Mordecai the Jew." For it does not at all matter to what nationality they belong—it

---

[1] Comp. the history which Dio Cassius gives of Scrib. Proculus, lix. 26.

[2] [Therefore in the liturgy for Purim it is said "Harbonah also is to be remembered for good."—TRANS.]

is not a question about certain persons, but a royal question which is dealt with here. Haman's offence consisted in wanting to slay the king's wife and the king's friends—this is accentuated. The Midrash (Yalkut Shimeoni, n. 1059) has a remarkable comment on this verse. Under Harbonah is to be understood the prophet Elijah, who assumed his appearance in order to effect Haman's death. They thought that חרבונה is derived from חרב, "sword." Haman is a type of Israel's adversary (Samael), of whom Jewish tradition says that he will at last be killed by Elijah. In the same way, in patristic writings, Elijah is represented as the great opponent of Antichrist at the last day (see the fragment attributed to Lactantius in *Baluzii Miscell.*, ed. Mansi, i. 12).[1]

" And the king said : Hang him thereon."

תלה means "to hang." The passage in Deut. xxi. 22 is well known: "And if a man have committed a sin worthy of death, and he be put to death, and thou hang him on a tree (ותלית אותו על העץ), his body shall not remain all night upon the tree, but thou shalt surely bury him the same day; for he that is hanged (תלוי) is accursed of God: that thou defile not thy land which the Lord thy God giveth thee for an inheritance." The condemned was drawn up upon a beam and nailed to it. This was a common mode of punishment among the Persians. The Greek writers when they mention it call it ἀνασταυρόειν, ἀνασταυροῦν.

The wood was called σταυρός. So narrates Ctesias, that the king had caused Inaros to be hung, ἀνεσταύρωσε ἐπὶ τρισί σταυροῖς ;[2] the same expression is used by Thucydides, ἀνεσταυρώθη (comp. 'Bähr, *zu Ctesiae Rell.* p. 176). What is expressed by ἀνά is reproduced in the Hebrew idiom by תלה, "to hang," as the beam was usually high, as is here expressly stated. Haman had one prepared fifty cubits high,

---

[1] We shall refer to this again when we consider the number 666.

[2] When Artayktes is punished we read (Herod. ix. 20): σανίδα προσπασσαλεύσαντες ἀνεκρέμασαν.

in order that the condemned might be seen from a distance,
and this fell upon his own head.

Haman's fate has a parallel in modern history.   Henry V.
of England had laid siege to Meaux in France, where the
cruel commander had hung all the English prisoners.   So,
after the king had taken the city, he caused him to be hung
on the same scaffold (Mensel, *Geschichte von Frankreich*, ii.
455).   When, therefore, the Jews call Christ a תלוי, there can
be no objection to it as far as the letter is concerned, as it
is the translation of *crucifixus*, "the crucified."   But the
objection is that they use the word as a term of reproach,
"But we preach Christ crucified, to the Jews a stumbling-
block, and to Greeks foolishness," etc. (1 Cor. i. 23).   When
the Jews also used, on the feast of Purim, to represent
Haman as crucified, the act contained a historical truth,
although the suspicion in ancient times may not have been
without foundation, that they also mocked thereby the
suffering of Christ; therefore the Roman emperors issued in
408 an edict against it, as follows: "Judaeos quodam festivi-
tatis suae solemni Aman ad poenae quondam recordationem
incendere et sanctae crucis assimulatam speciem in contemtum
Christianae fidei sacrilega mente exurere" (Cod. Theod., lib.
xvi. tit. 8. 18).

The allegory which the Jews have in connection with this
occasion is interesting.   It is told in the second Targum that
when Haman was about to be hanged in the garden, he
complained to the trees that he was to be hanged on one of
them, and especially on one which was fifty cubits high.   So
the vine, the Paradise-apple, the oak, and the pomegranate
refused out of pious motives to be used for that purpose.
The oak even averred that it could not have any one hung
upon itself, because it had served as a scaffold to Absalom,
the son of David.   Then the cedar came and offered itself, in
order that he may have the required height.   But later
homilies have taken away this office from the cedar, and
given it to the thorn bush, in order that it also may serve

a purpose in God's creation. "For equals meet together, one thorn should lie upon another thorn." The wicked are compared to thorns (*Mezahh Aaron*, p. 47). There is in this no doubt a hidden reference to the thorns of Christ. According to another allegory, when Haman was looking for the tree on which to hang Mordecai, and on which he was hanged himself, he could find no other but the fir tree for this purpose. In this is seen a German allegory. The fir is used as a Christmas tree; the Jews called Christmas נטל,[1] which properly comes from *natalis* (*festum natale*); but it admits a secondary meaning of "hanging" (תלה), by way of polemical play upon words.

Ver. 10. "*Then was the king's wrath pacified.*"

The remark is important for the statement that follows. In chap. ii. 1, after Vashti was removed, we read: "When the wrath of the king Ahhashverosh was pacified, he remembered Vashti!" He was sorry for her. But now—and on this the following is a commentary—his wrath is subdued; but Haman's fate caused him no sorrow, and this was fortunate for Esther and the Jews. The king's order was not yet revoked, and was still impending over their heads, and it would not have been difficult to find adherents of Haman who would have walked in his footsteps. The decision had only begun with the fall of Haman. If his execution had only been caused by the momentary anger of the king, the Jews would still have perished. Their destiny and that of Esther depended now on what the king was going to do after he calmed down.

[1] [This word is used by the Jerusalem Targum on Ex. xxx. 19: "Aaron and his sons shall wash." When applied to Christmas, it must announce to the Rabbis the glad tidings that Jesus came into the world to cleanse and to save sinners.—TRANS.]

CHAPTER VIII.

Ver. 1. "*On that day did the king Ahhashverosh give the house of Haman, the Jews' enemy, unto Esther the queen.*"

What is here narrated occurs numberless times in the histories of Oriental kingdoms. The will of the shah is law. What his servants possess, they have only through him. And this is also to some extent the case with their life. When they are to be punished their possession returns to him. The fall of a man like Haman is always considered in the light of a war—what he possesses is spoil. Haman falls, so his house is confiscated when the king wills it. When Sultan Suleiman caused the mighty vizier of the Turkish empire, his own brother-in-law, Ibrahim, to be strangled, he confiscated all his property, which was worth millions. And so when Shah Abbas ordered the execution of a certain prominent man on account of his haughtiness, Chardin, who informs us of it, adds : "I do not now say that the king put all his property under seal, because I believe I have said more than once, that the confiscation of goods almost invariably follows the loss of life, when it is lost by the order of the sovereign." The king Ahhashverosh confiscates Haman's house, not for himself, but for Esther. She and Haman carried on war between them, and she had conquered through the favour of the king, therefore she receives the war booty.

"*And Mordecai came before the king.*"

He had not come before the king when the king had learned from the chronicle that he had saved his life. Now he comes as Esther's uncle. It was now universally known to what nationality she belonged. She had therefore no longer any cause to conceal the facts, that her connection with the Jew Mordecai was of long standing, that he had brought her up, and that she had heard from him about the dangerous condition of her people. It made no difference to the king that she was a Jewess, for not the peculiarities of his subjects, but his own will was law (as is the case with all Oriental sultans). It was enough for him that Mordecai was her relation, that she liked him, and that he had obtained his favour.

He took off his ring and gave it to Mordecai, just as he did before to Haman. He gave the property of the defeated party to the conqueror. The persecutor (צורר) had fallen, and the persecuted came into power. The arbitrariness of the monarch became the instrument of retaliation. This also will not be strange to those who read Oriental history. In a story of the history of Harun Arrashid it is told that the governor of a prison was once though innocent punished by the governor of the State, and when his innocency was proved, he was set as inspector over his persecutor (ed. Habicht, xiii. 20). Abbas ordered Murchidealichan to be killed; and made his groom, who helped in the execution, governor of Herat in his place (Olearius in Meissner, p. 114).

The change was in itself radically not different from what takes place in modern constitutional States. In the place of the outgoing minister comes the leader of the opposition. Only here a matter of principle or ambition is involved in the change, but there a matter of life. In Europe it came to be a sign of the limited power of the monarch, while in the East it was a sign of the unlimited power of the shah.

Ver. 2. *"And Esther set Mordecai over the house of Haman."* It was given her as a present from the king, for she stood at the head of those against whom Haman conspired. But she cannot be the vizier, and so she nominates her uncle to the office. Therefore she gives him the house of Haman. He requires not only to have the ring, but also the property of

Haman, as the same grandeur which Haman possessed is
necessary to his (Mordecai's) position. Esther rewards
Mordecai for the love she had received from him. She is not
only a zealous daughter of Israel, but has also a grateful heart.
Through the education which she received from him she was
qualified to become a queen, and therefore in return he must
become her husband's vizier. But, with all this, she had not
forgotten the higher motive which was far above personal
triumphs.

It never occurred to the king that all was not yet
finished with the hanging of Haman. He saw that there
was war between Esther and his minister. The latter had
fallen in disgrace, for the king felt that he had assailed
his sovereignty, and now he thought that all was at an end.
It was not for the sake of the Jews that he had made such
an exhibition of his anger, but in vindication of his own
authority. Now the death of Haman had appeased him, and
he took no further trouble. But the queen could not yet be
satisfied with his condemnation. For what she had dared
and done was not so much to procure the fall of Haman, as
the deliverance of Israel. That Mordecai had the ring and
the house of Haman given to him could not satisfy her. The
cruel decree was still impending over Israel. It was yet in
full force though Haman was dead. And as long as this was
not repealed, the triumph of Mordecai and herself could not be
complete.

Ver. 3. "*And Esther spake yet again before the king.*"
She was not content with what she obtained in her first
audience with the king at the banquet. She besought him
again (ותוסף) to grant her a second audience. And she knew
well that this would be more difficult than the first, for the
very reason that the first was so successful. The means
which she on that occasion used could not be used again.
She could not invite to another banquet. To take the king
by surprise again was impossible. For this he had only given

her one opportunity. The personal consideration which induced him to grant the former interview was now wanting. The entertainment of tyrants becomes soon tedious when no character of novelty is introduced into it; they soon think they have had enough of it. The second appearance of Esther before the king was therefore more difficult and of more doubtful result than the first. She makes also now— as the narrator takes no pains to conceal—more exertions, in order that she may impress the king.

" She fell down at his feet, and besought him with tears."
She did not do so the first time. But at that time she did not know how much regard and affection the king had for her. And a weeping woman cannot invite to a feast. But now she knew that he loved her. One does not resist the tears of a beloved wife. And so she beseeches him even weeping, that he, the gracious and powerful, may now undo the evil (רעה) of the evil one (רע), viz. "the device that Haman had devised against the Jews." It is true that he is dead, but the arrow which he has thrown is still deadly poisonous. And she does not now say, as before, "we are sold," lest she should be misunderstood as if she was only anxious for personal freedom; but she entreats his help against the plan that threatens the Jews in general. This name was not even mentioned in the former conversation; but now, since it is known that she is a relative of Mordecai the Jew, she has courage to name them in the third person. The narrative indicates nicety of style, in that she is not represented as saying: "to do away the device which Haman had devised against us." For it would have been offensive to the king to entertain the idea that a plan of the execrable Haman could have touched the queen. The result of Esther's petition was still doubtful. She could not rely upon the humour of the Persian shah. During the interval between the fall of Haman and her present interview various influences might have been brought to bear upon the king's

mind. But she was mistaken in her fears. The king again held out the golden sceptre, as a sign that he regarded her graciously; and she recognised in this that he was favourably inclined to hear what she had further to ask of him.

Ver. 4. "*So Esther arose, and stood before the king.*"

As a suppliant she knelt, but in consequence of his favour she stood up as his wife, and more accurately formulated her petition. The speech which she now makes is a masterpiece of that prudence and humility with which the person of the shah must be addressed. The first words, "If it please the king, and if I have found favour in his sight," are, as it appears, the usual form of addressing the king. Similarly she spake to him on the former occasion; but now, bearing in mind the difficult matter that she had to lay before him, she adds, "and the thing seems right (כשר) before the king." This adjective occurs only here, but in later Hebrew of the Targum and the Talmud we meet with it frequently. The verb is etymologically cognate with אשר, ישר, meaning "right," "proper;" but the special sense in which כשר is used here, is the same as in later times. The Rabbis in the Talmud called that "*kasher*" which was permitted from a religious point of view. In the same sense Esther understands the word if the thing appears to the king such as, for his person, for his position and conscience, seems proper and allowable. She herself passes no judgment upon it,—this is his privilege, and he will in his wisdom know whether what she demands, is permissible and right. Then she goes on to say, "And I be pleasing (טובה), good, in his eyes." The word "good" is purposely chosen by her. According to the religious dualism of the Persian teaching, Ahriman is the evil, and Ahuramazda is the good god. Evil was therefore against the light and against the king, who represented the doctrine of Ahuramazda. Evil was the king's enemy, and good was the devoted adherent of the king. When Esther accuses Haman, she calls him הרע, "the evil one;" and in contrast to this she

says now, "And if I be good in his eyes;" if the king loves
me, and I appear as pleasing, submissive, and attached. She
prays him for the sake of the love which he has for her—
but, of course, after ascertaining that her demand is right—
that he should invalidate and revoke the edict, and destroy
the letters (ספר, "scroll," "letter," and "book" as *literae*)
which contain Haman's device to annihilate the Jews. She
adds wisely that they are מחשבת, the machination of Haman,
for in themselves they were the letters of the king; and
therefore she guards herself against implying that she meant
that the king's own work should be destroyed. Nothing of the
kind. For she knows well that a royal edict cannot be revoked,
and therefore she puts into the king's mouth a different interpretation of the character of the letters. They are entirely
Haman's work, of which the king knew nothing originally;
they had been smuggled in, and therefore he can revoke them.
When she adds: " son of Hamedatha the Agagite," it must be,
as already remarked, in allusion to his relation to a certain
party, which makes it more detestable in the eyes of the king.

Ver. 6. *" How can I endure to see?"* etc.

With rhetorical skill and force she continues to move his
heart. "Say not, O king, that thy favour protects my life,—
that is doubtless true,—but I have not prayed merely for
myself,—and how could I live in peace and enjoyment while
my poor people is slain; how unbearable would be to me thy
favour and glory, if I should have to witness the disaster
which befell my own kindred; how should I be ashamed to
be something to thee, when in spite of it I should have to
look at the destruction of the nation which gave me birth!"
(She uses the word מולדת for nation, from ילד, as *natio* is from
nascor.) She says, "endure to see," without being able to
help. Thus she gives the king clearly to understand that
she would be powerless and helpless, although she is the
beloved queen; and this powerlessness would be a reflection
upon him. She effectively shows him the contrast between

the favour that he had shown to her and Mordecai, and her possible helplessness in not being able to save her brethren from death and plunder. What would the people say, and what would be the general popular opinion if they should see that the great favourites of the king are inactive while their people suffer ?   Could Esther endure that people should say of her, that she was sitting and enjoying herself in the harem, and looking with indifference at the destruction of Israel ?   If so, thy favour, she gives him to understand, would be worse than thy wrath.   The adherents of Haman will avenge themselves on Mordecai and on us by killing the Jews before our eyes.   Not Haman but we would be the most unfortunate. His death would be better than our life.   For it is better to die with the others than to live in sorrow and contempt. " My people and I have not fasted and prayed that I should live, but that they should live.   My life is in thy hands. Save the poor people."

Vers. 7, 8. " *Then the king Ahhashverosh said to Esther the queen,*" etc.

The answer of the king manifests dignity and kindness at the same time.   He pacifies the excited Esther, and yet maintains his royal attitude.   It is difficult to see why Clericus finds the answer obscure.   His language is clear ; a revocation of the edict is impossible ; a rescript issued in the name of the king and sealed by his seal cannot be made void under any pretext whatever.[1]   And this rests upon the idea that a " decree," דת, is ideally to be looked upon in the light of an emanation from him.   Whether the writing and the plans originated in Haman's mind or not, is of no consequence. Suffice it that they bear the name and seal of the king. " But," says he, " you can obtain your wish very easily in another manner.   Mordecai is now the keeper of the seals, and he can issue any decree in my name that he likes.   It is now a

---

[1] What Brisson adduces from Diodor. xvii. 30 (not 14), has no reference to this (*De reg. Pers. princ.* l. i. c. 130).

well-known fact that Haman has fallen, that I gave to Esther
the Jewess his house, and that he was hung because of his
wanting to lay violent hands upon the Jews. Make this
known everywhere! This will show all over the Persian
kingdom what my will is, and where my interests lie. Then
my governors and officials, after hearing these reports, will
take care not to rise against the Jews. They will see from
this that another party has come to the helm of government,
and that it is not my will that the Jews should be wronged.
As soon as the officials hear that the queen and the vizier are
themselves of Jewish origin, they will instruct the people to
behave themselves to the Jews in general with proper decorum,
and not in the spirit of Haman. You can issue an edict in my
name, which will virtually annul the first, but the first cannot
be revoked. Write," says he, "now also to the Jews what you
please," just as he had before left Haman to do what he liked.
We observe in him the same arbitrary proceeding, the same
carelessness as to the lives of many people, the same tyrannical caprice now for Esther as it was before for Haman,—
all is easy in his hands, except to revoke his former edict,
which might be regarded as derogatory to the royal dignity.

Vers. 9, 10. "*Then were the king's scribes called at that
time, in the third month, which is the month Sivan, on the
three and twentieth day thereof,*" etc.

The name of the third month, Sivan, occurs for the first
time here. Its meaning, like that of most names of the old
calendar, has been entirely confused by Benfey and Stern
in the book, *Ueber die Monatsnamen.* According to them,
it is derived from an imaginary Iranian deity named
Çpenta. The meaning can easily be seen. The second and
the third month of the Jewish calendar were vernal months,
whose names were transferable to each other, as is the case
elsewhere. We frequently call June the second May. The
month May, which is called in the later Jewish calendar אִיָּר,
Iyar (ἔαρ, spring), goes in the Old Testament by the name of

זו (1 Kings vi. 1, 37), meaning blossom, the month in which
the trees are in bloom. Now, as the letters ז and ס are inter-
changeable (as in זהר and סהר), זו became סיו, to designate the
second spring month, and the third in the year. The Lettes
called it Seedu, month of blossoms (comp. my *Sunem*, 1876,
p. 182).

The decree which Haman obtained with subtlety dated from
the 13th of the first month Nisan, so that it was forty days
in advance of this. It was therefore the more necessary
to despatch the message without delay. For it had to be sent
all over the empire to all nations, as everywhere a rising
against the Jews was feared ; consequently we find here that
not runners only were employed, as in the case of Haman's
despatch, but also riders on swift steeds, mules, and young
dromedaries.   The expression רוכב הרכש is to show that
besides riders on ordinary horses, סוסים, there were others who
rode on race-horses.   The word רכש is found in two other
places in the O. T., in Micah i. 13 and 1 Kings v. 8, in
conjunction with סוסים, and appears to be cognate with *rachab*,
and to express "rash and fierce driving."   That, therefore,
the name of the famous horse of Rustem, Rekshh, is to be
derived from רכש there can be no doubt, and not from its
colour, as Vullers (*Lex. Pers.* ii. 24) asserts, for he himself
gives it the general meaning of horse.   It seems to me that
this word gives us explicitly the origin of the German word
Ross; Old High Germ., Old Low Germ. *hros*; Anglo-Sax.
hors. This explanation was overlooked even by Grimm
(*Gesch. d. deutsch. Spr.* p. 31).   In the translation into the
German language, the *chs* became an *s* or *sch*, as evidently is
the case in the relation between the Hebrew רחש and the
German *rauschen.*   These runners are further designated on
account of their excellence and swiftness as אחשתרנים.   All
recent commentators (as Bertheau, Keil, Schulz) have almost
literally accepted the view of Haug, which is expressed in
Ewald's *Annual* (v. 154), where he explained the word thus :
" It is an adjective form of *Kshatra*, ' dominion,' ' the king,'

with the termination *ana, na,* and signifies the 'royal State
horses.'" However specious this explanation may momentarily
appear, it awakens doubt after close observation. First,
because Haug himself explains in the previous page אחשדרפנים
from *Kshatra,* "land," "dominion," and it did not occur to him
that here in our text חשדר is with a daleth, ד, while in אחשתרנים
the same sound is given by a ת. Secondly, if it meant
"royal," it would have stood first in order by way of distinction. If it was not an official name, why did not the author
use the Hebrew word מלך, which he frequently uses? If
it were such, what does it mean? Were not the rest royal?
Or were all royal horses sent? Why is this expression not
used in connection with the State horse upon which Mordecai
rode? Then, again, the formation of the word is defective.
Kshatra means province, land (modern Pers. שהר). We do not
observe the meaning of "stately," "lordly," in it. It would
almost, on the contrary, express a contrast to what was royal,
and rather express that which was provincial and belonged to
a satrapy.

Now a closer observation will show that אחשתרנים is derived
from the Old Persian שתר with the prefixed syllable, and has
the signification of dromedary. The camel, which is swift in
running ("dromas velocissimi cursus," Vullers, ii. 411), has this
name (Zend. *ushtra, uschtur, uchtur*) *Schutur, Schtur.*[1] This
name of the camel is manifestly, as dromedary, from δρομέω,
"to run," derived from the habit of the animal. The Tigris is
therefore also called שתרב, because its current is swift. The
word is doubtless connected with τρέχω (for στρέχω), and
with the Zend. *takshra,* "to run" (Bournouf, *Sur le Yaçna,* p.
411). One is thereby reminded of the rapid running of a
stream (comp. Dieffenbach, *Goth. Glossen,* ii. 316). The camel
and the horse, on account of their swift running, have received
various exchanges in name. In Old German glossaries the
camel was called "wild horse." The name for horse in the
Middle Ages was *warannio;* Old High Germ. *reinneo, reinno*

_____
[1] [Sanscr. *açwatora.*—TRANS.]

(runner); *warani, waranah,* is used by Caucasian nations for camel (comp. my essay on the camel in *Märk. Forschungen,* vol. ix.). Accordingly, I translate אחשתרנים, "racers, horse-dromedaries," for this is the sense of the narrative, that they ran swiftly, which was of greater importance than that they should be of stately appearance.

Old Jewish commentators have really understood camel by the word, and the swiftness of the camel is well known (see Ritter, xiii. 639 and 734). But in the posts which the Persian kings in the time of Xerxes used, it does not appear that camels were employed. In *Mezahh Aaron* (p. 48c) there is the curious remark that the sort of camel that was employed in the transmission of this message had eight feet, so that when four of them got tired it ran with the other four, and that the riders were tied to them, and had no garments nor saddles, and that these Ahhashtranim are called "trampeltrarius." The Chaldean translators rendered the word by ערטולי, "naked," and the misunderstanding about the dromedary was added, because this loses its hair for some months, so that it appears as naked (comp. Oken's *Zusammenstellungen Naturgesch.* vii. 1270, and Ritter, xiii. 654).

To the above explanation what follows is very suitable, בני הרמכים, "sons of mares." רמך is "stud," Pers. *ramaká* (comp. Justi, *Zum Bundehesch,* 158); but it was not new that all were bred of the stud; but in רמך, Syr. רמכא, is repeated what Jacob Grimm (*Deutsche Gram.* iii. 327) remarks on the stud, that the word properly means, bred from the stud mares. רמכא also is stud, and *grex equarum, i.e.* "bred as a stud" (Castelli, 867). They were mares particularly trained as racers. Probably what Xenophon says about the places in which the postmen with their attendants halted, in order to receive directions, has some reference to this (comp. Brisson, *De reg. Persar.* n. 338, p. 312).

The sending of the letter took place on the 23rd of the month Sivan. The date is just as purposely chosen as that of the first message by Haman. That was despatched on the 13th

day of Nisan, which bore the name of Tir, "arrow," among
the Persians (see chap. iii. 12). Mordecai's message was sent
out on the 23rd day of the month Sivan, which corresponded
to the Old Persian month also called Tir, which was the name
among them for Mercurius the divine scribe (Hyde, *De rel.
Persar.*p. 264), and the 23rd day had the name of *Dai pa Din*, on
which day the Parsees pray for the expulsion of the evil of Satan.
Besides this, *Dîn* had the signification of justice and law, and
among the Jews דין meant judgment; it was then, indeed, for
Haman and his adherents a יום הדין, a day of judgment.

Vers. 11–14. "*Wherein the king granted the Jews which
were in every city to gather themselves together*," etc.

The edict of a Persian king was infallible and irrevocable;
consequently another must be published to remove the mis-
chievous effect of the former. In the first, direction was given
to the party of Haman to destroy all the Jews; the second
expresses that the king gives permission to the Jews to kill
their enemies. The king could not order the enemies of the
Jews to keep the peace, but could invest with authority those
who were appointed by them for the slaughter. He did not
literally take away the sword from the hands of the anti-Jewish
party; but he at the same time handed it to the Jews. On
the side on which the king lent his weight and authority
victory was sure. Therefore the edict in favour of the Jews,
according to the narrative, is verbally like the hostile edict
against them, with the exception of a few variations which
their peculiar position required. Because the Jews were
scattered in different places, the decree provided that they
should assemble themselves in localities and arm themselves
so as to be able to offer a collected national opposition or
assault. But they are authorized to exercise this power only
against the חיל העם, "the fighting men," of their enemies,
but not against any one else. They may only fight against
the party and adherents of Haman. They are the צרים, "the
enemies." This was to take place on the same day which

Haman had appointed for their destruction, on the 13th day of the month Adar. A day sooner would annul the former decree,—but the present was only another which supported the former. The month Adar (אדר) corresponds, according to its origin and meaning, with the month of March. The name already signified " fire " among the Chaldeans and Assyrians (Movers, *Phœnic.* i. 340). Adramelech, a name containing the word Adar, was an idol to which children were offered up in burning fire. It represented the consuming and warming power of fire, as well as the warmth which the earth possesses and makes use of in the vernal season. Therefore March is also so called from Mars, not on account of its warlike, but on account of its agricultural significance. He was invoked that he should protect the field from injury ; that he should give prosperity to the produce of the land, and to the cattle (comp. my *Drachenkämpfe*, p. 91). For Ares, whose power was transferred to Mars, means also nothing else but אר ,ער = אש, " fire " (comp. my *Esmun*, pp. 30, 31). He is the flaming god, and is represented on both sides of coins of Areopolis as holding weapons with burning torches. The genius of the modern Persian month Adar, although not corresponding now, as in olden times, with March (Hyde, *De rel. Pers.* p. 249), but with November, is yet connected with fire, the hearth, and the sun. The 9th of the month was illuminated by the festive fire, and all the altars were burning like funeral piles. According to Haman's opinion, Israel should be consumed in flames of war; but instead of this they became a consuming fire for their enemies.

While in chap. iii. 15 it is merely said of the messengers of Haman that they went forth in haste, דחופים, of these it is said, " they hastened and hurried on," מבהלים. The word דחף is only a transposition of פהד; " to be afraid," " to flee," " to hurry," are cognate ideas (comp. הפז = הפד, which means the same when the consonants are thus exchanged). The same is the case with the verb בהל, " to be anxious," " to flee," " to tremble." It contains the idea which is found in the Latin *halitus*, and expresses " panting for breath." The messengers

are breathlessly hurrying on, and anxious to carry out the
king's command.   The decree was published at Shushan, and
only through this the inhabitants of the capital learned what
had happened.   Not only the fall of Haman, but also of his
party, is but just now made known; but it is done in such
a way as to produce a visible and forcible impression of a
dramatic kind upon the great multitude.

Ver. 15. *"And Mordecai went forth."*
At the time (chap. iv. 1) when the dreadful decree against
the Jews was issued, Mordecai rent his clothes, and put on
sackcloth and ashes.   Now, being placed by the king in
Haman's position, he went out from the palace in official
uniform. " He went forth," he let himself be seen, and by
this the fall of Haman and the victory of his opponent
was shown, so as to leave no doubt in any one's mind.
He wore an apparel of blue and white. White and purple
or violet were the Persian State colours.   They have reference
to the Persian religious view about the world. White is
the colour of light, blue of the sky, purple of the sun.   He
wore on his head " a great crown of gold," עטרת זהב גדולה.
When the king asked Haman, on that eventful night, what
he should do to the man whom he wanted to honour, he
replied, he should put upon his head the כתר מלכות, " the
cidaris, which the king alone could wear," the straight one
($\grave{o}\rho\theta\acute{\eta}$).   It is not said that he conferred this honour upon
Mordecai.   He only granted him royal dress and a royal
horse.   And now is עטרת to be distinguished from כתר; the
first is a diadem twisted round about the head.   Verbally עטרת
and *tiara* (in Herod. $\tau\iota\acute{a}\rho\alpha\varsigma$ or $\tau\iota\acute{\eta}\rho\eta\varsigma$) seem to be the same
(Hyde, *De rel. Pers.* p. 369); but, in fact, it is more used and
described as a *cidaris*, and is really only a diadem, and
therefore must mean such in our passage, for only such
was made of gold.   With regard to the identity of the *tiara*
with the *cidaris*, Spanheim says (*Dissert. de usu et præst.
Nummor.* p. 770): " Conjuncta itaque in regione Persarum

aut Armeniorum etiam culta illa capitis ornamenta tiara ac
diadema non vero ut eadem, sed diversa."[1] In themselves
tiara and *cidaris* were not the same ; but they were bound
together, for the former was wound around the latter, and
appears also on the coins of the Arsacides without the *cidaris*
(comp. Vaillant, *Regnum Arsacidarum*, p. 1, etc.). So the name
tiara came to be used for the whole ornamentation of the
head, and appeared to signify כתר, a crown, while it was only
an עטרה or עטרת. Mordecai did not wear a high hat, which
the king alone could wear, but a princely *tiara*, which was big
enough, and embroidered with gold. A passage in Strabo (lib. xv.
c. iii. 19, ed. Paris, p. 625) clearly describes his uniform: "They,
the princes, have a lined robe with sleeves down to the knees
(χιτιόν), inside it is (חור) white, outside it is ἀνθινός,—better
to read ἰανθινός, viz. violet blue (תכלח); in the summer they wear
a mantle of purple, but in winter it is of a variegated colour
or blue (just according to the reading ἀνθινόν or ἰανθινόν)."

Mordecai was so dressed, and as it was summer, in the
month of Sivan, he wore a purple mantle. The name תבריך,
which occurs only here to denote the stately flowing robe, is
very frequently used by the Jews to signify a wrapping up
in general (as the case is with *instrumentum*), and specially
for the grave-cloth or shroud in which the dead are buried.
The second Targum renders it by גלימה, which Buxtorf and
Levy after him consider Hebrew (*Lex. Chald.* p. 143) ; but in
2 Kings ii. 8, it is a wrapping together of the mantle, which
appears as contrary to enveloping. The etymological explanation in the Talmud, Tr. Shabbath, p. 77b, that one appears in
such a mantle like a גולם,[2] " a puppet," shows that the meaning
was then obscure. It is nothing else but the Greek καλύμμα.

The Midrash Esther, ed. Amst. p. 95a, speaks of coins on
which the images of Mordecai and Esther were struck on each

---

[1] Comp. Sueton. Nero 13: "Dein precanti tiara deducta diadema
imposuit."

[2] [Rashi, *in loc.*, explains that it means a garment made of one piece of
cloth, without being cut for sleeves, etc.—TRANS.]

side. If such really existed, they must have been issued for political reasons in later times. It is quite probable, as we have instances of Oriental coins which represent a man on one side and a woman on the other, as Zenobia and her son, or Aurelian. But there can be no thought of authenticating the report of the Midrash, as Hottinger is inclined to do (Cippi, *Hebr.* p. 147).

"*And Mordecai went forth.*" יצא.

This expression is reproduced by John in chap. xix. 5, when he says: 'Εξῆλθεν οὖν ὁ 'Ιησοῦς, " Jesus therefore came out " from the palace of Pilate, as Mordecai from the palace of the Persian king. Mordecai with the golden crown and stately robe, and Jesus wearing the crown of thorns and also a purple garment; Mordecai triumphant, but Jesus mocked and scourged. Mordecai went out to avenge his people by imbruing his hands in the blood of their enemies; but Jesus went out to pour out His life-blood on the cross, in order to redeem all from eternal death. It is impossible that John should not have had this passage in mind, and it is strange that modern commentators of the N. T. have not referred to it.

Ver. 16. " *The Jews had light.*" אורה.

Light is salvation, redemption, happiness,—the preceding anxiety had been to them like night. The morning emancipates, spring redeems, and good news brings light and liberty. The placing of lights,[1] together with the expressions of gladness and joy and honour, is certainly peculiar to the book of Esther; and this is to be attributed to the influence of the view which the Persians took of the universe, according to which light was the present agency in everything good. Ahuramazda—אורמזד—was the antithesis of everything defiled and impure, and of all deceit and slander (comp. Hyde, pp. 161, 162).—ששׂון, gladness, is radically and essentially like the

---

[1] [This was probably also an illumination, as was the custom in the East on such occasions, and it became the pattern for the later Feast of the Dedication.—TRANS.]

German *jauchzen, juchzen, juzen,* Eng. "to shout," "to huzzah,"
Gr. ἰύζειν.

Ver. 17. "*And many from among the people of the land
became Jews.*"

Our text has the word מתיהדים.[1] And from this it was
inferred from very ancient times (even by the Targumim)
that there must be a verb יהד, from יהוד, to signify "the act of
making a proselyte to Judaism." But the word does nowhere
occur. Neither biblical nor post-biblical Hebrew knows it,
but rather for the said act the words גיר and מתגייר do everywhere occur. I cannot believe that the narrative meant to
convey the idea that "many became Jews," that they cut
themselves off from their national connection, and embraced
the Mosaic religion by circumcision, etc. This would not
have been recorded in one short sentence forming only half of
a verse in the original. Such an event would have excited a
great deal of comment and much material for the historian.
The removal of the wall of partition which separated the Persians
from the Jews by their respective rites and customs, would
have produced such a change among them both, that the fact
would not have been passed over so slightly as if it was of no
great importance. What the passage means in all probability
is this—that many Persians made common cause with the Jews,
that they became friendly to them, and united with them in
hostility against the party of Haman, as they saw that the Jews
had such high influence at court, and that their patron was a
great favourite of the king. I think, therefore, that we are to
read מתיחדים, from יחד, "to unite," which word occurs frequently
in this sense in the O. T., in the Targum, and in the Talmud.

---

[1] [Although the LXX. and the Syriac read as the Masoretic text, yet it
may be that the scribes had afterwards purposely exchanged the ה for a ח,
as some codices have even a circle to indicate that a ו is wanting. Haul
says: "None sine causâ circulum habent codices. Nam legendum
מתיהודים, inserta ו, quia τό ו non abest ab יהודים Judaeis." The author's
view gains support from the comment of Ibn Ezra, who makes a com-
promise by saying, that they only assumed the name of Jew.—Trans.]

CHAPTER IX.

Ver. 1. "*Now in the twelfth month.*"

The arrow which Haman was to throw on the 13th of Adar upon the people of Israel fell upon his own head, and upon the heads of his family and party. That day was to be the great day of battle against the Jews, and his own sons fell. He that digs a pit for others falls into it himself. What he wanted to do to others was accomplished in himself. As Adonibezek said, "As I have done, so God hath requited me" (Judg. i. 7; see my Comm. p. 7); so it was fulfilled on the 13th of Adar. In the book of Wisdom (chap. xi. 15, 16) we read, "But for the foolish devices of their wickedness, wherewith being deceived they worshipped serpents void of reason . . . thou didst send a multitude of unreasoning beasts upon them for vengeance: That they might know, that wherewithal a man sinneth, by the same also shall he be punished." The history of the artist Perillus, who had made a bull of copper for Phalaris of Agrigentum, in order to torture those whom he murdered, and was the first to suffer by it himself, is repeated in all legendary collections. The German imperial chronicle tells a similar instructive story of the Emperor Nerva, to whom an artist offered to manufacture a horse of a wonderful kind. It was so constructed, that if a knight should be placed upon it, the horse would fly in the air and the knight would be burned. Nerva tried this first on the artist himself (see Massmann, *Kaiserchronik*, iii. 747). It is not clear why the legend was transferred to Nerva. Probably he is confounded with Nero. But it is a matter of history that Louis XI., king of France, put Bishop Roland of Verdun in the iron cage which he had invented. — Comines reports, "Fecerat caveas ferreas

ligneasque ferreas laminis intra extraque inductas cum
terribilibus claustris, octo pedum amplitudine, unum altitudine
supra staturam hominis. Primus harum auctor Episcopus
Verdunensis fuit, qui in primam earundem ut primum facta
fuit missus quatuordecim annos habitavit" (*Rer. Gest. Ludov.
XI.*, lib. vi. c. xii.). Similarly it is told of Ezzelin, who made
the architect the first prisoner in the prison which he had
erected (Massmann, i. 1, quoted from Muratori). Massmann
has also overlooked a similar story of an artificial horse of
which Plutarch tells in connection with Aemilius Censorinus
in Egesta. This man was a cruel governor, and a certain
Aruntius Paterculus offered to make him a horse of metal
by which he might torture people. Then the tyrant tested
its efficacy upon the artist (Plut. *Comparison of Greek and
Roman Reports*, n. 39). The modern history of France shows
a remarkable retribution in name and in date. Louis XIV.
ordered on October 12, 1693, to demolish the royal tombs at
Spire. The man who was entrusted with the superintendence
of the work was called Hentz. On October 12, 1793, the
revolution began by the demolishing of the royal tombs at St.
Denis, and the French representative who undertook it had
also the name of Hentz. When the narrator in the book of
Esther rightly points to the retaliation which the tyranny
of Haman received, the Jews should not forget that they
experienced a similar retribution in their history. They
shouted triumphantly when Jesus was crucified. And so
the whole Roman army shouted triumphantly when Vespasian
and Titus returned as victors to Rome and there publicly
crucified Simon Giora. There were not trees enough at the
siege of Jerusalem on which to crucify all the prisoners of
war. I have referred to these wonderful retributions in my
small book, *Israel in der Weltgeschichte.*

Ver. 2. "*For the fear of them was fallen upon all the
peoples.*"

If the second edict had not come, Haman's party would

naturally have obtained the ascendancy. In such a despotic
country everything depended upon the knowledge which people
had of what was precisely the king's will and caprice. When
the people heard that Haman's party were in bad odour at
court, that their leader was killed, and that Mordecai was in
his place, and was ever gaining in influence, their intention
and desire of laying violent hands on the Jews was relin-
quished. True, the first edict was still valid according to the
letter; but the second showed that the party to be attacked
had now the upper hand, and although the first was not
revoked, it would be decidedly against the will of the king to
molest them. All the officials, from the satrap downwards,
had no other will but that which was in harmony with the
royal will (under עשׁי המלאכה are to understood those who
used to do the king's will).[1] Consequently they were now
just as disposed not to put any obstacle before the Jews, as
they were before to assume a hostile attitude against them.
Courtiers and officials are double-faced, according as they
receive sunshine or cloud from above, *i.e.* from the court.
The law is therefore to them only a bugbear; it frequently
changes its appearance; now it is a roaring lion, and now a
mouse, and so on. What will the satraps and pashas, whose
positions are entirely dependent upon the favour of the king,
what will they undertake against the Jews when they hear
that one of them is the favourite prime minister of the king?

A linguistic peculiarity is to be observed in the word הגיע,
by way of analogous expressions in other languages. נגע means
"to touch," and in the causative form הגיע, "touch in point of
time," "to arrive," and is used in ver. 26 in the same way as
the Germans say *Zustossen, Eintreffen;* R. V. had "come"
(reached) "unto them." Comp. chap. iv. 3, where מגיע ought
to be translated "reached." Not in the same manner do
accidere, συμβαίνειν, *evenire,* etc., agree, but ἱκνέομαι is doubtless from the same root as נגע, as well as of the same meaning.

---

[1] In the same sense the words are used in chap. iii. 9 of those who as
cashiers brought the money into the king's treasury.

נהפוך is, of course, an infin. absol. It is used in the sense of reverting, turning over, upside down. The obscure etymology of הפך becomes clear by a comparison with the Latin *vix*, *vice*, German *Wechsel*, English " turn." שלט, " to rule," doubtless reappears in the German *Schalten*, and in Sultan having the sense of ruling powerfully.

Ver. 4. האיש מרדכי —" *The man Mordecai.*"

This האיש is of special significance when it is joined to a proper name. It represents the person as distinguished, as a man of influence and name.—So in Num. xii. 3, the word man is applied to Moses by way of emphasis, that such a man as Moses was very meek above all. Of the false Micah it is said : " And there was a man of the hill country of Ephraim whose name was Micah," and he had his own house of worship, Judg. xvii. 1.

Of Jeroboam it is said, " And the man Jeroboam was a mighty man," 1 Kings xi. 28.

Especially significant is Dan. ix. 21 : " And the man Gabriel." So it is used here.

Mordecai had a name, position, importance, and influence, and was continually advancing.

Ver. 5. " *And the Jews smote.*"

The narrator lays stress upon the fact that the Jews were mowing down their enemies with great fury, and that they were not interfered with by the authorities of the land. Such party warfares in the Persian kingdom are quite authentic. The narrator characterizes their violence on the opponents as inflicting death and destruction. They not merely humiliated them, or put them to flight, but they exterminated them. The authorities were silent spectators, and did not come to the assistance of the defeated party. That is what is meant by the word כרצונם, " they did according to their good pleasure," without let or hindrance. The Persian authorities saw their countrymen and co-religionists in the hands of the Jews; but they feared the king—and he was more than God — more than love — he had given his consent, and therefore the victims must fall.

It was a battle between inhabitants of the same country, but they were not fellow-citizens. They were all fellow-servants under one master. Only the Jews had a God in heaven, but they did not imitate His reconciliation and love.

The names of the ten sons of Haman give occasion for interesting remarks. Very little has as yet been done for their interpretation. The explanations of Jules Oppert (*Extrait des Annales de philosophie Chrétienne*, Janvier 1864, p. 22) are mere guesswork, paying more attention to the sound than to the ideas contained in them. All the names are pervaded by religious ideas in connection with the fire-worship; they originated in the religion of the Magi, and their formation and composition bear that character. But the text does not give them in their purity; one feels that they have been tortured by the hands of the conquerors. As their houses have been sacked, so were their names deformed and caricatured. The popular custom to extend the strife so as to assail the honour and name of the aggressive or opposing party took place also here. I have shown elsewhere[1] how old the custom is, and that this is not the only place in which it appears in the Old Testament. The hostility of the two parties in the Persian kingdom went so far, that they trampled the names in the dust, and they revealed their wrath in caricatures upon them. If we prove this in the case of a few names, we shall have the probability that it was so with all. The last son of Haman is called וַיְזָתָא.[2]

The name evidently signifies son of fire, for נ means fire, and זת, *natus*, "son" (comp. Justi, *Zum Bundehesch*, p. 164). It was written ו, which means "woe" (see chap. i. 1), and this

[1] Comp. *Panthera, Stada, Onokotes, Caricaturnamen Christi*, Berlin 1875.
[2] Comp. Wahyazdata in the *Inscription of Bisutum*. Comp. Benfey, *The Persian Cuneiform*, p. 18.

woe was indicated by making the letter ו large, and the ר smaller than usual, for the same reason. The second name is דלפן. Even at present the Jews nickname a poor man by Dalphon, because דל means poor, miserable, wretched. This Persian name was properly Durpan, דרבאן, meaning "a guard of the temple." In the same manner they have in some names omitted the letter *d* in *data*, in order to get a secondary meaning. They call one Purta instead of Purdata, in order to obtain the meaning that he was one upon whom the *pur*, the lot, fell by the direction of God,—and because Purta is in Aramaic "little," "dirt," "distress," and "shame." They write אספתא instead of אספדת. The proper meaning of the name was (sun) horse-given (comp. *aspban*, Justi, 63); they make of it *asafta* in reference to the Aramaic word אסופי, meaning "a foundling." The first name is פרשנדתא. The Masoretes have written the ת at the end small, in order to make it appear like פרשנדא, for פרש again means "dirt," and נדא means "bespattering," or if thus written נדה, it means "uncleanness." In itself, it is either one born of a high-caste family, a פרשאן = פרזאן, *persona*, parson, person; or it comes from *bursin*, fire (Hyde, *De rel. Pers.* 362). Yet Vullers gives the last as meaning "a fire-worshipping priest" (*Lex.* i. 219). In the name פרמשתא, also, the ש was written small in order to pervert the sense. It evidently means one born of Behram (Behram = Mars, Atesh-Behram, πῦρ ἄρειον ; comp. Hyde, p. 533). They want to connect it with פרימה, "rending asunder," in a degraded sense. The names ארידתא (not אריתא, as in some editions), ארידי,[1] אריסי, Oppert brings together with Ariyadata, Ariyaçaya, Ariyadaya, but I would rather consider them as compounds of אור, fire. The Jews wanted to understand by ארידתא, "an offspring of a lion;" and by אריסי, "poison." In ארידי, I am not sure whether the last syllable was to point to דוי, "pain," "sickness," "trouble." Adalia was probably originally Adaria, derived from אדר, "fire." It is clear that they made an effort to heap upon the fire-

[1] Ἀρίζος, a Persian, Herod. vii. 38.

worshippers scornful epithets. This was not merely because
they were victorious over their enemies, but chiefly because
their hateful religion had received a blow. That the Jews
cared more for retaliating and avenging than for enriching
themselves, appears from the added clause: "but on the
spoil they laid not their hand." בִּזָּה, "spoil," from בַּז, "to
take spoil." So is ἅρπαγμα, from ἁρπάζω. To בַּז, without
doubt, belongs the German word *Beute* (English "booty,"
"butin"), as ז is frequently assimilated with ר and ט.

Ver. 11. "*On that day.*"

The news of the day was, of course, reported to the king
from every quarter of Shushan. He communicated it to
Esther with an air of the greatest indifference, as if he asked
her how she likes the handsome present he had given her.
He asks her caressingly: "Have I not done it well? 500
have been slain in Shushan, Haman's sons are dead; and if
this has happened here, what must have taken place in the
provinces?" He at any rate expected, as it seems, that Esther
would express her satisfaction. But the grand woman has
caught the spirit of a Persian queen. It was not for nothing
that she ascended the throne. She wants to use the favourable moment, and to carry on the war thoroughly to the end.
She fears the vengeance of some of the hostile party who had
not yet been vanquished. If these are not put down with a
strong hand, she is afraid that they will eventually retaliate,
—and how easy it is to change the mind of a Persian king,
she knows well from her own experience. He tells her that
500 have been slain in the citadel of Shushan—viz. on the
13th of the month. She asks him to issue an especial
decree (דת) to continue the battle on the next day in the city
itself. There is evidently a distinction between what took
place in the two days. The former decree was only valid for
the 13th, and therefore a new one was necessary if the war
was to be continued. The partisans of Haman were killed in
the citadel, but not in the city. - Hence Esther's petition.

She is not satisfied with the slaughter of Haman's sons.
They must also be hung up, as Haman was, on the gallows.
The people should see the destruction of the whole household.
They should be impressed with the fact that all the leaders of
the party met the same disgraceful end as their chief. This
she considers necessary, not only for accentuating her triumph,
but that it might have a deterring effect. They should have
a visible demonstration of the end of the enemies of Israel.
Esther must not be judged by the standard of the love of
Christ. She and her people were engaged in a battle against
a powerful party, at whose head was the king himself, and
she would have succumbed, had she not, in a wonderful
manner, won him over to her side, and enlisted his participation. But that there is a difference between the mode of
warfare of the Jews and that of their enemies, is seen from
this, that had they been defeated, all their property would
have been made booty (chap. iii. 13), while they do not touch
the property of their enemies.

That the ten sons of Haman were hung on the same
gallows as Haman, is not expressly stated in the text.
The Jewish commentators take the word העץ for the same
tree that was used at the hanging of Haman. The manner
in which the names of the ten sons of Haman are placed in
Jewish manuscripts and books, viz. in a straight column one
under the other, is owing to a Midrash. In fact, the later
Jews show more hatred against Haman and his family than
even his contemporaries did who were engaged in the strife,
for it is directed against those who had long ago been
judged. Yet this hatred is expressive of later experiences.
They narrate that the ten sons of Haman were so hung
under each other upon the gallows of fifty cubits, that each
took up the space of three cubits, leaving the space of one
cubit between one another, so that all the ten occupied
forty cubits. The remaining ten cubits on the top was
occupied by the body of Haman. Thus he crowned the
summit of the gallows. The picture of the gallows is indi-

cated by the large ؛ of the last name. They also tell of a
mocking conversation which Mordecai carried on with Haman
when he was on the gallows, and Haman's thoughts.   (It
certainly reminds us of the scorn with which they treated
Christ on the cross.) They said jestingly, As Haman was
one with his sons during life, so they must be united in their
death.   Even at the present time they read the ten names
in the synagogue in one breath, in order to intimate that they
were all made to expire at one and the same time, as a
punishment for their wanting to destroy Israel in one day.
So it was that the battle lasted two days in Shushan, while
in the other parts of the Persian kingdom it was confined
to the 13th day, in accordance with the letter of the law.
On the 14th quiet was to be restored. The number of the
slain, 75,000, sounds dreadful; but when 810 fell in the
capital alone, the number is proportionally not so large when
divided between the various places of the kingdom.   Human
life was very cheap in the eyes of a Persian tyrant.
75,000 men fell in a battle, whose only origin was in
the circumstance that a decree issued by the king was
irrevocable.

Ver. 17. "*And made it a day of feasting and gladness.*"
The historical celebration of the feast of Purim is treated
elsewhere.—We have here an unvarnished picture of the
life of the ancient world,—how the people, after the trouble
they had gone through, rejoice and express their joy by
eating and drinking, just as they before express their sorrow
by fasting.   Above, in the narrative of the fast, God is not
mentioned before whom they expressed their sorrow in heartfelt repentance; nor is God mentioned now, that they
expressed their gratitude to Him in the feast of rejoicing.
Yet there is no meal and no feast among the Jews without
reference to God and mention of His name.   But there is a
marked difference between the people in captivity and the
people which Moses brought out of Egypt.   The ancient

Jews used to say, that Haman was in his time the same to the Jews that Pharaoh was to that generation. They also made it a rule that on a leap year the feast of Purim should be kept on the 14th of the second Adar, which in an ordinary year would be the feast of Passover. But there is a great difference between the solemnity with which the Passover was observed and the giddy joy of Purim. In the first, the unleavened bread, the Passover lamb, the blood, the feast itself, reminded them of sin, repentance, reconciliation, and redemption, while in Purim only the voice of exultation was and is heard. Passover is therefore in the highest sense the feast in which confession is made. Purim represents more the character of a national holiday. Therefore also the Church of Christ gave great glory to the feast of the Passover, while of Purim she took no notice, as it had vanished even from the circle of the early Jewish Christians.

Therefore the Lord's Supper is and should be the fairest of all feasts. Nowhere else can or dare one better express his gratitude and his joy for redemption and salvation.

Ver. 19. "*The Jews of the villages that dwell in unwalled towns.*"

Hitherto פרזים and the ערי פרזות were taken as people and cities of the flat or open country, in contrast to Shushan. But the idea that these words are intended to convey is more precise. The narrator distinguishes three kinds of Jews. First, the Jews in Shushan; secondly, ver. 16, the Jews that were in the provinces, היהודים אשר במדינות. The contrast to Shushan is the Medina. Thirdly, the Jews who were reported הפרזים. If these were the same as those in the provinces, then they would be mentioned successively twice, for it is already said in ver. 17, that on "the 14th day they rested, and made it a day of feasting and gladness." Moreover, the word *Perazim* would have occurred in ver. 17. The word therefore, על כן, also shows that the Jews spoken of are others, who lived neither in Shushan nor in the Medinoth.

Undoubtedly ערי פרזות are unfortified towns and places in the
east country, in Turkestan and Turan, on whose extensive
prairies many Jews were scattered. These words are clearly
illustrated by Ezek. xxxviii. 11, where ערי פרזות are clearly
described by ארץ פרזות. He represents there a land having
cities without walls. The word פרז seems to be related to
the Greek πόρος, " a ford."

"*And of sending portions.*"

The portion or present מנה, both as a noun and a verb, is
the Greek νέμω, with the transposition of *m* and *n*. (Probably
originally μείρομαι, μείρω, belonged also to it, and their relation
to each is like that between *donum* and δῶρον.) The opinion,
which is also shared by Fürst, that Mammon (μαμμῶνα) is a
doubling of מנה, is erroneous. The expression Mammon is
formed of *nummus*.

Ver. 20. "*And Mordecai wrote.*"

This is a very remarkable fact. It was quite natural for
the Jews, after receiving the tidings that the king was
favourably disposed toward them, and that they had gained
the victory over their enemies, to express their joy by keeping
a feast. But that this feast should be instituted for all
times was nevertheless singular, inasmuch as Mordecai
possessed no spiritual authority to order such a perpetual
institution. The importance that he possessed, he only
gained through the influence of Esther. And now he did
not occupy the place of a synod of the elders, nor of a high
priest, but the place of the grand vizier at the Persian court.
It was this position which gave him the authority of ordaining
a perpetual feast for the Jews. He considered the King of
Persia as the king of the Jews, and as his representative he
possessed Jewish-national authority. For, indeed, it was only
to be a national feast, only a feast in remembrance of the
victory over their enemies. The letters of Mordecai do not
prescribe any prayers to be used on the feast, but only the

making of merriment. There is no reference to any passage
of Scripture in them, but only a reminder of the present
wonderful deliverance. Of course, by the remembrance of the
dangers they had gone through, he wants to strengthen and to
encourage the hearts of the Jews, but the authority by which
he commands is solely his own. Hitherto no feasts were
kept by them save those commanded by Moses in the name
and by the authority of God. It was to a certain extent a
feast of the exile, in which also the exiled men became the
means of deliverance. Mordecai, too, directs his writings
only to the Jews in the empire of King Ahhashverosh, " both
nigh and far."

It is to be observed that the ground here given for enjoining
the feast is not because the Jews had obtained predominance,
but the sudden change in their condition from trouble to
tranquillity, from sorrow to gladness. On such occasions they
sent to each other presents, according to the custom of the
times ;—but Mordecai was particularly anxious in his letters
that they should bestow gifts upon the poor. It does not
appear that Mordecai was conscious, when instituting this
feast, that he could not enjoin it in the spirit and authority
of Moses. True, it is added, "and the Jews took upon them "
(וקבל), they declared their readiness to comply with his order,
which was easy enough, for people are generally glad to have
an annual festival of rejoicing, especially under such circumstances; but there was yet wanting in it any previous consultation with the people as to whether they wanted to have
such a feast for all time. It was the same Mordecai that
ordained it who had procured for them the second decree of
the king.

Ver. 23. From the words, "and as Mordecai had
written," the editor of the book begins to write his
appendix. Thus far he has given the original narrative.
Now the style is quite different. He uses quite different
forms of expressions. The phrase אמר עם הספר, " he commanded
by a writing," ver. 25, is only found here. The same idea is

expressed above only by נתן דת‎, " he gave an order." Again,
when we read in ver. 24, "Haman devised to destroy them,"
he uses the להמם‎, which was not used above, and only because
it is of similar sound with המן‎. Further, when we read, ver.
26, they called these days Purim ; with regard to the events
of this אגרת‎, " letter," we must understand by the " letter "
the whole book of Esther, which was sent with a memorandum
to the Jews. The word does not occur above. Finally,
when it said (ver. 27), "the Jews took upon them, and upon
their seed, and upon all such as joined themselves unto them
(כל־הנלוים‎)," one understands by this word, which does not
occur in the real text, and especially from the same word in
Dan. xi. 34, that it refers to false associates. It appears that
it is applied not so much to such as were completely converted to the Jewish faith, as to such as had become friends
and helpers. The reason why they should also at all times
keep the feast, is because they must reflect that in case the
party of Haman had gained the victory, they as friends and
confederates of the Jews would have perished with them.
They were those of whom mention is made in chap. viii. 17 ;
and my hypothesis, that we are there to read מתיחדים‎, " they
united themselves," is thereby confirmed. Were it not so, we
should not have הנלוים‎, but נרים‎, " proselytes," or a similar word.

Ver. 28. " *And that these days.*"

The Jewish commentators conclude from these words that
the book of Esther was written by inspiration, because it is
here said, " these days should be remembered, and should not
fail from the Jews," which must be a prophecy.

They have indeed been fulfilled, for the feast of Purim
has never been forgotten by the Jews ; nevertheless, they
were not spoken in prophetical, but in legislative language.
These days of Purim shall not fail from among the Jews, nor
the memorial of them perish from their seed.[1]

[1] [Jewish tradition teaches that in the days of Messiah all the feasts shall
cease except the feast of Purim.—TRANS.]

Ver. 29. "*Then Esther the queen, the daughter of Abihhail, wrote.*"

This second letter proves more decisively that Esther and Mordecai assumed a special authority over the Jews, at least in so far as they were connected with the related events. The addition here of the words "daughter of Abihhail" is borrowed from the solemn introductory sentence of her own letter. But the object of the second letter was not merely to emphasize and to confirm the first. The emphasis consists chiefly in this, that Esther added her authority to that of Mordecai. Therefore she inserts the words בכל תקף, "with all strength or authority." The last expression occurs only once more in Daniel, and means "the royal authority," "the influence," "the order," of the shah. For the celebration of the feast of Purim, the royal authority of Esther was made use of. Therefore the first word of ver. 29 has in the text a large ת, thus ותכתוב, to emphasize that the queen herself wrote the letter with her own hand. This letter was sent like a royal decree to the Jews in all the 127 provinces, and contained only words of peace and of assurance. It was comforting news which Mordecai could communicate in the name of Esther. The more so—and this was the second reason for the letter—because the Jews, in consideration of what had happened, are requested not only to keep the feast with gladness, but also the previous fast, remembering that Mordecai and Esther have themselves fasted during the distress. They had in the hour of danger cried to God and totally abstained from food. This also should never vanish from the memory of the Jews.

After the despatch of the first letter of Mordecai, it became then a serious question whether it was possible to establish on his sole authority a feast like the Mosaic ones; therefore the influence of Esther was invoked—and should it be only a feast of joy! If they had passed from sorrow to joy (מיגון לשמחה), they should not only commemorate the experienced joy, but also the sorrow.

The duty was enforced upon the Jews to imitate everywhere, and at all times, the example of Esther and Mordecai, and to devote one day in the year to fasting and prayer. For this the authority of Mordecai alone was not sufficient. Therefore it is written (ver. 32), " the commandment of Esther confirmed these matters of Purim," and the fast is indeed called thè fast of Esther, the day before Purim. But that this day was originally the 13th of Adar is not expressly stated, but it may be supposed so, as the 13th day was the day of distress. It must not be overlooked in confirmation of this, that in ver. 31, Mordecai is mentioned before Esther, because Mordecai began the fast (iv. 1). We have the word צומות here, as in iv. 16, of Esther, and זעקתם, as in iv. 1, of Mordecai, ויזעק, " and he cried with a loud and a bitter cry."

The book properly ends with chap. ix. All is written in the book, the event, the help, and the feast. The contents of chap. x. are only a historical postscript.

CHAPTER X.

Ver. 1. "*And the king Ahhashverosh laid a tribute upon the land.*"

Short as the sentence is, it has yet caused a good deal of speculation. It was sought in various ways to explain why the narrator made this record. Jewish commentators wanted to assume that the king had put all under tribute except the Jews, which is by no means intimated. Grotius was of opinion that this is stated in order to enhance the merits of Mordecai. He exclaims: " Sunt enim Judaei, magni artifices talium."

More modern commentators, as Bertheau and Schulz, said the author wished to show the power of the king. Keil, as well as others, thought that he only communicated an item from the Persian annals.

The report must show the bias of the narrator; it contributes to magnify the wonderful change which the deliverance of Israel had brought about. The king had given up much when he had prevented the destruction of Israel. It was not alone that he had renounced the offer of Haman, but also the whole property of the Jews, which, if they had been cut off, would have become his own in all places of his dominion. All this was taken from him. The product of the plunder was so much loss for him. With this thought the narrator connects the report concerning the tribute. Instead of taking away the property of the Jews, he laid a tribute upon all. The whole kingdom must make up the deficiency which arose from his presenting the Jews with their own riches.

This application of the general historical fact agrees with

the spirit of the whole narrative.   In the texts in this verse
we find mostly אחשרש, while in the other passages it is written
אחשורש.   This is scarcely a mistake of the scribe, but is
intentional.   The two ו in the name Ahhashverosh express
the woe which the deed of Ahhashverosh occasioned.   I go
so far as to believe that the reading in this verse is the
proper one, and the other a homiletic corruption, although
in the last mention of the name it is pointed as in the
first.   In chap. v. 2 we have an imitation of the style of
the book of Kings.   פרשה, as was observed in iv. 7, is
used in the sense of "the full sum;" so here it means
"the distinguished," "the highest," influence of Mordecai.   It
is surprising that Mordecai bears no other title but Yehudi,
"the Jew."   But at that time it was only a national and
religious epithet.   It had not yet received the sarcastic and
annoying character which was put upon it in later centuries.
He calls Mordecai משנה למלך, literally, "the second to the
king."   By which is meant the king's grand vizier, his substitute, who was the keeper of the royal seal.   That it was a
general Oriental dignity may be inferred from 2 Chron. xxviii.
7, where it is told that Zichri slew Elkanah the משנה המלך.
It seems to have appeared strange to the narrator that Mordecai, although a captive Jew, should have become royal
vizier.   He was, says he, גדול ליהודים, "great among the Jews."
Just as the king of Persia and the king of Assyria were both
called מלך הגדול, "the great king," that is, the one who had
power over the others, so this expression is used with regard to
Mordecai, he was a great one for the Jews, viz. their representative and their prince of the captivity, as he proved by
his letters.—And, indeed, he was not like one of the many
ministers who as Jews held offices in Muhamedan or Christian
courts, for he had more power than they, and was elevated
for quite different reasons.   The others, not even excepting
R. Chisdai in Cordova, were raised to their ministerial offices
on account of their knowledge of finance; but not one of
them, however highly esteemed and appreciated, "was great

among the Jews" in the sense in which Mordecai was. He
was the acknowledged saviour of the life of his king and of
the lives of the Jews. His only great prototype was Joseph,
for Daniel, as it seems, possessed only spiritual authority in
Babylon.

And the power that Mordecai possessed over the Jews
was popular and pleasing, "accepted (רצוי) of the multitude."
He did not oppress them; they, his brethren (אחיו); he did
not assume a proud and overbearing air towards them, and
did not forget in the uniform of the grand vizier the garment
of the penitent. Why should he not be beloved by them
when he had promoted their safety and welfare, and made
arrangements that his posterity should maintain the peace?
For this is the sense of דובר שלום, "speaking peace." They
were not merely words of peace, but he laboured that the
peace should remain uninterrupted for the present and the
future, that is, for "his seed" (זרעו), viz. "the posterity of the
people," inasmuch as their enemies had received a mortal
blow.

Alas! the book closes without further information about
the end of the king, of Esther, and of Mordecai. But no
other disturbance occurred, and, in fact, the Jews enjoyed
prosperity and peace in the Persian kingdom beyond the
time of Alexander the Great. But we have no more information about such persons as Mordecai and Esther. Later times
have given us many speculative interpretations, but not facts
of authentic historical value.

APPENDICES.

I.

THE SECOND TARGUM.

(Translated from the Aramaic.)

§ I.

AND it came to pass in the days of Ahhashverosh, one of the ten kings [1] who once ruled and are to rule the world in the future. And these are the ten kings. The first kingdom is that of the King of kings, the Lord of hosts,—may it be speedily magnified upon us. The second is that of Nimrod, the third of Pharaoh, king of Egypt, the fourth of Israel, the fifth of Nebuchadnezzar, king of Babylon, the sixth of Ahhashverosh, the seventh of Greece, the eighth of Rome, the ninth of the King Messiah, the son of David, the tenth (again) of the King of kings, the Lord of hosts,—may it be speedily revealed to us, and to all the inhabitants of the earth. [2] When the kingdom of Babylon was about to be destroyed from the earth, and its dominion to pass away from it, the inhabitants of the country did not know whom they should place as king

---

[1] In Dan. vii. 24, Rev. xvii. 12, we have parallel passages in which the rulers of the world are spoken of as ten in number. The idea of such universal rulers is more peculiar to the East, where the great shahs have always pretended to be rulers of the world. Of Kai Kawus says Firdussi, among other things,—

> "Now Kawus as king in the place of his father succeeded,
> And all the world was to him subjected.
> Now he saw that the earth quaked and trembled."

This idea is more largely developed in a mythic-dogmatic way in the "Tshakravartins" of the Buddhists. Tshakravartin was lord of the wheel, *i.e.* of the world. Universal kings were the lords of the ages. It must be so understood if one of these Tshakravartins appears to be lord of the iron wheel, another of that of brass, another of that of silver, and another of that of gold (Remusat on *Foe-koue-ki*, Paris 1836, p. 134). Buddha had the choice, according to the legend, of becoming either a Tshakravartin or an ascetic. He chose the last (comp. Matt. iv. 8).

[2] Comp. 1 Cor. xv. 23-28.

over them.　And when Nebuchadnezzar, the king of Babylon,
died, Evil-Merodach succeeded him, and the inhabitants of
the country did not want to raise him over them.　For they
answered and said to him, "Thy father Nebuchadnezzar had
not his dwelling with men, and how shall we place thee
over us?　Thy father Nebuchadnezzar may perhaps of a
sudden turn up, and come upon us and kill us."　When
Evil - Merodach heard these words of the people of his
country, he said to them, "My father Nebuchadnezzar is
surely dead and is removed from the world, and yet until
now you do not believe it."　They rejoined, "Nebuchadnezzar
thy father made the whole earth tremble, and all the kingdoms thereof; for concerning him it is expressly written:
'Is this the man that made the earth to tremble, that did
shake kingdoms?'" (Isa. xiv. 16).　What did Evil-Merodach
do at that time?　He went to the treasuries of the king, and
brought out from these chains of iron and of brass, and threw
them upon the soles of Nebuchadnezzar his father,[1] and
dragged him out of his grave.　As it is written concerning
him: "But thou art cast forth away from thy sepulchre like

[1] It was the exposition of Isa. xiv. 19 that gave rise to the above legend,
which is mentioned by all commentators also on 2 Kings xxv. 27 (comp.
Munk, p. 12).　Nebuchadnezzar appeared as a type of all persecutors and
destroyers.　They saw in him a national warning for all time.　Moreover,
we have here represented historical experiences of the Jews.　Nebuchadnezzar, as is seen from Dan. iv. 30, had for a long time been subject to a
fearful disease which made him incapable of governing.　At that time,
says the legend, Evil-Merodach ruled in his stead.　But when Nebuchadnezzar recovered, and found his son upon the throne, he threw him into
prison.　When he again claimed the throne, the Babylonians, as is said
above, refused to reinstate him, and wanted to be certain that the king
was dead.　The Jews experienced a similar fate when a rumour was spread
for the purpose of raising a revolt that Herodos had died.　They were
severely punished for that (Josephus, Antiq. xvii. 6).　He also reports
that similar dangers arose with reference to Agrippa, the favourite of
Caligula, after the decease of the Emperor Tiberius (Josephus, Antiq.
xviii. 6).　The legend displays national animus when it represents Evil-
Merodach treating his father in such a manner as only enemies were
wont to do.　The narrative of Herodotus (iii. 16) is also important to the
expositor of Isaiah.　He tells of Cambyses, "That he caused the corpse of
Amasis to be taken out of the grave . . . and ordered to beat it, to tear

an abominable branch" (*ibid.*). And when the people saw that Evil-Merodach had done the will of his heavenly Father, they all rose up with great rejoicing, and they clothed him with the beautiful purple of the kingdom, and rendered him much honour and glory. Then Daniel, the man greatly beloved, said to Evil-Merodach : " Thy father Nebuchadnezzar never in all his days set the prisoners free, for thus Scripture says of him, 'that let not loose his prisoners to their home ' (Isa. xiv. 17). And when the enemies of the Jews filled up their measure of guilt,[1] then Nebuchadnezzar thy father equipped himself, and went up against them, and destroyed their land, and plundered the city of Jerusalem, and burned the holy house with fire, and took the people of Israel captive, and brought them to Babylon, and with them Jehoiachin, king of Judah, whom he bound and kept in prison for thirty-seven years, because he had not submitted to the will of his heavenly Father. Nebuchadnezzar was also exceedingly haughty, and said, There is no king and ruler beside me. As the Scripture expressly says concerning him : ' I will ascend above the heights of the clouds ' " (Isa. xiv. 14).

out the hairs, to prick it, and to treat it with all possible disgrace." Homer narrates at the end of the *Iliad* that the wrathful Achilles ill-treated Hector in a similar manner. The same happened among the Romans. The Roman people thus ill-treated Strabo, the father of Pompeius (Plut. *Life of Pomp.* cap. 1). When the Emperor Commodus died, we read (Lampridius, *Vit. Commod.* cap. xvii.) : " Corpus ejus ut unco traheretur atque in Tiberim mitteretur senatus et populus postulavit." The same was done before to Vitellius, as Suetonius (cap. xvii.) reports. Christian Rome and Constantinople have also witnessed such scenes.

[The friendliness with which the legend treats Evil-Merodach has its origin in 2 Kings xxv. 27. The Talmud (Berachoth 10*b*) records that Hezekiah dragged the bones of his father Ahaz on a bed of ropes. Munk may have understood it in a Rabbinical sense, *i.e.* when the Jews have to say something unpleasant of themselves, they speak in the third person. See Rashi on Ex. i. 11.—TRANS.]

[1] The expression וכדאתחייבו סנאיהון דיהודאי must be translated as we have done, and not as Munk (p. 14), " when the measure of the sins of the Jews was full." It expresses that when judgment should come upon the enemies of Israel they attacked them, for their judgment proceeded from their hostility to Israel.

In that hour Evil-Merodach did[1] the will of his heavenly Father, and went to the prison and liberated Jehoiachin, son of Jehoiakim, king of the tribe of Judah, and they brought out all the prisoners with him. What did Evil-Merodach further? He then went to the royal treasuries, and brought out from there the best balms and all kinds of aromatics, and then washed and anointed him (Jehoiachin), and put royal garments upon him, and allowed him to eat at his table all the days of his life. From him Darius the Mede received the kingdom.

That Ahhashverosh, the Persian king, son of Darius, the Median king, that Ahhashverosh (is it) who ordered wine to be brought from a hundred and twenty-seven provinces for a hundred and twenty-seven kings who waited before him, in order that every one of them should drink the wine of his own country which would not injure him. It is that wicked King Ahhashverosh, that fool, who said, "Rather let my kingdom be destroyed than that my decree should not be obeyed." That Ahhashverosh whose counsels were perverse, and whose orders were not right. That Ahhashverosh who commanded that Queen Vashti should appear naked before him, but she did not appear. That Ahhashverosh in whose time the house of Israel was sold for nought, as it is written: "Ye were sold for nought." That Ahhashverosh in whose time Israel's face became black like the sides of a cooking vessel. That Ahhashverosh who ordered to bring cedars from Lebanon and gold from Ophir, but it did not come. That Ahhashverosh in whose days was fulfilled what is written in the law of Moses concerning Israel: "In the morning thou shalt say, Would God it were even!" (Deut. xxviii. 67). There are five men in connection with whom the relative הוא is written who are called wicked, and five others who are called righteous. The righteous with whom הוא is written are: Abraham, Aaron and Moses, Moses and Aaron, Hezekiah, Ezra. The five wicked men are: Nimrod, of whom it is written, "He (הוא) was a mighty hunter"

---

[1] Some editions read סבר instead of עבד.

(Gen. x. 8). Esau, of whom it is written, " Esau (וישא) is Edom "
(Gen. xxxvi. 8) ; that Dathan and Abiram, that King Ahaz,
that Ahhashverosh. And as the last made promises and did
not keep them, his days were shortened ; yet he ruled from
Hodu in the west unto Cush in the east, over a hundred and
twenty-seven provinces. That Ahhashverosh was it who
killed his wife for the sake of his friend, and who killed his
friend Haman for the sake of his wife. That Ahhashverosh
who ruled from Hodu to Cush. But were not Hodu and
Cush near each other ? The sense is this : As he ruled
over Hodu and Cush, which are near each other, so he held
unlimited sway over a hundred and twenty-seven provinces
and the governments that belonged to them. Similar to
this, thou findest in reference to King Solomon, " He ruled
over the whole side of the river from Tiphsah unto Gaza "
(1 Kings v. 4). Were not Tiphsah and Gaza near to each
other ? But the meaning is, as he ruled over the Tiphsah
and Gaza, so he ruled over the whole region of the side of
the stream of the world. There were four men who ruled from
one end of the world to the other. Two of them belonged
to the nations of the world, and two to Israel. Solomon
and Ahab were of Israel. In connection with Solomon it is
written as said already. Concerning Ahab it is said, " Is
there anywhere a people or a kingdom ? " The universal
kings from the nations are Nebuchadnezzar and Ahhashverosh,
only the extent of the latter's kingdom was shortened, and
he ruled but over a hundred and twenty-seven provinces.
But why did he deserve to rule over a hundred and twenty-
seven provinces ? Because God said, " He will in the
future take Esther to wife, who is a descendant of Sarah that
lived a hundred and twenty-seven years, so she shall rule
over a hundred and twenty-seven provinces."

§ II.

In those days, when the king Ahhashverosh sat upon his
throne, which was prepared for him in Shushan the capital.

This throne was neither his own nor that of his father's, but it was the throne of Solomon, which Hiram, the son of a widow of Tyre, had made with great skill. It was this King Solomon whom the Holy One, blessed be He! set to reign from one end of the world to the other. He chose him before he was born, loved him when he was yet in his mother's womb, revealed to him hidden mysteries, and showed him deep hidden things. He gave him knowledge and wisdom, and an understanding heart from the very beginning. He looked through the persons who came to him to adjudicate their differences so that they could not say what was false before him, for he knew to distinguish between him who was right and him who was wrong. The Lord bestowed upon him splendour and glory, put the royal crown upon his head, and invested him with grace and mercy, as He did once to his father David all his days. He was twenty-three [1] years old on the first day when he received the kingdom. They called him Jedidiah (beloved), because he was beloved of the King of the world, of the Lord of hosts. Thus it is written (and the Lord loved him): " And He sent by the hand of Nathan the prophet, and he called his name Jedidiah" (2 Sam. xii. 25). They called him Solomon (peace), because there was peace in his days. For thus it is written: " And Judah and Israel dwelt safely." They called him Ben [2] (builder), because he built the temple,

---

[1] ת instead of מ.

[2] The glorifying of Solomon in the Jewish legend has its ground in its opposition to Christianity (see my *Kaiser und Königsthrone*, p. 60). What belonged to the Messiah, the son of David, was transferred to Solomon. The names in Prov. xxx. 1, with the exception of Agur, are here applied to Solomon. Ben is taken in the sense of builder (not son), to give the idea of stone, אבן (as Ben and Ibn). For Christ is also called stone (*lapis herillis*, in Isa.). When the Targumist says that he is called Yaka, because he was king and lord over the nations, it is because he sees in יקא חמשא a correspondence to מלך חמשא, and derives it from the Greek ἡγέω ἄγω, or we consider יקא = נקא = ἄναξ. In Bemidbar Rabba, cap. 10 (ed. Amst. 199a), seven names of Solomon are enumerated : Solomon Koheleth, Jedidiah, Agur, Ben, Yaka, Lemiel, and Ethiel, and so Ben and Yaka are not separated.

as it is written: " I have built Thee an house of habitation"
(2 Chron. **vi.** 2). They called him Ethi-el, "God is with
me," because the Word of God was his assistance. And
so it is written: "He was wiser than all men." He was
called Yaka (commander of obedience) because he was lord
and ruler over all the kings of the earth, east and west.
And so it is written: "Solomon sat upon the throne of his
father David." All the kingdoms feared him, nations and
languages were obedient to him; devils, demons,[1] and ferocious
beasts, evil spirits and accidents, were delivered into his
hands. Imps brought him all kinds of fish from the sea,
and the fowls of heaven, together with the cattle and wild
animals, came of their own accord to his slaughter - house
to be slaughtered for his banquet. He was rich and powerful
in the possession of much silver and gold. He explained
parables, solved hidden problems, and made known mysteries
without end. His enemies and adversaries became his
friends, and all the kings obeyed him. All came to see
his face, and longed to hear words of his knowledge. The
High One elevated and exalted him for the sake of David
His servant. His fame was spread among the kings, and
his power among the wise. He was perfect and true,
shunned evil, understood the mysteries of heaven, and was
wise in divine things. His kingdom was more powerful
than all the kingdoms, and his understanding was greater
than that of all the children of Mahhol (the globe). They
heard everywhere of his fame and of his wise sayings, and
all came to salute him. All the kings loved him; all
governors trembled before him; they brought him their
sons and daughters to be his servants, and to run before
him; they desired to sit before him, and yearned to hear
the words of his mouth and his wisdom. When he began
to speak, they knelt and prostrated themselves before him;
all who were about to come to him neglected and despised
their cities, even hated their places and countries, and came

[1] לילין is by mistake omitted in Amst. ed.

to hear amiable words of wisdom from his lips with which
he manifested the praise of the Lord of lords. When he
opened his mouth, he spake like a trumpet the praise to
the Most High King. To him was given a large key whereby
to open the gates of wisdom and understanding of the heart.
He understood the languages of birds and of animals, stags
and rams ran at his command, lions and tigers seized weapons
before him. He understood languages better than all nations,
he instructed all schools, all kings and queens trembled before
him. All rulers were seized with terror, to him was given
the crown of victory, he subdued all men, he was the head
of all kings, and (through his influence) no kingdom could
take up weapons against another.[1] All kings shook before
him, all countries revealed mysteries to him, so that he
knew all the secrets of men; because he did works of
righteousness and charity, he was from the beginning worthy
to be king in this world, and he shall be worthy in the
world to come.[2]

§ III.

This King Solomon was it who had caused a glorious
royal throne to be made, covered with gold from Ophir,
overlaid with beryl stones, brilliants,[3] marble, samaragel,
carbuncle, diamonds, pearls, and other precious stones.[4]

For no king was the throne made like it, and no kingdom

---

[1] To be read דינא.

[2] The discovery is highly interesting, that the praise here given to
Solomon consists of two alphabetical acrostics, which even compilers of
the Targums had failed to notice. The acrostic is forward and backward,
and can only be seen in the original. This also is a contrasting imitation
of the Byzantian acrostical song of praise in reference to Christ.

[3] The אבני ציצא are lustrous stones. יין=ציין, as נצר=נזר. ציין is
applied to things white and shining, to the ornament worn by the high
priest upon his forehead, and to white blossom; as נעץ, to shine, and
נץ, blossom (comp. my treatise on "Nazareth" in *Wege nach Damascus*,
p. 11).

[4] Read ברכודנין and not ברכודנין, viz. chalcedony, which the Targum
has for the Hebrew יהלם. For שהם it has בורלין, beryllus. From this is
derived the French word "briller."

could produce similar ones. This throne was made as follows: Twelve lions of gold stood upon it, and opposite to them twelve eagles of gold, a lion opposite an eagle, and an eagle opposite a lion. The right paw of the golden lion was toward the left wing of the golden eagle, and the left wing of the golden eagle was toward the right paw of the golden lion. The sum of all the lions upon it was seventy-two, and there were the same number of eagles. Towards the top, where the king's seat was, the throne was round. It had six steps of gold, as it is written: "The king made a throne of ivory, and this throne had six steps." Upon the first step lay a golden ox, and opposite to it a golden lion; upon the second step lay a golden bear, and opposite to it a golden lamb; upon the third step lay a golden panther, and opposite to it a golden owl; upon the fourth step lay a golden eagle, and opposite to it a golden peacock; upon the fifth step lay a golden cat, and opposite to it a golden hen; and upon the sixth step lay a golden hawk, and opposite to it a golden dove. Upon the throne stood likewise a golden dove, holding a golden hawk in its claws. Thus one day will all the nations and languages be delivered into the hands of King Messiah, and into the hands of the house of Israel. Upon the top of the throne stood a candlestick, properly arranged with lamps, ornaments (or pomegranates), snuffers, ash-pans, cups, and lilies. To one side of the shaft were attached seven pipes, upon which the pictures of the seven patriarchs were engraven. The names of these are as follows: Adam, Noah, his eldest son Shem, Abraham, Isaac, Jacob, and Job among them. To the other side of the shaft were likewise attached seven pipes, upon which were represented seven pious men of the world, whose names are: Levi, Kehath, Amram, Moses, Aaron, Eldad, Medad, and the prophet Haggai among them (or rather Hur).[1] Upon the top of the candlestick stood a golden

---

[1] The proper reading is חור, for Haggai was not, of course, in the time of Solomon. The reading of חני must have arisen from the word נביא. Hur

jar filled with the purest olive oil which supplied the lamps
of the temple; and under it was a great golden vessel containing the purest olive oil which supplied the lamps of
the candlestick, and upon it was portrayed the high priest.
Two branches proceeded from this great vessel, and upon
them were depicted the two sons of Eli, namely, Hophni
and Phinehas,[1] and out of these branches proceeded two
pipes bearing the pictures of two sons of Aaron, viz.
Nadab and Abihu. There were also upon it two seats of
gold, one for the high priest and the other for the vice high
priest. Towards the top of the throne were attached seventy
golden chairs, upon which sat the seventy Synhedrists
as judges before Solomon. Two doves were sitting, one on
each side of the ears of Solomon, in order that he should
not be frightened (at the tumult of the judges). On the
upper side of the throne were placed twenty - four vines
of gold, which formed a shade for the king. And wherever
Solomon wanted to go, the throne moved under him upon
wheels. When he placed his foot upon the first step, the
golden ox raised him to the second, and so it went from
the second to the third, from the third to the fourth, from
the fourth to the fifth, and from the fifth to the sixth, where
the eagles took hold of him and seated him upon the throne.
There was also a serpent of silver around the wheels.

When the kings heard the fame of the royal throne of

---

was the father of the architect Bezaleel, and stands everywhere near
Moses and Aaron. The Midrash represents him as a martyr. The
people wanted him to make the golden calf, which he refused to do, and
therefore they killed him. Shemoth Rabba, cap. 41, 42, ed. Amst. p. 139.
לא היה שם נדול מחור הרנו אותו. The legend seems to have arisen for
the sake of excusing Aaron, to show that his life also was in danger.

[1] From 1 Sam. ii. it appears clearly that the two sons of Eli were not
virtuous and exemplary characters. And yet the Midrash (Beresh, cap. 54,
ed. Amst. 49a) represents God as saying to Abraham : Thou hast offered
seven lambs, and so the Philistines will slay thy seven righteous (צדיקים),
among whom Hophni and Phinehas stand first. This legendary view of
their character, though in opposition to the view of Scripture, occasioned
their being depicted upon the candlestick. It displays a desire to
perpetuate the fame of their priest warriors.

King Solomon, they assembled themselves and came and bowed before him, and exclaimed : No such throne was ever made for any king, and no nation can manufacture its like ! And when the kings saw its glory, they prostrated themselves and praised the Creator of the World. As oft as King Solomon ascended the throne and sat down, the crown was placed upon his head, and after this a great serpent artificially wound itself, and also lions and eagles rose up and artificially shaded his head, a golden dove descended from one pillar, opened a cabinet and took out the book of the law and placed it in his hands, in accordance with the words of Moses : " And it shall be with him, and he shall read therein all the days of his life," that he and his sons may long reign in Israel.

When the high priest came to salute King Solomon, and all the elders sat on the right and on the left of the throne to administer justice, and there appeared witnesses who wanted to bear false testimony before Solomon, then the wheels moved artificially, the oxen lowed, the lions roared,[1] the bears growled, the lambs bleated, the panthers yelled, the owls hooted, the cats mewed, the peacocks shrieked, the cocks crowed, the hawks screamed, and the birds chirped, and caused terror in the hearts of the false witnesses, so that they said to themselves : " We must bear witness to the truth ; if not, the world will be destroyed on account of us." When King Solomon went up upon the throne, rivers of spices flowed ; and no other king had such a throne. And when the enemies of Israel reached the height of their guilt (see above), the wicked

[1] The words describing the voices of the animals are in my edition of the Targum emended. בעין is used of lambs, but of the panther should be used פעין (boare). In reference to the voice of cats, instead of טייסין read מייסין (misa mica, etc.). Of peacocks, instead of מיללין read מפללין (pupulare). Of a bear may be said מחטפין, but of a hawk must be מפפטין, as it is called pipitare, pipare, piplire. Comp. my Kaiser und Königsthrone, p. 140.

בני נצן, elsewhere בר נצא. Levi quotes a MS. on Job xxxix. 29, where the last occurs. The expression son of נץ is somewhat strange. It is certainly a kind of Nisus, by which the sea eagle, the sparrow, and the hawk is sometimes denominated. The name arises from the rapidity of the flight of the bird.

S

Nebuchadnezzar equipped himself.   He went up against them, destroyed their land, plundered the city of Jerusalem, burned the temple, took the people of Israel captive, and brought them to Diblah in the land of Hamath; and with them he also brought the throne of Solomon.   And when the wicked King Nebuchadnezzar wanted to ascend and seat himself upon the throne, he did not know that an ascent was effected by artificial means, and so when he put his foot upon the first step, a golden lion stretched out his right paw, and gave him a blow upon his left foot, so that he became lame until the day of his death.[1]

After the Babylonian King Nebuchadnezzar, came Alexander the Macedonian and took the throne of Solomon, and brought it to Egypt.   When Shishak, king of Egypt, saw this throne, and that it surpassed in beauty all the royal thrones, he wanted to seat himself upon it; but he also did not know that he must ascend by means of artificial wheels, and so when he put his foot upon the first step, a golden lion stretched out his right paw and smote him upon his left foot, and so he was called the lame Pharaoh unto the day of his

[1] These remarks are legendary, but they contain historical impressions. The occasion for them was given by King Necho.   He slew Josiah, and heavily taxed Jerusalem.   The name was translated the lame (as if it had been derived from נכא).   Another Egyptian king, שישק, plundered Jerusalem in the time of Rehoboam (1 Kings xiv. 26), and the quality of lameness was ascribed to him, as if his name is derived from שוק, "a leg." But although this is said of Nebuchadnezzar, yet a political allusion to a later time is easily discerned.   Nebuchadnezzar stands for the Roman emperor who also destroyed Jerusalem.   The war began under Claudius Nero, and Claudius is derived from Claudus, "lame."   It is interesting to note that the leader of the Vandals, Genseric (Geiserich), who took away from the Romans the Jerusalem temple treasures and carried them to Africa (Procop. Vand. ii. 9; comp. Papencordt, Vandalen, p. 350), was lame (Jordanes, Get. 53), "equi casu claudicans." A remarkable parallel to the throne of Solomon is found in the Mongolian legend (comp. Jülg, Mongalische Mährchen, p. 206).   A golden throne is shown; upon thirty-two steps stand thirty-two wooden figures.   It was the throne of the god Churmista, and after him the throne of the king Vikramaditja. When Ardshi Bordshi wanted to sit down upon it, the wooden figures did beat and push him, and said, "If thou dost sit down upon it, thou wilt die."   Then he and his people prayed.

death. And when Epiphanes,[1] son of King Antiochus, came to Egypt and destroyed it, he took with him the throne of Solomon and brought it into a ship. There a leg of the throne with the chain of gold was broken, and they brought all the artists and goldsmiths of the world to repair it, but they could not do it until this day.

And when his kingdom was at an end, and Cyrus the Persian rose up after him, he for the sake of building the temple had the merit of being able to ascend and seat himself upon the throne of Solomon, the like of which there was not in all the kingdoms.

§ IV.

In the third year of King Nebuchadnezzar the house of Israel wept, groaned, sighed, and exclaimed : " Woe to us ! the enemy has prevailed over us, he has plundered our land, destroyed our provinces, carried us into exile, and has done every injustice against us. Our old men he put in chains, our princes he dragged away, our young men he slew with the sword, and our children he took captive ! Ah ! the crown of our glory is taken from us." For when the kings of the house of David were in existence they reigned over the whole world. After David succeeded Solomon his son, whom the Holy One, blessed be He ! made to rule over all the beasts of the field, and over the fowls of the air, and over the creeping things of the earth, and over devils, demons, and spirits, whose language he understood as they also understood his. For thus it is written : " And he spake of trees " (1 Kings iv. 33).

And when the heart of King Solomon was once merry with wine, he sent to invite all the kings of the East and of the West who were near the land of Israel, and he lodged them in the royal palace.[2] And when again merry with wine, he ordered that the violins, cymbals, tambourines, and harps upon

---

[1] Read instead of אניפונים.

[2] Concerning the Solomonic legend, I have treated in my " Thron Salomo's " (*Wissenschaftl. Bericht der Erfurter Akadamie*, 1851) in my *Kaiser und Königsthrone*, Berlin 1873, and in the treatise *Schamir* (Erfurt 1856).

which his father played should be brought to him. And, further merry with wine, he commanded the wild beasts, the birds, the reptiles, the devils, demons, and spirits to be brought, that they should dance before him, to show his greatness to the kings who were staying with him. The royal scribes called them all by their names, and they came together without being bound or forced, and without even a man leading them. At that time, the cock of the wood was missed among the fowls, and was not found. Then the king commanded in anger that he should appear before him, or else he would destroy him. Then the cock of the wood answered and said to King Solomon: "O lord of the earth, incline thine ears and hear my words. Are there not three months since thou hast put counsel in my heart and words of truth upon my tongue? Since then I have not eaten any food, nor drank any water, and have flown all over the world and made an inspection. I thought, Is there a country or a kingdom which is not subject to my lord the king? Then I saw a certain country, the name of whose fortified town is Kitor,[1] whose

---

[1] קימור is from קטרת, "frankincense." Saba, in Arabia, was famous for frankincense. Many authors report of it (comp. Ritter, *Weihrauch und Weihrauchland in Arabien*, xii. p. 356). The note of Strabo is interesting when he says: "τοσαῦτα δ' ἐστὶ τὸ πλῆθος (of frankincense) ὥστ' ἀντὶ φρυγάνων καὶ τῆς καυσίμου ὕλης χρῆσθαι κινναμώμῳ καὶ λασίᾳ καὶ τοῖς ἄλλοις . . . ἐκ δὲ ἐμπορίας οὗτοι τε (the Sabeans) καὶ Γερραῖοι πλουσιώτατοι πάντων εἰσίν, ἔχουσι τε παμπληθῆ κατασκευὴν χρυσωμάτων τε καὶ ἀργυρωμάτων, κλινῶν τε καὶ τριπόδων καὶ κρατήρων σὺν ἐκπώμασι καὶ τῇ τῶν οἴκων πολυτελείᾳ καὶ γὰρ θυρώματα καὶ τοῖχοι καὶ ἐροφαὶ δι' ἐλέφαντος καὶ Χρυσοῦ καὶ ἀργύρου λιθοκολλήτου τυγχάνει διαπεποικιλμένα" (lib. xvi. 4, § 19, ed. Paris, p. 662). "There is such a great quantity of frankincense that they use cinnamon and cassia for fuel instead of faggots and other firewood. Through this commerce, the Sabeans and the Gerrhaons are the richest of all, and they have a great number of gold and silver vessels, of beds, tripods, basins, together with cups and the whole decoration of the houses. Even the doors, walls, and ceilings are decorated with gold, silver, and ivory." Remarkable details, which Ritter had overlooked, are in the fragments of Juba (*Fragm. Histor Graecor.* iii. 479). Strabo says also: "On account of abundance of servants, the inhabitants are lazy and careless in their manner of life." The authors from which Strabo drew his information tell indeed a strange story of a king of Saba: "It has a king who presides over the court of justice and other things. He is not allowed to leave the palace, the people would at

dust is more precious than gold, and where silver lies about like dung in the streets. Trees also are there standing from primeval times, and are watered from the garden of Eden. Great crowds of people are there from the garden of Eden, having crowns upon their heads, who know nothing of warfare, nor can they draw the bow. For, indeed, I have seen one

once stone him, in consequence of a saying of an oracle. Not only he, but also all his companions live in effeminate luxury." The Targum evidently regards Saba as Arabia. A curious opinion is found in the Targum on Job i. 15, where, on the words, "and the Sabeans fell upon them," it says : וּדְבֵרְתִינָן זְמַרְנָד מַלְכַּת לִילִית. This hitherto unexplained passage is interesting. It should be read, not וּדְבֵרְתִינָן, but וּדְמַרְתִינָן, viz. the Mauritians. The Targum Jerushalmi on Gen. x. 7 has for Saba and Dedan זְמַרְנָד וּמֹזָג. Instead of זְמַרְנָד should be read נְמַרְנָד or נְגְרָד, viz. Nigrotes, and מֹזָן for מֹזָג, the Musones, well-known Mauritanian nations. The Targum on Job understands the peoples who fell upon the sons of Job to have been Moors, black people (hence Nigros, from Niger, Mauritanians). From this is seen why the queen is called לִילִית, who is also understood as a night spectre, from לֵילָה, night. Such a one appears here as queen and murderess, because Satan, who is also called the black one (Shahhr), has caused her to be so. There was also a tradition that the Queen of Saba came from Ethiopia, as even Josephus reports (*Antiq.* viii. 6. 5). An opinion had therefore arisen that Cush stood at the head of the whole race. As לִילִית is here, and לִילִין, spectres, is in the text several times spoken of, I shall add a note upon the peculiar story of Jerushalmi Hhagiga, because the word אַיִּם which occurs there was not properly understood either by Rapaport (*Erech Millin*, *sub voce*) or by Wünsche (*Jerus. Talmud*, p. 181). It is there told that R. Simon ben Shetahh was judging eighty witches in Askalon. He went there with eighty young men whom he had concealed. He called the witches אַיִּם, אַיִּם ; but the name is not Greek,—it is not companions,—but rather refers to Jer. l. 39. The Arabic is *bne avri*, from morning, as Delitzsch has already explained it, according to Bochart (i. 848). Jerome renders this word by Fauni, "a spirit of the forest." The Syriac version renders it by Sirens, which on the whole is correct.

It is also instructive that the Targum on Jer. renders אַיִּם by חֲתוּלִין, cats. The witches, according to the opinion of the ancients, appeared in the form of cats (comp. Grimm, *Mythol.* 1051 ; also *Ausland*, 1855, Nr. 52, p. 500 ; my *Sunem*, vol. vii. 256). The people called the witches by such and other names (like weather-cats, thunder-cats, etc.). The saying also of Simon ben Shetahh to the young men, that they must lift them up from the earth in order that they should no more be injurious, was in accordance with the common notion. It was, *e.g.*, taught in connection with lawsuits about witches, that they should not be permitted to touch the ground, otherwise they would again become transformed (comp. Grimm, *Mythol.* p. 1028). We are reminded of similar ideas in the conflict between Heracles and Antaeus.

woman who rules over them all, and her name is Queen of Saba. Now, if it please my lord the king, I shall gird my loins like a mighty man, and shall arise and go to the city of Kitor, in the land of Saba, and shall bind its kings and governor in chains of iron, and shall bring them to my lord the king." This speech pleased the king, and royal scribes were called, a letter was written and tied to the wings of the cock of the wood, who lifted up his wings and soared up in the air, and compelled other birds to fly with it. Then they came to the city of Kitor, in the land of Saba. Toward morning the queen went out to worship the sea, when the birds obscured the sunlight, so that the queen out of astonishment took hold of her clothes and tore them in pieces. The cock of the wood now came down, and she observed that a letter was tied to its wings, which she at once opened and read what was written therein, as follows: "From me, King Solomon, peace to thee and to thy princes. Thou must certainly know that the Holy One, blessed be He! made me to rule over the wild beasts, over the fowls of the air, over devils, demons, and spirits, and that all the kings of the East and of the West, of the South and of the North, come to salute me. If thou wilt come and salute me, I shall show thee greater dignity than I shall show to all the kings that are sojourning with me; but if thou wilt not come to salute me, I shall send kings, legions, and riders against thee. But if thou wilt ask, What sort of kings, legions, and riders has King Solomon? So know, that the wild beasts are the kings and the legions, and the riders are the birds in the air. My army consists of devils, demons, and spirits, who will strangle you in your beds, the wild beasts will kill you in your houses, and the fowls of the air will devour your flesh in the field." When the queen heard the words of the letter she again rent her clothes. Then she sent for the elders and prominent men, and said to them, "Do you know what King Solomon has sent to me?" They answered, "We do not know Solomon, nor do we esteem his kingdom." But she did not trust them, nor listen to their words, but caused all the ships to be collected and loaded with presents of pearls and of precious stones. And she also sent him six thousand boys and girls who were born in the same year, month, day, and hour, and who were of the same stature and of the same proportion; and they were all dressed in purple.[1]

[1] לבושא ארגונא‎, purple garments. ארגון‎ is the known Hebrew ארגמן‎; the ן‎ and מן‎ are undoubtedly corresponding terminations. The letters m and n exchange in all languages (comp. heav-en and himmel, etc.). ארג‎ is found again in the Greek ἀλουργός, purple-dyed, namely ἀλ, sea, and ἔργ, which has nothing to do with ἔργον, work. Pape's explanation, that it means sea-work, is peculiar in connection with the significance of dye. It surely means the shell-fish from which the purple dye is extracted, just as in Latin murex comes from mare. The words לבושא ארגונא‎ correspond to blatteae vestes; blatta is also properly a worm. That blatteus came to mean purple, is to be explained from the use of purple silk. Silk and purple-silk are identical, and blatteus of silk is connected with words in which it means only purple-dyed, like blatteus colour. Eutrop. speaks of blattei funes. A senator was called blattifer. From this the use has arisen of even saying, sericoblatta and pallium blattoserium (comp. Gerard, Joh. Voss. de theologia Gentili, p. 1612). From this promiscuous use of purple dye and of silk material arose the expression of "silkworm" and "purple worm;" but we shall touch upon this afterwards. About the names of silk there is yet something to be said. In the Mishna (Kilayim, § 9. 1) the word כלך‎ stands near שירים‎, which scholars have long ago recognised as related to sericum. But the opinion that שירים‎ must be read somewhat like seris or serie cannot be allowed, for even the Armenians also, the great merchants, say sheram for "silk."[1] More interesting and difficult is the word which the Jerusalem Talmud has in the same passage, viz. מטבסא‎, which should be read מטבסא‎, Gr. μέταξα or μάταξα (ed. Krotoschin, p. 32a). Another passage in which it occurs is found in Bereshith Rabba, § 40, p. 35c (ed. Amst.). When Abraham was on his journey to Egypt he had locked up his wife in a box, in order to conceal her from the Egyptians. Arrived in Egypt, he was asked to pay duty for his goods. He said that he was ready to pay for everything, only they must not open that particular box. They said to him: "Hast thou gold in it (רהבאת טיען‎)? then pay duty; or hast thou silk (מטבסין טיעין‎)? pay duty." Metaxa was then here used for valuable articles which are taxed, as it stands between gold and pearls, מרגלין‎ (comp. Yalkut Shimoni, n. 67). There is a curious passage in Bereshith Rabba, chap. 77, p. 67c (comp. Yalkut Shimoni, n. 132, ed. Venice, i. 39a), where we read. "R. Hhiya Rabba and R. Simon had business with Metaxa, and they also

[1] [This evidently originated from the fact that the shell-fish from which the purple dye of the silk was extracted was first found at Tyre, which was pronounced in the original Sar or Sur, with a strong sibilant like Sc. The fish was likewise called Scar. Hence also the name scarlet.—TRANS.]

She wrote a letter and sent it through them, which ran as follows : "From the city of Kitor to the land of Israel is indeed a journey of seven years, but owing to the questions which I have to ask thee, I shall come in three years." After three years, the Queen of Saba really came to King Solomon,

found a forgotten parcel of silk (מחילא דמטכסין)." The word מחילא has not yet been explained. It is Persian and Arabic, חל is quilts and other utensils. מחלם is in Arabic *volumen*, "a book," as well as *storea* (comp. Freytag, *Lex. Arab.* i. 290a). Interesting is the mention of *Metaxa* by Gush Chaleb of Giscala in *Koheleth Rabba* (ed. Amst. 65b). The mentioning of the word in these passages is important, because it shows how groundless is the doubt which ancient scholars have thrown upon the use of *metaxa* in the title of Marcianus which was received in the Pandects (*De Publicanis et Vectiglibus*, lib. 39, iv. 16. 7), and which they held as interpolated. They assert that, in the enumeration of *metaxa vestes serica sub serica vel attincta*, Tribonian has interpolated the word *metaxa*. This opinion is groundless when contemporaries of Marcian (R. Hhiya) use the word. Rather are the words "Vestis serica" to be considered as a gloss. The word also occurs in Cod. Theod. (lib. 10, tit. xx. de Murilegibus ; comp. *Jus. Cib. Antejustin*, ed. Hugo, p. 777) in an edict of the year 406, and — which is not surprising—in Cod. Justin (lib. 8, tit. xvi. 28, de pignoribus) in an edict of the year 528. All these quotations are older than those which Du Cange has (*Gloss. Graec.* p. 917), where Hesychius and Menander occupy the first rank. Michaelis (in Castelli, *Lex. Syr.* p. 495) quotes it Syr. מטכסא, without giving the source of the quotation. It must not be overlooked that *metaxae* is used by Vitruvius, vii. 3, in the senses of "coil" and "skein." In Turkish Tartaric also, silk was originally called *ipek jipek* (Vambery, *Die primitive Cultur der Turktataren*, p. 88). *Metaxa* is also twisting (*stria taenia*), like twisting of hair (comp. Reiske, *Zu Constant Porphyr.* ii. 791). Festus quotes it from Lucillius, as is further to be seen by Alberti on Hesychius, *sub voce σής*. A sufficient etymological explanation of the word is not yet given. Ritter has found none in his sources (*Geogr.* viii. 708), and Lassen says (*Ind. Alterthumskunde*, i. 321, note): "The word μίταξα is still of obscure origin among the later Greeks." Salmasius (comp. *Vopisc. Aurelian*, ed. Haack, ii. p. 540) is of opinion that the name that was applied to a silk thread afterwards signified silk in general. This is improbable. He thought of a formation of μίτος (from μίω) like περίσσοι, and περιξ from περί, and like σμιλος and σμίλαξ. Braun, *De Vestitu Sac. Hebr.*, approved of this, and thought that μίταξα is for μίταξις, which is unacceptable. I think that the explanation of *metaxa* has its analogy in the other names which silk had in the East and in the West. The spinning of silk by a worm has ever been the astonishment of nations. Legend and fiction are connected with it. Gervasius of Tilbury has the strangest story in his *Otia Imprialia*, chap. lvi. (Leibnitz, i. 978): "Est enim a sui principio quasi semen sinapis minutissimum cumque tempus panniculum inclusum coactum illud semen in sinu dominarum ac virginum

who, when he heard of her arrival, sent Benayahu, son of Yehoyada, to meet her. He was beautiful as sunrise (or like Venus the lustrous star), and like the white lily which stands by brooks of water. Now when the Queen of Saba saw Benayahu, son of Yehoyada, she dismounted from her riding

tenetur; beneficio caloris vivifactum foliis mori supponitur et super tabulam vernuculi extensi nutrimentum folium mori in brevi crescunt ad grossorum vermium quantitatem," etc. According to the Arab legend, Solomon wanted to have a thread brought through a diamond, so he commanded Satan to bring a worm to do it. He brought the worm, which, after accomplishing the work, left a silk thread behind. When Solomon wanted to reward the worm, it besought him to be allowed to choose a fruit tree for its dwelling, and he assigned to it the mulberry tree (*Weil bibl. Legenden*, p. 263). Paulus Silentarius poetizes of silk, "Als dem Gespiunst der fremden emsigen Würmer" (ed. Kortüm. near Salzenberg, *Altchristl. Baudenkm.* p. xlvi.). In a Roman Catholic book of songs (Bamberg, 1628, p. 483, v. Degen) we read,—

> "Was ist der Seyden Pracht,
> Wer hat die Pracht gemacht ?
> Es haben Wurm gemacht
> Den ganzen Seydenpracht."

Even the traveller Olarius exclaims, "What wonderful work of nature there is in such a little worm in its variation, work, and production !" Owing to this, most of the names of silk are called after the worm. In Mahabarata, silk is called *Kitaga*, worm-product (comp. Lassen, *Ind. Alterth.* ii. pp. 564, 614, note). The well-known *Sericum* has long ago been derived from the name of the worm, called in Mongol. *sirkek*, in Mandshu *sirghi*, in Corean *sir*, in Chinese *sze* or *szu* (the Chinese have no *r*). From the Greek *bombyx*, caterpillar, silk dresses were called *bombycinius*. Hesychius adduces a name βρύδαξ (βρύδαχις) for silk stuff, from a form βούτον, which is a worm (perhaps the German *Brut*) (comp. Salmasius on *Tertullian de Pallio*, p. 240).

The Latin *blatta*, "moth," is in well-known use applied to materials of silk. As already remarked, we meet with *blattei funes, blattei, blattifer senatus*, with which the idea of purple-dyed is connected (comp. Voss, *De theologia gentili*, p. 1012). The best known name was *Seide* (silk), derived from the Greek σής (in older forms, gen. σεος and then σήτος), originally also the moth. In the MIDDLE AGES it was called *Seta*, and the name came with the silk from Byzantium (comp. Du Cange, and Ritter, viii. pp. 708–9). The *Aruch* also mentions the name as שירא in the twelfth century in Italy. The name passed then over into French, as *soie* (from *sida*, like *foi* from *fides*, and *vair* from *videre*). It is found as שייאה in Rashi on Ezek. xvi. 10. The Greek σής is the same as the Hebrew סס, for which also it is given in the Greek version on Isa. li. 8. Elsewhere it stands for עש (Isa. l. 9 ; Job iv. 19, xxvii. 18), and for רקב (Prov. xiv. 32, etc.).

Doubtful is the Persian *Ebrisim* (Vullers, *Lex.* i. 67), Armenian *aprsoum*

animal. "Why," asked Benayahu, son of Yehoyada, "dost thou dismount from thy riding animal?" She rejoined, "Art not thou King Solomon?" He replied, "I am not King Solomon, but one of his servants who attend upon him." Thereupon she turned to her great men, and said this proverbial saying: "If you do not see the lion, you see his lair; though you do not see King Solomon, yet you see a handsome man who stands before him." Then Benayahu conducted her to the king, who, when he heard that she was coming, went and sat down in an apartment of glass. When the queen saw the king sitting there, she thought in her heart, and in fact

(*eprsoum*), which also passed into Arabic (Freytag, i. pp. 2, 3). Also *Abreshum* (*Ebreshum*) in Georgian (Güldenstädt, *Reise nach Georgien*, ed. Klaproth, p. 93). The extensive and interesting explanation of Haug in the *Göttinger gelehrten Anzeigen*, 1854 (26, 27, Stück vom, 11 Feb. p. 259), is not decisive. אבריסם is nothing else than the Greek ἑρπετόν, "worm," "reptile."

According to these analogies, which show that the name for silk was derived from the name that was given to "worm" and "moth," there can now be no doubt that we must in the same way explain the word *metaxa*, and that from a name which was widely known, namely from the moth itself (with which probably the German word *Made*, "maggot," is related). It is called in Old North German *madkr*, Swedish *madk*, Danish *madike*, *maddik*. The Low German forms sound *maddik*, *meddike*, *metke*. It was rightly supposed that it is connected with the Sanscr. form *matka* and the Persian *miteh*, moth (comp. Vullers, ii. 1250). This derivation has also ethnographical value. When one meets in the East a name for silk having an Old Germanic origin, he is reminded of the Sers, who were always merchants of silk, of whom Pliny (*Hist. Nat.* vi. chap. xvii. No. 88, ed. Sillig, i. 434) says, that they were on this side of the Emodos: "Seras ab ipsis adspici notos etiam commercio . . . ipsos vero excedere hominum magnitudinem, rutilis comis, caeruleis oculis, oris sono truci, nullo commercio lingu de," which indicates a Germanic type. What Lassen says (ii. 359) cannot militate against this. The remarkable traits of nations often indicate names. The Germanic nations now call silk by a Greek name. The Byzantian ages transmitted a name which was essentially Germanic.

In English, silk is rightly supposed to have received the name from Sericus, which has come from the Chinese and Tartar peoples. In the Old Testament the word משי appears. This also has not been known until now. I hold it to be the same as μέταξα, also that מש=משי=ממשי, like the Persian *miteh*, Greek μίδας, Old High German *mizo*, French *mite*, *motte*, English moth, mite, and must be like the similar forms mentioned above which had received the letter *k* (comp. Dieffenbach, *Goth. Wörterb.* i. p. 6). In משי is clearly seen the meaning of worm.

said, that he was sitting in water, and she raised her dress to cross the water, when the king noticed that her foot was full of hair. He said to her, "Thy beauty is the beauty of women, and thy hair is the hair of men; hair is becoming to a man, but to a woman it is a shame." The Queen of Saba then said: "My lord king! I will give thee three riddles,[1] which if thou shalt solve, I will acknowledge

---

[1] The riddles which Solomon here solves are not like those which the Muhamedan tradition relates (comp. Hammer, *Rosenöl*, pp. 159, 160 ; Weil, *Bibl. Legenden*, p. 260), nor like those in the Midrash Mishle (comp. Wünsche, *Räthselweisheit*, p. 16). The Arabic riddles are poetic. That of the tear is also mentioned in the fable of Tewedud (*The Thousand and One Nights* of Hammer and Zinserling), which contains, apart from this, plenty of Arabian riddles. Of the riddles which are stated here, the author of a German translation of the Targum in the year 1698 says that he does not give them because they are different in various places, and also because he does not understand them. The same has happened to many others. The author of the מצח אהרן (Fürth 1768) explains the first thus : " It is a reed made of wood, in which is put dye for colouring the eyes ; and this dye is very hard, like a stone ; and when one wants to take out the stone, he must use an iron spoon to extract the colour, and when the eye is smeared over, then water comes out. Of the second he says, this is pitch, which is extracted from the earth like water, because it is thin and it will stick to a house." In imperfect language he rightly gives the old interpretations. But, on the other hand, he did not understand the beginning of the following riddle, which is the most interesting one. I must here remark that for the reading of ארקלין, which Rapaport (*Erech Millin*, p. 229) considered for *oraculum*, and was also obscure to Buxtorf, must be read פרקלין, viz. *procella*, and the passage should be translated : " In the storm moves and arises a great bitter cry." This reminds us of the praise given to flax by Pliny in his Introduction to *Bib.* 19, where he says : " Andax vita, scelerum plena, aliquid seri, at ventos procellas recipiat." But, also in the other passage which Rapaport quotes under ארקל, the reading is false. In Shirhashirim Rabba 3a, the Kiss of God must be spoken of. The reading therefore must be אבקולאין for *oscula*, instead of ארקולאין. Again, for הרימא, or הרימא, should be read אריסא, viz. *sponsio*. For the passage speaks of the kiss and the betrothal of God to man. The riddle itself is very suggestive. As a sail flaps violently in the storm the linen made of flax it bows low its head like a rush (comp. Isa. lviii. 5). Linen is a cause of dignity to the rich and free who wear byssus (there is a play upon the word חורין, free, with חור, white), a cause of shame to the poor who wear rags, an ornament for the dead in their shrouds—which are white as angels, and a mockery to the living (the rope of flax), a joy to the birds, who pick up the seed of flax, and a vexation to the fish on account of the nets. Flax is called in Greek and in Latin *linon*, *linum*. Hence it was that Yashua ben Levi (Bereshith Rabba,

that thou art a wise man; but if not, then thou art a man
like all the rest."

She asked, "What is berries of wood and buckets of iron
which draw up stones and pour out water?" He answered,
"A tube of paint." "What is," she asked again, "a thing
which comes as dust from the earth, eats dust, is poured out
as water, and sticks to a house?" He answered, "It is
naphtha." She further asked, "What is that which as an
oracle (or as a storm) goes at the head of all, cries loudly and
bitterly with its head bowed down like a rush, is a cause of
praise to the free, of shame to the poor, of honour to the
dead, of disgrace to the living, of joy to the birds, and of
grief to the fish?" He answered, "It is flax." She exclaimed, "I would not have believed it had I not come here
and seen it with mine own eyes; and behold the half has not
been told me, for thy wisdom and thy goodness surpass the
report I have heard. Blessed are thy people, and blessed are

§ 20) said : "God had made for them garments of לבוש, 'linen;'" for which
Wünsche (Midrash Rabba, p. 95), curiously enough, read לבנא, "garments
of the skin of a hare." The riddle which we have here is more intelligible and instructive than that contained in the symposium which is
ascribed to Lactantius,—

> "Major eram longe quondam, dum vita manebat
> Sed nunc examinis lacerata, ligata, revulsa
> Dedita sum terrae, tumulo sed condita sum."

Simrock made a peculiar mistake in his German book of riddles. In
No. 13 he gives us the riddle thus :—

> "In days gone by when young I was green,
> A robe for counts and princes I've been ;
> And when I am old and not much use,
> My learning then is great and profuse."

This is evidently flax. Linen becomes at last rags, and rags become
paper. But in the list of the solutions of the riddles, the cherry is given
for No. 13. On the other hand, riddle No. 22 is as follows :—

> "A damsel sits upon a tree,
> Her gown is red as red can be,
> Within her heart a stone I see,
> Guess now, I pray, what this may be."

The solution is a cherry ; but in Simrock's list, flax is given for it. The
copyist must have confounded the two solutions.

these thy servants who are about thee!" Thereupon he brought her into the tribunal[1] (or an apartment) of the royal palace. Now, when the Queen of Saba saw his greatness and glory, she praised the Creator, and said: "Blessed be the Lord thy God, whom it has pleased to set thee upon the throne of the kingdom to do justice and right." She then gave the king plenty of gold and silver, and he gave her what she desired. And the kings of the West and of the East, of the North and of the South, who heard of his fame, came tremblingly from their various places with extraordinary dignity, and they presented him with much gold and silver, and with pearls and precious stones.

§ V.

And when the enemies of Israel filled up the measure of their guilt (or when Israel were guilty), the prophet[2] Jeremiah uttered many prophecies to them; and as they did not listen to him, the Holy Spirit persuaded him, and led him away into the land of the tribe of Benjamin. Thus it is written:

---

[1] טרבונא can best be explained by reading טרבונא, *tribuna* = tribunal, of which Reiske (*Constant. Porphyr.* ii. p. 83) says: "Tribunal est omne aedificium excelsum, illustre, non tantum βῆμα in quo causae aguntur." In the same way explains Rashi: וכל טרבונא בלשון ארמי פלטין החשובין למלכות. That which Munk adduces (p. 24) does not explain it.

[2] This narrative about Jeremiah is owing to a curious homily upon two sentences in his prophecy. Tradition assumed that he really did what is told in the above quotation from Jer. xxxvii. 12, and it therefore understood by the "gate of Benjamin," not a city gate by which people went to Benjamin, but a gate in the country of Benjamin itself. It connected with this Jer. xx. 7, where the prophet exclaims: "O Lord, Thou hast persuaded me, and I was persuaded; Thou hast forcibly taken hold upon me, and hast prevailed," and understood by these words that Jeremiah was led by the Spirit to go to Benjamin, but his heart failed him, and he went instead to Jerusalem, and therefore it was conquered by the enemy. For this the prophet laments, "Thou hast persuaded me." A similar tradition is in Midrash Echa (i. 5, ed. Amst. 47a) concerning R. Zadok. About him said R. Johhanan to Vespasianus: "If such a man were yet in Jerusalem, thou wouldest not be able to take the city with double thy force." Another like saying is told of the siege of Bether, which, so long as R. Eliezer המודעי (not of Modin, as Wünsche says), lived in it, was preserved on account of his piety (Midrash Echa, ii. 1, ed. Amst., p. 52b).

"Then Jeremiah went forth out of Jerusalem to go into the land of Benjamin." But so long as Jeremiah was in Jerusalem he prayed to the heavenly Father, and the city was not delivered into the hands of the Chaldeans, and they did not destroy it. But when he went into the land of Benjamin, then came up Nebuchadnezzar, the king of Babylon, and destroyed the land of Israel, plundered the city of Jerusalem, and burned the temple with fire. While yet the tyrant Nebuchadnezzar was dwelling in Antiochian Ribla, he sent the chief executioner, Nebuzaradan, who razed the walls of the city Jerusalem to the ground. And when the prophet Jeremiah arrived, and saw that the city was destroyed, and that the Chaldeans surrounded it on every side, he cried aloud, and wept much and bitterly, and said: "Thou, O Lord, hast persuaded me, and I was persuaded; Thou hast forcibly taken hold upon me, and hast prevailed." And when the wicked Nebuchadnezzar, king of Babylon, heard that Jerusalem was conquered, he assembled all the troops of the Chaldeans, and came to avenge himself against the temple. He thoughtfully shook his head, and pointed with his hands here and there, as the fate of Sennacherib's camp was known to him, against which angels from heaven were sent, who slew eighteen myriads and five thousand riders, so that of Sennacherib's camp only he remained.

Then a Bathkol (an echoing voice) was heard, which exclaimed: "Nebuchadnezzar, king of Babylon, arise, and return to Ribla in the land of Hamath."[1]

---

[1] אנטוכיא רבלתא.
Ribla is the place where Nebuchadnezzar encamped, where Zedekiah's eyes were taken out, and his sons killed before him. It is supposed to be the same as the present Ribleh, 10 to 12 hours distant from Homs, on the Orontes (El Asy), in the northern part of Bekoa (comp. Robinson, *Palestine*, iii. 747). The Rabbis have identified it with Antioch, or Daphne near Antioch, where they think Nebuchadnezzar sojourned for a time.
The Midrash Echa states twice that he tarried ברפני של אנטוכיא (ed. Amst., 51a at the close of the Introduction, and 58c), where, by the way, Wünsche has not correctly rendered it by Daphne Antiochena. It is called in Greek, as by Josephus (*Jewish Wars*, i. 13. 5, etc.), 'Αντιόχεια Δάφνη, and

He cast arrows,[1] consulted the oracle; he threw an arrow
westward, and it fell in the direction of Jerusalem; then east-
ward, and it fell in the direction of Jerusalem; and then
again he threw an arrow towards the guilty city (*i.e.* Rome)—

not seldom 'Αντιόχεια ἐπὶ Δάφνη (see Ritter, xvii. 1163). The reason why
the Rabbis identify Ribla with Daphne is more of an ethical than a historical
character. What Ribla was for Nebuchadnezzar, the same was Daphne
for the Syrian and the Roman kings. There in the Orient was their seat.
Thence issued all the misery that came upon the besieged.

[1] In Ezek. xxi. 25 we have that grand passage which informs us that
Nebuchadnezzar was in doubt whether he should march against Rabbath
Ammon or against Jerusalem.

"He stood at the parting of the way, at the head of two ways, to use
divination; he shook the arrows" (קלקל חצים). Upon the meaning of the
word קלקל a good deal has been conjectured. It is of an onomatopoetic
kind, and is connected with Βάλλειν, "to throw." Throwing was used in
the sense of casting a die (comp. balloter), like the Latin *Alea*, has arisen
from the Greek ἰάλλω, "to throw" (comp. my *Spielhaus auf Monte Carlo*,
p. 23). The commentators have mostly been influenced by what Jerome
says on this passage, but they overlooked that he (ed. Migne, v. p. 206)
confounded *belomantia*, "arrow-divination," with mace-divination, which
was not, nor could be, the same. The examples of Arabic usage by Van
Dale (*De Orig. et Progr. Idolatriae*, etc. p. 456), and quoted from Herbelot,
do not appear to be applicable (*Voc. Acda.*). It was, on the other hand,
overlooked that Haman cast the lot, and chose the thirteenth day, which
was called Tir, "an arrow," for issuing his destructive decree. See my
Commentary on Esther, p. 103. There would be more ground for Chwolsohn's reminder of Sabian usage (*Sabier*, ii. 200) if he had not laid stress
upon the extinguishing of the torch. The ancient Jewish expositors are
right when they speak of "the shooting of the arrow." The decision
depended upon the direction in which the arrow fell. Rashi has well
translated the words "shooting an arrow" by the French טרא אית, which
should he read טרא טריח, "*tirer trait*." It was a kind of casting the lot
when Jonathan shot an arrow to give a sign to David (1 Sam. xx. 21), and
Elisha prophesied by the shooting of arrows concerning the victory of
Joash over Syria (2 Kings xiii. 15). The Targum uses the homily of the
Midrash as in Echa Rabbathi (ed. Amst. p. 39a), but gives it more correctly than it is in Midrash Echa. The latter appears to have taken the
word קלקל in the sense of *calculari*, "to reckon" the arrows. The Targum
is more explicit when it says, "He shot towards the west and the east, and
it fell towards Jerusalem; he then shot towards the city which is guilty,
that it should soon be rooted out from the world (by which it means Rome,
as is expressly said in Midrash Echa), and it rebounded towards Jerusalem."
The time for its destruction had come, and Nebuchadnezzar, as the tradition tells, was directed by his oracle to undertake the siege reluctantly,
for he remembered what had happened to Sennacherib. The Midrash Echa
speaks also of a divination, upon which both Ezekiel and the Targum are

may it soon be rooted out from the world !—and this also fell towards Jerusalem.

Then he arose and sent his generals against Jerusalem, whose names were Nargal, Sharezer, Shamgar, Nebosar, Sechim, Rabsaris, and Rabmag, *i.e.* Chief-eunuch, and Chief-magus. He

silent. It says : "Nebuchadnezzar lit candles and torches (נרות ופנסים), and appointed them for Rome, and they were extinguished ; for Alexandria, and they were again extinguished ; finally, he appointed them for Jerusalem, and they burned." Chwolsohn would have been right in connecting this with the Sabian custom, according to which an arrow was fastened to a torch, and if it burned, it bore an omen of good fortune ; and if it was extinguished, it bore an omen of misfortune (*Sabier*, ii. 26 and p. 201).

פנס, Syriac פנסא, occurs also in compounds, as in Midrash Koheleth, p. 63*a* (ed. Amst.), קספלפנס, viz. ξυλοφάνης, ξυλοφάνιον, a wooden torch (ξυλολύχνος, comp. Spanheim, *de Praest. Numism.*, ed. Amst., iv. p. 128). Through this rare word a passage in Hesychius is explained. He says there, under Ἴχθον : ἄστρον . . . ξυλοφάνιον. Some, like Spohn, corrected this by σκαπάνη, which is altogether unnecessary, as the passage in the Midrash shows. ξυλοφάνιον is, like ξυλοφάνης, "a piece of wood which was applied to torches." קספלפנס is here used in contrast to מקורתפנס. They are lanterns with net-laces. The Greeks also used with the word λύχνος such words as δίμυξος and πολυμώξος (see Stephanus, *sub voce* μίξα, and Wüstemann, *Der Palast. des Scaurus*, p. 133). Indeed, we also know from mediaeval legends, that arrows were applied to purposes of witchcraft. In the *Gesta Romanorum*, n. 102, we read of a certain cleric who wished to marry a man's wife during his absence in a distant place, so he placed a wax figure and shot an arrow upon it, intending thereby to kill the man in the distance. This man was just then in Rome, where he was warned by a wise man of the danger he was in. He showed it to him in a magic mirror while he was in the bath. He then dipped his head under the water, and thus escaped the danger, while the arrow which the cleric shot rebounded upon himself. Another wonderful story is told in *Gesta Romanorum*, cap. 10 f. There was once a beautiful secret chamber which contained an image with precious stones, into which a cleric entered clandestinely, with the intention of stealing. Then the image upon which was sculptured an arrow and a bow, shot an arrow upon a luminous carbuncle, and this caused thick darkness as in the night. In the eleventh narrative of the English edition (ed. Grässe, ii. 339) it is told : A knight once shot a beautiful bird that sang gloriously, in consequence of which a mountain was cleft in two, and then sank into the abyss. In the *Image du Monde* it is told that the Apostle Paul had visited the grave of Virgil to find his books. He entered it, and saw a lamp hanging from the roof, and an archer stood before Virgil ready to shoot. When he was about to take the books, the archer shot an arrow upon the lamp, and then everything was turned into dust (comp. *Virgili im Mittelalter übersetzt von Dütschke*, p. 265).

followed his generals and entered the temple, and thus exclaimed, "Art Thou the great God who has stirred us up, and brought us against Thy city and against Thy temple?"

But when the gate of the temple saw the unclean people standing against it, it shut itself, and would by no means open. Then came all the army of the Chaldeans, and brought with them three hundred and sixty camels laden with iron axes; but the external gates of the temple destroyed them, and continued not to open themselves until Parnitus [1] came and slew a swine, and sprinkled its blood upon the temple, and defiled it.

After the temple was defiled, the gate opened, and then the wicked Nebuchadnezzar went in and sat down in the hall of Zechariah, son of Yohoiyada the high priest, and he saw his (Zechariah's) blood moving upon the ground. So he asked the elders of Israel, "Whose blood is this?" They answered, "We had a prophet amongst us who reproved us; but we did not hearken to his words, but rose up and slew him in the temple." [2]

---

[1] This cannot be thought of Ptolemaeus Euergetes, for he was kind towards the Jews. Josephus acknowledges this (*Contra Apionem*, ii. 5, ed. Havercamp, ii. 472). The one who offered swine in the temple was Antiochus Epiphanes, as it is narrated in the book of the Maccabees and by Josephus. The Greeks called him instead of Epiphanes, Epimanes, viz. "the mad one." The same is expressed by the above name פרניטוס, the *effrenatus*, "the wild and unrestrained." We should gain the same sense if we should read פרנטיקוס, *phreneticus*, "Until the mad and the bold one come."

[2] The awful story about the blood of the prophet is in allusion to 2 Chron. xxiv. 22, where it is recorded that Zechariah, the slain prophet, uttered these last words: "The Lord look upon it (*i.e.* my blood), and require it." They connected this passage with Hos. iv. 2: "Blood toucheth blood." The underlying thought is, that blood boils up when the murderer comes near it. The blood of Zechariah continued to boil until Nebuchadnezzar came. Even then it was not pacified, however many were slain,—for the murderer was still there,—and only at last out of pity it became still (see my *Symboliks des Blutes*, p. 22, etc.). The story is told in various ways in Echa Rabbathi, p. 39*a*, *b*. Comp. Bab. Gittin, 57*b*; Sanhedrin 96*b*. [He appears to have been the same as in Matt. xxiii. 35. The first component parts interchange as in Jehoiakim, who was called Eliakim. Jerome says that the Gospel of the Nazarenes read the son of Jehoiada.—TRANS.]

When the wicked Nebuchadnezzar heard these words, he said to them: "Go and bring me four thousand young priests." These he slew over that blood, and yet it would not enter the earth, until Nebuchadnezzar rebuked it by saying, "Shall thy whole people be destroyed for thy sake!" After this it was absorbed by the earth. Then the high priest, seeing that the priests were killed, put on his upper garment and the ephod, took the keys of the temple in his hands, and went upon the roof of the temple and called out: "The house is now given back to its Lord, and the keepers are no more in it!" Thereupon he threw himself into the burning pile and was consumed. When the remaining priests saw that the high priest was burned, they took their violins and harps, and all their other musical instruments, and likewise threw themselves into the fire, and were burned.

When Nebuchadnezzar wanted now to enter the Holy of Holies, the doors closed and would not open until an echoing voice from heaven exclaimed, and said, "Open, Libanon, thy gates!" After this a door opened itself, and the wicked Nebuchadnezzar defiled the Holy of Holies by entering into it; and he saw there the glories of the King of all the worlds, of the Lord of hosts. But when he saw that the holy vessels which the priests and the kings of the house of David used were sunk into the earth, he was very wroth, and hastened away and slew a great number; and many others he took captive, and led the people of Israel into exile, bound in iron chains, naked, and carrying sand upon their necks. The prophet Jeremiah went with them until he reached the graves of the patriarchs. Here he wept, and cried: "O our merciful fathers, Abraham, Isaac, and Jacob! arise from your graves and behold your children, the people of Israel, are led into captivity!" Then answered the Holy Spirit and said to him: "I have long ago told thee, O prophet Jeremiah, that I have withdrawn my peace." He then rose up from the graves of the fathers and went to the graves of the mothers, and prostrated himself, and cried, "O merciful mothers, Sarah, Rebekah, Rachel, and Leah! arise from your graves and see your sons and daughters, the people of Israel, whom you have brought up in the truth, are going barefoot into captivity!" The Holy Spirit then answered: "A voice was heard in Ramah," etc. He then arose from the graves of the mothers, and went to the graves of the prophets, and prostrated himself, and cried: "O merciful prophets, Moses and Samuel! arise from your graves and see the people of Israel, whom you have led in the truth, are going barefoot into captivity." The Holy Spirit answered and said: "I have long ago told thee, O prophet Jeremiah, 'If even Moses and Samuel should stand before me,'" etc. He then rose up from the graves of the prophets, and went and prostrated himself in the house (or upon the graves) of the mourners, and said: "Bring me 'the bread of the mourners to eat, and the cup of comfort to drink,' for I mourn for the people of Israel who went into captivity." The Holy Spirit answered and said: "Do not go into the house of mourning." Thus Jeremiah mourned, wept, and groaned concerning the people of Israel who went into exile naked, and carrying sand upon their necks, they and their kings and princes and governors, until they reached a place which is called Beth-Coro,[1] where they changed their garments. Then Jeremiah said to Nebuchadnezzar the wicked, and to all the army of the Chaldeans who came with him, "Do not go to your idols and praise them. Rather know that you have only killed and taken captive a people which was already captured and killed." They then went on until they reached a certain country, where Jeremiah bitterly wept and sobbed. Two tears fell from his eyes, which became there two fountains that exist to this day.

---

[1] בית כורו. It would be difficult to identify this place. But the legend of the Jews has made the figurative prophecies of the prophets a reality. בית כור is "a furnace," of which the prophet says that the children of Israel must be refined in it (Isa. xlviii. 10). The legend considers this as a place. The exclamation of Jeremiah, "Oh that my head were waters, and mine eyes a fountain of tears!" was also made to refer to a place. Likewise the harps of which Ps. cxxxvii. speaks are historically placed together.

When the people of Israel had arrived at the rivers of Babylon, the wicked King Nebuchadnezzar said to them: "Let those singers who used to sing before your Lord in Jerusalem come and sing before me." When the Levites heard this, they hung up their harps on the willows which stood by the rivers of Babylon. For thus it is written: "By the rivers of Babylon," etc. The Levites, moreover, said to Nebuchadnezzar the tyrant: "Had we done the will of our heavenly Father, and had we praised Him in Jerusalem, we should not have been delivered into thy hands. But how can we now sing the praise of our Lord before thee?" For thus it is written: "How shall we sing the Lord's song," etc. When Nebuchadnezzar the wicked heard this, he said: "Kill them, for they have transgressed the command of the king!" Then an Israelite, by the name of Pelatya, son of Yohoiyada, said to him: "When one delivers his flock to a shepherd, and a bear comes and snatches away a sheep, of whom will it be required?" He answered, "From the shepherd will it be required." Pelatya then said: "Let thy ears hear what thy mouth has spoken." Then the king ordered to bring Zedekiah before him, and they removed the chains of iron and of brass from him, and changed his captive garments for others.

§ VI.

"In the third year of his reign, he made a feast for all the princes and ministers of Persia and Media, and for all the governors of the districts. They were clothed in silk and purple garments, ate and drank, and rejoiced before him."

It is not said here, he showed them his riches, but "he showed them the riches of his glorious kingdom." By which riches is to be understood, that which came from the temple. For a mortal eye has no riches, but all riches belong to God; as it is written, "Mine is the silver and the gold, saith the

Lord of hosts." During a hundred and eighty days he showed them daily six treasuries, as it is written, " riches, honour, dominion, glory, majesty, greatness " (Esther i. 4),—so then six expressions. But when the Israelites saw there the vessels of the temple, they did not remain any longer. The king was told that the Jews did not want to take refreshment, because they saw there the vessels of the temple, and so he ordered that they should have another banquet for themselves.

When those days were ended, the king said : " Now I will make a feast for all the inhabitants of my city, for all the people that are found in Shushan, both small and great." They were brought to the royal garden where fruit and spice trees stood, some of which were broken and arranged for arbours, and others were planted for shades; seats also were prepared, and the paths were strewn with costly stones and pearls.—And they drank out of golden cups and bowls ; and when one drank of a cup, he did not drink of the same again, but he was given a new cup. The cups were of various descriptions, as it is written : " And the vessels were diverse from one another." But when they brought out the vessels of the temple, and the heathen began to pour wine into them, the appearance of the vessels became different from what they were. And for this reason it is said : " The vessels being diverse from one another;" "And royal wine was (רב) in abundance." That is, the wine was older than the person who drank it. For example, the butlers asked a man how old he was, and he said forty years, and so they gave him wine forty years old ; and thus they did with every man. For this reason it is written : " And royal wine was in abundance." And the drinking was according to regulation, so that it could hurt no one. Why could it not hurt ? Because when at royal feasts generally, a cup was given to a Persian containing from four to five Hemins (a certain measure that was called Pithka[1]),

---

[1] פיתקא. Neither Buxtorf nor Michaelis nor Levi has properly explained this word, the reading of which is unassailable. It is the Persian drinking vessel βατιάκη, "περισκή τε φιάλη ἡ βατιάκη;" comp.

he had to drink the whole out in one breath.   Owing to this
the butlers used to become rich, for no Persian guest could
be found able to drink the whole cup at once, and therefore
they used to beckon to the butlers to take it away for a
certain sum of money.   But Ahhashverosh gave order that
no such cups should be given this time, but that every one
should drink as much as he liked.   Therefore it is written
"And the drinking was according to law."   Vashti also made
a feast for the women, and gave them red wine,[1] and seated them
in the palace, in order to show them its riches.   They asked
her various question, for they wanted to know everything, *e.g.*
where the king eats, drinks, and sleeps ; and she showed them
all the places.   Therefore it is written : "In the royal house."

On the seventh day, when the king and the hundred and
twenty-seven crowned princes who were with him were merry
with wine, a dispute arose among them about indecent things.
The kings of the West said, Our women are the handsomest.
The others said the same of their women.   Ahhashverosh also
took part in the dispute, and in his drunken freak said:
"There are no more beautiful in the world than the Babylonian;
but if you will not believe me, I shall send for the Babylonian wife which I have in the palace, and you shall see
that she surpasses in beauty all your wives."   Immediately
King Ahhashverosh sent seven eunuchs to the queen.   He
said : "Go and say to Queen Vashti : Arise from thy royal
throne, strip thyself naked,[2] put the crown upon thy head,
take a golden cup in thy right hand and another in thy left,
and thus appear before me and the hundred and twenty-seven
crowned kings, that they may see that thou art the fairest
of all women."   She refused.   Vashti answered to the seven
eunuchs : "O shame.   Go and tell your master, the fool,—

Casaubon on Athenaeus (pp. 484, 494).   In passing, I may remark that
כותא has no connection with χους, as Levi says.   It is the Greek κύαθος,
cup.   Comp. Athenaeus, p. 480.   ‡ stands for θ, *th.*

[1] [Read סומקא instead of אוכמא.—TRANS.]

[2] [This reminds one of the story of Lady Godiva, whom Leofric, her
husband, ordered to ride naked through the town of Coventry.—TRANS.]

you also are fools like him,—I, Queen Vashti, am the daughter
of Babylonian kings of more ancient times. My ancestor
Belshazzar drank as much wine as a thousand persons, and yet
the wine never made him so silly as to utter such improper
words as thou hast to me." Then they went and told the king
the reply of Queen Vashti. And when he heard it, his anger
was kindled, and he again sent the seven eunuchs, saying to
them: "Go and say to her, If thou dost not hearken to me,
and dost not appear before me and before these kings, I shall
cause thee to be slain, and thy beauty will perish." The
nobles came to her with the message, and she did not honour
them, but said: "Go and tell the foolish king, whose counsel
is as much folly as his command is unjust, I am Queen
Vashti, the daughter of Evil-Merodach and granddaughter of
Nebuchadnezzar. Ever since I was born no man has seen
my body except thou alone, and if I now appear before thee
and before the hundred and twenty-seven crowned kings, the
end will be, they will slay thee and marry me." Now a noble
Persian lady said to Queen Vashti: "Even if the king should
kill thee, and cause thy beauty to perish, thou must by no
means dishonour the name of thy ancestors, and thou must
not show thy body to any man, except to the king alone."

At the same time the nobles told the king that Vashti
refused to obey the command which he sent to her by the
eunuchs, and his wrath quite overpowered him. Then the
king laid the matter before the sages and statesmen, for royal
affairs are brought before those who are acquainted with laws
and statutes. There were some in the cabinet council who
were from near, and others who were from a distance. Those
from near were Carshena[1] from Africa, Shethar from India,

---

[1] The information about the countries of the seven officials is merely
for the purpose of showing the world-wide empire of the Persian king.
Carshena was an African, according to the meaning of the name.

The Targum does not use a scientific method in its explanation, but
rather bases it upon a fanciful hypothesis, that the names of these men
indicate the places they came from. Thus אדימתא has some similarity
with אדום, therefore he must be an Edomite. So also Carshana or

Admatha from Edomaea, Tarshish from Egypt, Meres-Marsena
from Meres, a distant country, Memucan from Jerusalem. To
those seven great Persians and Medes, who looked upon the
king's face and were of the first rank, he communicated the
royal order which he sent to Vashti by the eunuchs. Then
said Memucan, who is Daniel. But why is he called Memucan?
Because when the tribe of Judah were taken captive to Babylon,
—Hananiah, Mishael, Azariah were among them,—Daniel also
was exiled, through whom great, wonderful, and mighty works
were done, and again through whom heaven determined that
Queen Vashti should be killed, in consequence of which he
was called Memucan, i.e. "establisher." And Memucan spake
to the king and governors—there was a royal statute at the
time which provided, that in the cabinet consultations the
younger ministers should give their advice first. If it was

Carshena must be an African, because it sounds like Carthage. Near this
stands שְׁתָר, and he is said to have come from הנדקי. This is done on the
ground of the explanation of the Targum of the words "sons of Cush,"
viz. סינידאי הנדקי, סמידאי, ולובאי וזנגאי. The last זנגא are the Tingitani.
Zinghi. לובאי are the Libyans. For סמדאי must be read נמדאי, the
Numidians. הנדקי are the Hindoos=Ethiopians; and for סינדאי must be
read סרינא, the Cyrenians. On account of the vicinity of these in Africa,
the Targumist has assigned הנדקי to שְׁתָר, by which he thought of the real
India. In consequence of this he assigns מצרים, Egypt, to תרשיש. In
another place (1 Kings xxii. 49; Jer. x. 9) the Targum has for Tarshish,
Africa; and the LXX., too, renders it by Carthage. But this has already
been assigned to Carshena, and could not be made use of again for the
other ministers, who were all supposed to be sons of Cush, with the exception of Memucan. The explanation also of מרם by מרסנא shows this. It
is Maurusia, and the Greek name for Mauretania is to be understood by it.
The Targum also explains רעמה (Gen. x. 7) by this word. The name
Memucan is very artificially explained. Because the fate of Vashti was
decided through him, therefore he is compared with Daniel, and is called
Memucan, "the one who was appointed to this work." For the Hebrew
הכין, part, Mucan is usually reproduced in the Targum by תקן, hence מתקנן
=ממוכן. This connecting of Memucan with Daniel is more remarkable
than that which the Targum ascribes to Daniel, which does not redound
to his honour. The explanations in Midrash Esther are quite different.
Memucan is not there identified with Daniel. In the first Targum he is,
on the contrary, compared with Haman (comp. Megill. p. 12b). Mordecai
is explained by מראדביא, "pure balm," in allusion to Ex. xxx. 23 (comp.
Bab. Chulin 139b).

a proper one, they carried it into execution; but if not, the
older ministers gave their advice. And as Memucan was the
youngest of them all, he gave his advice first. It so happened
that Memucan had married a Persian wife who was richer
than himself, and she refused to speak to him in any other
language but her own, and so he thought to himself, now
is the opportunity to compel the wives to honour their
husbands. Therefore he said to the king and the nobles:
"Not against the king alone has Queen Vashti failed, but
also against all the nations and governors that are in the
empire of Ahhashverosh. For the answer of the queen will
be spread among all the women who now honour their
husbands, and every woman will say to her husband, 'Art
thou perhaps worthier than King Ahhashverosh, who commanded that Queen Vashti should come before him, and she
refused to come?' Even this day the noble women of Persia
and Media repeat the language of the queen to the royal
governors in such a manner that it causes contempt and
occasion for wrath." But at the very time when Memucan
gave this decision, he was anxious about himself. He thought,
perhaps the king will not issue a decree, and Queen Vashti
may hear of my advice concerning her, and she will judge me
severely, and cause me to be killed. I will therefore see that
the king should not order her to appear before him, by binding him by an oath which the Persians and Medes fear (to
break). Hence he further said: "If it please the king, let
this decree be issued, and this oath be written in the statute
book of the Medes and Persians that it should not be
invalidated, namely, that Vashti should no more come before
the king, and that her kingdom should be given to her companion, who is better than she. And let this decision be
proclaimed in all the empire, however great it may be, and
all the women, great and small, will honour their husbands."
This advice pleased the king and his governors, and he acted
according to the words of Memucan. The king sent letters to
all the provinces, to each according to its writing, and to

every people in its own language, to the effect that every husband should be honoured in his house, and that he should speak his native tongue.

§ VII.

After these things, when the wrath of King Ahhashverosh was pacified, he sent and called his nobles, and said to them : " I am angry, not against Vashti, but against you; I have spoken a word when drunk with wine, but why have you provoked me that I should kill Vashti, and blot out her name from the kingdom ?   Now I shall also kill you, and blot out your names from the kingdom."   After the nobles were killed, Vashti was remembered, and that which was decreed concerning her, that she herself did not deserve punishment of death, but that it was so determined in heaven, in order that the posterity of Nebuchadnezzar, king of Babylon, should perish.

Then said the royal young men and servants : " Let fair young virgins be sought for the king, and let the king appoint officers and trustworthy men in all his dominion who should collect fair virgins and bring them to Shushan to the harem, and that Hega, the royal eunuch, be appointed to guard them and to provide for them.   And the virgin that shall please the king shall reign in place of Vashti."   The king was pleased with these words, and he did so.   There lived a Jewish man in the capital Shushan, and his name was Mordecai.   But why was he called a Jewish man ?   Because he feared to commit sin.   Concerning him David prophesied when he said : " Shall there die on this day a man of Israel ? "   And from that man descended the man ˙Mordecai, son of Yair, son of Shimei, son of Shmida, son of Baanah, son of Elah, son of Micah, son of Mephibosheth, son of Jonathan, son of Saul, son of Kish, son of Abiel, son of Zeror, son of Becorath, son of Aphia, son of Shehharim, son of Uziah, son of Sheshak, son of Mica, son of Elyael, son of Amihud, son of Shephatyah, son of Pethuel, son of Pithon, son of Malich, son of Yerubaal, son

of Yeruhham, son of Hhanayah, son of Zabdi, son of Elpaal,
son of Shimri, son of Zecharyah, son of Merimoth, son of
Hhushim, son of Shehhorah, son of Gazah, son of Azah,
son of Gera, son of Bela, son of Benjamin, son of Jacob, who
was also called Israel. But why was Mordecai called the
son of Shimei? For this reason. When Shimei despised
David, king of Israel (on his flight), and said to him, "Go
away, thou wicked man, who deservest to be slain!" then
Abishai, son of Zeruyah, said to David, "I shall go and take
off his head." But David saw prophetically that Mordecai
would descend from him. And foreseeing this, he commanded
his son Solomon that he should only then kill Shimei in case
he would cease to beget a son who would be worthy to bring
him to the world to come (he should spare him), because
from him would come a righteous son, by whose instrumentality wonders would be done to Israel in four exiles; and
this is Mordecai, *i.e.* pure myrrh, son of Yair, son of Shimei, son
of Kish, of the tribe of Benjamin. But Shimei did indeed
deserve punishment of death, as it is written in the law of
Moses: "A righteous judge shalt thou not vex, and a prince
of thy people shalt thou not curse." Yet David had pity on
him and spared him, because he foresaw that two righteous
persons would one day descend from him, through whom
Israel would be delivered. Mordecai and Esther were from
Jerusalem, and were banished into exile together with
Jeconiah, king of Judah. Mordecai returned with those
people who volunteered to go up and build the temple a
second time, when Nebuchnadnezzar again banished him.
Yet again in the country of the children of the exile he did
not cease from doing wonderful and mighty works. Mordecai
brought up Hadassah. This is Esther; and she was called
Hadassah, because as the myrtle spreads fragrance in the
world, so did she spread good works. And for this reason
she was called in the Hebrew language Hadassah, because
the righteous are likened to a myrtle. In reference to her
Isaiah prophesied, saying: "Instead of the Naazuz (the thorn)

shall come up the Berosh (fir-tree), and instead of the Sarpard (briar) shall come up an Hadassah." That is to say, instead of Naazuz, the thorn, shall grow up a tamarinth, *i.e.* instead of the pious Mordecai the wicked Haman shall ascend the scaffold. Sarpard is a willow;[1] instead of the willow shall grow up the myrtle, *i.e.* instead of Vashti, Esther shall ascend the throne.

For the sake of this Esther, Mordecai went into exile. He said: "I will rather go into exile and educate Esther than remain in the land of Israel." She was called Esther, because she was like the planet Venus, which is called in Greek Astara. But her name Hadassah was on account of her piety, for the righteous are called so, like Hananiah, Mishael, and Azariah, of whom it is said: "And he stood among the myrtle trees that were in the captivity" (R. V. "bottom" or "shady place") (Zech. i. 8). And Zula, "bottom," "shady place," is Babylon, for thus it is written, "that saith to the deep, Be dry"[2] (Isa. xliv. 27). She was also called Hadassah, because as the myrtle does not dry up either in summer or in winter, so the righteous have a share in this world and in the world to come. This Esther was the daughter of Mordecai's father's brother; she remained the same in her youth and in

---

[1] אוּרבִּינָא. About the various forms, see Löw, *Aram. Pflanzennamen,* p. 54, who yet overlooks that the Lat. *Rubus* is connected with it. I cannot agree with him in finding fault with *Kohut* in the *Aruch* because he placed *acantha* for הִינְתָא, for it is no other word (p. 145).

[2] The explanation that צוּלָה is Babylon, is a figurative rather than a verbal one. They took this idea from the context of the above passage, which speaks of Cyrus as the deliverer. With the word צוּלָה they identified מְצוּלָה of Zech. i. 8 [see also D. Kimchi, *in loco.* — TRANS.], where myrtle trees are spoken of, and hence the Targum applied it to Esther, who came from Babylon. In reference to the meaning of the word צוּלָה, it is generally in modern times translated by "the bottom," "the deep," which meaning is to my mind an improbable one. It surely refers to the wonderful conquest of Babylon by Cyrus, when he dried up the inundation which protected it, as Vitringa already has inferred this from Herodotus and Xenophon. צוּלָה cannot mean anything else but "water," "sea," and is connected with θαλ(αssα). R. Moses ha Cohen (quoted by Ibn Ezra on Zechariah) considered the word מְצוּלָה as equivalent to בְּרֵיכַת מִים, "a pool of water."

her old age, and never ceased from doing good. She had
neither father nor mother, was fair in appearance and graceful
in figure, and when her father and mother died, Mordecai
adopted her as his daughter.

Now when the royal decrees were made known, and virgins
were gathered to Shushan through Hega the royal eunuch
and keeper of the women, and when Mordecai heard that
virgins were forcibly demanded, he took Esther and withdrew her from the royal messengers, that they should not
carry her away. He hid her in a summer-house, that they
should not see her. The daughters of the heathen used to
dance and show their beauty through the windows when the
royal messengers passed by, therefore the messengers brought
many virgins from the provinces. And the messengers knew
Esther, and when they saw that she was not among these
virgins, they said one to another: "In vain have we exerted
ourselves to bring virgins from the provinces, when we have
in our province a virgin who surpasses in beauty all those
whom we have brought." And when search was made for
Esther and she was not found, they made it known to the
king. When the king heard it, he issued an order[1] that
every virgin who shall conceal herself from the royal messengers, shall be punished with death. Mordecai, hearing
this order, was afraid, and he conducted his uncle's daughter
to the market, and so Esther was brought by Hega, the
keeper of the women, unto the king. And the girl pleased
him, and was by him rewarded with favours; he was zealous
in giving her presents of ornaments and portions, likewise seven virgins were appointed for her from the royal
house. Yet she gave her portions away to the heathen
virgins, because she did not want to taste of the wine which
came from the house of the king. He distinguished her as
the best of all the women. Esther did not tell who her
people or her family were, for Mordecai had commanded her
not to tell. Day by day Mordecai passed by the seraglio, in

---

[1] Instead of דינטסים read ריטנסים, i.e. διατάξῃς.

order to learn how Esther fared, and what wonderful things were accomplished through her. Now when the time had come that these virgins should appear before King Ahhash-verosh, for according to the custom the women had to remain twelve months, of which six months were spent in using unguents and oil of myrrh, and six months in using spices and other female preparations. Then the girl came before the king, and whatever she wished to take from the harem to the king's house was given her. In the evening she went there, and in the morning she returned to the harem, accompanied by Shaashgaz, the royal eunuch and keeper of the women. Her name was inscribed in a book, and she could not come again to the king unless he wanted her, and called her by her name. But when the time had arrived that Esther, the daughter of Abihhayil, Mordecai's uncle—who had in truth brought her up like his own daughter—had to appear before the king, she did not ask for anything but what Hega, the royal eunuch, wished her to have; and Esther found favour in the eyes of all who saw her. Esther was then led to the King Ahhashverosh into the royal palace, in the tenth month, the month Tebeth, in the seventh year of his reign. And the king loved Esther more than all the wives, and she was rewarded by him with more grace and favour than all the virgins; and he caused her to reign in the place of Vashti. The king made a great feast, the feast of Esther, for all his lords and statesmen, and distributed many presents in the provinces. On the occasion, he said to her: " Pray tell me, who are thy people, and what is thy family ? " She replied : " I am ignorant both concerning my people and concerning my family, because when I was quite a child, my father and mother died and left me." Now when the king heard these words, he universally remitted the taxes, and gave presents to the provinces, because he thought and said to himself, I will do good to all the nations and governments, among whom is certainly the people of Esther.

When the virgins were again gathered, and this second

gathering was only because Esther was living in the palace of the king, and he loved her more than all the wives, and had put the royal crown upon her head. Yes, the second gathering was, because the governors said to the king: " If thou wilt that Esther should reveal to thee her nation and family, cause her to be jealous by gathering other women, and then she will reveal both." So the virgins were gathered a second time, and, just then, Mordecai sat at the royal gate. Nevertheless, Esther did not tell concerning her people and her origin, but was doing just what Mordecai commanded her; for as she was modest in her youth, so she remained even when she became queen. Therefore Scripture says : " Esther did the commandment of Mordecai, like as when she was brought up with him."

In those days when Mordecai sat at the gates of the royal house, Bigthan and Teresh, two of the royal eunuchs and keepers of the wardrobe, were wroth, and wanted to lay violent hands upon and to kill King Ahhashverosh, having devised a plan of putting a poisonous snake [1] in the golden cup from which Ahhashverosh drank, in order that it might bite and kill him. This affair was revealed to Mordecai by the Holy Spirit, and he told it to Esther, who communicated to the king in Mordecai's name. The matter was investigated and found true, and they were both hanged on a scaffold; and the event was recorded in the chronicle of the king.

§ VIII.

After these events, King Ahhashverosh promoted Haman,[2]

---

[1] חורמן, a snake. The expression in Syro-Chald. came from Persia. It is nothing else than " Agramainyus," " Aharman," " Ahriman," the evil spirit, who, especially as a serpent, was thought to bring death. This is well to be assumed, and not the contrary (Spiegel, *Eranische Alterthums-kunde*, ii. 122).

[2] The genealogy of Haman is most interesting, because it enumerates all the enemies and oppressors of the Jews who have oppressed them in the Holy Land. It discloses impressions which date from before the destruction of Jerusalem. It is not indeed very easy to restore the

son of Hamdatha the Agagite, son of Stench, son of Robbery, son of Pilate, son of Lysius, son of Florus, son of Fadus, son of Flaccus, son of Antipater, son of Herod, son of Refuse, son of Decay, son of Parmashta, son of Vajasatha, son of Agag, son of the Red, son of Amalek, son of the concubine of Eliphaz, the eldest son of Esau. He made him great, and placed him upon a throne higher than all his nobles and ministers. And all the servants of the king who sat at the gate of the royal palace bowed down and prostrated themselves before Haman, because the king had commanded it; but Mordecai did not kneel before him, nor salute him. Then the servants of the king who sat at the gate of the royal palace said to Mordecai: "What privilege hast thou above us, that we should make obeisance before Haman, and that thou shouldst not kneel before him? Why dost thou transgress the command of the king?" Mordecai answered and said to them: "You are foolish, and without understanding! Hear me, and tell me, you hypocrites (or coal blacks), Where is there a man who dares to be so proud and haughty? He a man born of a woman, and his duration but a few days! He who at his birth weeps and cries,

corrupted names, yet the whole underlying thought supports and confirms the emendation. Instead of אפלטוס must be read פלטוס, Pilatus the governor, who was not the less hated by the Jews when he assumed the fatal position in the history of Christ. Instead of דיוסיס must Felix (פלסיס) be placed (Joseph. *Ant.* xii. 7. 3 ; 1 Macc. chap. iii.), the remarkable and cruel brother of Pallus. Instead of פרוס is to be read פלרוס, Florus. Under Gessius Florus broke out the Jewish war (Joseph. *Ant.* xx. 10. 11). For מעדי is to be read פעדי, Fadus the procurator of Judea under Claudius (Joseph. *Ant.* xx. 1. 1, etc.). For בלעקן is to be read פלעקן, Flaccus the governor of Syria (Joseph. *Ant.* xviii. 6. 2). For אנטימרוס is to be read אנטיפטרוס, Antipater, as this clearly appears from his being connected with Herod. Agag is called בר סומקי, the son of the red, viz. Rufus. The name Rufus was not merely the name of the enemy in the Jewish war, but it is a translation of Edom, Esau himself. Rome was understood to be a successor to Edom (comp. my *Chazar. Königsbrief*, Berlin 1876, p. 53). בר שנר means a young calf, and refers to Vitellius. בר ננר refers to Cestius Gallus, for ננר means a cock (ננר טורא, cock of the wood). With respect to the meaning of the names of Haman's sons, see the commentary.

in his youth mourns and sighs, and during all his days is
full of trouble and vexation, and at last returns to his dust !
And shall I kneel before him ?   Never !   I only bow before
the one great and living God in heaven, who is a consuming
fire and whose angels are fire, who holds the earth in His
arm, who spread out the heavens by His mighty power,
who by His will makes the sun to be darkness and the
darkness to be light, who by His wisdom surrounded the
ocean with sand, provided the sea with odorous salt and
with banks, keeping the waves bound in the deep as with
chains that they should not overflow the land and not pass
their limit.   By His word He created the firmament and
spread it as a cloud in the air, yea, He spread it as a
vapour upon the world, and a tent upon the surface of the
earth, and by His power He carries the things that are above
and below.   Before Him the sun, the moon, and the Pleiades
run their course, and the stars and planets are not for a
moment inactive.   None of them rest, but all run before
Him as His messengers, who go right and left to do His
will.   To Him who created them belongs praise, and before
Him one must bow."   They replied to Mordecai : " Nevertheless, one of thy fathers bowed before one of the fathers of
Haman !"   " Who was it," exclaimed Mordecai, " who bowed
before the ancestor of Haman ?"   They rejoined : " Was it
not thy father Jacob who bowed before his brother Esau,
the ancestor of Haman ?"   He in reply said, " I am of the
posterity of Benjamin,[1] and when Jacob bowed before Esau,

---

[1] It appears from the above that in the days of the Targum Jacob's
bowing before Esau, who was identified with Rome, was not looked upon
by the Jews with a favourable eye.   But this happened when Benjamin
was not yet born, therefore Mordecai his descendant was justified in
refusing homage to Haman, Esau's descendant.   Nor was Benjamin
present when the children of Jacob sold Joseph, therefore his descendant
Mordecai becomes the deliverer of Israel whom Haman had sold.   The
silence of Esther concerning her origin was referred to as typified in
the silence of Rachel when Jacob searched for the teraphim of Laban,
and especially to Benjamin.   The latter was on the ground, that the stone
for his [Benjamin's] tribe in the breastplate of Aaron (Ex. xxviii. 20)

U

Benjamin was not yet born, and he never in all his life bowed before a man. Hence an eternal covenant was made with him while he was yet in his mother's womb, until the time that Israel shall go up to their land and build the temple in his territory, and that the Shechinah shall dwell in his border, and that all Israel shall rejoice there, and that the nations shall bow and prostrate themselves in his land. But I shall not bow before the wicked Haman, this enemy!"

Day by day they thus spake to him, and he did not hearken to them. They then reported him to Haman, to see whether the words of Mordecai will stand, in that he told them that he was a Jew. When Haman saw that Mordecai refused to bow before him, he was full of wrath against him.—But he was too despicable an object in his eyes to lay violent hands on him alone, and he wanted rather to destroy all those Jews who were sojourning in the empire of Ahhashverosh. In the first month, which is the month Nisan, in the twelfth year of the reign of Ahhashverosh, he cast the lot, in order to destroy the holy people. Then an echoing voice from heaven resounded, and said: "Fear not, congregation of Israel! If you turn with repentance to God, then the lot will fall upon him instead of thee." The scribe Shamshai began to cast the lot before Haman day by day. He began on the first day of the week, but did not succeed, because on that day were the heavens and the earth created. The second day was likewise unpropitious, because on it the firmament was created. He failed on the third day, because on it the garden of Eden was created. The fourth day was unfavourable to him, because on it were created the sun, the moon, the seven stars, and the twelve planets. The

was a jasper (Heb. יָשְׁפֵה), which was interpreted as composed of two words יֵשׁ פֶּה, "he had a mouth," and yet he was silent (Midrash Esther 92b; comp. R. Behhai on Yalkut Reubeni 104c). From this etymology plainly comes that which Pliny observes (lib. 37, § 118): "Libet obiter sanitatem magicam hic quoque coarguere, quoniam hanc utilem esse concionantibus prodiderunt."

fifth day [1] did not serve his purpose, because on it were created the leviathan and the cock of the wood, which have been appointed for a feast to the congregation of Israel on the great day.

The sixth day was unfavourable, because on it Adam and Eve were created; and likewise the seventh day, because it is a covenant between the word of the Lord and the people of Israel. He then left the days and began with the months.

---

[1] The legend of the leviathan and cock of the wood being created on the fifth day, in order that Israel should feast on them on the great day (יומא רבא), is very remarkable, and betrays Christian influence. In Gen. i. 21 we read that on the fifth day were created the ocean monsters (תנינים). The Targum Yerushalmi adds, that the leviathan was also created on the fifth day for the purpose of serving a feast on the great day. But no mention is made of the cock of the wood (תרנגל ברא). The passages which are generally adduced from the O. T. for the great feast, viz. Isa. xxvii. 1, Job xl. 26, etc., do not give in the slightest way any information concerning a banquet of leviathan and the cock of the wood. The passage here is to be understood as a contrast to Christian symbolism. The leviathan is the opposite of ichthys [fish], which is the emblem of Christ, and contains the acrostic of His name. Joshua (ישוע), the conqueror of Canaan, was also the son of Nun, which means fish. On the fifth day—on Thursday, which is called the great fifth (μεγάλη πέμπτη)—Christ constituted the Lord's Supper, when He said, "Take, eat, this is my body." The idea of the feast of the leviathan was started as a counterpart to the supper of the ichthys. That this is really so, is seen from the addition of the תרנגל ברא, which is only found in this place. The cock of the wood, or "wild cock," stands for the cock in general. It is well known that the Jews have on the eve of the Day of Atonement a cock for every male as an atonement, when they say : "This is my substitution, this is my vicarious sacrifice, this is my atonement, this cock shall go to death, and I shall enter into life." That this act is vicarious may be seen from the fact that the cock is called Geber, i.e. "man," and has special reference to Christ, who is called Geber in Zech. xiii. 7. Certainly most Jews are not acquainted with the fact that these Christian ideas are contained in that ceremony ; but learned Jews have perceived the hidden meaning, and have consequently discouraged the use of the ceremony altogether. It is remarkable that it was customary to use a fish for the same purpose, in case a cock was wanting. It had the same symbolism. Julius Africanus says also : "Christ is the fish who nourishes the world." Upon pictures of the Lord's Supper are found a fish instead of a lamb on the dish. It is likewise the custom among the Jews to have fish and cock in their Sabbath meals. The feast of the leviathian represented the same as that of the cock. The Targumist unites the two, in order to indicate that the feast will consist of fish and meat. Concerning the symbolism of the fish, see my *Eddischen Studien* pp. 118-121.

Nisan was not appropriate, because of the meritorious influence of the feast of the Passover. Nor Iyar, because during this month fell the manna. Nor Sivan, because in it was the Law given on Mount Sinai. Nor Tamuz, because in it were the walls of Jerusalem broken, and two evils cannot take place in the same month. Nor Ab,[1] because in it the Israelites in the desert ceased from dying away, and the Shechinah of the Lord of the universe began again to speak with Moses. Nor Elul, because in it Moses went up on Mount Sinai to bring down the second tables. Nor Tishri, because in it the sins of Israel are forgiven. Nor Marhheshvan, because the flood ceased in the same month, when Noah and all his were saved. Nor Kislev, because in it was laid the foundation of the temple. Nor Tebeth, because in it the wicked Nebuchadnezzar went up against Jerusalem, and this tribulation was sufficient. Nor Shebat, because this month is the new year for the trees, of which the first-fruits are offered. When he finally came to the twelfth month, the month Adar, he said : " Now they are caught by my hands like the fish of the sea." But he did not know that the children of Joseph are likened to fish, as it is written : "They shall multiply like the fish of the sea, among men upon the earth."

And Haman spake to King Ahhashverosh : " There is a certain people of the Jews, scattered and thrown about among the nations in all the provinces of the empire ; they are proud and haughty, they bathe in Tebeth in tepid water, and in Tamuz they sit in cold baths. They practise laws and customs which are different from those of every other nation and country, and do not walk according to our laws, nor have pleasure in our customs, nor do they serve the king. When they see us they spit on the ground, and consider us in the light of an unclean thing. When we go to them and order them to do some service to the king, then they jump down the walls, break down the fences, and make their escape through the gaps. When we try to catch them, they turn

---

[1] This significance of the month Ab appears only in this place.

round and stand staring at us, gnash with their teeth, stamp with their feet, and so frighten us that we are not able to take hold of them. We do not marry their daughters, and they do not marry ours. Is any of them taken for the service of the king, he passes the day in idleness, with all kinds of excuses, such as to-day is the Sabbath, to-day is Passover. The day on which they want to buy from us they call a lawful day, and the day on which we want to buy something from them they call an unlawful day, and they close the market for us. In the first hour of the day they say, 'We must read the Shema' (Deut. vi. 4); in the second hour they say, 'We must pray;' in the third, 'We must eat;' in the fourth they say, 'We must thank the God of heaven for having given us bread and water.' In the fifth they go out for a walk. In the sixth they come back. In the seventh they go to meet their wives, who say to them, 'Here is some soup to refresh you after the heavy toil which the tyrannical king put on you.' One day in the week they keep as a day of rest, in which they go to their synagogues, read in their books, interpret their prophets, curse our king, imprecate our rulers, and say: 'This is the seventh day, in which the great God rested.'

"Their unclean wives go after seven days, in the middle of the night, and defile the water. On the eighth day they circumcise their sons, without any pity upon them, in order, as they say, thereby to differ from other nations. Thirty days they call a month, and they say one month is complete and another is defective. In the month of Nisan they keep a feast, lasting eight days, when they remove and burn everything that is leaven, and cleanse their utensils, and say, 'This is the day in which our fathers were redeemed from Egypt;' and they call this day Passover, and go to their synagogues, read their books, interpret their prophets, curse the king, imprecate the governors, and say, 'Like the leaven is removed from that which is unleavened, so may the kingdom of the tyrant be removed from among us, and so may we be delivered from this foolish king.' In the month Sivan they keep a feast of two days, in which they go into their synagogues, read the Shema, pray, read their law, interpret their prophets, curse the king, imprecate the governors, and call it the day of convocation.[1] They then go up to the roof of the house of their God, and throw down pomegranates and apples, and then collect them, and say, 'Like as we gather these pomegranates and apples, so may their sons be gathered out from amongst us.' They also say, 'This is the day in which the Law was given to our fathers on Mount Sinai.' A certain time they call new year, viz. the first of Tishri, in which they go to their synagogues, read their books, interpret their prophets, curse the king, imprecate the governors, blow the trumpets, and say, 'On this day the remembrance of our fathers comes up before our Father in heaven. May our remembrance conduce to our good, and that of our enemies conduce to their evil.' On the ninth of the same month they slaughter geese and animals, eat and drink sumptuously—they, their wives, their sons, and their daughters. The tenth of this month they call a great fast day, on which they, their wives, and their sons and daughters fast; and they harass even their children and sucklings, without pity upon them, and they say, 'On this day are our sins atoned, yea, our sins are collected and added to the sins of our enemies.' They go to their synagogues, read their books, interpret their prophets, curse the king, imprecate the governors, and say, 'May this foolish kingdom be blotted out from the world;' and they pray and supplicate that the

---

[1] On the יומא דעצרתא they go to their synagogues and throw apples. The Feast of Weeks was called Azereth, "convocation," like the last day of the Feast of Tabernacles. The former is a commemoration of the giving of the Law, the latter is devoted to rejoicing for the Law. In the West the throwing of apples takes place on the latter feast, on שמחת תורה, which is in the autumn. The Tania (p. 129a) speaks of מנדים, "fruit," which the חתן תורה caused to be thrown. Of this also speaks the Minhagim (p. 47), and therefore the דוכן, the priestly benediction, does not take place at מוסף, "the supplementary service." The use of תפוח was chosen in allusion to Prov. xxv. 11.

king may die, and that his government may be destroyed. On the fifteenth day of the same month they erect booths on the roofs of their houses, then they go into our orchards, cut down our palm leaves, pluck down our citrons, break our willows (or spice trees), destroy our gardens and our fences without any pity, and then they make of the branches hosannas,[1] and say, 'As the king does among the arrayed army, so do we.' Then they go to their synagogues, read their books, pray, rejoice, go around with their hosannas, jump and dance like goats, and we do not know whether they curse or bless us. They call this feast the Feast of Tabernacles, and do not perform the work of the king, saying to us, 'This is a forbidden day.' Thus they spend the year, with the excuse of 'Sheehy, Pheehy,' i.e. 'To-day is a Sabbath, to-day is a feast.'[2]

[1] [Hosanna means, Save now. It was first used as a prayer in Ps. cxviii. 25. Secondly, as a Messianic acclamation when Jesus entered triumphantly into Jerusalem. Thirdly, the five twigs of willow tied with a palm leaf, and smitten in the synagogue on the Feast of Tabernacles to symbolize the defeat of the Satanic kingdom by the Messiah, are called hosanna.—TRANS.]

[2] The speech of Haman before the king, as given by the Targum, is very remarkable. It vividly describes the accusations which were brought against the Jews in the time of the Targumist, and which are still brought against them by their enemies. Whatever they did is taken amiss. They are represented to live extravagantly, because, forsooth, they bathe in the summer in cold, and in the winter in tepid water. They are reproached for feeding upon roast geese before the fast day. They are further reproached that they have no relish for the service of the king, that they hate other nations, curse the kings, and that they continually have holidays as an excuse for not doing loyal service to the government. We must remark upon some of the items of this speech, because they are not without historical interest. It is said twice that they spent their time with שהי פהי instead of doing some useful service. The same expression is found in Bab. Megilla 13b (דמפקא לכולא שתא בשהי ובשהי). Rashi explains the words as initial letters of פסח היום שבת היום, as if they always excused themselves with the saying, "To-day is Sabbath, to-day is Passover." Though this explanation is given above, yet I do not agree with it. Levy in Chald. Lex., voce פהי, says that Rashi's explanation is forced. I now think it an impossible one. First, because the feast of the Passover happens only once in the year, and they could not excuse themselves the whole year round by saying: "To-day is Passover." Secondly, such an acrostic abbreviation may look well to the eye, but sounds badly to the ear. It is plainly an alliterative formula, expressing "doing nothing," or "doing useless things," as we have in

" Fifty years they call a jubilee ; seven years, a jubilee week ;
twelve months, a year ; thirty days, a month ; the seventh day
they call a day of rest, and they keep it as a feast day, in which
the Lord of the universe rested.   When their kingdom was
yet standing, there arose a king among them whose name was
David, who harboured thoughts of evil against us, and wished
to kill us and to exterminate us from the world.   Two parts of
us he killed and rooted out, and one part he left.   Yet of
those he left he made servants.   As it is written : ' And he
measured them with the line, making them to lie down on
the ground ' (2 Sam. viii. 2).   After him rose up one of the
kings who were thy predecessors ; his name was Nebuchadnezzar, and he went against them, destroyed their temple,
plundered their city, and led them into captivity, and still
they are high-spirited and have not given up their haughtiness till now, but say : ' We are the children of renowned
fathers, and we have never subjected ourselves nor bowed to
kings, neither have we obeyed governors.'   They send letters
to every place, asking for prayers to God that the king may
die, and that our rule may be destroyed ; and this they do
without our knowledge.   When their forefathers came down
to Egypt they were only seventy persons, but when they
went up (out of Egypt) they were sixty myriads.   And even
now, though they are likewise in captivity, and have nothing,
yet they say : ' We are the children of pious and good people.'
But, in fact, there is not a more poor and faulty people in the
world than they are.   This people is in all the towns ; some
of them are dealers in wax[1] and candle provisioners, and some

German *Larifari* and *Schnickschnack*, and in English shilly-shally and
helter-skelter.   I remark, in passing, that *Larifari* comes from the Greek
λῆρος, which Grimm and others have overlooked.   The Romans said
butu batta.   It is, moreover, interesting to note that such meaningless
alliterations, like *Phehy*, generally begin with *F*, thus : *Foxen, floccus,
flyaros, larifari*, and therefore *Sheehy, Phehy*, may mean useless words in
reference to Pe, month.

[1] זבני קירא.   When the Targumist makes Haman complain that some
are dealers in wax and candles, and that others are rich, but that they
obtain their riches in a wrong way, he shows that Haman's intention

of them are great men. Everything they sell, they sell at an overcharged price, and everything they buy, they do not pay its value; they do not observe the laws and ordinances of the king, and the king has no advantage in tolerating them or in allowing them to exist.

"If it please the king, let him write an order for their extermination, and I will give thee for every one of them a hundred zuzin; and as the total number of their ancestors when they went out from Egypt was six hundred thousand men, and ten thousand kikar silver are equal to six hundred thousand zuzin, so if it please the king I will deliver this money from my treasury into thy treasury. It needs only a stroke of the pen, and the silver in full weight shall be delivered through the officers of the mint into the treasury of the king." Then the king of kings answered and said: "They have long ago paid a sela (half a shekel) per head, when they went out of Egypt, and the sum amounted to one hundred kikar, and one thousand seven hundred and seventy-seven selas. Thou hast therefore no right to sell them, nor has Ahhash-verosh a right to buy them." Then the king took off his ring from his hand and gave it to Haman, son of Hamdatha the

was to make the Jews appear contemptible. He represents them on the one hand as poor miserable people, who maintain themselves as dealers in a small way, and on the other hand as usurers. The trade in wax, קירא (cera), did not bring large profits. The Jews were in the habit of using many wax candles in their service in the synagogue as well as at home, especially on the Day of Atonement; and the singling out of this trade seems to be a mocking allusion to it. This is seen in Sanhed. 95a: "Thy grandson buys wax, and art not thou sorry?" In the Minhagim of the year 1692 (Dyhernfurt), p. 38, we read: "On the eve of the Day of Atonement it is necessary to light a candle, for the candle atones (מכפר) for the soul (נשמה), which is also a candle. It is also an honour for the synagogues to have many candles." A curious story is told that in אשכנז, Germany, candles were only lighted for men and not for women. The man has 258 members in his body; add to this his soul and spirit, רוח and נשמה, the initials of which are נר, candle, and numerically also 250. In other countries, candles are lighted for the women also, though they have four members more in their bodies than the men. As זבני קירא, "buyers of wax," and תלין בוצין, "those who hang up candles," are connected together, so in the usage of the Byzantine Church κηροι and υλιχνοι stand together.

Agagite, the oppressor of the Jews. And the king said to Haman: "The money is given to thee, and the people too, to do with them as it seems best in thy sight."

But thou, Ahhashverosh, hast neither acted like a buyer nor like a seller, for a buyer gives money and a seller takes money; but thou hast given thy ring to Haman, and hast said to him: "Thy money is given thee and the people, to do with them as it seems best in thy sight." In thee is the verse verified which says: "As a ring of gold in a swine's snout (Prov. xi. 22). As rings do not befit swine, so the kingdom does not befit thee, and thou art like a beautiful woman of bad morals."

Then the scribes of the king were called together on the thirteenth day of the month Nisan, and everything which Haman commanded concerning the Jews was written down, for all the dignitaries of the king, and for all the great men in every province, and for the rulers of every people. In the writing and language of each country and people it was written in the name of King Ahhashverosh and sealed with the royal seal. And letters were sent by swift messengers to all the provinces of the king to destroy, to kill, and to exterminate all the Jews, from boys to old men, infants and women in one day, namely, on the thirteenth day of the twelfth month, the month Adar, and also to plunder their houses. The writing was explained, and its object was revealed and published to all the nations in every province, that they should be prepared for that day. All this happened that thou (reader) mayest know that God never fails to punish with measure for measure. You have seen that because the brethren of Joseph sold him into a strange land, therefore their descendants were likewise sold into a strange land; but as Benjamin did not take part in this transaction with his brethren, for that reason two of his descendants, viz. Mordecai and Esther, became redeemers of Israel. The swift messengers hastened on with the decree of the king, and it was also published in the capital Shushan, while the king and

Haman sat down to eat and to drink, and the city of Shushan was in a state of lamentation.

§ IX.

And Mordecai, the righteous, saw by the Holy Spirit everything that had been done, viz. that the king had sent word from his palace by his servants to the righteous Haggai, Zechariah, and Malachai, who were in the chamber of hewn stones, and were prophesying on the great wall of Jerusalem, that they should stop the work of building after seventy-two towers were already built. The wicked Ahhashverosh also fetched a hundred and twenty-seven scribes from a hundred and twenty-seven provinces, every one of whom had a roll and a book in his hand. They sat at the gates of Shushan and wrote, and sent out grievous decrees concerning the Jews and their laws. The first letter written in the name of the king, and sealed with his signet-ring, they despatched by swift messengers, and the contents were as follows :—" From me, King Ahhashverosh, to all peoples, nations, and languages who live in all the land, peace be multiplied. I make known to you, that a certain man came to us, who is not from our place nor from our province, and he came for the purpose of joining us, that we might prevail against our enemies. We have made investigation concerning him, and (we find) that his name is Haman, son of King Agag, son of the great Amalek, son of Reuel, son of Eliphaz the first-born of Esau, in fact, a descendant of prominent lords and wealthy people. This man asked of me a small and insignificant petition, and informed me concerning the Jews and their blameworthy laws and affairs. He said, 'When they came out from Egypt they numbered six hundred thousand men, and so I will give thee six hundred thousand minas[1] of silver, a

---

[1] [Mina was a certain weight of silver, variously estimated as consisting of from fifteen to one hundred shekels. Comp. 2 Chron. ix. 16 ; 1 Kings x. 17 ; Ezek. xl. 12, etc.—TRANS.]

mina for every man;' for which sum he desired that I should sell this people to him to be killed. Then I, Ahhashverosh, greatly rejoiced, and after mature deliberation, I took the money from him and sold the people to him to be slaughtered. Therefore, eat and drink and be merry, as I eat and drink and am merry. He that understands to handle the bow, let him use the bow; and he that can fight with the sword, let him seize the sword, and go you out and overpower them on the fourteenth and fifteenth days of the month, which is called in our language Adar. Do not spare either their princes, their rulers, their great men, nor even their little children, but kill them and spoil their goods. I, King Ahhashverosh, do therefore hereby decree for all nations, languages, places, provinces, and for every tribe and family and town, that wherever a Jewish man-servant or a Jewish maid-servant is found, their masters shall slay them at the gate of the city, because they have not obeyed the order of the king which was issued by me, that no Jews should be found upon the soil of my empire."

And when Mordecai, the righteous, heard of the decree which was issued, and of the letters which were sealed, he rent his garments in the front and behind, and put on sackcloth and rolled himself in ashes, and lifted up his voice and cried, "Woe! how great is this decree which the king and Haman have decreed against us! Not a half of us has he condemned and a half spared, no not even a third or a fourth part has he spared, but the king and Haman have determined that we should all as a body be killed, destroyed, and rooted out." Now, when the people of Israel saw the righteous Mordecai, who was a greatly esteemed Rab[1] over them, they assembled together and came to him in very large multitudes. Then Mordecai stood up in the midst of the assembly and addressed them as follows: " People of

---

[1] [This title may also help us in deciding as to the age of the Targum. It shows that it was written outside of Palestine, for there the same title was Mar.—TRANS.]

Israel, beloved and dear to the Father in heaven! Do you
not know, and have you not heard, that the king and Haman
have determined to destroy us from off the face of the earth,
and to exterminate us from under heaven? Alas! we have
no king on whom we can rely, nor a prophet who should
pray for us, nor a place into which we can flee, nor a
country where we would be safe, for to every place it was
written, and to every province a message was sent concerning
us! We are like sheep without a shepherd, and like a ship
without a pilot. Yea, we are like orphans without a father,
and like suckling babes whose mother has died." Immediately the holy ark was brought out to the gates of Shushan,
and the book of the Law was taken out, and they covered
it with sackcloth, and ashes spread upon it, and then they
read therein : "When thou art in tribulation, and all these
things have come upon thee, etc., thou should turn to the
Lord thy God; for the Lord thy God is a merciful God"
(Deut. iv. 30, 31). Mordecai again rose in the midst of the
congregation and said : "People of Israel! Beloved and dear
people! Beloved and precious to God! Let us look for
an example to the people of Nineveh! When the prophet
Jonah, the son of Amittai, was sent to announce to them that
the city of Nineveh would be destroyed, and when the tidings
reached the king of Nineveh, he arose from his throne, laid
aside the royal throne, put on sackcloth, rolled himself in
ashes, and issued a proclamation in Nineveh, saying : 'The
decree of the king and his nobles commands thus: Let
neither man nor beast, herd nor flock, taste anything; let
them not feed nor drink water. Let them turn from their
evil ways, and from the violence that is in their hands.'
'And the Lord turned by His word from the evil which He
thought He would do unto them, and He did it not.' Let
us also do as they did, and institute and proclaim fasts,
because we are banished from Jerusalem; and because of
Israel's guilt, an echoing voice called upon wicked Nebuchadnezzar, and said : 'Nebuchadnezzar, king of Chaldea! Arise

and go against Jerusalem, and destroy it, and burn the
temple with fire!' At that time Nebuchadnezzar shook
his head and wrung his hands, knowing well what was the
fate of Sennacherib's army, when an angel was sent down
from heaven who killed eighteen myriads and five thousand
of them, so that none remained alive but he himself." While
Mordecai was thus speaking, he rent his garments, put on
sackcloth, sat down in the dust, rolled himself in ashes, and
burst into tears, and cried: "Woe to you, O house of Israel,
that such a decree has been issued against you!" He then
went into the city and cried loudly and bitterly. Then he
went to the gate of the royal palace, because there was a
decree which ordered that no man should come to the gate
of the house of the king clothed in sackcloth. When, now,
an Israelite came to a heathen and said to him: "I pray
thee, let me and my wife and children be thy slaves, only
that we may be delivered from being killed," then the
heathen answered: "Seest thou not what is written in the
decree which King Ahhashverosh has published, that if a
Jew is found with any of our people, that man shall be
killed like him." Whereupon the Jew went home in great
distress. At this time was verified that which is written in
the law of Moses concerning Israel: "Ye shall sell yourselves
unto your enemies for bondmen and bondwomen, and no
man shall buy you" (Deut. xxviii. 68). Day by day every one
of them went and read the published royal decree, and then he
knew how long he had yet to live in the world. Thus again
was realized what is written in the law of Moses: "And thy
life shall hang in doubt before thee; and thou shalt fear
night and day, and shalt have none assurance of thy life; in
the morning thou shalt say, Would God it were even! and at
even thou shalt say, Would God it were morning! for the
fear of thine heart which thou shalt fear, and for the sight of
thine eyes which thou shalt see" (Deut. xxviii. 66, 67).

In every place and province where the king's decree came,
there was great lamentation amongst the Jews, consisting of

fasting, weeping, wailing, mourning, sackcloth, and, among
many of them, lying in ashes.

And Esther's maidens and her chamberlains came and told
it her; and the queen was exceedingly grieved, and she sent
raiment to clothe Mordecai, and to take his sackcloth from off
him, but he received it not. Then called Esther for Hathach,
one of the king's chamberlains, whom he had appointed to
attend upon her, to charge him to go to Mordecai, to know
what this was, and why it was. So Hathach went forth to
Mordecai, unto the broad place of the city, which was before
the king's gate. And Mordecai told him of all that had
happened unto him, and the exact sum of the money that
Haman had promised to pay by weight to the king's
treasuries for the Jews to destroy them. And he gave him
an explicit copy of the writing of the decree that was
published in Shushan, to destroy them, to show it unto
Esther, and to declare it unto her; and to charge her that
she should go in unto the king, to make supplication unto
him, and to make request before him for her people. And
Hathach came and told Esther the words of Mordecai.
Then Esther spake unto Hathach,[1] and charged him to say
to Mordecai: "All the king's servants, and the people of
the king's provinces, do know that whosoever, whether man or
woman, shall come unto the king into the inner court who is
not called, there is one law for him, that he be put to death,
except such as to whom the king shall hold out the golden sceptre,
that he may live. And behold, I have been praying for thirty
days, that the king should not ask for me and cause me to sin ;
for as I was trained by thee, thou didst say to me, that every
woman of the daughters of Israel who of her own free will co-
habits with a heathen, has no part among the tribes of Israel."

And because Hathach was a messenger between Esther and
Mordecai, Haman was very wroth against him, and killed
him. The words of Esther were then reported by writing to

---

[1] It is inferred that Haman caused Hathach to be killed, because he
is no more mentioned. But in Megilla 15a he is identified with Daniel.

Mordecai.   And Mordecai said in reply to Esther as follows
" Perhaps thou imaginest that thou at any rate art safe, and
sayest to thyself, I need not pray for Israel; but when only
a foot of one Jew is struck, do not think that thou, of all
Jews, shalt escape.   For thy ancestor Saul caused this evil to
Israel, because if he had done what the prophet Samuel told
him, then the tyrant Haman would not have sprung from the
children of the house of Amalek; and if he had killed King
Agag, this son of Hamdatha would never have risen against
us, and would never have sold us for ten thousand kikar of
silver to King Ahhashverosh, and the Holy One, blessed
be He! would not have delivered Israel into the hands of
two tyrants.   Nor, at the beginning (of our history) would
Amalek, the ancestor of Haman, have come against Israel and
carried on war against Joshua, son of Nun, at Rephidim,
though, through the prayer of Moses, the memory of Amalek
was blotted out from the world.   Arise, therefore, and pray
to thy heavenly Father for the people of Israel.   He who did
justice to the first generation will also do justice to those
who came after them.   Is, then, Haman the tyrant stronger
than another?   Or is his decree of greater duration?   Is he
stronger than his ancestor Amalek, who came against Israel,
but whom the Lord removed from the world?   Is he stronger
than those thirty-one kings who likewise came against Israel,
but against whom Joshua, instructed by a word from heaven,
went and killed them?   Is he stronger than Sisera, who
came against Israel with nine hundred iron chariots, and closed
the cisterns against them, in order that their wives should
not bathe, . . . that they should not multiply and increase
in the world, but whom God delivered into the hand of a
woman, and she killed him?   Is, indeed, this wicked Haman
stronger than Goliath, who came and blasphemed the armies
of Israel, but who was delivered into the hands of David, and
he killed him?   Is he stronger than the sons of Orphah, who
came and carried on war against Israel, but who were delivered
into the hands of David and of his servants, and they killed

them. Therefore withhold not thy mouth from prayer, nor thy lips from interceding for mercy from thy Creator. And pray that, for the sake of the righteousness of our fathers' Israel, we may be delivered from slaughter; and He who has at all times done wonders for them will also deliver our enemies into our hands, and we shall do with them as we please. But, O Esther, do not fancy that thou, of all the Jews, shalt be saved in the house of the king. For if thou neglectest thy opportunity at this time, He who is the Holy One, and the Redeemer of the Jews at all times, will cause redemption to spring up for them from another place, but thou and thy father's house shall perish. And who knows whether thou hast not come to the kingdom because the sins of thy father's house are called to account."

Then Esther answered Mordecai by letter: "Go gather together all the Jews that are found in Shushan, and fast for me, and neither eat nor drink three days and three nights; and I also and my maidens will fast in like manner, and so will I go in unto the king without being summoned; and if I perish in this world for your sake, I shall have a portion in the world to come. Hitherto I went to the king against my will, but now I go willingly. And a daughter of Israel who is violated by a Gentile is a lawful wife to her husband. Let the bridegroom go out from his sleeping-room covered with sackcloth, and let the bride likewise leave her nuptial chamber with her head covered with ashes. Let men and beasts and sheep not taste anything for three days, and let the babes be separated from the breasts of their mothers."

Immediately they inspected the assembly, and they found in it twelve thousand young priests. These seized trumpets with their right hand and the books of the law with their left, and then wept and cried towards heaven, and said: "O God of Israel! behold the law which Thou hast given us. Behold, Thy beloved people is about to cease from the world. Who will read therein and speak of Thy name? The sun and moon will be dark, and not give their light, for they were created but for Thy people Israel." They then fell upon their

X

faces, and cried: "Answer us, O Father, answer us! Answer us, O King, answer us!" And they blew the trumpets, and the people cried aloud after them, so that the hosts of heaven wept, and the patriarchs were moved in their graves.

Mordecai went and did everything which Esther charged him to do. And it was on the third day, after Esther had three successive fasts, she arose from the earth where she was sitting, bowed down in dust and ashes, not having changed her raiment, and she put on royal apparel, which was embroidered with gold of Ophir, adorned herself with a fine silk dress wrought with diamonds and pearls that were brought from Africa,[1] and put the golden crown upon her head, and shoes of pure refined gold[2] upon her feet. After this she prayed thus: "O Thou who art the great God of Abraham, of Isaac, and of Jacob, and the God of my father Benjamin, it was not because I was right before Thee that I came to this foolish king, but for the sake of Thy people Israel, that they should not perish from the world. For the sake of Israel the whole world was created, and if Israel should perish from the world, who will say before Thee thrice every day, 'Holy, holy, holy'? Save me from the hand of this foolish king, as Thou didst once save Hananiah, Mishael, and Azariah from the burning furnace, and Daniel from the den of lions, and cause me to find favour and grace in his eyes." She broke forth into tears, and further prayed and earnestly supplicated: "I beseech Thee, hear this prayer, hearken to my supplication at this time, when we are banished and removed from our land. Ah! on account of our sins hast Thou delivered us, that that which is written might be fulfilled in us: 'And then ye shall sell yourselves unto your enemies for bondmen

---

[1] That pearls should have been brought from the land of אפריקי would be surprising, were it not that in the ethnographical tables, Gen. x., the Targum Yerushalmi in some copies puts under sons of Cush the countries lying between Cyrene and Numidia. The Indian pearls were considered in ancient times as the most famous (Pliny, lib. ix. c. 45). Aelian says (*Thiergesch.* x. 13) that the pearls of India and the Red Sea are the best.

[2] [אברין is probably derived from Ophir; the פ is changed into a ב.— TRANS.]

and bondwomen, and no man shall buy you.' A law has been issued to kill us, and we are all appointed to the sword and to utter extermination. The children of Abraham are clothed in sackcloth, and they have thrown ashes upon their heads. If our forefathers have sinned, why are the children guilty ? If we are destroyed, who will then praise Thee ? If the children have sinned and provoked Thine anger, what have the sucklings done ? The inhabitants of Jerusalem have moved from their graves because Thou hast delivered their children to the slaughter. Thou makest us vanish away like the clouds of heaven. How few are our days of joy ! To the wicked Haman hast Thou delivered us—to our enemy—to be slaughtered. I will remember before Thee the deeds of Thy beloved. Of Abraham I will begin to say : Thou hast tried him with all trials ; Thou hast proved him, and found him faithful. Oh, assist and support his beloved children, whom Thou hast brought to Thyself by the seal of the covenant. Demand an account from Haman for our disgrace, and take vengeance on the son of Hamdatha by the hands of Thy people Israel, whom he wants to cut off like a lamb, and whom he oppresses grievously in all their places.

"Thou hast made an everlasting covenant with us. By the binding (sacrifice) of Isaac do thou raise us up ! Behold, Haman has offered the king ten thousand talents of silver to buy us ! Hear us, and bring us out from tribulation into freedom. Break down the mighty, yea, break down Haman, that he should not rise from his fall." And Esther lifted up her voice and cried aloud, and lamented bitterly. With tears she prayed fervently, so that her throat and lips became dry, and her eyes became dim from weeping. Esther thought in her heart, and said : " It may be when I go to the king he will not listen to me. Nevertheless, I shall go to the king to pray for mercy upon mine inheritance, and may an angel of mercy go before me, and grace and favour accompany me, the righteousness of Abraham prevent me, the sacrifice of Isaac support me, the goodness of Jacob be given into my

mouth, and the gracefulness of Joseph upon my tongue.
Happy is the man who trusts in God, for he that trusts in
Him shall not be confounded.   He will extend to me His
right hand and His left, with which He created the whole
world.   You, all you Israel, pray for mercy for me (for I rely
upon your kindness), as I also pray for mercy on your behalf.
For whatever a man asks in the time of his distress from the
Holy One, blessed be He ! his prayer is heard.   Let us see
that we do the (good) deeds of our fathers, and He will
answer our petition.   The left hand of Abraham seized Isaac
by the throat, and his right hand held the knife.   He willingly did the will of Thy word, and did not delay to carry
out Thy message.   Heaven opened its windows to give place
to the angels from on high who cried bitterly, and said thus :
' Woe to the world if this deed be done ! '   I also call upon
thee, O answer me !   For Thou answerest the prayer of him
who is oppressed and afflicted.   Thou seest the afflicted soul.
Thou art called the merciful and the gracious ; Thou art slow
to anger, and plenteous in mercy and truth, and forgivest
iniquity and transgression ; Thou keepest the covenant of grace
to those who love Thee and keep Thy commandments for a
thousand generations.   Yea, by our fathers wast Thou called
the merciful.   This covenant which Thou hast made was with
them.   Thou hast heard the voice of Jonah, when he sat and
wept like a woman in childbirth ; hear also our voice and
answer us, and bring us out from tribulation into freedom.
Three days I have already fasted before Thee, what can I do
more ?   Lord of the universe ! I have forgotten the fast of the
fourth and the fifth, but I fasted three days according to the
three days in which Abraham went to bind his son upon the
altar before Thee.   Thou didst then make a covenant with him,
and didst promise him : ' Whenever thy children shall be in
tribulation, I will remember them favourably for the sake of
the sacrifice of their father Isaac, and will redeem them.'
Again, I fasted three days in reference to the three divisions,
the priests, Levites, and Israelites, who stood at the foot of

Mount Sinai when they said: 'All that the Lord hath spoken, we will do and obey.' Therefore redeem them from this oppression!" And Esther continued to pray, and said: "O God, Lord of hosts! Thou that searchest the heart and reins, remember in this hour the righteousness of Abraham, of Isaac, and of Jacob, and do not turn away from my petition, nor delay an answer to my request!" Esther then put on royal apparel and stood at the gate of the royal palace of the inner court, opposite to the royal palace, and the king sat upon his throne opposite the gate. And when the king saw Queen Esther standing in the court, she found favour and grace in his sight. But the royal executioners[1] who stood there were ready to kill Esther; then the king stretched out the golden sceptre which he held in his hand to her, and she approached and touched the top of the sceptre.

Then the king said to her: "What wilt thou, Queen Esther? and what is thy request? It shall be given thee even to the half of the kingdom." When Esther heard these words she trembled, and said: "I ask for nothing else, but if it please the king, let the king and Haman come this day unto the banquet that I have prepared for him."

And the king said: "Call Haman, and make him hasten to do as Esther has said." So the king and Haman came to the banquet that Esther had prepared. And the king said to Esther while drinking wine: "What is thy petition? and it shall be granted thee; and what is thy request? even to the half of the kingdom it shall be performed." Then

---

[1] The אספקלטורי of the king would have killed Esther had not the king intervened, because she came to the king without being summoned. Levy in his *Chald. Lex.* reads speculator. But it must be spiculator, the lance-bearers which the Greek Onomasticon calls δορυφόροι, of whom we read in Sueton. Claud. cap. xxxvi.: "Neque convivia inire ausus est, nisi ut spiculatores cum lanceis circumstarent" (comp. Sueton. Galba, cap. xviii.). It is, indeed, true that we find in manuscripts speculator and spiculator are often interchanged, but in no place is speculator used for a lance-bearer. The ideas of spy (speculator) and of bodyguard (spiculator) are quite different. Even Salmasius on *Spart. Hadrian* (cap. xi. ed. Haack, i. 107) has not clearly distinguished the one from the other.

answered Esther and said: "My petition and my request?
Thou, O king, art good without parallel, and if I have found
favour and grace and mercy before thee, and if it please the
king to grant my petition and to perform my request, let the
king and Haman come to the banquet that I shall prepare for
them, and I will to-morrow do as the king has said." For three
reasons Esther invited Haman to the banquet. First, because
Esther knew that Haman was angry against Hathach, and
was about to kill him, for his going on errands between her
and Mordecai, and therefore she thought: " I will invite him
to the banquet in order to appease him." Secondly, she
thought: " I may eradicate the hatred from his heart, and again
I shall excite the jealousy of Ahhashverosh against Haman,
for the king will say: ' What must be the reason that of
all my governors Esther invited none but Haman to the
banquet ? '" Thirdly, she thought: " The eyes of all Israel
are directed towards me, that I should request the king to
kill Haman ; I will therefore invite him to the banquet, in
order that the heart of Israel may be changed and directed
to the heavenly Father to ask for mercy from Him." Then
went Haman forth that day joyful and glad of heart ; but
when Haman saw Mordecai in the king's gate, that he stood
not up nor moved for him, he was filled with wrath against
Mordecai. Nevertheless, Haman restrained himself and went
to his house, and he sent and fetched his friends and Zeresh
his wife. And Haman recounted unto them the glory of his
riches, and the multitude of his children, and all the things
wherein the king had promoted him, and how he had
advanced him above the princes and servants of the king.
Haman said, " Moreover, yea, Esther the queen allowed no man
to come in with the king unto the banquet that she had prepared but myself ; and to-morrow also I am invited by her
together with the king. Yet all this gives me no joy, and I
am not pleased so long as I see Mordecai the Jew sitting
at the king's gate." Then said Zeresh his wife and all his
friends unto him : " Thou canst not throw him into fire, be-

cause his ancestor Abraham was delivered out of it. Thou canst not kill him with the sword, because his ancestor Isaac was delivered from it. Thou canst not drown him in water, because from water were Moses and the children of Israel saved. Thou canst not throw him into a den of lions, because Daniel was saved from it. Therefore, make a gallows fifty cubits high, and in the morning speak to the king that Mordecai may be hanged thereon. For thus far not one of them who was hanged on the gallows was delivered. After that, go with the king to the banqueting-house with joy." This advice pleased Haman, and he made a gallows for himself.

§ X.

In that night great lamentation of the infants of Israel went up to heaven, and it resounded before the Lord of the universe like the voice of kids and goats, so that the angels from on high were moved and trembled, and said to one another: " Has, perchance, the time come that the world should be destroyed?" Then they assembled and went before the Lord of the universe. The Lord asked them : " What is this voice of kids that I hear?" Then the attribute of mercy answered: " It is no voice of kids which Thou hearest, but the voice of the infants of Israel, against whom the wicked Haman issued a decree that they should be killed." Immediately, the Lord of the universe was full of compassion and goodness, and He commanded to tear the seal which sealed Israel's evil destiny, and ordered the angel who is in charge of confusion to confound Ahhashverosh, and to deprive him of his sleep. Very early in the morning Ahhashverosh rose with a sad countenance, and gave order to Shimshe the scribe to bring the Chronicle in which were recorded the events that took place in Medo-Persia from the earliest times. When Shimshe the scribe saw what was told concerning Mordecai in the affair of Bigthan and Theresh, he turned over the leaves and did want to read them ; but it was the will of the Lord of the

world that the leaves should open and read of themselves
before the king the record written on them. He then saw
and considered what was written in the Chronicle, that it
revealed concerning the deed of Mordecai in the matter of
Bigthan and Theresh, two officers of the king, keepers of his
head, that they wanted to stretch out their hands and kill
King Ahhashverosh. And the king said: " What honour and
dignity hath been done to Mordecai for this ? " Then said
the young men of the king that ministered unto him:
" Nothing was done for him." And the king said: " Who is
in the court ? " Haman was come into the outward court of
the king's house to speak to the king to hang Mordecai on the
gallows that he had prepared for him. And the young men
of the king said to him: " Behold, Haman stands in the court."
And the king said: " Let him come in." So Haman came in.
Then the king said to him: " What shall be done to the
man whom the king desires to honour ? " Now Haman
thought in his heart, who among all the king's servants are
so worthy as I am, and to whom would the king delight to
do honour more than to myself ? Haman answered and said
to the king: " For the man whom the king wishes to honour,
let royal apparel be brought which the king is accustomed to
wear, and the horse that the king is accustomed to ride, and let
the crown of the kingdom be placed on his head, and let the
apparel and the horse be delivered to the hand of one of the
king's most noble princes, that they may array the man withal
whom the king delights to honour, and cause him to ride on
horseback through the street of the city, and proclaim before
him: ' Thus shall it be done to the man whom the king
delights to honour ! ' " Then the king gazed upon Haman, and
thought in his heart: " Haman wants to kill me and to reign
in my stead, as I see in his face." And the king said to
Haman: " Make ready, and go into the royal treasury and
take from the wardrobe a purple covering, an apparel of fine
silk, adorned with fringes and costly stones and pearls, having
bells of gold on its four corners, and pomegranates on every

side. Bring also from there the great golden Macedonian
crown [1] which was brought to me from the province on the
first day that I was raised to the kingdom. Further, bring
from there the sword and the coat of mail which were brought
to me from the country of Cush, and the two royal veils
embroidered with pearls which were brought to me from
Africa; then fetch from the royal stables the horse whose
name is Hippus Regius [2] (royal horse) which I rode on my
coronation day, and go and invest Mordecai with all these
marks of distinction." Haman answered and said: "There
are many Jews in Shushan, the capital, by the name of Mordecai, to which of them shall I go?" The king said: "Go
to Mordecai, the Jew who spoke good about the king, and
who sits at my gate." When Haman heard these words he
was in great trouble, his countenance was changed, his sight
became dim, his mouth became distorted, his thoughts confused, his loins languid, and his knees beat one against the
other. He then addressed the king: "My Lord King, there
are many Mordecais in the world, and I do not know of which
of them thou hast spoken to me." The king in reply said:
"Have I not told thee that I mean Mordecai who sits at my
gate?" "But," rejoined Haman, "there are many royal gates,
and I do not know of which gate thou hast spoken to me."

---

[1] כלילא דהבא מוקדניא must be read μακρυκορώνη. See the Introduction
to my edition of this Targum. Though, indeed, Macedonia was famous
for gold, as Strabo expressly says (lib. vii. fragm. 33, ed. Paris, p. 280),
especially the territory of Datum (Δάτον), whence came the saying Δάτον
ἀγαθῶν, in reference to the Lat. datum, from dare. Comp. 34 on the gold
mines in the neighbourhood of Philippi. Yet this is not the case of the
imperial time; and the name "Macedonian" is not found for the above
word, "a golden crown."

[2] הפרנו should be read instead of שיפרנו. The lexicographers—Levy
also—have given up the interpretation of this word in despair. My
suggested reading stands for ἵππος ρηγός, horse of the king. The word
rex has passed into Greek (comp. Du Cange, Gloss. Gr.). Of the horse
of the King of Byzantium, says Codin (de officiis, cap. xvii., ed. Bonn,
p. 97), that it wore pearls and diamonds περὶ τράχηλον, and upon the back
the so-called χαιώματα. Around the ankles were tied red silk ribbons,
which were called τούβια.

"Have I not told thee," said the king, "that I mean the gate which is passed from the harem to the palace?" Haman said: "This man is my enemy, and the enemy of my fathers; I will rather give him ten thousand talents of silver, only let this honour not be done to him." The king replied: "Go and give him ten thousand talents, and he shall rule over thy house, and this honour also shall not be withheld from him." Haman said to the king: "I have ten sons, let them run before the horse (another reading, thy throne), but let not this honour be done to him." The king replied: "Thou and thy sons and thy wife shall be slaves to Mordecai, and this honour shall not be withheld from him." Haman continued: "He is only a common man; place him over a province or over a district,[1] but let not this honour be done to him." The king answered: "I make him to rule over provinces and districts, and all my possessions upon land and sea shall obey him, and this honour shall not be withheld from him." "My fame and thy fame," said Haman, "is spread in all the country, may thy fame and his be spread in all the world, only let not this honour be done to him." The king answered: "A man who spoke good of the king, and has saved him from being killed, his fame shall be spread all over the world, and this honour shall not be withheld from him" Haman said again: "Messengers with letters are already sent out to all the provinces of the king to destroy the people of Mordecai, and yet this honour shall be done to him?" The king answered: "The messengers and the letters which I sent out I invalidate, and this honour shall not be withheld from him." Then the king for the second time rebuked him, and said: "Haman, make haste! Be quick! Do not fail to do all that I command thee!" Now when the wicked Haman saw how his words were received by the king, and that he did not pay any attention to his speech, he went to the royal treasuries bowed

---

[1] The word רסתקא, which appears to be used for an estate, has not this sense, nor is the reading רסתקא, but רסתרקא, viz. *districtus*, district. So are all the passages in which רסתקא or רסתקא are found to be explained.

down and sad, his head being covered like that of a mourner, his ears deafened, his eyes dim, his mouth distorted, his heart oppressed, his bowels aching, his loins weakened, and his knees beating one against the other. And he took from there the apparel of the king which was brought to him on the first day of his reign, and all sorts of royal things, according as he was commanded, and hastened to the royal stables and fetched the king's horse, which stood at the head of the stable, upon which were suspended stirrups of gold. He then took hold of the horse's bridle, and carried the saddle and harness upon his shoulder, and went to Mordecai, and said to him as follows: "Arise, righteous Mordecai, thou son of Abraham, of Isaac, and of Jacob. Thy sackcloth and ashes have won the victory over the ten thousand talents of silver which I promised to deliver from my treasury into the royal treasury, but which were not accepted, because you are beloved by your Father in heaven, who hears your prayers at all times when you come before Him, and delivers you from your enemies. Now arise from your sackcloth and ashes, and put on the royal garment, and ride upon the royal horse." The righteous Mordecai answered and said to the wicked Haman : "Haman, wicked descendant of Amalek, wait one hour, that I may eat food of wormwood and drink bitter waters, and then lead me out and hang me on the gallows." Haman answered and said : "Arise, righteous Mordecai, descendant of a noble generation ; so long as you exist, miracles were done for you. The gallows which I erected I have erected to my misfortune. Now stand up, and put on the royal apparel and ride the royal horse, and do not frustrate the words of the king." But Mordecai answered and said to Haman : "He that fasted three days and three nights, how can he mount the royal horse?" When Haman heard these words he went to the royal stores, and brought from there all kinds of spices and ointment, and anointed him and bathed him, put the royal apparel upon him, dressed him up in the nicest fashion, and brought him food which Esther had sent for him.

But before he mounted the royal horse there were sent to
him twenty-seven thousand choice young men from the king's
house, who carried golden cups in the right hand and golden
goblets in the left, and they went before Mordecai and praised
him, and proclaimed: " This is done to the man whom the king
delighteth to honour!" When the Israelites saw this they
went on his right and left hand, and cried: " This is done to
the man whom the King who created heaven and earth
delighteth to honour!" And when Esther observed Mordecai,
the son of her father's brother, dressed in royal apparel,
wearing the royal crown upon his head and riding upon the
royal horse, she thanked and praised the God of heaven for
this redemption, and she said to Mordecai: " In thee is fulfilled
the Scripture which says: ' He raiseth up the poor out of the
dust, and lifteth the needy from the dunghill, that He may
set him with princes, and put him in possession of a throne of
honour.'" Mordecai also praised, and said: " Thou hast turned
my mourning into joy ; Thou hast taken away the sackcloth
from me, and hast clothed me with royal apparel. I praise
Thee, O God, for my redemption, and that Thou hast not caused
mine enemies to rejoice over me." Then Mordecai returned
to the gate of the palace with great honour and dignity; but
Haman went to his house covered with leprosy, sad, and his
head wrapped up. He had at that time to perform four
offices for Mordecai—(1) He was his barber, and had to shave
him; (2) he then was his attendant at the bath ; [1] (3) his groom,
for he led the horse; (4) his herald, for he proclaimed: " This
is done to the man whom the king delighteth to honour."
Haman told Zeresh his wife and all his friends what had
happened unto him. Then said his wise men and Zeresh his
wife to him: "Hast thou never heard of the three Jewish
men in the country of Babylon, Hananiah, Mishael, and

---

[1] באניא is one who washes in a bath or baptizes another. John was a
באניא. His imitator was Banus, whom Josephus mentions as his teacher
—while at the same time he gives a true copy of John (*Life of Josephus*,
chap. i.). גוליר, Galearius, probably *caballarius*, *cavalarius*, groom, and is
to be read גֻלִיר.

Azariah, who, because they did not obey the command of
Nebuchadnezzar, were thrown by him into a burning furnace;
but they came out from the flames without being hurt, yea,
the flames consumed their oppressors, but they were delivered.
Now, if this Mordecai is a descendant of these men, his deeds
are like theirs; and if thou hast begun to fall before him, thou
shalt not prevail over him, but shalt continue to fall and
not rise any more." While they were yet speaking, the king's
courtiers came and hastened Haman on to come to the banquet
which Esther had prepared. And the king and Haman went
to dine with Queen Esther. And the king said to Esther
also on the second day of the banquet of wine: "What is
thy petition? and it shall be granted thee; and what is thy
request? even to the half of the kingdom it shall be performed."
Then answered Esther and said: "If I have found favour and
mercy in thy sight, O king, and if it please the king, let my
life be granted to me at my petition, and the life of my people
at my request: for we are sold, I and my people, to be destroyed,
to be slain, and to perish. But if we had been sold for bondmen
and bondwomen, I had held my peace. Verily, the adversary
does not care for the king's vengeance (or jealousy)." King
Ahhashverosh then spake to an interpreter, and the interpreter
asked Queen Esther: "Who is this man, and whose son is he,
that durst presume in his heart to do so?" And Esther
said: "A bad man and an adversary, even this wicked Haman!"
And why is he called Haman, because it means הא מאן, i.e.
"this one who wanted to lay violent hands" on the people of
the Jews, who are called the children of the Lord of All, and
to kill them. Then Haman was afraid before the king and
the queen. And the king arose in his wrath from the banquet
of wine, and went into the palace garden, where beautiful
trees were cut down to appease his wrath; but it would not
be appeased. Haman stood up to make request for his life to
Esther the queen, for he saw that there was evil determined
against him by the king. When the king returned from the
palace garden to the place of the banquet of wine and saw

that Haman was fallen upon the couch whereupon Esther was sitting, he said to him: "Dost thou also want to force the queen before me in my palace?" Scarcely had the words gone out from the king's mouth when they covered Haman's face. Then said Hharbonah, one of the king's eunuchs—this Hharbonah is elsewhere mentioned for evil, because he was in the counsel of Haman for hanging Mordecai, but here he is mentioned for good; for when he saw that misfortune had befallen Haman and his house, he went of his own accord to the king, and said: "Thee also Haman wished to kill, and to take the kingdom from thee; but if thou wilt not believe me, send some one to see the gallows which Haman had erected for Mordecai, who spake good for the king. It stands in his house, and is fifty cubits high." Then said the king to Mordecai: "Hang him thereon." In Mordecai was the Scripture verified which says: "When God is pleased with the ways of a man, He makes his enemies also his supporters." The king then said further to Mordecai, who had saved the king from being killed: "Go and take Haman, the enemy and the oppressor of the Jews, and hang him on the gallows which he has now prepared for himself, punish him terribly, and do with him as it seems good to thee." Presently, Mordecai went from the king and fetched Haman from the gate of the palace, and said to him: "Come with me, Haman, thou wicked enemy and oppressor of the Jews, and I shall hang thee on the gallows which thou hast erected for thyself." Then the wicked Haman answered righteous Mordecai: "Before I am brought to the gallows, I ask of thee, righteous Mordecai, do not hang me on the same gallows on which common criminals are hanged. For I have not held in esteem famous men, and governors of countries were subject under me. I have made kings tremble by a word of my mouth, and countries to be afraid by an utterance of my lips. I, Haman, had the title of viceroy, and was called father of the king. I am afraid that thou wilt do to me as I intended to do to thee. O pity my nobility, and do not kill nor destroy me in the same manner as my ancestor Agag

was destroyed !   O Mordecai ! show me kindness in not slaying
me as a murderer does, for there are no murderers among you !
Remember not the hatred of Agag and the envy of Amalek
against me.   Take no vengeance of me as an enemy, and do not
have a rancorous feeling against me, as my ancestor Esau had
[against Jacob].   Great wonders have been accomplished for
thee, as once for thy forefathers when they passed through the
sea.   My eyes are too dim to see thy face, and I cannot open
my mouth before thee that I should take counsel concerning
thee from my friends and from my wife Zeresh.   I pray thee
lord, righteous Mordecai, to have compassion upon my soul,
and not to blot out my name so quickly as they blotted out
that of my ancestor Amalek, and do not hang my grey head
upon the gallows.   But if thou art determined to kill me,
then cut my head off with the sword of the king, with which
all the nobles of the kingdom are beheaded ! "   Then Haman
began to cry and to weep, but Mordecai gave no heed to him.
And when Haman saw that his words were not heeded, he
lamented bitterly in the midst of the palace garden, and cried :
" Hearken unto me, ye trees and plants which I have planted
of old, when I, the son of Hamdatha, wanted to go to the
Exedra[1] to Bar-Panthera !   Assemble yourselves together and

---

[1] Levy is of opinion that we must read Alexandria ; but this is impossible (comp. my "Jüd. Gesch.," *Ersch u. Gruber*, xxvii. p. 28, Nr. 40). Instead of
אבסנדריא the reading is evidently אבסדרא, a well-known word for Exedra,
" hall," "lecture-room."   The passage in Shabbath (104a) about witchcraft
of Bar-Pandira has no reference either to Alexandria nor to Haman.   The
sense of the above address of Haman to the trees is as follows : " I have
planted you when 1 went for instruction to Bar-Pandira, consequently I
must be hanged on one of you, as he was."   We have here a latent attack
upon Jesus, whom the Jews call son of Pandira.   The Targum insinuates
that all the Hamans were educated in the Exedra, or school of Pandira.
One can understand the national ill-humour in the midst of dire persecutions, but it is deplorable enough to remember that those who treated Him
whom they call son of Pandira, like Haman, have suffered worse than the
latter.   At the destruction of Jerusalem there were not sufficient trees on
which to crucify all of them.   Those who bear the character of Haman do
not go to the Exedra of the son of Pandira, but rather keep far away from
it.   המן is in Gematria = הין, Judenhetze.   I have written a special treatise
concerning son of Pandira and son of Stadah.   Suffice it here to say that

take counsel, if any of you has fifty cubits in height, upon it
Haman's head shall be hanged." The vine said : "I am too
short, and, besides, he cannot be hanged upon me, because
from me is taken wine for oblations." The fig tree[1] said: " He
cannot be hanged on me, because from me was taken the first
fruit-offering, and from me Adam and Eve were clothed."
The olive tree said : "He cannot be hanged on me, because
from me was taken the oil for the lampstand in the temple.
Besides, He to whom all the mysteries are not hid created me
to pay the bill of debt of the prophet Obadiah. Let, therefore,
another be taken to hang him on." The palm tree said to
his keeper (God) : "All men know that the tyrant Haman is
descendant of Agag and of Amalek, and all kings acknowledge
that Thou alone art God, and none beside Thee, and it behoves
Thee to redeem Thy children as Thou hast once redeemed their
fathers." God answered : "Thou art right in what thou hast

---

these names originated in the early times of Christianity. בר פנדירא
stands for בר פרדינא, "the son of the virgin" (παρθίνος), and בר סטדה
stands for Bar, סטרה, "the son of the star."

[1] ארא. From what follows, it undoubtedly appears that the fig tree is
meant, and therefore the reading must be ארנא, viz. ὄρνος, ὄρνεος, the later
Greek name for the wild fig tree. The remarks of Levy (Chald. Lex. p.
12) are not to the point. I embrace this opportunity to explain an
important passage about the names of trees, the reading of which has thus
far not been understood. It is in Rosh Hashanah 23a, where we read :
" There are four sorts of cedars." These are : ארו, קתרוס, עין שמן ,ברוש.
קתרום is citrus (citron orange). When we there read that Rav says קתרום
is ארא, and the school of Shila say it is מבלינא, we must read for the
former קדרא, viz. κίδρα or κίδρα ; for the latter must be read מבלונא,
malon, or rather lemon. Malus lemon, μῆλον λιμωνίον. Further on, שיתא
is explained by תורניתא, which should be read חרניתא, viz. ἀρκευθος, the
juniper tree. For שאנא must be read פאנא, fagus, beech tree ; for שוריבנא
must be read שובריגא, viz. suber, the cork tree. For נולמיש, which Löw
(Aramaische Pflangennamen, p. 60) leaves unexplained, must be read נלמיש,
viz. keltis, the other name for lotus (Columella de re rust. ix. 7b); comp.
Langkawel, Botanik der Spätern Griechen, p. 93.

In Shabb. 157a occur the words ארן ואשוחי. It appears to me that אשוחי
is meant for the ash tree. The פקסינן, which Löw quotes from Tanchum
is to be taken as fraxinus, and therefore the reading is פרקסינן. The
word אספנדרמן in Tanch. is σφίνδαμνος, the maple in Sinope. Acer pseudo
platanus occurs in forms like σπδουμνον, ἀσφίνδυνος, and σφίνδαμνος.
Langkawel, p. 16.

said, and in hesitating to be the gallows for Haman, because thou art considered as the companion of the congregation of Zion." The citron tree or paradise apple said: "He cannot be hanged on me, because from me all the people come to take my fruit wherewith to praise Thee" (on the Feast of Tabernacles). The myrtle then opened its mouth, and said: "He cannot be hanged on me, because with me they say joy and gladness,[1] and I am also an associate of the paradise apple tree." The terebinth cried: "On me he cannot be hanged, because Deborah, the nurse of Rebekah, was buried under me." The oak called out: "On me he cannot be hanged, because Absalom, the son of David, remained suspended upon me." The pomegranate tree said: "On me he cannot be hanged, because the righteous are likened to me." The cedar then said: "Hearken to me. Hang the wicked Haman and his ten sons upon the gallows which I have prepared for him." So they hanged Haman upon the tree which he had prepared for Mordecai, and the wrath of the king was pacified. And in Mordecai was fulfilled what is written in Scripture, "The righteous is delivered from oppression, and in his place comes the wicked."

§ XI.

On that day did the king Ahhashverosh give the house of Haman, the Jews' enemy, unto Esther the queen. And Mordecai came before the king; for Esther had told what he was unto her. And the king took his ring, which he had taken from Haman, and gave it to Mordecai. And Esther set Mordecai over the house of Haman. And Esther spake yet again before the king, and fell down at his feet, and besought him with tears to put away the mischief of Haman the Agagite, and his devices that he had devised against the Jews. Then the king held out to Esther the golden sceptre. So Esther arose, and stood before the king. And she said: "If it please the king, and if I have found favour in his sight, and the thing seem

---

[1] [Here is allusion to weddings, in which myrtle was used.—TRANS.]

right before the king, and I be pleasing in his eyes, let it be
written to reverse the letters devised by Haman the son of
Hamdatha the Agagite, which he wrote to destroy the Jews
which are in all the king's provinces: for how can I endure
to see the evil that shall come unto my people?" Then the
king Ahhashverosh said to Esther the queen, and to Mordecai
the Jew: "Thou hast from the outset committed a fault, for
when I asked thee from what nation thou art, in order to
make of them kings and princes, and from what family thou
art, in order to make some of them governors and generals,
thou saidst to me, 'I have not known father and mother, for
they died and left me when I was a little child.' But now,
behold, I have given Esther the house of Haman, and him they
have hanged upon the gallows, because he laid his hand upon
the Jews. Write to the Jews, as you think best, in the name
of the king, and seal it with the king's ring; for a writing thus
written and sealed is irrevocable." Then were the king's scribes
called at that time in the third month, which is the month
Sivan, on the twenty-third day thereof; and it was written,
according to all that Mordecai commanded, unto the Jews, and
to the satraps, and the governors and princes of the provinces
which are from India unto Cush, a hundred and twenty-seven
provinces, unto every province according to the writing thereof,
and unto every people after their language, and to the Jews
according to their writing and language. And he wrote in
the name of the king Ahhashverosh, and sealed it with the
king's ring; and sent letters by posts on horseback, riding
on swift steeds and young dromedaries: Wherein the king
granted the Jews which were in every city to gather themselves together and to stand for their life, to destroy, to slay,
and to cause to perish, all the power of the people and province that would assault them, and to take their little ones
and women, and households and servants for a prey, upon one
day, in all the provinces of the king Ahhashverosh, namely,
upon the thirteenth day of the twelfth month, which is the
month Adar. The contents of the published royal circular

were as follows: " King Ahhashverosh sends a letter to all the inhabitants of the isles and countries, to all the rulers of districts, nobles, and generals who dwell in every country. May your peace be multiplied. I have written this document to apprise you, that although I rule over many nations, and upon the inhabitants of land and sea, yet I am not proud about my power, but will rather walk in lowliness and meekness of spirit all my days in order to provide for your peace and prosperity, and to all who live in my dominion, that there may be free intercourse between those who want to trade by land or by sea between the various peoples and languages. I am the same from one end of the land to the other. It is further made known to you, that in spite of the sincerity and truthfulness of those who love all the nations, revere all kings, and are loyal to all the governors, there are others who stand near to the king, and to whose hands the government was entrusted, who have by their intrigues and falsehoods led the king astray, and have written letters which are not right before heaven, and which are bad before men, and cruel before the king. And this is the petition which they asked from the king, that righteous men should be killed, and much innocent blood should be shed of people who have neither done any evil nor were guilty of death, but were rather righteous. Such are Esther, who is famous for all virtues, and Mordecai, who is expert in every science; and there is no blemish to be found in them nor in their people. I thought to myself that I was requested concerning another nation, and did not know that it concerned the Jews who are called the children of the Lord of all that created heaven and earth, and who led them and their fathers in greater and mightier kingdoms than mine. Haman also, the son of Hamdatha from India,[1] a descendant of Amalek, who came to us and enjoyed

---

[1] In this peculiar letter the king says that Haman is from הנדיא. This is to be distinguished from the הנדיא רבא by which the Targumist translates הדו. This India, הנדקי, is identical with Ethiopia, and is therefore in some copies of the Jerusalem Targum put in the ethnographical table as the son of Cush. Cush is the son of Ham. It should be said of Haman

much kindness, praise, and dignity from us, whom we made great, and called him 'father of the king,' and who sat at the right of the king. He did not know how to appreciate his dignity and how to conduct himself in the kingdom, but harboured thoughts in his heart to kill the king and to take the kingdom from him. Therefore we have caused the son of Hamdatha to be hanged, and all that he deserved we have brought upon his head; and the Creator of heaven and earth brought his machinations upon his own head."

The swift messengers upon dromedaries hastened on with the king's commandment, and the decree was published in Shushan the capital.

And Mordecai went forth from the presence of the king in royal apparel of blue and white, and with a great crown of gold, and with a robe of fine linen and purple: and the city of Shushan rejoiced and was glad. The Jews had light, and gladness, and joy, and honour. And in every province, and in every city, whithersoever the king's commandment and his decree came, the Jews had gladness and joy, a feast and a good day. And many from the peoples of the land became proselytes; for the fear of the Jews was fallen upon them. Now, in the twelfth month, which is the month Adar, in the thirteenth day of the same, when the king's commandment and his decree were to be put in execution, in the day when the enemies of the Jews hoped to have rule over them, in the same day the opposite happened—the Jews ruled over their enemies. The Jews gathered themselves together in their cities, throughout all the provinces of the king Ahhashverosh, to lay hand on such as sought their hurt, and to kill them: and no man could withstand them; for the fear of them was fallen upon all the peoples. And all the princes of the provinces, and the magistrates, and the governors, and they that did the

that he came from the land of Ham, and was a descendant of Amalek. He was called אבא דמלכא, "father of the king." It is well known that father was a title of honour, and the Arab women call their husbands "father." So also the Turkish sultan called Ferdinand III. father after the war, when he took Hungary from him (Hammer, *Gesch. des osman. Reichs*, iii. 140).

king's business, praised the Jews; because the fear of Mordecai
was fallen upon them.   For Mordecai was mighty in the
king's house, and his fame went forth throughout all provinces: for the man Mordecai waxed greater and greater.   And
the Jews smote all their enemies with the stroke of the sword,
and with slaughter and destruction, and did what they would
unto them that hated them.   And in Shushan the capital, the
Jews slew and destroyed five hundred men.   And they slew
also the ten sons of Haman, son of Hamdatha, the oppressor
of the Jews; but on the spoil they laid not their hand.   And
on the same day the number of the slain in Shushan the
capital was given to the king. . . . And the king commanded
to do so, and the command was explained in Shushan. Haman
was hanged within three cubits. Parshanandatha a cubit distant from him.   Parshanandatha was hanged within three
cubits.   Dalphon a cubit distant from him, and was hanged
within three cubits.   Aspatha a cubit distant from him, and
was hanged within three cubits.   Poratha a cubit distant
from him, and was hanged within three cubits.   Adalya was
hanged within three cubits.   Aridatha a cubit distant from
him, and was hanged within three cubits.   Parmashta a cubit
distant from him, and was hanged within three cubits.   Arisa
a cubit distant from him, and was hanged within three cubits.
Arida a cubit distant from him, and was hanged within three
cubits.   Vaisatha, the tenth, a cubit distant from him, and was
hanged within three cubits.   And so all the ten sons were
hanged on the gallows.   The gallows was sunk in the earth
three cubits, and Haman's last son was three cubits distant from
the earth, and so they were hanged within forty-four cubits;
for the length of the gallows was fifty cubits.

Now, when Mordecai came and saw Haman and his sons
hanging on the gallows, he addressed him as follows: "Thou
hast thought to do evil to the people of Israel, but He who
knows the hidden and the revealed things has brought thy
design upon thine own head.   Thou hast desired to kill us,
and to remove us from under the wings of our Father in

heaven; but now have we dealt kindly with thee, and have
hanged thee, and thy sons under thy wings." And the Jews
that were in Shushan the capital again assembled themselves
on the fourteenth day of the month Adar, and killed in
Shushan three hundred men; but on the spoil they laid not
their hand. And the rest of the Jews that were in the king's
provinces gathered themselves together, and stood as masters
for their lives, and had rest from their enemies, and slew of
them that hated them seventy and five thousand; but on the
spoil they laid not their hand. These are the men whom
they killed in Shushan, namely, those of their enemies who
had said to them: "In a few days from now, we shall
kill you, and shall dash your children to the ground." This
was done on the thirteenth day of the month Adar, and on
the fourteenth day of the same, they rested and made it a
day of feasting and gladness. Therefore the Jews who were
in the villages and in the small towns, made the fourteenth
day of Adar a day of feasting and gladness and a good day,
and sent portions one to another. And Mordecai wrote these
events, and sent letters unto all the Jews that were in all the
provinces of the king Ahhashverosh, both nigh and far, to
enjoin them that they should keep the fourteenth day of the
month Adar, and the fifteenth day of the same, yearly, as the
days wherein the Jews had rest from their enemies, and the
month which was turned unto them from sorrow to gladness,
and from mourning unto a good day, that they should make
them days of feasting and gladness, and of sending portions and
presents one to another, and gifts to the poor. And the Jews
undertook to do as they had begun, and as Mordecai had
written on their behalf. Because Haman the son of Hamdatha, the descendant of Agag, the oppressor of all the Jews,
had devised against the Jews to destroy them, dipped the dice
(*i.e.* cast the lot), threw the ring, that is, "the lot," in order
to confound and to exterminate them.

When the royal scribes of Haman saw him and his sons
hanging many days on the gallows, they asked: "Why does

Esther transgress what is written in the law, 'Thou shalt not let his body remain all night upon the tree'?" Esther answered them: "Because King Saul had killed the proselytes of the Gibeonites, his sons hung upon the gallows from the beginning of barley harvest until the day when rain came down upon them, which lasted six months; and when the Israelites came up to appear before the temple, the nations asked them: 'Why do these hang?' The Israelites answered them: 'Because their father has laid his hand upon the proselytes of the Gibeonites and killed them.' How much more does the wicked Haman and his sons, who wanted to destroy all Israel, deserve to hang on the gallows—yea, for ever!" When Esther came to the king, she said what is written in the book: "Ye shall blot out the remembrance of Amalek from under heaven;" and as Haman was of the seed of Amalek, and had devised an evil device against Israel, it fell upon his own head, and he and his sons were hanged on the gallows.

Therefore, because this has happened to them, they called these days Purim, on account of the lot and of the oppression which befell them, as it is written and explained in this letter (concerning all that the fathers had seen, which led them to appoint a day in commemoration of the miracles which the Lord of heaven did for them), and that their children might know of the past events. The Jews took upon themselves and their children, and the proselytes that shall be added to them, that they shall never cease to keep these two days, in their season, year by year, according to Scripture. And these are remembered and kept in every generation by every family, in every province and in every city; and these days of Purim shall not pass away from the Jews, and their remembrance shall not cease from their children. Then Esther the queen, the daughter of Abihhail, and Mordecai the Jew, wrote with all authority, to confirm for the second time the ordinance of Purim; and they ordained that in a leap year the scroll (of Esther) should not be read in the first, but in the second Adar.

He sent letters to all the Jews, to the hundred and twenty-seven provinces of the kingdom of Ahhashverosh, which contained words of peace and truth, to confirm these days of Purim in their appointed times, according as Mordecai the Jew and Esther the queen had enjoined them, and as they had ordained for themselves and for their seed in the matter of their fastings and prayers. And the commandment of Esther confirmed the matters of these days, and it was written in the book of the Scroll (of the Chronicle). And the king Ahhashverosh put a tribute upon the inhabitants of the land; but when he knew who the people and family of Esther were, he declared them free, and set them over all the nations and over the whole kingdom, and laid that tribute upon the inhabitants of the land and upon the merchants of the sea. And all the acts of his power and of his might, and the full account of the greatness of Mordecai, whereunto the king advanced him, are they not written in the books of the Chronicles of the kings of Media and Persia? For Mordecai the Jew was viceroy of King Ahhashverosh, president and elder among the Jews, and supreme over all the nations. His fame was from one end of the world to the other. All kings were afraid of him, and trembled when they saw him. This is that Mordecai who is like the star Noga that glitters among the stars, and like the dawn of the morning. He was the Master of the Jews, who had pleasure in the greatness of his brethren, who sought the good of his people, and spoke peace to all his seed.

MITHRA.

1. THERE can be no more erroneous opinion with regard to the book of Esther than that given by Zunz in his *Gottesd. Vorträge* (pp. 14, 15), where he remarks: "The book of Esther is especially a monument of obscurity and of deficiency in the prophetic spirit. For although it was scarcely necessary to mention the Persian king and kingdom 187 times, and his name twenty-six times, yet it found no opportunity to mention the name of God even a single time." This very fact, that it omits to mention the name of God, is rather to be taken as the best testimony concerning the age and the originality of the little book. The name of God could not have been mentioned without awakening a sense in the heart of Israel that the king is *far beneath* His glory and power. The reproach which Haman made to the Jews consisted just in his saying, "that they do not keep the king's laws," chap. iii. 8. This could not have referred to their not paying taxes, or to their refusal to render any other service to the State which they were obliged to render, but it referred to the religious laws of the country, according to which the Persian king was to be regarded by the people as the human representative of Mithra the sun-god, and they could not possibly so regard him.

That the king of Persia was so regarded, and that Mithra was the image of the sun,[1] will be seen in the following :—

All qualities which occur in the Zendic writings, especially

---

[1] The treatise of Windischmann, *Mithra ein Beitrag zur Mythengeschichte des Orients*, Leipzig 1875, which was considered of first-rate importance among the treatises on the Orient, is a distinguished book, and is still of great value. Just with respect to it, or, properly speaking, against it, are

in the Mihryast, are such as are everywhere ascribed to the sun. The same can be observed in the accounts of the Greek and Roman writers. The Mihr (Mithra) yast (Windischmann, 1; Spiegel, *Avesta*, iii. 79) reads: " Ahuramazda spake: ' When I created Mithra, who possesses wide pasturages, I created him as laudable as myself.' " Ahuramazda signifies the " lord of light," and not " wise lord," as Spiegel, *Eran. Altherthumsk.* i. 10, says, for it is derived from אור, light, just as Nairyoçagha connects נר with fire.

He perfectly resembles the Greek Zeus, who no less signifies the heavenly light, and is like him the father of Apollo, and of noble sun heroes (Hermes, Bacchus, Heracles, Perseus), and of Vulcan,—so also the progenitor of Mithra as sun and of fire.

Of Mithra it is said in the Mihryast, as well as in the Quarret-nyasis (Spiegel, iii. 9) and elsewhere, that " he has 1000 eyes and 10,000 ears," who sees all and hears everything, as Aelios is called the shining eye (Sophocles, *Antig.* 870, etc.), and as we read of him in Homer: " Who seest and hearest all" (ὃς πάντ᾽ ἐφορᾷς καὶ πάντ᾽ ἐπακούεις). The horse in the sun-car is called in the Edda, *Alswidr*, " Omniscient." Therefore is Mithra also called " wide ranging," for he shines and sees over all, just as Odin sees over all with the eye of the sun.

Hence he is called a sleepless, vigilant scout, a penetrating one, and a thousand scout (Wind. *Mihryast*, x. p. 6), like as the

the above remarks written. Space is wanting to enter upon an extensive exposition. It would become an Oriental mythology; but I believe the task is in a manner accomplished—to refute the opinions and elucidations of Windischmann, particularly in reference to the identity of Mithra and the sun. This might also be done according to Spiegel's *Eranische Alterthumskunde*, ii. 70. Further proofs are reserved *s.d.v.* for another occasion. For more information, which owing to the brief space granted me I cannot here adduce, I refer to my following writings :—"*Esmun eine archaeologische Untersuchung aus der Geschichte Phöniciens und Kenaans*"; 2. "Kaiser und Königsthrone," in *Geschichte, Symbol und Sage*; 3. *Drachenkämpfe*, Berlin 1878; 4. *Der Phöniz und seine Aera*; 5. *Löwenkämpfe von Nemea bis Golgotha*; 6. *Weihnachten Ursprünge, Bräuche, Aberglauben*; 7. *Kittim Chittim*, Berlin 1887, etc.

sun is called in Homer: "Who espies the gods and men" (θεῖον σκοπὸς ἠδὲ καὶ ἀνδρῶν, Hymn in Ceres, 63). The ten thousand eyes are only the images of affluence and power, as Ardviçura Anahita has 1000 canals, the three-legged ass needs as much space with his feet as 1000 sheep, or the tree at the Bouru-Kasha produces every year 1000 branches (Spiegel, *Alterth.* p. 118).

Very remarkable is the passage in the Mihryast which speaks of the eight friends of Mithra, but which neither Wind. nor Spiegel could explain. Damascius says (comp. my Esmun, p. 35): "To Sadukos are born sons, which they call Dioscuri and Kabires, but the eighth is called Esmunus." The Kabires (חברים) are none else than "the friends" spoken of above. The number eight was that of the stars, including Esmun. We read already in Xenophon that they used to swear by Mithra (Μὰ τὸν Μίθρην, Cyrop. viii. 5. 53; Windischm. p. 55). Plutarch reports that Artaxerxes swore also by Mithra; and Darius demanded of the eunuchs to give testimony, looking reverently at the great light of Mithra (σεβόμενος Μίθρου τε φῶς μέγα). Just so was in Homer the sun invoked at taking an oath (comp. Preller, *Myth.* p. 292; Nitzsch, *Nachhomerische Theol.* p. 118, etc.). In the Mihryast, § 15, we read: "Mithra the espy, . . . who causes the water to stream, the trees to grow, and who makes the furrows," which is a more correct translation than that of Spiegel. In Aeschylus (*Agamemnon*, 633) it is said that no one can announce this but Helios, who nourishes the nature of the earth (" τρέφοντος Ἡλίου χθονὸς φύσιν ").

He cannot be deceived, he is called Adaoyamna; as the proverbial saying of the sun is: "Nothing is so finely spun, but what is exposed to the light of the sun." Innocent people can in their sufferings call the sun to witness. The sun has seen the act of murder, and brought about its punishment. Pindar speaks of the sun as the measure and the source of all wisdom.

Mithra is an enemy of long sleep. Owing to this, the cock,

who, as the watch and the symbol of the sun, drives away evil
spirits and wakes men, is his type. In the Vendidad (Spiegel,
Avesta, i. 237) we read : "This bird raises his voice on every
divine dawn crying : Get up, ye men, praise the best purity,
drive away the Daevas; *Daeva Bushyancta dareghogava* is
running towards you; he lulls again to sleep the whole
corporeal world when it awakes. Long sleep is not becoming
to thee." In all folk-lore the cock is the symbol of the sun,
and by his crowing drives away evil spirits (comp. my *Edd.
Studien*, pp. 53, 54, etc.). Mithra goes as a victorious warrior
to battle against the evil spirits, with a carriage of four white
horses, which calls to mind the sun-carriage of Helios. White
horses are always everywhere symbols of light. The sun was
always a warrior, and Apollo no less then Heracles and Perseus
were combatants against the dragons and lions of the night.

2. The Persian king manifests himself as the image of the
sun-god Mithra. The king had also " eyes and ears," namely,
officers through whom he was made cognizant of everything
that was going on. Apuleius says : " He was believed by
men as a god, as he through the report of those eyes and
ears knew what happened everywhere." No event in his
country could be hid before him, as before the sun.

It was a witty remark of Vespasian, who said of a comet
with long hair that appeared in his time, that it belonged
to the king of Persia, *cui capillus effusior*,—just as Helios
is represented with curly hair. They used to worship the
king from a distance, as if by reason of the glow which
proceeded from him. Even modern etiquette in the Persian
court requires that no one come near before the order to do
so is repeatedly given. A young courtier made his fortune,
because on the occasion when he was called to come near, he
replied : " *Misusum* (I burn); I pray not to command me to
come near." The king appeared upon the golden throne
like the sun in the sky ; behind him stood umbrella carriers,
[as depicted] upon Persepolitan and Assyrian monuments.
Of the education of Minuntshehr, Firdussi muses,—

"A silk umbrella shaded his head." But not for the sake of the shade which he needed, but for the sake of the world, which without the shade would be consumed by the sun. The servants held the sunshade over him as a perpetual sign that he as a sun might, if he were so disposed, burn up the world. All royal usage was transferred from Persia to the modern Oriental lords; just as the carriage of Mithra was drawn by white horses, so are the carriages of kings—as it is more specially told of Cyrus and Xerxes that their carriages were drawn by Nysaeic white horses. He sat behind his seven councillors, as the sun behind the stars. So general became this image, that even a German monk describes an audience which the Greek Embassy had with Charlemagne in this manner : "They saw the emperor at the splendid window, covered with gold and precious stones, shining as the rising sun, and surrounded as by a heavenly host." Strabo has a remarkable notice, to the effect that owing to the continual sun in Shushan, no serpents nor lizards are found there. This is a misunderstanding of the author, who understood in a literal sense what was meant figuratively. Of all the cities of the sun and of Apollo, the saying was, that no serpents could live in them, neither in Delos, nor in Claros, nor in Crete. This is also in Christian legend said to have been the case in more famous spiritual places, and especially in Jerusalem.[1]

3. Much more significant appears the identity of the king, Mithra, and the sun, upon important figures and in customs, which are generally misunderstood. In the great hall of the ruins of Persepolis, the king is represented as carrying on a combat with three animals, which stand erect and defend themselves with their forelegs as with hands; all three have each one horn and wings. The king seizes with one hand the horn, and with the other he thrusts the sword into the body. They are now photographed in the great work of

---

[1] [The Talmud asserts that serpents and scorpions never hurt any one in Jerusalem (Yoma, p. 2a).—TRANS.]

Stolze, though they were very clearly portrayed in former works, such as of Ker Porter and Chardin, and also nicely reproduced by Kossowitz. The opinions about them are curious enough. The whole tableau indicated that the king fights against an enemy endowed with animal qualities and symbolized by it. The wings are everywhere signs of an inhuman nature. With peaceable animals they refer to holy divine nature, but with wild creatures they are signs of demoniac and Daeva nature. So likewise the horns in them are not merely natural signs, but also symbolic. They signify the destructive will of force, for which we have an instructive example in Dan. vii. The horn indicates evil thoughts; the king breaks it: the belly is the seat of carnal lust and uncleanness; the king pierces it with the sword.

It is Mithra the sun-hero who is depicted in the king;— of the animals is represented the nature of the wolf, the lion, and the dragon, which are representatives of the night, and of the enemies of the gods of light. So Odin in the northern doctrine combats the evil spirit in the wolf; and the wolf is also characterized as a special enemy in the thirteenth Fargard of the Avesta. In the dream of Astyages there appear three hostile men riding respectively upon a lion, a leopard, and a dragon with wings. Diodorus describes monuments in Babylon which represent Semiramis fighting with a leopard, and Ninus with a lion. In the vision of Daniel, also, appear lions, bears, and leopards with wings. The wild creatures are the attributes of the national as well as of the spiritual antithesis. The lion especially is the type of Ahriman, as the king is depicted upon a seal fighting a lion; and he is in various other groups represented as seizing the bull, the sacred animal of Iranian thought. Hence Apollo combats the dragon, and Heracles combats both the lion and the dragon.

Apollo is especially surnamed " the archer; " the arrows were figures of the sunbeams; therefore he is called ἕκατος, ἑκάεργος, ἑκατήβολος, τόξιος; the arrows rattle in his quiver, he shoots and sends arrows for deliverance and for destruction. It is therefore interesting to observe that the coins of the Arsacide kings usually bear the image of the king carrying a bow in his hand. Mithra was particularly much spoken of at that time, and he appears in names of kings. One of the kings calls himself Mitraetus (*Vaillant Imp. Arsac.* p. 246). The king intimates that he is the image of the sun Mithra with the bow, and the more so as the use of the bow was much in vogue among the Persians and Parthians. It is to be assumed that the name Mithra also signifies this.

By the transition of Mithra into Mihr, one is reminded not only of the Hebrew verb מהר (to hasten), as the arrow flies, but even more so of מורה, meaning an archer. One may also compare the Latin *mittere*, which is used to denote sending an arrow, as missile itself means arrow, dart.

Though, indeed, we read in Plutarch (*De Is. et Os.* cap. 46) : " Therefore the Persians call Mithra a μεσίτης, mediator ; " yet this is not to be understood verbally, but essentially. To ascribe the meaning of mediator to the name Mithra, would be just as erroneous as to explain Christ by μεσίτης, because He is called so. The sun is a mediator, because he is the visible light of Ahuramazda, who manifests himself through his medium. What is called here Mesites is given in the surnames of the Parthian and Syrian kings as Epiphanes, as the one Arsaces calls himself "Αρσάκος μιτράητος ἐπιφανής," namely, he is the visible representative of Mithra himself. That was, too, the arrogance of that Antiochus, who as Epiphanes wanted to destroy the religion of Israel. Just as the throne-culte was transplanted from the Persians to the Western nations, so also the opinion that kings are visible representatives of the sun, or aped the gods—like Mithra the Mesites of Ahuramazda. The name Mesites has had indeed a great significance in Christian doctrine. When the apostle (Gal. iii. 20) says: " ὁ μεσίτης ἑνὸς οὐκ ἔστιν, ὁ δὲ Θεὸς εἷς ἐστιν," we obtain from the use of the word a clear idea of

Mithra. Neither is he ἑνός, for he is only as sun the visible operating agent of Ahuramazda; nor is Christ ἑνός, for what He is, that He lives and works as the visible and incarnate Logos. The apostle could therefore say : For there is one God, one Mesites also between God and men (1 Tim. ii. 5); just as Jesus says to His disciples, "He that hath seen me, hath seen the Father" (John xiv. 9). Precisely from this idea of Mithra is seen that his name included the essence of the visible sun.

4. A peculiar but instructive report is given by Ctesias in Athenaeus (comp. *Ctesiae fragm.* p. 79, ed. Paris), that it is permitted to the king of Persia to get drunk on the day when offerings are made to Mithra; and from Duris it is reported, that the king does this on the feast Mithra, when he also dances the Persian dance. This report has not been quite understood. The month Mihr (Mithra) corresponded to the month Tishri in the Jewish calendar, and was the beginning of the civil year. I have through this circumstance explained the name itself (*Lit. u. Gesch.* p. 319); it corresponded to October, which was everywhere the proper month for vintage. It is indeed called by the Anglo-Saxons Vinterfylled, that is, vintage month, and also Vindumemanoth or Winmanoth, from the Latin *vindemia*. The feast of the sixteenth day in the month Mihr is called *mihr rúz*, and lasted to the twenty-first, which was high festival. These days correspond to the Feast of Tabernacles, which obviously was originally a nature feast, and only through the Mosaic law was elevated to the position of a religious feast. It is at any rate interesting that Plutarch in his Table-talk speaks of the Feast of Tabernacles "as falling in the midst of the time of vintage," and is of opinion that it was dedicated to Bacchus.

So then we see that the king's conduct on the Mithra-feast was connected with the feast of vintage. The vine thrives through the sun; he produces the juice in the grape; Mithra, the sun, drinks the wine, his production,—this the king as his representative imitates; it is the portion of victory by which Mithra celebrates the victory of the sun over the nightly darkness. Of such a feast of victory the Persian tradition rightly reminds. It is said, that on this day the kings were anointed with oil, and adorned with the crown upon which was to be seen the image of the sun. Then a dish containing fruit, white grapes, seven berries, myrtle, citrons, sugar, and other things was brought to the king—all signs of productiveness which the sun caused to the earth.

The tradition, that on that day Feridun was victorious over Dahak agrees with this; they saw in it an act of emancipation and deliverance, which has its Biblical counterpart in the words of the Psalmist: "I will take the cup of salvation, and call upon the name of the Lord" (Ps. cxvi. 13).

The dance of the king on the Mithra feast signifies the dance of the sun himself.

Mithra rejoices over his victory. So King David dances before the ark; and a Latin hymn calls upon the east and the west, upon heaven and earth, mountain and river, to move their hands for joy. On this rests the old popular notion, that on the feasts of Christ the sun dances and leaps for joy. In Silesia and other places they used to place a tub of water in the court, in order to see in it the skipping of the lamb-offering. People were so sure that the leaping of the sun became signs of the calendar, as to be quite certain that the introduction of the Gregorian calendar was faultless. In the Christian Church the Feast of Tabernacles was not preserved, and its place is occupied by Christmas. This has occurred not without deep thought. When paganism was still prevalent, there was a repeated attempt to dedicate Christmas day to the sun instead of to Christ. Indeed, it was notably Julian, who fell in the war against the Persians, who exerted himself to make January 1 as a sun-feast, in order thereby to displace Christmas day, which was then on January 6. It is probable that a trans-

ference of New Year from October to January had also taken
place among the Persians. When Golius says the Arabs
called the feast Mihragzan, the sixth day of the feast, " night
of the kindling of the fire," he appears to confound this with
January 6, viz. Epiphany, which was in fact called Phota
(feast of lights). The drinking of the king on the Mihragzan
illustrates a peculiar popular custom in connection with January 6, which was especially preserved in the Netherlands in
quite a different manner. They proceed to the election of a
king; and that person is chosen who finds a bean in the royal
cake given to him, or who draws a royal figure from a bag
containing other figures. The chosen king is then duly
crowned and his court established; after which follows feasting on good and sweet things, as on the day of Mithra; and
when the king raises his glass, all shout with joy, "The king
drinks." Thus the Occident gives a mirror of ancient Oriental
usage.

A much-spoken-of myth of Mithra is, that he was born of
a rock, ἐκ πέτρας γεγένησθαι, as Justin says. The poet
Commoedianus calls him " Invictus de petra natus." Even
John Lydus calls him πετρογενής. It did not suggest itself to
the expositors that the same is said of the Greek gods of light.
Apollo was born in Delos, an unsightly rocky island. The
island in which Aesculapius, son of Apollo, was worshipped,
כם, Cos, means a rock. The Dioscuri were born upon a cliff
near Pephnos. Parallel to this, might be considered the
reported solemnities as held in his honour in a cave (σπήλαιον)
out of which he came forth. "Everywhere," says Porphyrius,
"where Mithra is known, God is propitiated by a cave."
And he adds that such caves were consecrated to Zeus in Crete,
to the moon and Lightpan in Arcadia, and to Dionysus in
Naxos. The writer overlooked that Hermes was in a hidden
grotto of a hill; and that Perseus, who appears as a Greek
Mithra, of whom the oracle speaks as of "a winged lion,"
whose name reminds the ancients of Persia, came into the
world in a subterranean dungeon. The births in rocks and in

caves represent both the battle and the victory of the god of light. As the demigods must fight against the giants of the rocks to secure their existence. The sun rises out of obscurity Out of the crags of the rocks, where nothing thrives, rises the light, in order to make everything fruitful, just as the spark issues from the stone.

This is spiritualized in the Old Testament. The whole of theology had its birthplace in isolated localities. The whole doctrine about God was hidden at the beginning. Moses came from the rigid desert in order to educate his people in the desert. On a hidden rocky mountain (Sinai-rock) God was revealed.

What could be more hidden than Bethlehem and Nazareth? The stable is like a cave, out of which came the Light. As Moses brought forth water out of the rock, so Jesus says that He will make disciples of stones if men will not hear. Peter was a man of flint.

The report of Elisaeus the Armenian, that Mihr was a divine incarnation, and that he was a king of divine descent, has its origin in the tendency to find Mithra again in Christ. The sun comes forth out of the obscure deep, just as the spiritual light of the nations comes out of the hidden corners of the nations. That which is told of the cattle robbery which Mithra has committed, certainly signifies the deliverance of the fertility of the earth from the hands of darkness and frigidity. For, as we saw above, cattle and earth mean the same thing. So Perseus delivers Andromeda, who represents the earth as sustaining men. The sun has herds of cattle with which Hermes has his lively game. Geryon is a lord of the nether world, from whom Heracles robs his flock, and gives back to the earth, as agriculture, fertility.

Least of all, in our opinion, has the so-called Mithra-offering, whose relief is in the Louvre in Paris, been understood. Mithra as a youth, dressed in Oriental costume, pierces with his sword the neck of a bull, while he lifts the head upwards. Blood streams. There are the words: *Nama sebesio.*

A dog, a serpent, and a scorpion are present. The tail of the bull ends in the form of a bundle of corn. A raven sits upon a rock behind Mithra. Two genii with erected torches stand there, upon one the sun with the morning star, upon the other the moon with the evening stars. There was always the mistake committed in assuming that Mithra does violence to the bull, which is otherwise ascribed to Ahriman. Just the contrary is the case. What he does is a benefit. Therefore he is worshipped. It represents the consecration of his life. The bull is the earth, his blood is the water, without which the earth cannot thrive. Mithra is the sun, who with golden sword, his ray, opens the earth. Its being apparently wounded, is its safety. The bull has therefore a sheaf of corn on his tail, as a sign of the fruit which Mithra produces. The wolf (which may more properly be instead of the dog), the serpent, and the scorpion are hostile creatures which defile the earth and desire to destroy Mithra's work. The raven behind Mithra belongs to the sun - worship. It is the servant of Apollo, as Coronis, the crow, is his beloved. Where there is a service of Apollo there are ravens, as hence two ravens, "Hugin and Munin," accompany Odin. *Nama sebesio* is not difficult to explain. *Nama* expresses celebration, *sebesio* is equivalent to Sabazios. It well belongs to the Hebrew שבת, not because it contains the idea of rest, but of celebration. It is Mithra's feast,—the deeds of his power, the nature of his life, that he displays when he kills the bull from morning till evening.

5. Much has been written and copied about the mysteries and the solemnities of the worship of Mithra. The central point in all the writing is Mithra as a sun. This is recognised in the names of the animals, or in the masks of animals in which the initiated appeared. The famous passage of Porphyrius (*De Abst.* iv. 16) has from this side not yet been understood. What is remarkable in it is, that it is influenced by Persian as well as Egyptian interpretations. In Egypt especially the lion was sacred to the sun, because when he

entered the zodiacal sign of the lion, the Nile began its fertilizing inundation. Horapollo says, that when the Egyptians pray for a full Nile, they bring the image of a lion. It is therefore the image of the Sphinx, as Arnobius calls it: "that of a fruit-producing lion" (*leonis frugiferi*). The Egyptian hieroglyphic has no connection with the general nature of the animals, so also not here with the rapacious lion, but only with the one thought, that it is the sign of the happy inundation; hence all wells spring from the jaws of lions. Indeed, Heracles also, who conquers the lion, wears his stamp; and Dionysus, too, appears as a terrifying lion. The initiated went to meet the novice in masks of lions; the mysteries themselves were types of nature's production through the sun. Of these Tertullian says, the lions philosophize (*Ad. Marcion,* i. cap. 13); but they were not destitute of a natural ethic. As Tertullian reports, the warrior of the mysteries was obliged to throw away his usual wreath, for Mithra was his wreath. There rests upon him to a certain extent the disc of the sun, like a nimbus (as Porphyry narrates, iv. 16);[1] the attendants were called ravens. We have already explained the ravens before. The fathers they call eagles and hirakes (hawks). Of the eagle, who is called

---

[1] The passage literally reads: "While they call those who are initiated into the sacred acts (ὀργίων μίστας;) lions, the women hyenas, the servants have the name of ravens. As concerning the fathers (ἐπί τε τῶν πατέρων . . .), they are called eagles and hawks (ἰέρακες). And who that takes upon himself the order of the lions (λεοντικά παραλαμβάνων), invests himself everywhere with the appearance of the animals." The supposition that λεαίνας is to be read for ὑαίνας originated with Felicianus, who translated Porphyry into Latin, but did not, like Hercher, insert the conjectural reading into the text. Hercher states that he has done it on the authority of Kircher. He thinks that the ὑαινικά of Salmasius rests only upon this passage, which may not be correct, for the old inscription has also *hienocoracica* (comp. the *Comm. of Hieronymus,* ii. 869, ed. Migne; the edition of Porphyry, *Trajecti ad Rhenum,* ed. Jacob. de Rhoer, p. 350).

With respect to the marks of the animals, compare especially (p. 351) with the passage of Diodors. i. 62, where he narrates: "It is the custom among the lords of Egypt to put on masks of the head of lions, bulls, and dragons as symbols."

ἀετός (עיט), as of the rapacious bird in general, it was thought to resemble the sun in seeing at a distance. The eagle, says Aristotle, compels his young ones to gaze at the sun. When the Egyptians, says Horapollo, wished to designate a far-seeing man, they called him a vulture (γύψ). Sacred above all was the hierax, "hawk." Horapollo says: "When one wants to draw the victory of the sun-god, it is done by drawing the hawk." Therefore the image of the Phoenix as a figure of the course of the sun is represented by a crowned eagle, or hierax.[1]

Why the Egyptians regarded birds of prey so sacred was, as it is taught, because these birds have a great relish for carcases, around which gather ravens, eagles, and hawks. Among the quadrupeds is the hyena, which has relation to these.

It is interesting information that the female initiates appeared in masks of hyenas; though, indeed, R. Hercher (in the Paris edition, 1856) read λεαίνας instead of ὑαίνας, but he only followed a conjectural reading; the codices have rightly ὑαίνας. There is in themselves no difference between the masks of lions and lionesses, but the myth which touches upon the hyenas gives sufficient support to the idea, that just they were the proper images for the initiated. Of them it is

---

[1] Jerome writes to Laeta (*Epp.* n. 107, ed. Migne, ii. p. 869 (679)): "Nonne specum Mithrae et omnia portentosa simulacra, quibus Corax Nymphus (*al.* Nyphus, Gryphus), Miles, Leo, Perses, Helios, Dromo, Pater initiantur." The text is not quite clear. For Niphus, Nymphus, Gryphus, should be read Eniphus, namely, the Egyptian Cneph, which is connected with כנף, "wing" (בעל כנפים), and signifies here the hawk of which Porphyry speaks. Perses is Perseus. Dromo is explained by the commentators of Jerome as δρόμος, crab. The crab has indeed some relation to the sun, but only a hostile one, for it helps the hydra against Heracles. Again, *dromos* is only a sea-crab, in reference to which there are certainly quite other legends (comp. my *Drachenkämpfe*, p. 50). Apart from this, it is improbable that the name of an animal stood between Perseus, Helios, and Pater. It must be read: Bronios, viz. Dionysus, who would stand well, near Pater (Pater Liber). It is also false that Dionysus has no relation to the mysteries of Mithra. The sun, Mithra, Dionysus, were one there. They all merged in the sun-worship.

said that they are of a double gender, and can be man and wife.

The hyena appears in the legend a decided enemy of the dog, and the dog again was, as an animal of the nether world, obnoxious to the sun and his heroes.

It was said that even the shadows of the sun made dogs dumb. We have indeed but one notice of Porphyry which speaks of the hyena in the mysteries of Mithra; but Salmasius, too, cites ὑαίνικα. In the Latin translation of Palladius (*Histor. Lausiaca*, cap. 20; comp. Bochart, *Hieroz.* i. 835) there is an anecdote told, that he once healed a young hyena, and out of gratitude its mother brought him a sheep-skin. The saint said: " Where didst thou get the skin, if thou didst not rob the sheep from some one ? What is wrongly obtained I do not accept." The hyena with dejected head prostrated itself before the feet of the saint, and laid down the skin. The saint said again: "I do not accept it unless thou swearest solemnly not to vex the poor by devouring their lambs." The hyena bowed its head as a sign of consent to the words of the saint. It appears to me that this is a story of the conversion of a hyena which originated among the adherents of Mithra.

I was thus far concerned to prove that Windischmann is mistaken in his opinion that Mithra was ever anything else but the sun, and invoked independently from the sun. They are both identified everywhere, although it cannot be contested that some authors have not understood the significance of Mithra. Even if the passage in Curtius (*et Solem et Mithrean invocans*, iv. 48. 12) were genuine, it could only prove their identity, but not their distinctiveness— because it speaks only of the sun and fire. Strabo is surely a sincere witness to this when he plainly says: " They worship the sun, which they call Mithras." When some say that Mithra was also held as fire, it is to be understood that Mithra was the visible representative of Ahuramazda, who was identified with fire. Mithra, as sun, was identified with

Titan (with Osiris, as Statius calls him *torquentem cornua*,
which may just as well refer to the sun as to the bull, the
symbol of the fertile earth).   And the heretical early Christians found that Mithra signified as much numerically as the
mystical Abraxas, namely 365, as the number of the days in
a solar year.   The Church Fathers have rightly laid stress
upon the fact that the heathen of the first centuries, like
Julian, upheld the sun-worship in opposition to the doctrine
of Christ.   Justin Martyr affirmed that there was an imitation
of the Communion in the mysteries of Mithra.   Tertullian is
of opinion that there was also in them an imitation of baptism,
the signing of the forehead and of the resurrection of Christ.
Dionysius the Areopagite speaks also of such an imitation
among the Magi, who celebrated the memory of a threefold
Mithra (τριπλασίου), which was obviously only borrowed
from Christianity.   But not only was the sun everywhere
understood by Mithra, but also the opinion was universally
held, that the king, and therefore also the Roman emperor,
assumed to himself the attributes of Mithra.   Dio Cassius
narrates that King Tiridates, at his coronation in Rome, said
to Nero that he came to worship him as Mithra (προσ-
κυνήσων σε ὡς καὶ τὸν Μίθραν).

Specially noteworthy is the fact that the inscriptions which
were designed for Mithra: *Deo soli invicto Mithrae*, were
by Roman emperors entirely appropriated to themselves.
Particularly since Commodus they called themselves *invictus*
—a term with which even a month was designated.   Cara-
calla was addressed: *invicte imperator!*   Constantine still
bore that title, and Arcadius and Honorius were called
invictissimi.

Joined to this by way of a brief reminder, is the strange
opinion which wandered from one book to the other, that the
Romans kept a Mithra-feast on the 25th of December, which
is not merely a fable, but also a striking testimony of the
rapidity of bookmaking.   The remark of the Roman Calendar
of the year 354 to the *VIII. Cal. Jan.*, which read *N. I.*, was

understood as *Natalis Inocti*, viz. Solis, regardless of the fact
that this is the only designation of this day—as there is no
similar notice in existence. But *N. I.* only signifies *invicti
imperatores*, and refers to Constantine, who celebrated on the
25th December 351 the decisive day of his assuming the
government. Yet even at present one can find in compiled
books that Christmas is for this reason observed on the 25th
of December, because it was once the day of the Mithra-
feast.[1]

[1] [The author has, in the above essay, thrown much light on the
omission of the name Jehovah or Elohim from the book of Esther. Had
they inserted the sacred name, it would either at once have provoked the
just appeased king, or it would have been associated with Mithra, and
perhaps have been perverted into the same. We know that the heathen
have turned the ineffable name into Jove. Macrobius quotes an oracle:
Ἰαω ὁ πάντων ὕπατος Θεός. According to Jerome, the cultus of Mithras
lasted till 377 A.D. It has left its traces even in Germany on the
monuments at Hedernheim, near Frankfort-on-the-Main. What a
wonderful providence it was which caused the Jews to exercise their usual
cleverness in omitting both the name of their God and of the god of the
country from this book! Had they done the latter, we should have had
many Jews named Mithridates, as we have many named Jehoshua.—
TRANS.]

THE WINGED BULLS OF PERSEPOLIS.

THE monuments which were discovered in the last century in Persia, and in recent years in Assyria, have received great and well-deserved attention, but the knowledge of them is yet incomplete. Those of Persepolis and Nineveh, around which all the monuments of every place may be grouped, have for the culture of all times another importance than is the case with the Greek monuments. Almost all of them disclose indications of the intellectual life of great nations. No writings existed to give us in any way these indications before the monuments were discovered and deciphered. No trace of them is found in all the rich literature which reflects Hellenic art. The scanty information which we possess about some feature of these nations, is not derived from their sentiments, and shows only the smallest part of their spiritual nature.

That the Iranic nations excel the Assyrian by means of religious writings of the Avesta, is of great importance to us; but these writings, owing to the difficulty of the idiom, are still of little use. Therefore a thorough examination of these monuments reveals to us, as it were, antiquity alive again. Sixteen hundred years ago, when Charon, the ferryman in the infernal regions (Lucian), paid a visit to the world, in order to see for himself whether it was so magnificent as the dead had described it to him, his guide, Mercurius, had then to report to him about the monuments of Nineveh. "Nineveh, my dear ferryman, is destroyed, and one cannot even say where it stood. That large city with many towers and high walls is Babylon, whose locality will soon be sought as that of Nineveh." But fortunately Mercurius can now receive information from us. We now know more of Nineveh than it ever seemed probable that we should. Our old philologians were not in a position to regard the artistic monuments of Greece in their relation to the history of the country. They had indeed the hoary sketcher of Grecian art, Homer, whose pictures and statues date of the most ancient time. But this is quite different with respect to the mentioned Asiatic nations. The Oriental monuments not only supply us with the lost literature of poets and describers of art, but they have also done this in ancient times. They were themselves a kind of art literature. Everything may be described in a few words. To express one's thoughts properly and in elegant language is the highest art. So also it is the greatest difficulty with the artist to give a complete expression to the general idea which his mind has grasped, and at the same time to delineate beautifully all the qualities. Homer was the teacher of all the artists of Greece. With the artist in colour and marble, who has carried out his thoughts in the minutest stroke and shade, the general idea is uppermost in his mind. Of this Schiller says, "that it is the germ in the plant which produces the work of art and gives an inexpressible charm to the whole." This cannot be otherwise. The descriptive arts do not in their works create books, in which one should so read that nothing etherial should remain. The silent beauty which does not need letters and syllables, and which speaks in summary forms, can be more easily brought nearer to completion than the speaking and syllabic beauty. Hence the language in figures is the elementary language of man, and therefore hieroglyphics are attempts of thoughtful people to express their ideas in a beautiful and tangible manner. They have hence become the elements of a sacred language, because they appeal to the soul without effacing the tender pain of the idea through a disguised and confused manner. Next to them was no literature which either did or could communicate what they expressed. Therefore a

symbol is like a fleeting hieroglyph of life, and the language
of the greatest master is not capable so much as to fathom
the depth of this word and reproduce it in a plain and perfect
definition.   Therefore it would be to make life shallow and
dam up its streams, if its symbol should be removed.   They
would destroy the copious activity of the musing soul, who, if
it were possible, could have dissolved it by sober reflection.
From this deficiency of language, which is the characteristic
of all uncultured nations, but which does by no means imply
a want of ideas, much of the life and of the views of the
ancient nations is to be explained.   In considering the
sources of art, we are unable to pursue here all the stand-
points which suggest themselves, but it is certain that the
chief source of *pagan art* in all its religious and national
relations lies in *the need felt of giving utterance by its means.*
In the Orient especially, which was the cradle of man and
of his thoughts, this cradle remained, and in its elementary
conditions.   This also accounts for the Oriental languages
being in relation to ours what a figure of speech is in relation
to a word.   Hence a metaphor was more used in the East by
way of making clear an idea symbolically, than as an object
in which a word is incorporated for the sake of its beauty.
In communicating his religious views the Oriental was satisfied with a symbolic representation, and had no other intention
in it.   So, then, we also mean when we speak of the relics
of Nineveh and Persepolis, that in their discovery we have
not lost such descriptive writers as Pausanias and Philostratus,
for such writings as these produced, did not exist.   The want
of such was essential to the mode of life in the East.   There
was no literature to excite their production, the monuments
were the only literature.   Some things have been found,
dating from later times, which might illustrate the past, but
they are only isolated ruins which remain from the flourishing
time of life—groups upon a tablet, representations in relief
upon disinterred walls of a palace, monumental stones which
form a path to themselves, and in which we recognise remains

of another alphabet of ancient thoughts than that of the
cuneiform which our experts have deciphered.   This is not
the case with all, and indeed the same rule and test cannot
to most of them be applied.   But the already accomplished
investigation of single monuments establishes the fact, that
they offer us a greater insight into ancient views and fancies,
than even was possible to have by the writers of monumental
inscriptions themselves.   We shall consider one such single
monument by way of attempt.

On the plain of Merdosht, thirty-five English miles north-
east of Shiras, lie the grand ruins of Persepolis.   He that
was so fortunate as to see them was quite struck by their
phantastic bulk.   The ruins stand upon an artificial even
platform, hewn out of the rock; on the south side 802, on
the north 926, and on the west 1425 feet long.   The platform is ascended from the plain by means of double marble
steps, which travellers describe as the finest in the world.
On the front of the gate, which is reached after climbing up
the steps, there are figures in bass-relief of animals of colossal
dimensions, which deserve special attention.   The columns
upon which they appear are immense blocks of marble of $27\frac{1}{2}$
feet in length, 5 feet in width, and 30 feet in height.   The
animals cover them almost entirely, and only the heads, which
are now broken plastically, protrude.   Various opinions have
been expressed as to the kind of animals they are.   But a
careful inspection of the cloven hoofs, the powerful jaws, and
of the form of the tails, shows to a certainty that they are
bulls.   This is confirmed by a similar bass-relief of the hinder
gate.   Here huge bulls are clearly recognised.   The legs and
bodies are those of bulls, the neck is striped, the ears have
ornaments in them.   On the head appears a tiara in the form
of a cylinder, at both of whose sides are clearly-marked horns,
rising from near the eyebrows upwards to the heads of the bulls
which, though injured, still disclose human faces, and from
their backs proceed gigantic wings; and they are adorned with

curled beards. The true meaning of these rare and artistically splendid figures has become more apparent since the finding of similar winged bulls in Chorsabad and Nineveh. The attempts at an explanation hitherto made are acknowledged by the learned themselves as unsatisfactory, because they proceeded from too narrow a standpoint. For it has been disproved that the Persians adored the bull, seeing that in Egypt they scoffed at the worship of Apis, and destroyed the idols. That these winged bulls represent any specific heroes is doubtful, as they are also found in Assyria. Again, to assume, with Lassen, that they are of Babylonian-Assyrian origin, because the Assyrians are older than the Persians, would explain very little why the palace of the Persian kings was chosen as the place for these monuments.

We have already made some remarks above on the figurative language of the Orient. Its soul speaks in images, symbols, and hieroglyphics. Life in the East has from very ancient times another relation to the animal world than it has in the West, not only because of the want of culture there, but also because of the abundance and the variety of animals which are within reach of man. Language, by means of animal designation, or the expression of one's thoughts through animal symbols in a simple or complex form, is therefore of Oriental origin, and is to be considered as a contrast to the Greek Mythos, which first issued from man, and was then applied to the animal symbol. The difference between the Hellenic and Oriental culture is especially to be seen in the different manner in which the Greeks and the Orientals did speak. The Greek spoke, the Oriental symbolized. Hence the conceptions of the Greek became men, those of the Oriental became animals. The fulness of thought which in Greece found its expression in language, was reproduced by the Asiatic in nature, in especially exhausting the animal and vegetable kingdoms. Herodotus says, the Persians had no gods which they thought to be in the form of men. Quite right. But the Persians, who paid homage to the

Iranic idea of God, expressed their views in reference to the
origin and conditions of the world, in the same manner
through the medium of symbolic animals as the Greeks did
through symbolic men. The figure of language and of the
word was to them still merely an image. Just as the
Egyptian wrote by means of figures, notably figures of animals, so the Oriental generally thought that the bird, horse,
wolf, lion, etc., are terms capable of containing and giving
expression to a whole series of thought. Now, without
pursuing this subject in its wide range, we return to the
bull-figures, concerning which we are of opinion that they
do not represent animals as objects of idolatrous worship, but
hieroglyphs and symbols typifying and portraying ancient
thought. It is not difficult to recognise which thought the
bull was symbolically intended to express when it could not
fail to be on the portals of Persepolis. The bull was especially
the symbol of the *Iranic-Zoroastrian Theology*, which we have
still preserved in a remarkable though covered and obscure
manner in the Zendavesta. The doctrine of Zoroaster, in so
far as we gather it from these books, represents a warfare,
not merely between virtue and vice, but a strife especially
between the civilised agricultural life and the wild, rough,
natural, hunting life. Ahuramazda, *i.e.* Ormuzd, therefore
always appears under the figure of tame domestic animals,
and when we read in the Third Fargard of the Avesta :
Creation of world filled with bodies. What is the third most
agreeable thing to this earth ? Ahuramazda answers as
follows : Where agriculture mostly abounds, and holy Zarathustra blesses the land with corn and fruitful trees. What
is the fourth thing most agreeable to this world ? When there
is plenty of cattle and beasts of burden, etc. All things,
therefore, that are sinful, injurious, and imperfect in life are
expressed through animals, which are hindering and destructive to agriculture. Therefore Ahuramazda declares that
the animals which are most disageeable to this world are
those which Ahriman created, like the wolf and the serpent.

Hence it was imposed upon the Persians as an atonement
for a sin, to kill ten thousand lizards (which evidently means
a great many sexcents), ten thousand ants, which carry away
the grain, and ten thousand gnats. The regular order of
things, rich possession of fields and animals, health, good
weather, everything which is favourable to the villager and
townsman, was created by Ormuzd, and was represented in
such images; and the opposite, the mortality of man, and
adversity in life in every possible form, was considered as
the creatures and weapons of Ahriman. All existent things,
only Ahriman hinders their prosperous development. According to these ideas the bull was the picture of happiness, and
peculiarly appropriate to designate the earth itself. In the
thousands of years before power was given to Ahriman, there
lived through Ormuzd, Willca the original bull, *i.e.* the world
was without sin and misery. When the wicked appeared,
he poisoned the bull, that he died. From his ribs proceeded
man, and from his tail fifty-five kinds of corn, and also the
good trees sprang forth. From the seed of the original bull,
when purified by the light of the moon, proceeded again a pair
of bulls of both sexes, from which all the animals descended.
The soul of the first bull after being poisoned went to Ormuzd
and said: Whom hast thou appointed for the globe? Ahriman hastened to destroy the earth. Is it man of whom thou
hast said, I will create him, that he may learn to protect
himself against evil? Ormuzd replied: The bull has become
weak through Ahriman's weakness, but man is preserved for a
globe, and a time when Ahriman will not be able to exercise
his power. Ormuzd is therefore called also in prayers the
protector of the soul of the bull, and the seed of the latter is
called effulgent, holy, and exalted. It is not the place here
to show fully the analogous views of other ancient nations,
and we shall only touch upon what is necessary to our purpose. One who was well acquainted with Egypt has
collected many passages, according to which Isis, by which
name the Egyptians understood the earth, was designated by

the picture of a cow. Plutarch plainly says that βοῦς, the ox, was among the Egyptians a symbol of Isis and the earth. It has also long ago been noticed that the Greek word γῆ, earth, comprises the Sanscrit *ga*, the common name for kine, masculine and feminine. Jacob Grimm has noticed the connection between Old High German *Rinta*, " earth," and *Rind*, " kine." So likewise the Sanscrit *bhumi*, " earth," reminds one of the Greek βοῦς. The old doctrine as, *e.g.*, it is manifested in the Zendavesta, has *expressed* the bull, but *understood* the earth. It was an ancient hieroglyphic picture, which the language perhaps occasioned, and later on drew a view from the picture. It was at all times the custom to borrow such hieroglyphic pictures and symbols from analogy of language. Well-known instances are the emblems of many cities of antiquity, which were later called in heraldry " speaking coats of arms," " armes parlantes." Euboea had for its emblem a bull, or a bull's head, βοῦς Εὔβοια ; the island Aegina was represented by a goat, which is in Greek αἴξ, αἰγός. Rhodes had the rose (ῥόδον) ; the city of Cardia, in Thracia, was symbolized by a heart; Melos by an apple ; Myrina by a wolf, which is in Greek μυρίνη ; Selimos by parsley (σέλινον); Side, in Pamphylia, by a pomegranate (σίδη), as also Granada in Spain. With this is to be compared the better known coats of arms, as of Berlin and Berne, which are represented by a bear, and Bieberach by a beaver. It is an established fact that the bull, as it represents the sense of γῆ in the Zendavesta, is always called by corresponding words which have a similar sound in Zend, Pehlevi, and in Persian. Only in later times was the symbol petrified, and the literal sense of the bull was received into the cult. This appears in the ceremonies which the Avesta prescribes, and which is still carried out by the Parsees, namely, the use of the water of the bull for purification. It almost excites merriment when reading through the treatises concerning this custom, and applying to it the rule of decency. Undoubtedly the ancient idea was, that the water of the bull purifies, viz. in the sense that the bull and the earth are the same. The *water that springs from the earth* was meant. In this sense the bull became the emblem of the Iranic-Zoroastric faith, and it can be established and explained in various ways. One of the badges of the Persian kingdom is still the club-shaped part of a bull's head. With it Feridun killed the old Persian hero, the wicked Zohak. The later legend explained the origin of the club as coming from the cow which he sucked as a child. In the sacred writings of the Persians the tauriform club is mentioned with which Guershasp killed the demons. It was the chivalrous adornment of all the ancient Persian lords and kings. They bore it on their thrones and into war. It was the formidable weapon of Rustem when he accomplished his herculean deeds, as Firdussi sings,—

> " Brandishing the tauriform club with his right hand,
> He gave them no respite or ground to stand,
> But fiercely attacked the whole band."

In connection with this we mention for the present that the Indian Çiwa is likewise joined with productive nature. Therefore he is called Paçupati, the " lord of the animals," and the bull is his symbol ; whence comes his name Vrishadhvaga, the bearer of the bull banner. To this may be added the hitherto unexplained image of a bull's head upon old Indian coins. Images of Minerva have the shield-emblem of a bull's head, of which the explanation of our well-known student of art Gerhard, is certainly insufficient. Less obscure is it upon the shield of the Geryones who defend themselves against Heracles. An Etruscan bronze figure at Gori has a bull's head ; whilst Pausanias tells of a statue of Apollo on which the foot of the god stands upon a bull's head. From this is explained the heads of oxen on coins of Phocis. Coins of Caligula have sometimes the impression of a whole bull, and sometimes only the head of a bull. We know a coin with a fine bull's head, having upon the shield a female figure and circular inscription : Britannia. After these apparently unconnected notices, we cannot leave unmentioned that in the description of the throne of Solomon, which seems to have been after the model of a Persian one : a bull is at the head of the whole order of tame animals which stand under the protection of the king.

Be it also noted that Mirkhond narrates that the Byzantian emperor had caused the Sassanide king Shapur (Sapor) to be sewn up in a skin of a bull and there imprisoned. That the bull was really considered as symbol of the Iranic-Zoroastrian system, and that other nations and tribes had certain animals as symbols upon coins, as, e.g., the Greek-Indian kings were depicted on coins in Cabul hunchbacked upon elephants, which signified the Indian Peritapotamia,[1] is clearly evident from the combination in the bull statues of human heads with wings. The figures are to be regarded as congruous symbols with hieroglyphics. The union of attributes in various kinds of animals upon one figure indicates a union of various thoughts in one symbol. The human head with horns in the front signifies that the enormous strength of the bull is also symbolized in man. Man has and comprehends that which is inherent in the bull. So also was the symbol of the king who represented the land and the Zoroastrian faith. Only heads of such figures appear on coins as that which is ascribed to Pacorus the Arsacide. A coin of the Bactric king Eukratides shows a king with ear and forehead of a bull. Eckhel reports of a fighting bull with a human face upon a Parsee figure, and also refers to the existence of such upon other coins of Cretan colonies, as upon those of Gela, Agyrium, and Tauromenium. The attribute of the wings is likewise significant. It signifies the connection of the celestial with the terrestrial. By their medium the possibility of harmony between heaven and earth is indicated. For this reason superhuman beings have wings, as also Bundehesh expressly says is the case with daevas. On the other hand, they are expressive of the possession of the power over the kingdom of the air. As the bull's head with

---

[1] [This name still appears in the name of Punjab.—TRANS.]

the tiara was the symbol of royal power over the Iranian empire, inasmuch as the bull comprised the possessions, the crop, and the earth, so the wings on the same indicated that the king claimed to have dominion over the air. This Firdussi expresses when he represents King Kaikawus, who ruled over the whole world, as being persuaded by a daeva to conquer also the heaven,[1]—

"O Lord (spake the daeva), thy will caused the earth to shake ;
As a shepherd does his flock, so leadest thou mankind in thy wake.
To only one thing thou mayest lay claim,
Then shall all the universe be filled with thy fame.
Hast thou observed the course of the sun,
And knowest thou how his rise and set do run ?
Thy rule upon earth thou dost well accomplish,
What is wanting is that thou dost also heaven vanquish.
The heart of the king is thus enticed to undertake the deed,
And he meditates whether somehow he will succeed
To reach the air with wingless feet ;
Then inquires of his sages how far
From here to the moon, and thence to some star."

Then he ordered to catch eagles and to tie them to a throne, and thus to be carried to heaven. This perhaps gave rise to Lucian's representation of the philosopher Menippus catching an eagle and a vulture, and severing the right wing from the one and the left from the other, and then fastening them with a string strapped to his shoulders, and thus flying to the assembly of the gods in heaven. Lucian further narrates, that Jupiter did not receive Menippus in a very friendly manner, for fear that in a short time all mankind might in this way fly to him ; and so when he was to depart he clipped his wings and let him be carried by Mercury to the earth.

It is remarkable that the use of wings in Grecian art came only in vogue in the Persian war. But when the scholiast on Aristophanes, whom Gerhard quotes, mentions that only in later times did Nike and Eros appear with wings, he means

[1] [A similar though somewhat different story is told in the Talmud Tamid, p. 32a, about Alexander the Great, and had perhaps this for its source.—TRANS.]

just simply that wings represent heavenly might. For Nike
the goddess of victory, and Eros the god of love, have special
rule over man.

We will not further enter fully into the domain of Greek
and Roman works of art, and upon thoughts in connection with
them, which apply wings in manifold ways, but one thing
which has remained obscure we must add. An Etruscan
vase picture represents the giant Geryon and winged bulls
carrying on war against Heracles, as if the same was attributed
to them as to the daeva and demon, though this is only
corroborated elsewhere by a reported observation upon an
Egyptian two-handled vessel called *amphora*. Wings appear
upon other figures of animals, in so far, which we here do not
consider, as they in the views of the nations represented the
symbol of *heavenly* or *demoniac* power.

But the bull, with or without wings, appears as the symbol
of Iranic Zoroastrianism, as it is represented in its sacred
books. So likewise the opponents of this faith and state, are
designated by animal symbols that are hostile to the bull.
Here, too, the opposition of the religious and political state is
compressed into one element and picture. The traveller Ker
Porter found depicted upon the bas-relief on the west end of
the platform, a king in the act of fighting with animals, a
closer description of which we here omit, and only remark
that they represent the lion, the wolf, and the ass, with wings
and heads of the eagle. The king appears as the conqueror.
Of course the wings do also signify service, civility, or
respect, but the political enemy is no less emblematically
expressed in them. To this may be compared the dream
of King Astyages, of which Moses of Chorene speaks. In
it he saw a woman who had three sons. One riding
upon a lion hastened to the west, the second upon a leopard
ran to the east, and the third upon a dragon, with the
wings of an eagle, rushed towards him. Attention needs only
be called to the wonderful prophecy of Daniel. A lion with
the wings of an eagle, a bear, and a panther, together with a

strange wild animal, rise from the sea.   The prophet himself
interprets them as symbols of great empires and kings.   In
the second dream this is still more clearly represented,—the
Ayil (ram) with two horns, as it appeared to him one higher
than the other, and he saw him push westward, northward,
and southward, so that no beast could stand before him.   But
a he-goat with two horns came against him from the west, and
vanquished him, and brake his two horns.   Of his conquest it
is said : "he touched not the ground," as if he had a swift-
winged victory.   It is the war of Alexander (Deul Karnain)
against Media and Syria which Daniel predicts.   All who
have seen the winged bulls and lions, or who have read a
description of the same, have been reminded of the prophetic
mysterious vision of Ezekiel in its entire greatness and wonderful spiritual application.   He speaks of figures of animals with
wings which had the face of a man, the face of a lion, the face
of an ox, and the face of an eagle, upon which the glory of
God passed.   It is remarkable about this, that while in the
first chapter of the prophecy which proceeded by the river
Chebar, the word cherubim is not even named, on the other
hand, in chap. x., in which the prophetic vision in Jerusalem
gets an insight into the mystery, the animals are called Cherubim.   Although it was the same animal which he saw by the
river Chebar, in the place of an ox appears a cherub, while the
lion, man, and eagle are also so called.   The significance of
this symbolizing, which expressed at the same time the worldly
power and the religious view, had an extensive influence
upon ancient legends as far as the West.   Through its
elucidation the monuments of Nineveh will gain in light ; its
contents are the more important the higher one ascends into
the obscure walks of antiquity.   And there could not have
been merely the simple combination of art and artists, which
created figures and porticoes in Nineveh and in Persepolis.
The combination and the contrast that there exist between a
lion and a bull, as they are represented in a Persepolitan figure,
engaged in battle with one another, testify, what may be more

fully dwelt upon elsewhere, to the contrast of principles at stake, of which the one which is hostile is always considered as the evil and Satanic one. Art gave expression to the language of these symbols, and without it symbolic representation would have remained inexplicable. On the other hand, the artistic monuments upon which the symbols of remarkable animals are portrayed, elucidate a series of historical information which till then had remained obscure; of which we only mention a few. It has been affirmed of Grecian monuments of art, that they reacted upon life, as representations upon marble were transported into fancy and knowledge. This also Oriental art has done. The symbol which it has laid down in the figures of the above description, passed into legendary lore without being understood and explained. Rustem the great hero was so strong, that he engraved with his nails figures of eagles and the like upon rocks. The wonderful animals which natives and strangers long centuries after have seen in their gigantic and violent forms upon walls and rocks, were taken up by fancy and by this winged messenger carried farther. After they were found in isolated places, they came forth, loosed the bonds which had kept them tied to the marble, and passed into actual life as pictures of former living and wonderful creatures. Much of the truth of this kind which ancient tales and legends contain has arisen in this manner. The stranger who travelled in the country looked upon the figures as types of existing animals, and could speak of them at home without properly saying what was false. What effect ancient art in the Orient as well as in the Occident produced through the influence of human fancy upon the culture of the nations, has not yet been sufficiently proved, nor applied by authors in criticism. Old Berosus says this in Eusebius clearly enough: "Once when all things were yet in obscurity and chaos, there were also animals of other sorts . . . men with two wings, others with a double pair of wings and two faces, others again who had one body and two heads, one of a man and one of a woman; other men had a sort of roebuck's legs upon their heads, others had legs of horses, and again others were half horse and half man. *Bulls had human heads,* and dogs had four bodies with tails of fish; there were horses with dogs' heads, men and animals with heads of horses, and their lower parts were formed like a fish; and still many more creatures which united in themselves the appearance of animals of many sorts. There were also fish, dragons, serpents, and other wonderful kinds of animals, *whose images were severally preserved in the temple of Bel."* Berosus evidently assumed, that the images of the various symbols of animals were such as had actually existed and lived in hoary antiquity. So misunderstood things become by and bye false, the more so when one takes a false way to establish their truth. Only a few years ago, the famous Indologian Lassen declared Ctesias to be a liar, because he says he had seen the Martichoras with the king of Persia, to whom the Indian king gave it as a present. I believe that he may be freed from this reproach. " Here is," says he, " an Indian animal of enormous strength, larger than the largest lion, red of colour like vermilion, and with thick hair like dog's. Among the people of India it is called Martichoras, which translated means 'man.' The head is not like that of an animal, but it has a human-like face. Its legs are like those of a lion, on its tail it has a sting like that of a scorpion."

Who does not see in this a description of some old image of a lion with a human head such as is still found on the monuments of Persia and Assyria? The notice becomes more interesting from the addition of the name. Martichoras is unanimously explained as Martijakara, " killer of man." We have thus an image of an evil demon for the Iranians, as is also clear from the scorpion-like tail. The form of a lion, as already remarked above, indicated in the animal kingdom hostility. Grotefend has long since found upon an ancient seal Ahriman depicted in a lion. According to the Bundehesh, Ahriman created the scorpion. Its title in the Avesta is: " He is the

fulness of death, the destroyer of man, the bringer of unhappi-
ness generally." Ctesias had seen such an image: and when
he asked what it meant, he was told that it was Martichoras;
and he went home with the impression and the name of an
animal which he had never known. In this it is very interesting to notice that we definitely learn to know Ahriman
in the form which Heeren wished to explain the Persepolitan
giant animals. Now we can explain Martichoras more
accurately from the figures. So here also the world since
1814 has turned round. The ancient authors whose credi-
bility has been much doubted, because true descriptions of
actual life was missed in them, will receive a new charm
when they shall be regarded as guides (*Perigeten*) and
reporters of the truth of art. They made of the picture, life:
we shall do well if we make life a picture.[1]

---

[1] The above essay could not be carried out so far as it deservedly
requires. It was also not possible to add the scientific references and
quotations. Much of that which is above indicated is more fully explained
than I could do in the continuation of the *Hierozoikous* (*Lowenkämpfe*).

ZOROASTER.

HIS NAME AND TIME.

THE name Eran (Iran) does not occur in the book of Esther. Classic authors also are unacquainted with it as a title applied to the entire Persian empire. It could not possibly have been so used at the times of Graeco-Persian wars. Doubtless it would otherwise have been mentioned in the records of the Old Testament and by Herodotus, as there seems to be no scarcity of personal names even in the book of Esther, in whose composition it occurs as $ari = ariya$.——Now, just as Strabo makes record of a province called Ariana, so also we should surely have heard of the name for the whole empire if it had been of a like sound. It is therefore not extraordinary that Spiegel should have found no trace that already in the ancient times such a name was used for the whole empire. It is quite true that, according to the cuneiform versions, King Darius calls himself an Aryan; but he does not give a like term to his whole empire. It is not simply by chance, but for political reasons, that only the title King of Persia or Persia and Media (פרס ומדי) occurs in the proper official documents and inscriptions. But taken on its own merits, the name Aryan seems to me to give the best proof that in researches for the home of the Aryan tribe the account of the O. T. has been unreasonably neglected. The cognate sound in the name Ararat (אררט) is beyond doubt.

1. The Scriptures describe the nations as coming down from Ararat. That Ararat means high land is indisputable, especially when one takes into account the various names, such as

Aram and Armena, which that district has borne in the past and present. And to interpret *Aryans as highlanders* is certainly possible, which in later times appears by an abstract form as high, or the honourable one.

Whatever of common culture and religion Aryans and Indians had in common proceeded thence. Aryan conquerors descended to India, just as Mahmud of Gazna and Islam have done.

Herodotus has the remarkable memorial that the Medians were called Aryans in former times, and connects the myth of Medea and Colchis with the change of name. And this is not preserved by him alone. — Diodorus also gives us the sayings of others about a Medus, a son of Medea, who was said to have become king of Media.—That, however, there really are Aryan traces in the legend of Medea is quite clear from the report of Pausanias. He tells us that in Corinth, where Medea lived with Jason, she hid each of her children in the temple of Juno, being under the impression that they would become immortal; that Jason had discovered her engaged in the act, and that their separation followed thereupon. We should not be able to understand what constituted Medea's offence in Jason's eyes if we did not remember the Indian story of Ganga, who, reborn as a human being, weds Santanu, the son of Pratipa. She puts her children into the river to make them immortal; and when Santanu surprises her, she has to separate from him.

It is also noticeable that in the ethnographic table of Genesis, Media (מדי) alone appears as the son of Japhet, and that in the immediate neighbourhood of יון (Javan), that is to say, of the Ionic-Greek nation. Up to the time of Cyrus it has the palpable precedence of Persia. Its name also points to the meaning of central position which it possesses. Without doubt Media (מדי) signifies Zend. *maidhya = medius, maidhyana*, the middle, a meaning which may have been not alone local, but national and religious as well. A land specially praised and holy, situated between the Jamuna and the

Ganges, is called Madyadeça by the Indians, *i.e.* "land of the middle."

A name of like meaning is applied to China (Tschung Kue). The Greek Messene stands for Middleland (legend tells of a woman of this name, as of Medea). It was said of Delphi, that Apollo there inhabited the earth's navel, which, however, Varro somewhat prosaically denies. So the Jewish commentators called the Holy Land the navel of the earth (טבור),—ideas which seem to have been held concerning the Kaaba in Mecca by the adherents of Islam.

The ancient central place occupied by the Medes is proved by this circumstance, that even during the most flourishing period of the Persian empire and during the Persian wars the word "Median" was used by the Greeks, and interchangeably for Persian, in the same sense as one now uses "Iranic" or "Aric." This application is not limited to poetic usage, as when Aeschylus says, "Such an host as has already inflicted great damage on the Medes," or as it occurs in Roman poets (cf. Catull. 67 : "Cum Medi irrupere novum mare," etc. ; cf. again, "Otimu Medi pharetra decori," which was also poetic usage, even when historians like Arrian and Aelian and others use "*Median*" for "*Persian*"). So also it is only poetic metaphor when Tertullian exclaims, "Alexander vicerat medicam gentem et victus est medica veste."

But the word has a deeper signification when Herodotus not only makes Themistocles speak of a "king of the Medes" (viii. 5), but also places a Greek and a Median party spirit in antithesis. He tells us, for instance, that the Phocians would not become "*Median*" because they were hostile to the Thessalians, the latter being Median. Had these been of the Greek party, he surmises that the Phocians would have become "*Median*" (viii. 30). In like manner he says later on of the Boëtians that they are "*Median*" in their entirety. This is the more peculiar as it is Herodotus specially who records the distinction between the Persians and Medes.

2. The fall of the Median supremacy was, as is well known, brought about by Cyrus.—But it was obviously no mere political revolution. Just as in later times the Sassanides introduced not only a new dynasty, but also a new religious era, so did also the Persians when they became masters of the Median dominion. The folk-lore and science-system, which we call (Zarathustra) after Zoroaster, first came to power over the whole empire with Cyrus.

Through him a political and religious revolution of extraordinary importance in Asiatic and general history was introduced, and which was only fully accomplished by Darius Hystaspes.—I think that even a few historical fragments and legends should suffice to make this probable.

We read in Herodotus (i. 20) that the Magi address Astyages in the following fashion: " King, it is very important to us that your mastership should continue.—For in the other case we shall become slaves of the Medes and lightly esteemed by the Persians. But as long as you are king we participate in the government, and win honour from you." And when, as Herodotus further records, after the death of Cambyses, pseudo-Smerdes the Magus usurped the throne, it was considered as an attempt on the part of the Medes to regain the mastery,—e.g. Gobryas says (iii. 73) : " For now we Persians are being ruled by a Mede, a Magus."

For this reason the discovery of the fraud caused a universal bitterness among the Persians.

The Magi that could be reached were put to death ; and like a Persian Purim, the death of the Magi was long celebrated as a national liberation festival.

According to Herodotus, the Magi formed a tribe of Medes ; they represented a sort of priest caste. In the Old Testament, on one occasion Rab-Mag, a Magus, appears in the train of the Babylonian king Nebuchadnezzar. When later authors call also the Zoroastrian priests by the name Magi, it is only a general term in accordance with old habits.—In itself it was not a name for them. Rather with the mastery

of Cyrus there was introduced a Persian hatred against the
Magi, as they were identified with the Medes. Could one
rely on the interpretation of the Bisutun cuneiform inscription,
this would be strikingly confirmed. Darius recounts in it his
conquest of pseudo-Smerdes (Bartiya).

"The mastery, which had been snatched from our race, I
have brought back again ; I restored it happily as it had
formerly been ; I ordered that what Gumata the Magus had
professed should not be honoured ; I have the service and
temple of the protector of the state, and have given back to
the gods what Gumata the Magus had robbed them of . . .
and so through the grace of Ahuramazda I have won back
that which was lost."

This much is certain, that in this inscription a victory of
Ahuramazda over his enemies is celebrated for the reason that
Darius had dethroned the Magus.

The historic legend of the rise of Cyrus, as it is recounted
by Herodotus and in later Persian poetry, doubtless supports
the view that the victory of the old Persian empire was also
shared by the Zoroastrian system.

Firdussi recounts from the traditions known to him that it
was Kai Khosru (Khosrav) who built the temple in Bahmandiz
for the "Adar Gushasp" (the holy fire). The worship of the
latter is always preferred before his. The Bundehesh says
that (cap. 17) the fire Adar Gushasp was a friend of Kai
Khosru, and that when he destroyed the idol-temple, the fire
took its seat on the mane of his horse. Only through his
service to the fire Kai Khosru gains the right of succession to
the throne. He is the first shah of whom this is told.

There is no doubt that Herodotus's accounts of Cyrus are
reflected in the legends of Kai Khosru. It is not only the
name that reminds one of this. Kai Khosru is the grandson
of the ruler whom he serves, just like Cyrus. As a child he
is placed amongst shepherds, and is brought up unrecognised.
His royal demeanour soon shows itself. A dream declares
his royalty. Kai Khosru alone has the Quarenô, the divine

nimbus, which proves him to be a destined king. His grand-father Kai Kaus has no nimbus, and indeed retires deeply into the background as one who has injured his grandson. Quarenô is derived from Khar, "to shine." It is connected with the Hebrew קרן (Karan), which is used (Ex. xxxiv. 29) when Moses's face shone so divinely that every one feared to draw near to him. It is manifestly from this that Apollo derives his name Karneios, Karnose, the shining god. It is certain that from this the house of Cyrus or כרש is derived, who manifested himself as the rightful and appointed sovereign. Of course many details diverge in the brilliant mixture of Firdussi's poem, but the groundwork of similarity cannot be mistaken.—The fact that Herodotus's account declares Cyrus to have been reared by the woman Spako, or bitch, may be referred to the honours which, as we shall see later on, are paid to the dog in Zoroastrianism. By the action of youthful Cyrus in causing the Persians to till a thorny field one day and enjoy its fruits the next, the essence of Zoroastrianism is really portrayed, which represents the cleansing of the earth from thorns and vermin as religion, in order to have a joyful life later on.

As regards Cambyses, one must not overlook the fact that his killing of apes and burning of the Hephaestos image recall the ideas of the bull and the fire which appear in Zoroas-trianism, and concerning which the necessary remarks are given in the preceding Appendix. One must also notice the words which, according to Herodotus (iii. 65), Cambyses addressed to the Persians on his deathbed: "Now therefore, whilst invoking the royal gods (θεοὺς τοὺς βασιλικῶς ἐπικαλέων), I lay it on your consciences — that you do not allow the supremacy to pass again to the Medes. If ye observe this, may the earth bring forth fruit for you, and may you have fruitful vines and herds, and may you be free (in this consists the blessing of Zoroastrianism). And if not, then I invoke on you the contrary of all this."

3. In a special sense Darius is called the son of Hystaspes.

Darius is the real architect of the great Persian empire, and under him also Zoroastrianism attained its permanent success. The name Hystaspes (Viçtaçpa, Gustasp) is connected with the origin of Zoroastrian teaching. We do not think that he could have been the father of Darius; but this is certain, that through the circumstance that he is called the son of Hystaspes, his adherence to Zoroastrianism receives accentuation, and through that, attainment of royal dignity became easy.

In Viçtaçpa appears the connection with asp, horse. According to the legend of Herodotus, Darius becomes king through the neighing of his horse.

In one of the legends of his life Zoroaster demonstrates upon a horse of Gustasp the truth of his doctrine. Its four feet shrinking into its body disappear; Zoroaster restores to the horse its natural existence; on account of this, Gustasp enlists himself and his son Isfendiar in the service of the new teaching. The consequence of this is that the separate feet emerge again.

I consider in these legends the horse to be the symbol of Persia itself. Many records of the ancients show that Persia is a very special horse-raising country. In the legends of heroes the horse is a prominent associate of the Iranian conquest. Kai Khosru could not become king unless he obtained the horse Behzad which had served his father Siawusch (Syawaksch). The horse, however, quickly allowed the son to catch it when it saw the rein and saddle that had belonged to the father.

But this is not the case with Viçtaçpa alone; also his father Lohrasp and the chief antagonist of Zoroastrianism are named after horses in the legend "Arzasp of Turan," just as the good and the bad genii Tistrya and Apaosha contend with each other in the shape of a white and a black horse.

Persia itself as פרס signifies nothing but horse-land, and is identical with פרש (horse, horseman), just as in modern Persian it means horse and Persian.

In like manner in the various terms of the Hebrew records כרש (Cyrus, shine) and חרס (sunshine) converge. But con-

tained therein is a deeper symbolical thought.   The horse,
especially the white one, was the type of the sun.   Sun-steeds
were known to all Oriental nationalities.

In the march of Xerxes and his army, Herodotus describes
(vii. 40 and 55) the holy chariot of Zeus drawn by eight
white horses, which was followed by the royal chariot.——What
Herodotus here ascribes to Zeus is told of Mithra in the
Persian sacred scriptures, before whose chariot four gleaming
steeds are harnessed; a like chariot is ascribed to Ardviçura
Anahita, who resembles Mithra in conception.

It is therefore no wonder that the sun is said to be possessed
of swift steeds.   Xenophon also expressly calls the chariot
that preceded the king's that of the sun.   It was a most
ingenious combination of the ancients which joined together
the name of Perseus with Persia.   The legend of this hero is
Oriental.   Perseus is nothing but פרש, the knight.   He comes
from heaven a sun-hero on the steed which overcomes the
dragon.   So the Persian heroes overcome the Azhis dahaka, the
evil serpent, of which it is said that it slays men and horses,
even as Andromeda is called the rescued " bearer of men."

The famous hero Kereçaspa, who conquers the terrible
Çruvara, signifies perhaps nothing else than the horse, as we
shall see farther on.

Also when Herodotus has the statement that the Persians
had formerly been called Kephenes by the Greeks, we must
not regard this as simply a playful idea.   We are reminded
of the legends about the conquering smith Kawi and the
royal family of Kawi Kawata (Kai Kobad), Kaviuça (Kai
Kaus), and Kawi Huçrava (Kai Khosru).   The father of
Zoroaster is called Purushaçpa (comp. Prexaspes).   The
translation, " possessing many horses," does not seem to be the
correct one.   I would rather suggest here "*purus*," pure, and
$\pi\hat{v}\rho$, fire, if indeed the name is ancient.   But when the
Persians have the names of their horses as symbols of the
victory of the sun, it is only natural that in the time of their
power they should emphasize these names.

Of Çraosha, who in reality is perhaps nothing else than
Mithra, we are therefore told in the 11th Yaçna (after
Spiegel), "whom the four horses guide (carry), without speck
(pure), brightly shining, beautiful, holy, wise, swift, obeying
the heavenly behest." What he sees in Eastern India (hendu,
הודו), he seizes; what in the Western (כוש), he strikes (conquers).
He is the type (ensample) of the king of Persia, who from out
of his chariot judges (governs) the Oriental world.

Hitherto I have frequently, and I think justly, used the
treasures of the Semitic languages for the explanation of
Persian names. It is legitimate *per se*, because the real
relations of men and nations were much freer and wider
than the modern science of language seems to be inclined
to assume. But there is a reason for it in a narrower
sense. It is remarkable that while Media (מדי) appears
already in the table of nations in Genesis, the name of
Persia (פרס) appears only late in the time of the captivity,
when Israel got into relations with the great empire.
Instead of it, however, we find another. At the head of
the sons of Shem appears, on the side of Ashur, Arpachshad,
Lud and Aram, the name of Elam (עילם). It occurs in
Gen. xiv., in company of ·Amraphel king of Shinar, Arioch
king of Elasar, Tidal king of Goyim, as כדרלעמר, king of
Elam. It is the opinion of all tradition that this Elam
stands here for פרס, Persia. Scripture itself gives us a proof.
In Isa. xxi. 2 and Jer. xxv. 25, Elam stands in the same
conjunction with Media as usually is the case with Persia.
In Isa. xxii. 6 it stands in conjunction with Kir, reminding
us either of the Kuran, a tributary from Khusistan to the
lower Schatul - Arab, or perhaps of Kur, Kyros, another
tributary from the Bhaktegan lake in Fars. The prophet
depicts the Elamites as Persians with quivers, chariots, and
horses. Finally, Daniel sees his vision in Susa, in the land
of Elam, on the river אולי (Eulaeus or Choaspes).

The Scriptures, in counting Elam amongst the descendants
of Shem, and Media amongst those of Japhet, wish to indi-

cate thereby a difference in language and people. Every Elamitic signification can be explained by Semitic language. In Elam we find high land or plateau, as the name seems to be derived from עלה, to mount, and brings us to Asia, just as Elyon means high or exalted (as it is explained of Ariya). Shushan (שושן) gets its name from the lily, combined with שש, white. In Eulaeus we find another form of a Semitic name, Uval, אבלי=אולי, Juval, the river; while Choaspes was the Arian name, mountain-horse, since the horse was compared to rivers springing from hills.

Highly interesting is the explanation of כדרלעמר. Schrader has compared with it kings' names from other inscriptions; so Kudur-nanhundi; he also thinks Kudur-Mabuk an Elamitic king. It is related of Kudur-nanhundi that he had robbed an image of the goddess Nana, which returned again to Babylon, and that he laid hands on the temple at Akkad. Kudur-Mabuk calls himself Ruler of the West country. Schrader, however, has not interpreted the name itself. Thirty years ago I called attention to the fact that the names of the ancient kings of Mesopotamia are compounded with those of the gods. This is seen in Kudurlaomer. Kudur occurs in נבוכדרצר = נבוכדנצר. Benfey reads Nabucodrossor; in the inscriptions, Nabokudurriussur; in Schrader's version, Nabu Khadrachara. It is composed out of Nabo, Zar or azar and Kudur, Kudan, or Adon, Lord; Adir, mighty one. In Laomer we recognise El Amir, "God, Prince." In Kudur-nanhundi, who robbed Nana, I see a composition with the name of the goddess Anahita, the same as Nana, called in the Avesta, Ardviçura Anahita, the goddess of fertility. For this reason I consider the Semitic derivation of פרס as the most likely.

In Persia, Elam was the Semitic element; through the preponderance of the Median-Arian tribe, the Arian language became the prevailing one. However, it was only by means of the old reminiscences of Persian life as far as the spirit of the matter required it, especially in worship, which seems to have proceeded from Elam, that the Semitic vocabulary was used.

II.

When Aristagoras came to Sparta to persuade King Kleomenes to war against the Persians, he described to him the condition of the great empire : " They have more good things than all others taken together ; beginning with gold, silver, brass, many-coloured garments, cattle, and slaves."

The empire was indeed well cultivated, not only in the Provinces of Asia Minor, but also in Mesopotamia and Persia.   All the gifts of the earth were well cultivated. Through good communication the nations were joined to each other.   Roads led, as Herodotus describes (v. 25), through inhabited and safe countries.   Even the way through the desert to Egypt was made easy by the quantity of water led into the desert (Herod. iii. 6).   The remark of Xenophon, that the Persians, wherever they are or come to, have gardens laid out, and make the land beautiful and fertile, characterizes Persian life in manners and morals.[1] The so-called Paradises (פרדס, fenced gardens) show more than the desire after luxury and pleasure.   The chase of wild animals was not only a warlike game.   When Lysander, visiting the younger Cyrus, found him in his garden, he was astonished at the costly culture, the beauty of the trees, the careful tilling of the ground, fertility, and beauty. Hearing that the prince had ordered all, and even worked at it himself, he burst out in the following words : " Rightly I call thee happy, because thou joinest virtue to riches ; not understanding that Cyrus followed a still higher motive—— a kind of moral obligation.   When Xenophon depicts Dascy- lium, the capital of a mere satrap, Pherenbazes, as wonder- fully cultivated, endowed with gardens and lakes, fit for

---

[1] [The Talmud testifies to this by representing the Persians pleading on the day of judgment before God that they were busy in making bridges, etc., for Israel. Abvodah Zarah, p. 26.—Trans.]

chase and fishing, with its rich landscape, what must the
royal gardens of Susa have been, which the book of Esther
praises! Everywhere were trees and gardens found in the
splendour of Persian royalty. Firdussi sketches them in his
poetical traditions. Art imitated nature in poetry and reality.
Firdussi says that when Kai-Khosroe gave a feast,—

" A tree was erected, opaque in its branches, the summit
inclining to the throne, the stem of silver, the branches
of gold, rubies formed the flowers, fruits of carniol and
sapphire smiled out of the dark-green leaves of emeralds."

The splendour of the palaces and thrones of the caliphs
later on, was only a remembrance of the old Persian glory.
Caliph Al Moktader had a silver tree; in its branches
sat birds of silver and gold, which sang automatically, and
were able to move about. Hammer considers the gardens
of Chumaruye in Egypt as the first botanical garden, and
the type of those in the *Arabian Nights*. But the Persian
kings, in doing these things, did not think of splendour
and pleasure only; not of pleasure - gardens only, but the
tilling of fields, the culture of meadows, — and not only
profit even, but the profit to religion was the real motive.

The teaching of Zoroaster is the religion of a national
tilling of the land. To plant trees, make use of forests, to
plough the land, to regulate rivers, were the fundamentals
of their religion.

What was serviceable to this culture was good; what
contrary to it, bad. Animals helping therein were good;
those that hindered, demoniac. For a rational, well-con-
ducted life they wanted fire, water, the plough, the ox, the
horse, and the dog. Before all, they symbolized the idea
of good. Only the useful was good. The Persians explain
Miçvana, one of their deities, as " *a perpetual usefulness.*"
One of the attributes of Ahuramazda was Cevista, "the most
useful." The Anushaçpentas have the cognomen "always
useful;" Arstat, "helping on the world;" fire, "affording use
to all." Spiegel thinks "Çaoka" is nothing but utility. The

egoism peculiar to the farmer, according to which weather, time, the field and animals are good according to their usefulness, is the chief doctrine of Zoroastrianism, out of which has been developed its dualism, ethical and historical, social and historical.

A similar view of nature appears, indeed, among all heathen nations. Originally there was a contrast in Zeus and Hera, night; their children were enemies; Zeus represented Ahuramazda; Heracles was victorious over serpents. As the hero of civilisation, he conquers rapacious night, waterless deserts, poisonous swamps, and illness. In the Greek view of the world, these contrasts are united harmoniously. Hera and Zeus marry. Hephaestus becomes a member of the Olympic "round table." Prometheus is taken into favour with an iron ring on his hand. The contrast is also harmonised in Indian mythology, for even the serpents are made alive again through the Amrita.

Neither does the northern legend maintain the full contrast. Loki is one of the Asi, i.e. demigods. In order to free the world-views of the other Aryans of these irreconcilable contrasts, historical events had to take place in them and around them. Nowhere else do we find this sharp contrast but in the dualism of the Persians. The same corresponds only with the view of Holy Scripture. But here the contrast is between spirit and nature, Creator and creature; but there, within nature—profit or hurt of the agriculturist.

This doctrine was brought to a height through the Persians, whose first dynast was Cyrus, and was in opposition to the Hamitic Baal service, ruling from the Euphrates to the Mediterranean, from Babylon to Egypt, with which, however, it must have had, notwithstanding the antagonism, many features in common. This doctrine is ascribed to Zoroaster, who is said to have lived in the time of Gustasp (Hystaspes). Nobody, however, is able to give the meaning of his name, his home, or his generation with certainty. The legend of Zoroaster indicates this doctrine in all its points. His mother has dreams in which lions, tigers, wolves, and dragons attempt to rob her of her child; they can, however, do nothing to her, for all wild animals are driven away by his doctrine. The child is the only one, born, not only without tears, but coming laughing into the world. This legend is told already by Pliny and Solinus. Tears and pains belong to that hostile nature which he attempts to conquer. Other miracles related of his youth have all the character of his teaching. He sleeps quietly in the fire; cows and horses minister to him; the former give him their milk; wolves have to flee; as man he has to contend with countless serpents, which dare not hurt him. Vohu-mano commands him to tell the people to take good care of useful animals, and especially not to kill young lambs. Another genius tells him to plant (extend) fire and fire-altars. Cpenta-armaiti tells him not to defile the earth with blood, nor to heap impure matter upon it, but to cultivate it diligently at any price. The care of water, plants, and trees is recommended to him.

In one legend we have a peculiar notice. His mother is told she will be pregnant with her child five months and twenty-three days, i.e. on the twenty-third day of the fifth month she will become mother of a great man. The first month from which to reckon the time of his development can only be December, when the sun appears smallest; the fifth is the spring month (Ardibihist), corresponding to our April. On the 23rd the Mohammedans celebrate the feast of Khisr, when the horses are taken to the pastures; spring-day has conquered. Khisr corresponds with St. George, the George of farmers and gardeners, who conquers the dragon—winter. On his day, the 25th of April, the Emperor of China celebrates the initiation of spring, guiding with his own hand the agricultural plough. In the legend also the victory over winter is thereby transferred to Zoroaster. His name also can alone be explained out of the spirit of his doctrine. Many attempts, it appears to me, have been made to do this, without having regard to harmonious connection with the spirit of his doctrine.

Windischmann and, following him, Spiegel reject the deriva-

tion generally given, without putting something more satisfactory in its place. Windischmann, following Burnouf, demonstrates that in the name Zarathustra the last part, *ustra*,
may mean camel. As there are names composed with *agpa*,
horse, or *ukhsan*, ox, so also may Zarathustra be a compound of
usthra, camel. Fr. Müller translates therefore : " possessing
courageous camels," which Spiegel thinks the most likely.
But horse and bullock frequently occur in the teaching of
Zoroaster, while camel never occurs in his writings. One
ought to find some traces of it ; but, on the contrary, it
appears to me that the camel, as the animal of the desert and
of the hostile Arabs, is repugnant to Zoroaster's views. The
name has still less an ideal sense, as "rich in gold," which Bar
Bahlul gives; or "gold pure," which Hyde quotes from a Persian;
or " gold-star," which Windischmann thinks not problematical,
as adduced by Lassen. The opinion of Deinon (fourth century
B.C.) inclines to star, who suggests ἀστροθύτης, " sacrificing to
stars ; " while Bochart reads ἀστροθεατης. One cannot agree
to this, as it does not regard the nature of the name; but
Bochart is right, that the reading of Deinon is capable of
emendation. Had Deinon known anything of Zoroaster's
cultus, he would not have called him ἀστροθύτης, " a sacrificer
to stars." Most likely his true reading is ἀστροφύτης, born
of stars. Windischmann wonders why the Greeks have not
pronounced Zarathystres for Zarathustra, rather than Zoroastros
or Zoroastres. The reason is, that they recognised in *thustra*
the name of the star, and indeed that of Sirius the Dog-star,
as Anquetil and Wahl thought, Tistrya or Teshtri. Sirius
was frequently called simply *aster*, as, *e.g.*, sunstroke is called
ἀστροβλησια, from Sirius, under whose light is the greatest
heat. I am the more inclined to this interpretation, because
Sirius plays an important part in the doctrines of Zoroaster.

It is well known which signification it had in Egypt. People
saw in it the forerunner of the Nile-flood and the guardian
of its approach. They saw in the manner of its rising a sign
of the year's fertility brought about by the flood. From thence

began the world's birthday. Thence Jablonski explains its
name, Sothi, "beginning." Thence also Plutarch derives the
name from κυειν, to bear, and therefore was called Κυων, Canis
Major. But we cannot doubt that the star got the name of
Dog from being heaven's guardian. Κυειν and κυων not only
depend upon each other, but in Sanscrit also çua and çvajate,
to swell, are related to çvan, çvni, dog, as Plutarch himself,
speaking of Horomazes (Ahuramazda), the god of the Persians,
says, "he placed a star, Seirios, as guardian, φύλακα, and overseer." The name Seirios itself is very instructive. It is
specially brilliant; in 3rd Yaçna, "the brilliant shining;" in
17th Yaçna, "the splendid, majestic." In the Khordavesta
its splendour is praised repeatedly. The name is derived from
the Semitic זהר (סהר, Syr. סהרא, similar to the Arabic word for
moon = Isis, whence the connection of Isis and Sirius). Comp.
Jablonski, *Pantheon*, ii. 25. The Greek σειριος, "hot, burning,"
is taken from the Dog-star. I am the more astonished that
Spiegel could doubt whether Sirius and Tir are different in
Persian names and texts. Sirios and Tir stand to each other as
זהר and טהר (Sir—Tir), splendid and pure. The names of Tiri-
bazus and Tiridates are taken from Sirius = Tir. That Tir
appears as Counter-Sirius may be explained in the same way as
that Mithra occurs as an opponent, on account of the damage
which the Dog-star heat sometimes occasions. While it brings
blessing as "lord of the water," its heat is burning and
hurtful. For this reason are the old Bactrian texts right to
translate the month Tir with Tistrya. This identity appears
plainly in the Tistar-yast of the Khordavesta. Tir is "the
arrow," and of Tistrya it is said therein, according to Spiegel,
"who is a fearfully flexible arrow, very supple, gliding along
like an arrow."

The festival of Tiraghan is therefore most likely placed in
the month of Tir, which festival is otherwise called "âbriza-
ghân," sprinkling of water; reckoned from April, the month
of Tir falls into the Dog-star season. I see in Tistrya,
"Tistar," a compound of Tir and *aster* (*stara*), and it means

nothing else than Sirius-star, as (in Greek) Astrokyon = Dog-star.

The importance of Tistar for the teaching of Zoroaster is eminent. He is praised like Ahuramazda himself. For him the highest genii prepare the way. Above all things his is the task to further fertility by water, like the Egyptian Sothi; he draws out the clouds; animals and plants yearn for him (cf. Spiegel, *Avesta*, iii. 22). Zoroaster is, so to say, his image. As he, Zoroaster, is overseer over men, so is he over stars; it is therefore natural that Zoroaster's name as benefactor and teacher is taken from him. I see in the name of Zoroaster a formation similar to that of Zerubbabel. זרובבל is derived from זרע, seed, *sperma*, Zerubbabel, therefore son, seed, or power from Babel. The same word appears Iranic in Bundehesh as *zôr, zôrmed*, powerful, *zôrs*, power; cf. Justi on Bundehesh, 170. 71; in modern Persian זור, power, just as זרוע means both power and arm. The son and offspring is a sign of manhood, as Jacob says, Gen. xlix. 3: "Thou marrow and firstling of my power." Zarathustra-Zoroaster might therefore express the meaning that he should be a "Son of, or power of, the star;" just as the celebrated pseudo-Messiah of the Jews called himself Barcochba (Son of a Star), referring to the words of Balaam, Num. xxiv. 17: "There shall come a Star out of Jacob," and like the star seen by the Magi standing over the hut of Jesus.

In the foregoing I have changed the reading by Deinon into ἀστροφυτης. It would mean the same, offspring of [a] star; but the meaning found in the *Recognitions* of Clement has hitherto not been regarded profoundly enough.—If there the name of Zoroaster is expounded by *vivum sidus*, it does signify "living bodily and incarnate star," which is, indeed, the true sense of the name. This is made plainer still when it is said in the Clementines (l. ix. c. 51), "He is called thus, because a living river of the star had come upon him." Zoroaster is, as it were, the incarnation of the Tistar-spirit.

As in Tistar is understood the fertilizing of the earth and

watcher over the earth-blessing in heaven, so Zoroaster is to be understood as he who by his doctrine fertilizes the earth and watches over its safety. It may be asserted with almost certainty that thence is derived the honour shown to the dog in the cultus of the Persians.

We cannot agree with the researches made by Windischmann on the other names which appear to have been in use about Zoroaster. Porphyry confounds him with the Chaldeans when he says: "In Babylon he met with the Chaldeans and came to Zabratos" (read Zaratos). The dualistic doctrine quoted by Aristoxenus as the teaching of Zaratas, who taught Pythagoras, can only be referred to the opinion held concerning the teaching of Zoroaster. This dualism was known as his peculiarity. Whenever the name of Nazaratos occurs, Zaratos is not to be read, for otherwise he could not have been held to be the prophet Ezekiel. When Clement says, Pythagoras has been a zealous follower of Zoroaster, he means nothing else than that he had been his disciple. There is therefore no reason why Zaratus, Zarades, or Zaras should not be considered identical. Windischmann might, indeed, think Apuleius an offensive talker, but he is not the only one who considers Pythagoras a disciple of Zoroaster. The formation of the names Zaratus and Zarades are interesting even in a higher degree. They indicate that the sources from which they are drawn knew the name of Zarathustra, and as they recognised in *ustra* or *astra* the sense of star, they obtained by omitting *ustra* the abbreviation in Zarath.

It seems to have escaped Windischmann that the narration given by Plato of a man of the name of Er, son of Armenios, killed in battle, picked up uninjured ten days later on the battlefield, revived after two days on the funeral pyre, telling what he had seen in the other world, is, indeed, given by Moses of Chorene as an Armenian tradition. Ara, son of Aram (from whom Armenia derives its name), was loved by Semiramis on account of his beauty, but he rejected her offer. In the subsequent war Ara fell in battle, though the queen had given orders to spare him. Moses of Chorene relates, though he disapproves of it, that the queen by incantations and sorcery had brought Ara again to life. When Clement Alexandrinus, telling the story of Er (Ara), adds, "this is Zoroaster," it proves that the learned Father knew the legend of Zoroaster which is left to us.

There is one account, that Turberatus, a warrior of the army of Aryasphad, killed Zoroaster with the sword. Another relates that Ahuramazda, in compensation for not having made him immortal, had given Zoroaster, a moment before his death, the gift of omniscience, so that he (Zoroaster) had seen the joys of Paradise and the torments of hell, and gained an insight into the wisdom of Ahuramazda.

The accounts of his home, indicate Aramean influences in his teaching. When we are told in Avesta and Bundehesh, that Zoroaster had lived in Airiyana Vaeja, *i.e.* in the country of the sources, Airyana (cf. Justi, p. 265), we have a reference to the country of Ara in Armenia, which is also a land of springs. He is born near the river Dâraja, flowing out of this Airyana. This seems to be the Tigris, called justly the Master of the Bâra rivers. The name in modern Persian is Tir, the arrow, as Tigris is explained by the ancients, just as Tir is Sirius.

It may be added to the above notices on Er, son of Armenius, that he is called a Pamphylian. Such a statement cannot be without reason; but it seems that he became a $\pi \acute{a}\mu\phi\nu\lambda o\varsigma$ because he was $\pi \acute{a}\mu\phi\iota\lambda o$, *dilectissimus*, much beloved, as he appears in the legend.

Pliny has a remarkable notice, that Zoroaster came from Prokonnesos, which is the same as Elaphonnesos, isle of stags. *Prox* signifies stag (*hinnulus*), which is a sun-animal, the enemy of the serpent; its skin was the garment of the Eleusinian Mysteria. Mithridates, calling himself Dionysus, had a stag in his coat of arms on his coins. The horn was an old symbolical image for light. Alexander was called the two-horned, because he wore the Persian Quarenô, the divine nimbus of royalty. Zoroaster descends, according to the

legend, out of the country of this light. The doctrine
of Zoroaster may have appeared as a reformation of the
Babylonian Magismus. The enmity against the Magi, of
which there are still traces under Darius, is certainly much
older. The remembrance thereof is shadowed in the accounts
which we have of the contest of Semiramis with Zoroaster.
Ctesias tells of a war of Ninus and Semiramis with Oxyartes,
a king of the Bactrians, in whom appears no identity with
Zoroaster. When later writers tell the same of Zoroaster, we
can only explain that Babylonian enmity of the teaching of
Zoroaster was identified with this Bactrian as it had proceeded
as far as Bactria (Balkh). Moses of Chorene tells of a war
of Semiramis with the Median magus Zoroaster, in which she
is beaten. Arnobius says in his remarkable notice, that there
had been contests between Assyria and Bactria, not only with
the sword, but also with different religions. According to a
later legend, Zoroaster is killed by Aryasp at the conquest of
Balkh (Bactra). The whole story of the Bactrian origin of
Zoroaster arose out of this interpretation of Ctesias. Later
religious phenomena were by historical learning transferred
to these early days.

But into what times ought we to place the actual rise of
Zoroaster's teaching, and therefore also his life? I have
already stated above that Windischmann attempts to make
Apuleius alone responsible for the statement that Pythagoras
had been a disciple of Zoroaster. But how should Apuleius
get this notion? It cannot be denied that Porphyry means
the same; Clement Alexandrinus communicates the same in
his learned collections. Other circumstances agree to make it
likely that at the beginning of the sixth century before Christ
the new movement had arisen. It is Kyros whom I have
placed with Kawe Uçrawa (Khosru), who founds the Persian
empire. Under Khosru the services of Adar Gushasp become
paramount. That the restorer of the Zoroaster-cultus is called
a Darius, the son of Hystaspes, shows at least that the doctrine
which arose in the time of an Hystaspes cannot have been

very far off. From this we can explain how not only Apuleius, but also later writers like Abulfarage and Eutychius make him live under Cambyses. The question is, whether their sources do not refer to Cambyses the father of Cyrus, as Cambyses, in the cuneiform inscriptions Kabuyija, is surely the same as Kave-Uça = Kai Kaus. Agathias relates that he lived under an Hystaspes, but does not know whether he was the father of Darius.

I should like to add another consideration, resting on the spirit of Zoroaster's doctrine, affording an important proof that Zoroaster lived in the beginning of the sixth century. It is not necessary to speak here of the high importance of astronomy and astrology amongst both Chaldeans and Persians. Horoscopy and belief in a man's nativity reach surely into high antiquity. Zoroaster was the Star-son. Upon him flowed the Star-soul. He was the animated Tistrya or Sirius. His life also must come in contact with the Dog-star. Just as the star of the Magi appeared at Christ's birth, so likewise is for Zoroaster's appearance obtained the division of a star period. The cycle of a Dog-star period is, according to Tacitus, well known. He confounds it indeed with the Phoenix period from which it differs. But similar things are predicted of either. Geminus says, that the festival of Isis (identical with Sirius) ran in 1460 years through the whole cycle of the seasons. Ideler, according to Censorinus, has determined that in the year 1322 B.C. a Dog-star period began, which closed 139. But these periods fell into divisions in which the same was celebrated. When, e.g., Tacitus relates that there had been Phoenix appearances under Sesostris, Amasis, Ptolemaeus, and Tiberius, the times which lie between are not full Phoenix periods, but only portions of the same. Between Amasis and Ptolemaeus elapsed as much time as between Ptolemaeus and Tiberius, i.e. 280 years, in round numbers the twenty-ninth portion of a period of 7000, according to Chaerephon, or the hundred and twenty-fifth portion of one taken at 35,000 years. Half of a

Dog-star period is 730, which, beginning at 1322, would bring
us to about the year 590. Regarding this as the beginning
of Zoroaster, this would agree with all the given data, easily
bringing out the contemporaneous existence of Pythagoras.
The other notices about the life of Zoroaster teach us that these
hypotheses delivered to us by antiquity are not without reason,
and are more valuable than has hitherto been supposed.

These are three : the first, according to which Hermodor
places in a highly valuable note, Zoroaster 5000 years before
the destruction of Troy; the second, according to which
Eudoxus and Aristotle have fixed the same 6000 before the
death of Plato ; the third, where Xanthus states Zoroaster's life
6000 years before the campaign of Xerxes. These dates can
be judged rightly, only if one calculates them as cycles, having
formed a foundation for the teaching of Zoroaster.   The
events which with the Greeks were used as aids of calculation,
are in themselves very interesting. People saw in the Trojan
and the Persian war political combinations, the latter as a
kind of revenge for the former ; both were regarded as
conflicts of the East with the Greek West. Plato's pre-
visions, and the opinions about his divine origin, make him,
as a Greek prophet, appear as counterpart of Zoroaster the
Oriental. In effect, the death of Plato forms an epoch in
the Dog-star period, closing 139 B.C. The period, consisting
of 1461 years, is divided in halves (730½ years), thirds of
487 years, and sixths of 243½ years. That they fixed the
death of Plato correctly at 348 B.C. is evident. For from
B.C. 348 to A.D. 139 is just 487 years, i.e. a third of a Sirius
period. By the exact mention of the death of Plato it
appears that the above dates have reference to the Dog-star
chronology. When Hermodor places Zoroaster 5000 years
before the fall of Troy, one must remember that the same
was believed in ancient times, as Clement Alex. tells
us to have happened 417 before the first Olympiad, i.e.
1192 B.C. Four Dog-star periods amount to 5844. Take
their beginning as the commencement of Hermodor's 5000

years, and deduct 844 from 1192, you obtain 348, the
year of Plato's death, from which it is evident that this date
is also reckoned by the Sirius cycle. From its beginning
till A.D. 139 four periods and a-half have elapsed.

The death of Plato has a still nearer relation to the year
indicated above as the eventual time of Zoroaster. Half of
the Sirius period beginning B.C. 1322 falls in $591\frac{1}{2}$. Thence
to the death of Plato, 348 B.C., elapse $243\frac{1}{2}$ years, just one-
sixth of the Sirius period. When one sees the death of
Plato reckoned as an epoch in this chronology, one is
entitled by the hypothesis (it being two-thirds of the Sirius
period) to find therein Zoroaster, "the son of Sirius." When
Eudoxus and Aristotle speak of 6000 years before the death
of Plato, they make use of a round number instead of 5844,
where, indeed, the accuracy of Hermodor is not shown. Such
round numbers in chronological data are not uncommon, as
when the divisions of the Phoenix period are given at 500
years, while they really amount to 560.

Very remarkable is the statement by Xanthus, who gives
6000 before Xerxes' campaign, anno B.C. 480, showing a
richer knowledge of the current Persian chronology. Ideler
has shown it probable that the Persian before Mohamed had
a cycle consisting of twelve intercalary periods of 120 years.
In a cycle of 1440 years the intercalary month ran through
the whole year. This cycle stood to the Sirius cycle, having
also 365 days, but without intercalation 1440–1461, or every
intercalary period of 120 years counted $121\frac{3}{4}$ in the Sirius
cycle. Xanthus has surely made use of this chronology.
6000 is 50 × 120, and it is remarkable that B.C. 480 is
made the boundary whence four intercalary periods run to
the star of the Magi. This star, place it exegetically where
you like, must be considered not only as a heavenly star, but
also as characterizing a new era, and it could also not have
been without a reason that the Magi had seen it. It is not
without interest that the reign of Cyrus is 560 years, a period
of the Phoenix cycle before it.

GRIMM'S LEXICON.

Just published, in demy 4to, price 36s.,

GREEK-ENGLISH LEXICON OF THE NEW TESTAMENT,

BEING

Grimm's Wilke's Clavis Novi Testamenti.

TRANSLATED, REVISED, AND ENLARGED

BY

JOSEPH HENRY THAYER, D.D.,

BUSSEY PROFESSOR OF NEW TESTAMENT CRITICISM AND INTERPRETATION IN THE
DIVINITY SCHOOL OF HARVARD UNIVERSITY.

EXTRACT FROM PREFACE.

'TOWARDS the close of the year 1862, the "Arnoldische Buchhandlung" in Leipzig published the First Part of a Greek-Latin Lexicon of the New Testament, prepared, upon the basis of the "Clavis Novi Testamenti Philologica" of C. G. Wilke (second edition, 2 vols. 1851), by Professor C. L. WILIBALD GRIMM of Jena. In his Prospectus Professor Grimm announced it as his purpose not only (in accordance with the improvements in classical lexicography embodied in the Paris edition of Stephen's Thesaurus and in the fifth edition of Passow's Dictionary edited by Rost and his coadjutors) to exhibit the historical growth of a word's significations, and accordingly in selecting his vouchers for New Testament usage to show at what time and in what class of writers a given word became current, but also duly to notice the usage of the Septuagint and of the Old Testament Apocrypha, and especially to produce a Lexicon which should correspond to the present condition of textual criticism, of exegesis, and of biblical theology. He devoted more than seven years to his task. The successive Parts of his work received, as they appeared, the outspoken commendation of scholars diverging as widely in their views as Hupfeld and Hengstenberg; and since its completion in 1868 it has been generally acknowledged to be by far the best Lexicon of the New Testament extant.'

'I regard it as a work of the greatest importance. . . . It seems to me a work showing the most patient diligence, and the most carefully arranged collection of useful and helpful references.'—THE BISHOP OF GLOUCESTER AND BRISTOL.

'The use of Professor Grimm's book for years has convinced me that it is not only unquestionably the best among existing New Testament Lexicons, but that, apart from all comparisons, it is a work of the highest intrinsic merit, and one which is admirably adapted to initiate a learner into an acquaintance with the language of the New Testament. It ought to be regarded as one of the first and most necessary requisites for the study of the New Testament, and consequently for the study of theology in general.'—Professor EMIL SCHÜRER.

'This is indeed a noble volume, and satisfies in these days of advancing scholarship a very great want. It is certainly unequalled in its lexicography, and invaluable in its literary perfectness. . . . It should, will, must make for itself a place in the library of all those students who want to be thoroughly furnished for the work of understanding, expounding, and applying the Word of God.'—*Evangelical Magazine.*

'Undoubtedly the best of its kind. Beautifully printed and well translated, with some corrections and improvements of the original, it will be prized by students of the Christian Scriptures.'—*Athenæum.*

PÜNJER'S
CHRISTIAN PHILOSOPHY OF RELIGION.

Just published, in demy 8vo, price 16s.,

HISTORY OF THE
CHRISTIAN PHILOSOPHY OF RELIGION,
FROM THE REFORMATION TO KANT.

By BERNHARD PÜNJER.

Translated from the German by W. HASTIE, B.D.

With a Preface by Professor FLINT, D.D., LL.D.

'The merits of Pünjer's history are not difficult to discover; on the contrary, they are of the kind which, as the French say, *sautent aux yeux.* The language is almost everywhere as plain and easy to apprehend as, considering the nature of the matter conveyed, it could be made. The style is simple, natural, and direct; the only sort of style appropriate to the subject. The amount of information imparted is most extensive, and strictly relevant. Nowhere else will a student get nearly so much knowledge as to what has been thought and written, within the area of Christendom, on the philosophy of religion. He must be an excessively learned man in that department who has nothing to learn from this book'—*Extract from the Preface.*

'Pünjer's "History of the Philosophy of Religion" is fuller of information on its subject than any other book of the kind that I have either seen or heard of. The writing in it is, on the whole, clear, simple, and uninvolved. The Translation appears to me true to the German, and, at the same time, a piece of very satisfactory English. I should think the work would prove useful, or even indispensable, as well for clergymen as for professors and students.'—Dr. Hutchison Stirling.

Just published, Vol. I., in demy 8vo, price 10s. 6d.

(Completing Volume in preparation),

HANDBOOK
OF
BIBLICAL ARCHÆOLOGY.

By CARL FRIEDRICH KEIL,
DOCTOR AND PROFESSOR OF THEOLOGY.

Third Improved and Corrected Edition.

Edited by FREDERICK CROMBIE, D.D.,
PROFESSOR OF DIVINITY AND BIBLICAL CRITICISM, ST. ANDREWS.

Note.—This third edition is virtually a new book, for the learned Author has made large additions and corrections, bringing it up to the present state of knowledge.

HISTORY OF THE CHRISTIAN CHURCH.

By PHILIP SCHAFF, D.D., LL.D.

New Edition, Re-written and Enlarged.

APOSTOLIC CHRISTIANITY, A.D. 1–100. In Two Divisions. Ex. demy 8vo, price 21s.

ANTE-NICENE CHRISTIANITY, A.D. 100–325. In Two Divisions. Ex. demy 8vo, price 21s.

NICENE and POST-NICENE CHRISTIANITY, A.D. 325–600. In Two Divisions. Ex. demy 8vo, price 21s.

MEDIÆVAL CHRISTIANITY, A.D. 590–1073. In Two Divisions. Ex. demy 8vo, price 21s.

'*Dr. Schaff's "History of the Christian Church" is the most valuable contribution to Ecclesiastical History that has ever been published in this country. When completed it will have no rival in point of comprehensiveness, and in presenting the results of the most advanced scholarship and the latest discoveries. Each division covers a separate and distinct epoch, and is complete in itself.*'

'No student, and indeed no critic, can with fairness overlook a work like the present, written with such evident candour, and, at the same time, with so thorough a knowledge of the sources of early Christian history.'—*Scotsman.*

'In no other work of its kind with which I am acquainted will students and general readers find so much to instruct and interest them.'—Rev. Prof. HITCHCOCK, D.D.

'A work of the freshest and most conscientious research.'—Dr. JOSEPH COOK, in *Boston Monday Lectures.*

'Dr. Schaff presents a connected history of all the great movements of thought and action in a pleasant and memorable style. His discrimination is keen, his courage undaunted, his candour transparent, and for general readers he has produced what we have no hesitation in pronouncing *the* History of the Church.'—*Freeman.*

Just published in ex. 8vo, Second Edition, price 9s.,

THE OLDEST CHURCH MANUAL

CALLED THE

Teaching of the Twelve Apostles.

The Didachè and Kindred Documents in the Original, with Translations and Discussions of Post-Apostolic Teaching, Baptism, Worship, and Discipline, and with Illustrations and Fac-Similes of the Jerusalem Manuscript.

By PHILIP SCHAFF, D.D., LL.D.,

PROFESSOR IN UNION THEOLOGICAL SEMINARY, NEW YORK.

'The best work on the Didachè which has yet appeared.'—*Churchman.*

'Dr. Schaff's "Oldest Church Manual" is by a long way the ablest, most complete, and in every way valuable edition of the recently-discovered "Teaching of the Apostles" which has been or is likely to be published. . . . Dr. Schaff's Prolegomena will henceforth be regarded as indispensable. . . . We have nothing but praise for this most scholarly and valuable edition of the Didachè. We ought to add that it is enriched by a striking portrait of Bryennios and many other useful illustrations.'—*Baptist Magazine.*

In demy 4to, Third Edition, with Supplement, *price 38s.,*

BIBLICO-THEOLOGICAL LEXICON OF NEW TESTAMENT GREEK.

By HERMANN CREMER, D.D.,

PROFESSOR OF THEOLOGY IN THE UNIVERSITY OF GREIFSWALD.

TRANSLATED FROM THE GERMAN OF THE SECOND EDITION
By WILLIAM URWICK, M.A.

THE SUPPLEMENT WHICH IS INCLUDED IN THE ABOVE, MAY BE HAD SEPARATELY, price 14s.

TRANSLATOR'S NOTE.

SINCE the publication of the Large English Edition of Professor Cremer's *Lexicon* by Messrs. T. & T. Clark in the year 1878, a third German edition (1883), and a fourth in the present year (1886), have appeared, containing much additional and valuable matter. Articles upon important words already fully treated have been rearranged and enlarged, and several new words have been inserted. Like most German works of the kind, the Lexicon has grown edition by edition : it is growing, and probably it will still grow in years to come. The noble English Edition of 1878 being stereotyped, it became necessary to embody these Additions in a SUPPLEMENT involving the somewhat difficult task of gathering up and rearranging alterations and insertions under words already discussed, together with the simpler work of translating the articles upon words (upwards of 300) newly added. The present Supplement, extending over 323 pages, embodies both classes of additional matter.

To facilitate reference, a NEW and very copious INDEX of the entire work, Lexicon and Supplement, has been subjoined, enabling the student to consult the work with the same ease as the earlier edition, the arrangement of words by Dr. Cremer not being alphabetical save in groups, and requiring in any case frequent reference to the Index. Here at a glance it will be seen where any word is treated of in either Part.

One main feature of Dr. Cremer's additions is the consideration of the HEBREW EQUIVALENTS to many Greek words, thus making the Lexicon invaluable to the Hebraist. To aid him, the very full and important Hebrew Index, embracing upwards of 800 Hebrew words, and extending over several pages, is appended.

'It is not too much to say that the Supplement will greatly enhance the value of the original work; while of this we imagine it needless to add many words of commendation. It holds a deservedly high position in the estimation of all students of the Sacred tongues.'—*Literary Churchman.*

'We particularly call attention to this valuable work.'—*Clergyman's Magazine.*

'**Dr. Cremer's** work is highly and deservedly esteemed in Germany. It gives with care and thoroughness a complete history, as far as it goes, of each word and phrase that it deals with. . . . Dr. Cremer's explanations are most lucidly set out.'—*Guardian.*

'It is hardly possible to exaggerate the value of this work to the student of the Greek Testament. . . . The translation is accurate and idiomatic, and the additions to the later edition are considerable and important.'—*Church Bells.*

'We cannot find an important word in our Greek New Testament which is not discussed with a fulness and discrimination which leaves nothing to be desired.'—*Nonconformist.*

'This noble edition in quarto of Cremer's Biblico-Theological Lexicon quite supersedes the translation of the first edition of the work. Many of the most important articles have been re-written and re-arranged.'—*British Quarterly Review.*

HERZOG'S ENCYCLOPÆDIA.

In Three Volumes, imperial 8vo, price 24s. each,

ENCYCLOPÆDIA OR DICTIONARY

OF

BIBLICAL, HISTORICAL, DOCTRINAL, AND PRACTICAL THEOLOGY.

BASED ON THE REAL-ENCYKLOPÄDIE OF HERZOG, PLITT, AND HAUCK.

EDITED BY PHILIP SCHAFF, D.D., LL.D.,

PROFESSOR IN THE UNION THEOLOGICAL SEMINARY, NEW YORK.

'As a comprehensive work of reference, within a moderate compass, we know nothing at all equal to it in the large department which it deals with.'—*Church Bells.*

'The work will remain as a wonderful monument of industry, learning, and skill. It will be indispensable to the student of specifically Protestant theology; nor, indeed, do we think that any scholar, whatever be his especial line of thought or study, would find it superfluous on his shelves.'—*Literary Churchman.*

'We commend this work with a touch of enthusiasm, for we have often wanted such ourselves. It embraces in its range of writers all the leading authors of Europe on ecclesiastical questions. A student may deny himself many other volumes to secure this, for it is certain to take a prominent and permanent place in our literature.'—*Evangelical Magazine.*

'Dr. Schaff's name is a guarantee for valuable and thorough work. His new Encyclopædia (based on Herzog) will be one of the most useful works of the day. It will prove a standard authority on all religious knowledge.'—HOWARD CROSBY, D.D., LL.D., *ex-Chancellor of the University, New York.*

'This work will prove of great service to many; it supplies a distinct want in our theological literature, and it is sure to meet with welcome from readers who wish a popular book of reference on points of historical, biographical, and theological interest. Many of the articles give facts which may be sought far and wide, and in vain in our encyclopædias.'—*Scotsman.*

'It is with great pleasure we now call attention to the third and concluding volume of this work. . . . It is a noble book . . . For our ministerial readers we can scarcely wish anything better than that every one of them should be put in possession of a copy through the generosity of the wealthy laymen of their congregation; such a sowing of good seed would produce results most beneficial both to those who preach and to those who hear. But this Cyclopædia is not by any means for ministerial students only; intelligent and thoughtful minds of all classes will discover in it so much interest and value as will make it a perfect treasure to them.'—*Christian World.*

SUPPLEMENT TO HERZOG'S ENCYCLOPÆDIA.

Just published, in imperial 8vo, price 8s.,

ENCYCLOPÆDIA OF LIVING DIVINES AND CHRISTIAN WORKERS,

OF ALL DENOMINATIONS IN EUROPE AND AMERICA.

Being a Supplement to 'Schaff-Herzog Encyclopædia of Religious Knowledge.'

EDITED BY

PHILIP SCHAFF, D.D., AND REV. S. M. JACKSON, M.A.

'A very useful Encyclopædia. I am very glad to have it for frequent reference.'—Right Rev. Bishop LIGHTFOOT.

'The information is very lucidly and compactly arranged.'—Rev. Canon DRIVER.

'Very useful, and supplies information not elsewhere obtained.'—Rev. Dr. HENRY ALLON.

In Twenty Handsome 8vo Volumes, SUBSCRIPTION PRICE £5, 5s.,

MEYER'S
Commentary on the New Testament.

'Meyer has been long and well known to scholars as one of the very ablest of the German expositors of the New Testament. We are not sure whether we ought not to say that he is unrivalled as an interpreter of the grammatical and historical meaning of the sacred writers. The Publishers have now rendered another seasonable and important service to English students in producing this translation.'—*Guardian.*

A Selection may now be made of any EIGHT VOLUMES at the Subscription Price of TWO GUINEAS. Each Volume will be sold separately at 10s. 6d. to Non-Subscribers.

CRITICAL AND EXEGETICAL
COMMENTARY ON THE NEW TESTAMENT.
BY DR. H. A. W. MEYER,
OBERCONSISTORIALRATH, HANNOVER.

The portion contributed by Dr. MEYER has been placed under the editorial care of Rev. Dr. DICKSON, Professor of Divinity in the University of Glasgow; Rev. Dr. CROMBIE, Professor of Biblical Criticism, St. Mary's College, St. Andrews; and Rev. Dr. STEWART, Professor of Biblical Criticism, University of Glasgow.

1st Year—Romans, Two Volumes.
   Galatians, One Volume.
   St. John's Gospel, Vol. I.
2d Year—St. John's Gospel, Vol. II.
   Philippians and Colossians, One Volume.
   Acts of the Apostles, Vol. I.
   Corinthians, Vol. I.
3d Year—Acts of the Apostles, Vol. II.
   St. Matthew's Gospel, Two Volumes.
   Corinthians, Vol. II.
4th Year—Mark and Luke, Two Volumes.
   Ephesians and Philemon, One Volume.
   Thessalonians. (*Dr. Lünemann.*)
5th Year—Timothy and Titus. (*Dr. Huther.*)
   Peter and Jude. (*Dr. Huther.*)
   Hebrews. (*Dr. Lünemann.*)
   James and John. (*Dr. Huther.*)

The series, as written by Meyer himself, is completed by the publication of Ephesians with Philemon in one volume. But to this the Publishers have thought it right to add Thessalonians and Hebrews, by Dr. Lünemann, and the Pastoral and Catholic Epistles, by Dr. Huther. So few, however, of the Subscribers have expressed a desire to have Dr. Düsterdieck's Commentary on Revelation included, that it has been resolved in the meantime not to undertake it.

'I need hardly add that the last edition of the accurate, perspicuous, and learned commentary of Dr. Meyer has been most carefully consulted throughout; and I must again, as in the preface to the Galatians, avow my great obligations to the acumen and scholarship of the learned editor.'—BISHOP ELLICOTT *in Preface to his 'Commentary on Ephesians.'*

'The ablest grammatical exegete of the age.'—PHILIP SCHAFF, D.D.

'In accuracy of scholarship and freedom from prejudice, he is equalled by few.'—*Literary Churchman.*

'We have only to repeat that it remains, of its own kind, the very best Commentary of the New Testament which we possess.'—*Church Bells.*

'No exegetical work is on the whole more valuable, or stands in higher public esteem. As a critic he is candid and cautious; exact to minuteness in philology; a master of the grammatical and historical method of interpretation.'—*Princeton Review.*

In demy 8vo, price 10s. 6d.,

REVELATION;
ITS NATURE AND RECORD.
By HEINRICH EWALD.
TRANSLATED BY REV. PROF. THOS. GOADBY, B.A.

CONTENTS.—Introductory: The Doctrine of the Word of God.—PART I. The Nature of the Revelation of the Word of God.—PART II. Revelation in Heathenism and in Israel.—PART III. Revelation in the Bible.

NOTE.—This first volume of Ewald's great and important work, 'Die Lehre der Bibel von Gott,' is offered to the English public as an attempt to read Revelation, Religion, and Scripture in the light of universal history and the common experience of man, and with constant reference to all the great religious systems of the world. The task is as bold and arduous as it is timely and necessary, and Ewald was well fitted to accomplish it. . . . . The work has not simply a theological, but a high and significant apologetic value, which those who are called upon to deal with the various forms of modern scepticism will not be slow to recognise.—*Extract from Translator's Preface.*

'This volume is full of nervous force, eloquent style, and intense moral earnestness. There is poetry of feeling in it also; and, whilst it manifests an original mind, it is accompanied by that spirit of reverence which ought always to be brought to the study of the Holy Scripture. A masterly intellect is associated in Ewald with the humility of a child.'—*Evangelical Magazine.*

'Ewald is one of the most suggestive and helpful writers of this century. This is certainly a noble book, and will be appreciated not less than his other and larger works. . . . There is a rich poetic glow in his writing which gives to it a singular charm.'—*Baptist Magazine.*

In Two Volumes, demy 8vo, price 21s.,

ENCYCLOPÆDIA OF THEOLOGY.
By J. F. RÄBIGER, D.D.,
Professor of Theology in the University of Breslau.

Translated from the German,

And Edited, with a Review of Apologetical Literature,

By REV. JOHN MACPHERSON, M.A.

'It is impossible to overrate the value of this volume in its breadth of learning, its wide survey, and its masterly power of analysis. It will be a "sine quâ non" to all students of the history of theology.'—*Evangelical Magazine.*

'Another most valuable addition to the library of the theological student. . . . It is characterized by ripe scholarship and thoughtful reflection. . . . It would result in rich gain to many churches if these volumes were placed by generous friends upon the shelves of their ministers.'—*Christian World.*

'One of the most important additions yet made to theological erudition.'—*Nonconformist and Independent.*

'Rabiger's Encyclopædia is a book deserving the attentive perusal of every divine. . . . It is at once instructive and suggestive.'—*Athenæum.*

'A volume which must be added to every theological and philosophical library.'—*British Quarterly Review.*

In Two Volumes, 8vo, price 7s. 6d. each,

HANDBOOK OF CHURCH HISTORY.
By REV. PROFESSOR KURTZ.

VOL. I.—TO THE REFORMATION. VOL. II.—FROM THE REFORMATION.

'A work executed with great diligence and care, exhibiting an accurate collection of facts, and a succinct though full account of the history and progress of the Church, both external and internal. . . . The work is distinguished for the moderation and charity of its expressions, and for a spirit which is truly Christian.'—*English Churchman.*

In One Volume, 8vo, 640 pp., price 15s.,

HISTORY OF THE SACRED SCRIPTURES OF THE NEW TESTAMENT.

By Professor E. REUSS, D.D.

TRANSLATED FROM THE FIFTH REVISED AND ENLARGED EDITION.

CONTENTS.—Introduction. BOOK FIRST:—History of the Origin of the New Testament Writings—History of the Literature. BOOK SECOND:—History of the Collection of the New Testament Writings—History of the Canon. BOOK THIRD:—History of the Preservation of the New Testament Writings—History of the Text. BOOK FOURTH:—History of the Circulation of the New Testament Writings—History of the Versions. BOOK FIFTH:—History of the Theological Use of the New Testament Writings—History of Exegesis.

'It would be hard to name any single volume which contains so much that is helpful to the student of the New Testament. . . . Considering that so much ground is covered, the fulness and accuracy of the information given are remarkable. Professor Reuss's work is not that of a compiler, but of an original thinker, who throughout this encyclopædic volume depends much more on his own research than on the labours of his predecessors. . . . The translation is thoroughly well done, accurate, and full of life.'—*Expositor.*

'One of the most valuable volumes of Messrs. Clark's valuable publications. . . . Its usefulness is attested by undiminished vitality. . . . His method is admirable, and he unites German exhaustiveness with French lucidity and brilliancy of expression. . . . The sketch of the great exegetic epochs, their chief characteristics, and the critical estimates of the most eminent writers, is given by the author with a compression and a mastery that have never been surpassed.'—Archdeacon FARRAR.

'I think the work of Reuss exceedingly valuable.'—Professor C. A. BRIGGS, D.D.

'I know of no work on the same topic more scholarly and at the same time readable, and I regard the work as one of real value to scholars.'—President ALVAH HOVEY, Newton Theological Institute.

'A work of rare and long-tested merit. . . . I am sure that every theological teacher will be glad to be able to refer his students to it.'—Professor P. H. SKENSTRA, Cambridge, Mass.

In crown 8vo, price 3s. 6d.,

THE RELIGIOUS HISTORY OF ISRAEL.

A Discussion of the Chief Problems in Old Testament History, as opposed to the Development Theorists.

By Dr. FRIEDRICH EDUARD KÖNIG,
THE UNIVERSITY, LEIPZIG.

TRANSLATED BY Rev. ALEXANDER J. CAMPBELL, M.A.

'An admirable little volume. . . . By sincere and earnest-minded students it will be cordially welcomed.'—*Freeman.*
'Every page of the book deserves study.'—*Church Bells.*

In crown 8vo, price 5s. 6d.,

CREATION;

OR, THE BIBLICAL COSMOGONY IN THE LIGHT OF MODERN SCIENCE.
WITH ILLUSTRATIONS.

By Professor ARNOLD GUYOT, LL.D.

'Written with much knowledge and tact, . . . suggestive and stimulating.'—*British Quarterly Review.*
'The issue of this book is a fitting conclusion to a beautiful career. . . . This, his last book, coming from the author's deathbed, will serve two causes; it will aid science by showing that it is a friend of the faith, and it will aid Christianity by showing that it need not fear the test of the latest scientific research.'—*Presbyterian Review.*

Just published, in crown 8vo, price 3s. 6d.,

SECOND EDITION, REVISED
THE THEOLOGY
AND
THEOLOGIANS OF SCOTLAND,
CHIEFLY OF THE
Seventeenth and Eighteenth Centuries.
Being one of the 'Cunningham Lectures.'
BY JAMES WALKER, D.D., CARNWATH.

CONTENTS.—CHAP. I. Survey of the Field. II. Predestination and Providence. III. The Atonement. IV. The Doctrine of the Visible Church.
V. The Headship of Christ and Erastianism. VI. Present Misrepresenta-
tion of Scottish Religion. VII. Do Presbyterians hold Apostolical
Succession?

'These pages glow with fervent and eloquent rejoinder to the cheap scorn and
scurrilous satire poured out upon evangelical theology as it has been developed north
of the Tweed.'—*British Quarterly Review.*
'We do not wonder that in their delivery Dr. Walker's lectures excited great interest;
we should have wondered far more if they had not done so.'—Mr. SPURGEON in *Sword
and Trowel.*
'As an able and eloquent vindication of Scottish theology, the work is one of very
great interest—an interest by no means necessarily confined to theologians. The history
of Scotland, and the character of her people, cannot be understood without an intelligent
and sympathetic study of her theology, and in this Dr. Walker's little book will be
found to render unique assistance.'—*Scotsman.*

Just published, in demy 8vo, price 10s. 6d.,

THE FIRST EPISTLE OF PETER:
REVISED TEXT,
WITH
Introduction and Commentary.
BY ROBERT JOHNSTONE, LL.B., D.D.,
PROFESSOR OF NEW TESTAMENT LITERATURE AND EXEGESIS IN THE
UNITED PRESBYTERIAN COLLEGE, EDINBURGH.

Just published, in demy 8vo, price 7s. 6d.,

STUDIES ON THE BOOK OF PSALMS.
THE STRUCTURAL CONNECTION OF THE BOOK OF
PSALMS, BOTH IN SINGLE PSALMS AND IN
THE PSALTER AS AN ORGANIC WHOLE.
BY JOHN FORBES, D.D., LL.D.,
EMERITUS-PROFESSOR OF ORIENTAL LANGUAGES, ABERDEEN.

'A glorious book. We know not when we had such a treat as we have enjoyed in
reading this fine exposition. . . . It is the production of a scholarly man, and cannot fail
to be an enrichment to the intelligent reader.'—*Methodist New Connexion Magazine.*